MW01074211

The Officer's Wife

Adrienne D'nelle Ruvalcaba

Adrienne D'nelle Ruvalcaba

Indigo
Plume

THE OFFICER'S WIFE

Copyright © 2012 by Adrienne D'nelle Ruvalcaba.

Excerpt from *The Prostitute's Daughter* copyright © 2012 by Adrienne D'nelle Ruvalcaba.

All rights reserved. No part of this book may be used or reproduced in any manner whatsoever without written permission except in case of quotations embodied in critical articles or reviews. For information contact The Indigo Plume Publishing Company at indigo.plume@gmail.com.

ISBN: 978-0-9854672-0-3

Printed in the United States of America

Cover design by Byron Livingston.

Also available as an eBook distributed to major online retailers by Smashwords.com. (eBook ISBN: 978-147-625-0847)

Thanks to Marisa Winegar, Erica Peterson, and Maggie Barnes for all the editing, proofreading and invaluable encouragement along the way.

Chapter 1

"I didn't know it was yours!" Jenny whined as she looked into her roommate's face.

"You stupid little bitch! You're always stealing my shit!" Kanicker yelled as she swung her fist and struck Jenny across the face.

Immediately, Rebecca and the two ladies from the night shift separated the girls. Jenny was escorted down the hall as she held her cheek and cried, and Kanicker was taken down to the floor in the protective hold that all the employees at the mental health facility were required to learn.

"Get off me! Get off me! I hate you bitches! I hate all you bitches!" Kanicker screamed as Ms. Jones held her arms and Rebecca held her legs.

"Get the radio and call for a nurse," Ms. Jones huffed out to Rebecca.

"I already did before I grabbed her legs," was Rebecca's out of breath reply.

"Well call again! And hold her legs better!" Ms. Jones instructed over the noise of Kanicker's hysterics.

Rebecca struggled to grab the radio and hold Kanicker's legs at the same time, but it was difficult because the child was almost six feet of aggression and out of control rage.

"We need a nurse to the female unit," she managed to say as Kanicker quieted briefly to take a breath.

"...on the way," was the barely discernable response that crackled through the radio. Less than a minute later, one of the nurses came bustling down the hallway with the paperwork that was required after the initiation of a protective hold.

"I want my mommy! Please! Please get off me!" Kanicker wailed now. Tears streamed across her cheeks as she attempted to slam her face against the hard floor, but the small padded mat used by the staff during protective holds prevented her from injuring herself.

"Kanicker, you're going to have to calm down if you want us to let you up," Rebecca said in a quiet tone.

"Fuck you! I hate you!" Kanicker continued to scream and beat her forehead against the mat.

"Check the capillary refill on her hands," the nurse instructed as Kanicker continued to scream.

Rebecca let go of the child's legs and complied.

"It's good," she said, and the nurse made a notation on her chart.

"Kanicker, do you know why you're down here like this?" Ms. Jones demanded over all the screaming.

"Because that bitch stole my jacket and you stupid fuckin' staff don't do shit about it 'cause she's white!" Kanicker screamed.

"You're down here because you attacked another resident, and as soon as you calm down I'll let you up," Ms. Jones replied to Kanicker's tirade.

Kanicker screamed, "I can't breathe! Get off me you fat bitch!"

"Obviously you can breathe if you're screaming like that," Ms. Jones pointed out.

"Kanicker, you're going to have to calm down," Rebecca said again close to her ear. "Whatever happened with Jenny can be dealt with, but right now all you're doing is making it harder on yourself."

"I can't breathe!" Kanicker screamed again.

"Please Kanicker... please just take a deep breath and at least try to calm down," Rebecca said gently. She watched the girl's tears fall on the little blue mat and felt a moment of sadness for her. "When's the last time you talked to your mother?" Rebecca asked as she continued to lean close to Kanicker.

"Last Sunday," Kanicker sniffed.

"Don't you want to get your phone call this week?" Rebecca asked gently.

"Yes," Kanicker moaned as she rested her head against the mat and stopped struggling.

"Relax your arms. You still have all day and the rest of the week to get back on track, but first you need to assure us that you're calm enough for us to let you up."

"I'm calm Miss Rebecca," Kanicker said with considerably less heat than before.

Rebecca scooted away from the child's ear and looked at Ms. Jones who was now sweating from the strain of holding her arms. A small moment of mutual respect and understanding passed between the two women. Protective holds were always difficult to deal with on both an emotional and physical level.

"Okay Kanicker," Ms. Jones began. "I'm going to release your left arm first, and I need you to keep it flat on the floor."

"Okay," the girl sniffed.

"Good," Ms. Jones continued, "now I'll do the other one."

A few minutes later Rebecca escorted Kanicker to the time out room to continue the de-escalation process. Ms. Jones retired to the break room to fill out the incident report and clock out. Her shift had been over for fifteen minutes already, and she was more than ready to go home.

As for Rebecca, she still had sixteen more hours to get through before she could go home, and the day promised to be as busy as ever.

Around midnight Rebecca finally made it home from her trying day at work. The drive from the youth center usually took about forty five minutes, but tonight's dense fog had caused the trip to take an entire hour.

She got out of her car with a headache and a sad feeling in her heart. After a double shift of dealing with the product of the inner city ghetto mentality, Rebecca was physically, mentally, and emotionally exhausted.

All day she'd heard the same thing, "I don't care about this place... I don't care about these bitches in here... I don't care about no damn points!" None of the teenage girls at the treatment facility cared about their future... at least not in any discernable way. Most of them came from environments where the prevailing mentality could be summed up with the simple quote, "If you were born in the ghetto and raised in the ghetto, you're gonna die in the ghetto."

The first incident with Kanicker and Jenny had merely been a prelude to the rest of the day. Between seven a.m. and eleven p.m.

there had been numerous arguments, three fights, and one small riot between rival clique members on the girls' unit. This job was not for the faint of heart, and Rebecca, as quiet and soft spoken as she was, often wondered what in the world had possessed her to get this job... and then to keep it.

In her childhood years, Rebecca's softer nature had always been a problem for her. She was the only child of an unconventional mother who had moonlighted as a professional kick boxer for a number of years. Rebecca's mother had tried to toughen her up, but she eventually gave up trying to train her when it became clear that Rebecca was not a fighter. It just wasn't in her nature to hurt anything or anybody. She thought about her hostile work environment all the way home and wondered what her mother would say about it. Her heart was in the work, but she also knew that on some level she was still trying to live up to her mother's impossible standards.

Once inside her quiet apartment, she undressed and took a quick shower. Usually she would have gone straight to sleep, but tonight she was still too stressed from work. She took her laptop with her to bed and stayed up surfing the internet for awhile.

A few weeks ago she'd made a personals profile on a popular dating site, and every once in a while she checked to see if any single men had looked at her profile. This week nobody had looked, and the few messages she'd sent out had gone ignored again. After such a day at work she almost didn't care anymore whether or not she ever went on a date, but it would be nice to have someone to talk to at times like this.

Here she was, a twenty two year old woman who had never been in a serious relationship. All she did was work and go to school, and even then she hardly ever talked. Sometimes her own voice sounded foreign to her from lack of being exercised. Nothing was wrong with her other than a little bit of social ineptitude. That was why she'd decided to try online dating. She'd rather get past the awkward stages of "meeting" and arranging a first date behind the safety of her computer.

Tonight she browsed through the local profiles. Every few minutes she came across a man who had taken the time to write more than just, "Here for a good time," or, "Looking for a cute girl to hang out with." The problem with those was that the guys who wrote them were usually divorced men with children, and Rebecca wanted a simple uncomplicated relationship with a man who wasn't some other woman's reject.

After looking at all the men close to her age for half an hour she decided to expand her search to include older men. Not quite sure what to expect, she typed in 30-40 for the age range and clicked on the search button. Instantly over two hundred profiles came up in a list that was organized by how far away they lived. She changed the sort criteria so the best matches were at the top of the list.

To her surprise, the profile at the top featured a very handsome man. The best looking one out of all the profiles she'd seen so far. His introduction line simply said, "Hey!" His short paragraph about himself was vague. All it said was that he was a divorced dad of two wonderful kids, and that he'd been in the military for fifteen years. She clicked on the photo tab and looked at several pictures of him holding his kids. In one picture he was wearing his uniform and looking a little sad. The date at the bottom of the picture showed that it had been taken right around the time the local military division had last deployed to Iraq. Obviously he was sad to be leaving his family. Something about his face captivated her the moment she saw it. It was a face filled with character. He was handsome, but not in the classic sense. His features were rather severe and tended to look more stern than normal in all the pictures. In the only picture where he smiled, he actually looked a bit like he was grimacing.

Rebecca stared at his pictures for about ten minutes before she realized that she'd looked at only one profile. She began to scan through the others, but she repeatedly came back to the first one. Something about this man's face made her want to continue looking at it. She read his physical appearance info after staring at his picture for a few more minutes. He was 6'5" tall, and he had muscles everywhere. Obviously he worked out more than the average man. His hair was worn short in a military style cut, and his eyes appeared to be light in color. His bio said he had brown hair and blue eyes, but they looked more gray than blue to Rebecca.

After a few minutes of reflection, she decided to send him an email. She typed a short message that said, "I think it's sweet that you refer to your kids as wonderful. Would you like to talk sometime?"

It was simple and to the point, and she hoped he would respond.

The next day work was only slightly less dramatic. Breakfast and lunch passed without any fights, but there was a big one right before shower time.   One of the newer residents, a big girl who had been charged with armed robbery and assault, had found out that her girl friend was talking to another girl at the same time. The entire sordid affair was made worse by the fact that several staff members actually found it funny. Rebecca was thoroughly disgusted by their attitude. She didn't see anything funny about troubled teenage girls wanting to sexually dominate each other while in a treatment facility.

The big girl's name was Veronica, and besides her name there was no other indication that she was even a girl. She had a more masculine build than the other girls, she dressed like a male thug, she wore her hair in rough looking prison style braids, and there was no discernable femininity in her features. Even her voice sounded manlier than some of the grown men who worked there. She walked around with her hand near her crotch as if she thought she actually had something down there that needed adjusting.   In addition to her thuggish demeanor, she also had a way of looking at everyone that made it obvious she would just as soon stab them as talk to them.

Veronica thought she owned the place from the night she got there. She was bigger and stronger than most of the other girls, and she had more street credibility because her crimes had been more vicious than many others'.   In addition, the fact that she was from Philly commanded respect from more than half the girls on the unit.

The rest of the girls were loyal followers of another girl from Philly who had been at the center longer. This one's name was Shirelle. Shirelle looked more like a girl than Veronica did, but she had almost the same type of attitude. She thought she ran things on the unit, and when Veronica arrived flexing her own muscles there was instant conflict between the two.

The drama for the day had started late, but once it got going it was like a juggernaut that threatened to flatten the entire girls' unit. After the shower time fight, the girls were all taken into the day room for their nightly hour of recreation time. Some of the girls read, but most of them watched the movie the treatment team had selected for them. Rebecca sensed that some of them were still on edge, but there weren't any obvious indications that another fight was imminent.

Rebecca and another staff member, a nice older lady named Mrs. Krenshaw, were sitting in the day room monitoring the girls as they watched the movie. Rebecca was busy filling in the information on the point sheets for each of them when Veronica suddenly stood up and aggressively advanced towards another resident. The other resident just happened to be Shirelle's thirteen year old roommate Kenya, a big-boned, southern girl with the mental capacity of an eight year old.

Kenya always became easily upset, but most of the older girls on the unit tended to leave her alone. They knew she was slow and her family didn't want her, so most of them tried to help her calm down when she got upset...Kenya was also firmly on Shirelle's side of the unit.

Rebecca looked up just as Veronica said, "Somebody better get this stupid bitch away from me before I swing on her!" She advanced toward Kenya as she talked.

Kenya immediately responded with a great deal of heat, "Do somethin' then! Do somethin'!"

"That's enough!" Rebecca said as she ran towards the girls to keep them from fighting. As Ms. Krenshaw and a male staff member grabbed Veronica, Rebecca grabbed Kenya and escorted her into the timeout area.

"Kenya, what's wrong?" Rebecca asked while they stood in the small, white six by six foot room.

"They always talkin' about me Miss Rebecca," Kenya drawled out with her southern accent.

"What exactly did they say?"

"Veronica and Diamond were over there laughin' at me. They say my pussy stank," she admitted as she started crying.

Many of the girls were on hygiene monitor status, because they had problems with body odor, especially during certain times of the month.

"Did you take a good shower tonight?" Rebecca asked gently.

"I don't get enough time!" Kenya whined.

"If you get straight in the shower without messing around you get ten minutes, that's enough time to scrub yourself good," Rebecca replied.

"No it ain't" Kenya whined again. "I'm tired of them bitches always talkin' about me."

"They'll be dealt with, but you need to focus on you right now. You know that everyone in here talks about everyone else. You need to try harder not to let it get you upset to the point where you get yourself in trouble. Do you understand?"

Kenya nodded.

"You're in here to learn to control yourself; staff members won't be around for the rest of your life to control you. Can you promise to at least try?"

Kenya nodded again.

"If you need another timeout just let me know, don't let it get to the point where you're about to fight. And if someone is picking on you come tell me so I can do something about it."

They stood in silence for a few minutes. Rebecca watched Kenya for some indication that she was ready to rejoin the group. She was still crying and in an obviously agitated state, so Rebecca said nothing for a while. It took about twenty minutes, but Kenya's breathing eventually returned to normal and she no longer appeared to be in an agitated emotional state.

"Can I go back in the day room and watch TV?" she asked.

"Okay," Rebecca said, because it seemed that she was calm enough to rejoin the group.

Once they returned, Kenya took a seat on the far side of the room from Veronica. Rebecca resumed the task of filling out the point sheets. Things seemed calm.

After a few minutes, Veronica approached the staff table.

"Miss Krenshaw, can I get some water?" she asked with attitude.

"Yeah, but hurry up," Mrs. Krenshaw responded sternly.

Veronica walked across the room without incident. She took a moment to drink a cup of water before coming back into the day room, but by the time she got to the doorway Kenya had jumped up and grabbed a chair.

"I'm 'bout to kill this bitch!" Kenya screamed as she attempted to attack Veronica with the large wooden chair.

Rebecca was younger and in better shape than Mrs. Krenshaw, so she was able to leap directly over the table to get to Kenya first. She immobilized her arms, but was unable to get her to let go of the chair. Rebecca was only 5'2" tall, but Kenya was a very stout 5'11". It was almost impossible for Rebecca to hold her without getting tossed around a little.

"Kenya, you need to calm down!" Rebecca screamed at her over all the yelling. Kenya was screaming, and still trying to get at Veronica. Veronica was now advancing toward Kenya, and all the other girls were either encouraging the fight or screaming in fear.

"Dog! What's wrong wit you man?! Why y'all always gotta be drawlin," one of the other residents from Philadelphia screamed out.

Rebecca had no idea which girl she was talking to, because she was still occupied with trying to keep her feet on the floor and subdue Kenya. Suddenly Kenya twisted wildly, and Rebecca's leg slammed into the corner of the table. The pain was so sharp she momentarily lost her grip on Kenya's arms. Kenya twisted free and tried to advance toward Veronica again. Rebecca once again managed to leap in front of her, but this time she shoved her as hard as she could towards the nearest corner. Once she got her in the corner she simply held her there, and hoped that someone would grab Veronica before she got too close.

During the entire scuffle Kenya and Veronica had been screaming at each other as the other girls whooped and hollered all kinds of incitements.

"Kenya! Stop it!" Rebecca shouted repeatedly. Nothing seemed to be working until a male staff member showed up to assist them.

"I got her," he said as he quickly immobilized her arms and roughly pressed her up against the wall.

By this time the nurse had come to observe the protective hold, and Mrs. Krenshaw was nowhere to be seen.

"Kenya, if you don't calm down I'm going to have to take you all the way down to the floor," Mr. Thomas said to the still screaming and fighting child.

"Aaaaaaaah!" she continued to scream, but she was unable to get out of Mr. Thomas's firm grip.

Rebecca turned around to see Veronica pacing nearby in an agitated state. She looked like she was on the verge of attacking somebody, so Rebecca rushed towards her. Rebecca wondered why no one else had bothered to escort Veronica to the time out while she'd been busy with Kenya.

"I swear, I'm 'bout to kill that bitch," Veronica said to herself as she paced back and forth while pounding her fist into her hand over and over again in a threatening manner.

"Veronica," Rebecca said as she inched closer to the girl. "You need to calm down. Would you like to come with me to the back to take a time out?"

Veronica stopped pacing and menacingly approached Rebecca.

"Did you see that Miss?! She tried to throw the damn chair at me!"

"Yes I saw, but right now you still need to calm down before you end up on the floor like she did," Rebecca said firmly. She was surprised her voice wasn't shaking, because Veronica actually intimidated her. Up close she was even more frightening than normal. Tonight, her face looked like anger and aggression personified, and her eyes seemed to lack all human kindness. Rebecca had no doubt that if she dealt with this child the wrong way she would more than likely be on the receiving end of a vicious punch to the face.

"I ain't goin' down for something I didn't start. I didn't even touch that dumb girl!" Veronica's heavy breathing reminded Rebecca of an enraged bull ready to charge.

Rebecca's first instinct was to step back from such raw hostility, instead she reached out and took Veronica by the hand as she said, "I'm giving you the chance to come to the back and talk to me before you get yourself in a lot more trouble." Then she simply turned around and pulled Veronica along.

Relief flooded through Rebecca as Veronica followed her to the back instead of resisting.

Chapter 2

Monday dawned gray and chilly. Autumn had just set in, and all the leaves were beginning their annual descent towards the ground. The chill in the air was actually welcome for Rebecca's morning run. Usually she ran along the path at the riverside fairgrounds park in Clarksville Tennessee, where the terrain was characterized by gentle slopes and lots of trees in the background. It was an easy running route, the scenery was nice, and there weren't usually too many other people there early in the morning.

This morning she'd felt like challenging herself a bit more than normal. Rather than going down to the riverside park, she went to Ft. Campbell to run on the Air Assault road march route that she'd become all too familiar with during her years in the service. Instead of gentle slopes, it included some challenging hills that were daunting just to think about. The scenery was just as beautiful, but instead of a picturesque path lined with a few trees, the road-march route went straight through several large wooded areas that isolated her from the world so she could be alone with her thoughts.

Ten minutes into the run, Rebecca started sweating. She was thankful for the cooler temperatures and lower humidity as she kept to a steady pace and tried to concentrate on her breathing and on lengthening her stride. The first hill wasn't so bad; she was still fresh and there was still a spring in her step as she made it to the top. Her breathing became slightly more labored, but she felt mostly okay. The downhill on the other side gave her a much needed break.

As she ran, Rebecca thought about her job. She knew she didn't have what it took to be stern enough with those kids. She hated seeing them physically restrained, and she hated even more having to be the one to do it. Pain compliance was something she just didn't agree with, despite the fact that it was widely used in mental detention facilities to keep the residents under control. While she had no problem restraining a child who was an immediate physical danger to herself or another person, she balked at having to restrain them when they simply failed to comply with instructions.

The next hill loomed up ahead of her, much longer than the first. As she looked up at it, she felt a moment of hesitation. It seemed to stretch on forever, her legs burned, her breathing pattern had become sporadic, and she felt mentally and physically drained from work yesterday. She felt like she just didn't have enough in her to make it to the top. She was on the verge of stopping to walk when she decided to make herself run slightly faster instead.

"You can do it," she huffed out the words of encouragement to herself, feeling slightly ridiculous. Surprisingly they helped a little bit, so she kept repeating them as she struggled up the massive never ending hill.

"You're almost there! You can do it," she said again with more conviction as she neared the top.

"Yes you can," a male voice said suddenly beside her. In the next stride she was passed by a man wearing a rucksack that looked almost as big as she was. He ran past her and reached the top of the hill almost effortlessly. He was dripping sweat from everywhere, and he seemed to have been born to run. He hadn't even sounded out of breath when he'd spoken to her in passing. Rebecca looked ahead with a mixture of embarrassment and unwilling admiration.

As she watched him run ahead of her she momentarily forgot about her own discomfort. He was a fine specimen of manhood. He was huge, and he had well defined muscles everywhere. The sweaty shirt he wore clung to him like a second skin and he looked so incredible from behind Rebecca wished she could have seen his face. Rebecca had never been the type to ogle attractive men, but something about this man had definitely caught her attention. He was perfectly proportioned and symmetrical. His shoulders were huge and strong, he had a lean tapered waist, and his legs propelled him forward with power and grace. His body reminded her of Michelangelo's "David," arguably one of the most beautiful sculptures ever made of the human form.

His stride was strong and swift, and as it carried him farther away from her, Rebecca wondered if she would ever see him again. If she were the fearless type, like the women glamorized in magazines and television shows, she would have at least attempted to make a witty response... but she was no TV vixen with playful banter always at the ready, she was simply a quiet, hardworking person whose favorite thing to do was mind her own business. She was also very shy, and she knew that no man would want to talk to a woman who had serious trouble coming up with a response to, "Hi."

She'd run almost three miles by the time she got to the top of the next hill, and the man who had passed her was no longer in sight. No one was in sight. According to the distances spray painted on the path, it was time for her to turn around and head back. She was only running six miles today, the furthest she'd run in a long time.

When she turned around and gazed at the hilly three miles that seemed to stretch forever she thought about walking the rest of the way back. Then she had to give herself a mental shake to go on. She concentrated on simply breathing and putting one foot in front of the other. Hardly noticing as the first mile passed, she allowed her thoughts to drift into a short fantasy involving the man from online. Perhaps he had sent her a nice email expressing an interest in getting to know her, or perhaps not. The latter was more likely.

The last half mile wasn't as hard as the rest had been. Now that she could see relief just over the horizon her feet picked up speed seemingly of their own accord. As her pace quickened she imagined how good it would feel to be proud of herself instead of disappointed. Just over one more small hill and she would be finished... As she neared the top she broke into a sprint to get it over with, and after a moment of intense exhilaration she was done.

Rebecca walked for another ten minutes to cool down. Now that she wasn't running anymore she shivered in the cold air. She stayed near the path as she stretched. Part of her hoped to see the man who had spoken to her run by again. As she stretched, more than half of her attention was fixed on the top of the hill in anticipation. Eventually, she got in her car and drove home to shower, and she had to laugh a little at herself for being so fanciful.

Once she was home, Rebecca took a long relaxing shower. Today was the day she usually washed her hair, so she didn't have any plans to go out. It usually took a few hours for all of her waist-length hair to dry. During that time she would relax and clean up around her apartment. It was her day off... no school, no work, no anything except the chance to relax and reflect on the status of her life. As she stood in front of her bedroom mirror brushing her hair, she took a critical look at herself. She wore no makeup, and she had been cursed with such bad vision as to need glasses. Her face was feminine enough, and she had a nice smile. There was nothing wrong with the way she looked, but her infernal shyness always prevented her from talking to men, let alone actually dating any.

When she got around to checking her personals inbox there was one new message waiting to be read. Her heart beat a little faster as she thought about the email she'd sent a few days ago. He had replied! The handsome soldier had actually replied! She opened the message and read it three times before it finally sank in.

"I'm sorry, but I just don't think we're a good match," it stated. It wasn't even a real email; it was just one of the courtesy replies that the site asked users to select from when deleting messages they didn't want to pursue.

Rebecca was surprised by the amount of disappointment she felt at that moment. For some reason she'd taken it for granted that he would at least reply. Now she felt irritated and more than a little foolish for getting her hopes up too much. It was no great loss because she'd never even met the guy, but part of her felt like she was going to miss out on something. Every time she'd looked at his picture she'd felt moved by the character and the expression in his face, but apparently he wasn't interested.

A week later, she had managed to put him completely out of her mind. She had plenty of other things to focus on besides men. She was still having trouble adjusting to her hostile work environment, and she'd just decided to run her first marathon. Since she'd never run more than 12 miles in her life she had serious doubts as to whether she had the heart to do it. It was the biggest split second decision she'd ever made, but she was determined to stick to it.

It was now five a.m. and Rebecca was about to go for another six mile run along the Air Assault road-march route. This time she hoped to do better than she had last week. The morning air was crisp and chilly, and the sky was still mostly dark. There was just enough light to see the path as she started running.

The past week at work had been a rough one. Shirelle and Veronica constantly tried to attack each other, and every girl on the unit had taken sides. Rebecca thought of something she could say to get through to them as she ran, but nothing came to mind. She was so deep in thought she hardly noticed the sound of footsteps approaching from behind.

"You always run alone in the dark?" a male voice suddenly asked from beside her.

Rebecca was too startled to make a sensible reply. She stopped running and said, "Jeez! You scared me!"

"Sorry," he said without looking back.

Now irritated, Rebecca started running again. She had renewed energy from the adrenaline rush. His pace was only slightly quicker than hers, and he remained in sight as she trudged along up the hill behind him. He was the same man who had passed her last week, except today he wasn't carrying anything on his back. She would recognize his body anywhere. He was uncommonly tall and well proportioned.

He seemed to be taking it easy today. Rebecca knew he could have easily run far ahead of her, and she wondered why he was running so much slower today than he had been the first time he'd passed her. She ran close enough to hear his feet hitting the path and the steady even sound of his breathing, and for some reason his presence soothed her instead of intruding on her solitude. She ran behind him watching his graceful stride until she reached the turnaround point. At three miles she turned around without a word and started to run back. It took her a little less time today than it had last week. She looked at her watch and estimated that she had run at a nine minute mile pace. Not too bad, but there was still lots of room for improvement.

The sky brightened into full morning light while Rebecca walked an extra mile to cool down. Despite wearing shorts and a short sleeved shirt, she'd managed to sweat so much that her clothes clung uncomfortably to her. Her body temperature quickly cooled down in the crisp air, and she shivered as she approached her car. Tomorrow would be soon enough to do it again.

Norman turned around only a minute or two after Rebecca did, and he watched her run the last three miles. He had only planned on running four, but he had changed his mind at the last minute. He knew it was none of his business what women did with their time, but he wouldn't approve of his sister running alone on such a dark, isolated route, and he didn't really like the idea of any woman, especially one who was so small, putting herself in such a vulnerable position. He'd seen enough in his life to know that not all guys were trustworthy, but apparently she didn't know that. He ran this route every day, and usually there were no women. When they did show up on this path, they came later in the morning when it was light and they travelled in little packs. Today, he had considered running next to her to keep her company and maybe give her a few pointers, but he'd accidentally startled her instead. As he watched her drive away, he wondered if she would be back tomorrow.

The next day Rebecca decided to wait until it was almost light outside to start her run. She sat in her car listening to one of her favorite CD's until she saw the first light of dawn appear on the horizon. She was cold and tired, and her motivation level was somewhere around the soles of her feet.

Right around 5:30 she got out and started stretching. Today she was only running three miles, and then she was going home to do some strength training exercises. Her schedule was full today. She had to attend verbal de-escalation training at work, and then she had to go to a developmental psychology class tonight. After that she would be able to go home and study for an upcoming midterm.

Being a psychology major wasn't that hard academically, but it was difficult on a personal level. Her job was the main thing that made it hard, because she was able to see firsthand the way counseling affected those who needed it. Many of the girls at the youth center had come from horrific child neglect and abuse, and the mental health services they received might be able to change their lives for the better. Rebecca was working towards becoming a school psychologist, but she had to finish her master's degree and gain a few years of experience to qualify for such a job. Working with the girls at the youth center was equally challenging and rewarding, at least that's what she told herself when things got to be too intense at work.

The three miles went by very quickly. Rebecca half expected to see Michelangelo's "David" again, but she'd also deliberately chosen a different route to prevent such an occurrence. Today she ran in complete, uninterrupted solitude, but it wasn't as nice as she'd thought it would be. If she was completely honest with herself she'd have to admit that it had been a little boring.

According to her newly acquired training schedule, Rebecca needed to run seven miles on Wednesday. Since she also had to study for her statistics mid-term exam, she decided to start early. She was out at her chosen route at just after five a.m. Following a quick stretch and warm up, she ran up the hills she was coming to loath.

She didn't start to sweat until the middle of the second mile. As always, she had trouble staying focused on her breathing, and she almost stopped completely while running up one of the hills. It was the huge, never ending hill that always killed her. Every other time she'd walked part of the hill or at least slowed to the point where she was barely running. Today, she made up her mind to run all the way to the top without slowing down to a snail's pace.

"It's just a stupid hill," she muttered to herself as she began the long trek to the top. She kept encouraging herself until she made it. A little bit at a time she saw some improvement in her running. Today her pace was slower overall, but she had managed to make it to the top of the biggest hill, and she was running one mile more than she had in over three years.

After the first three miles she got into the rhythm of her breathing and the sound of her feet hitting the pavement. She concentrated on that rhythm, and tried to keep it steady. Every two steps she breathed in through her nose, and every other two steps she breathed out through her mouth. *In, in, out... In, in, out...* she repeated over and over in her head.

Once she reached her turn around point, she felt almost proud of herself. She went back over the giant hill, and it didn't intimidate her quite as much now that she knew she could do it.

In, in, out... In, in-

"The hills are easier if you keep your posture nice and straight."

Where in the world did he come from?! Rebecca thought as he fell into step beside her. Not only had he startled her into forgetting her breathing pattern, but her heart felt like it was about to jump right out of her chest.

"You always so quiet?" He didn't even have the decency to sound out of breath when she was obviously struggling.

"Yes," Rebecca huffed out with great difficulty. Even if she hadn't been running, she probably wouldn't have been able to come up with anything else to say. Blasted shyness!

Surprisingly he ran the last three miles right beside her. He encouraged her every time they came to a hill. It was actually kind of fun having someone to run with, and the fact that he was an excellent runner was an added bonus. He didn't sound out of breath, and he had slowed down considerably to keep pace with her.

On the last half mile when Rebecca picked up her pace he said, "There you go, finish strong!"

She smiled when she finally stopped running. She still had to walk another quarter mile to get to her car. When he started walking beside her, she was surprised again. She glanced over at him just long enough to see that he had a powerful chest. It was right at her eye level, because he was so much taller than she. He was the tallest man she'd ever stood right next to, but despite his size she didn't feel threatened at all by his presence. She did, however, feel mighty awkward about talking to him.

"How many miles did you run today?" he finally asked after the lengthy silence.

"Seven," Rebecca said quietly.

"That's pretty good. I don't see many people running this route, especially not this early," he said in a friendly manner. They still hadn't looked at each other, other than the occasional, furtive sidelong glance.

"Do you run here every day?" she asked cautiously.

"Yeah," he said.

Rebecca could see her car now, so she decided to introduce herself before she had to leave. She stopped walking and turned to face the stranger.

"So, what's your name?" she asked as she looked up at him. Her brown eyes instantly recognized the bluish gray eyes set in the stern yet handsome face of the same man who had rejected her at the personals sight. Embarrassment set in immediately, and she looked away.

"Hey, you look familiar! Do I know you from somewhere?" he asked as he studied her face. Did he honestly not recognize her?

"Yes you do," she said, "and that's exactly why I don't go there anymore."

He looked confused for a moment as if he wasn't quite sure if she had been kidding. Her half smile probably didn't help at all, and he looked like he thought she might be joking.

"Well whatever I did, please allow me to make it up to you sometime. Maybe I could buy you some breakfast... I'm sure you must be hungry. Right?" He smiled, and managed to look so charming that

Rebecca almost forgot that he had rejected her, and that she had a mid-term to study for.

"I have too much to do," she said and quickly turned around, walked to her car and drove home.

Norman stood glued to the same spot and wondered what had just happened. He had asked a cute young woman out, and she had treated him like she hadn't even noticed him. Usually he had more problems getting women to stop flirting with him. That had been a factor contributing to his divorce. No matter how much he'd paid attention to his ex-wife, she'd never stopped being jealous and demanding.

As he turned around to run back towards his truck, he thought again about the young woman he'd run with. What had he been thinking? First of all, he'd never tried to talk to an African American woman before, and secondly once he'd gotten a good look at her face it was obvious that she was way too young for him. She looked like she was nineteen at the most. The last thing his kids needed right now was their thirty six year old father lusting after some young girl. He drove home trying to remember where he'd seen her before.

Chapter 3

The verbal de-escalation training didn't last as long as Rebecca thought it would. The human resource department had accidentally scheduled her to attend three classes, but she was only due for one. By eleven a.m. she was clocking out. Usually she spent her mornings volunteering at a local elementary school. She acted as a teacher's aide helping the kids who needed some extra assistance with their math and reading skills. Today she could only be there for an hour, but she still wanted to stop by and read with the children for a while.

Rebecca had been working with Mrs. Martin's second grade class the longest. There were twenty seven children in the class, and the teacher simply didn't have enough time in the day to tutor all the ones who needed extra help and still keep the rest of the class moving forward.

Rebecca was well acquainted with three of Mrs. Martin's students. A cheerful little blond boy named Dylan who needed help with his reading skills, a shy girl named Peggy who suffered from obvious neglect, and a cute little African-American boy named Darius whose only problem was a propensity towards being a class clown. Darius was smart, but he'd rather disrupt class than let the other students know that his reading level was one of the highest in the class. Peggy was always a little grubby, and needed to brush her teeth more, but other than that she seemed like an average second grader. Rebecca had a feeling that she was one of the brightest students in class, but she was just too shy to answer when the teacher called on her. Rebecca identified with Peggy's reluctance to talk, because she'd often done the same as a child.

The only child needing special attention Rebecca didn't understand was Dylan. He came to school neat every day, he was never tardy, he wasn't shy, and he seemed like an intelligent little boy. So, why was he reading below his grade level? Rebecca had been working with him for a few months now, and she still didn't understand. He'd made some progress while in the tutoring program, but it was obvious that he was getting little help from home.

"I can't sound it out. I don't know that word," Dylan whined as he looked down at the literature book.

"You can do it," Rebecca encouraged. "Look, all you have to do is sound out each part one at a time. I'll help you." She covered half of the word 'swallowed' with her finger. "What does that part say?" she asked.

"Ssss-Wa-All....Swal?" he sounded out cautiously.

"Good!" Rebecca smiled at him. "Now try this part."

"Llll-oh-wa-e-d....lo-wed?" he asked.

"Not quite, but almost. This part is only one syllable," she replied.

He sounded the whole word out again, and eventually said, "Swallowed!"

"That's right!" Rebecca said with more enthusiasm than she actually felt.

By the time he'd labored through the entire story, it was time for Rebecca to go. She still had to do a little bit of last minute studying for her midterm.

When the alarm rang at five a.m. on Saturday morning Rebecca sprang out of bed with an uncharacteristic amount of energy. Today she was looking forward to her job. Maybe she would be able to deal with Veronica and Shirelle a little better. All the way to work she hoped for a good day.

By 6:45 she was sitting in the staff break room listening to the morning briefing about the status of all the girls on the unit and taking notes. During the week there had been two new admits, and no discharges. There were now 30 girls in residence. Shirelle and Veronica were on ten feet restriction, which meant that they had to be ten feet away from each other at all times to prevent a fight. Rebecca had no doubt that they had found ways to get at each other during the week, and they would continue to try all weekend. She would just have to stay prepared.

"Ladies, you need to line up for breakfast!" Rebecca heard Miss Parker yell as she approached the section of the building that held the female bedrooms. Miss Parker had been working at the youth center for more than three years, and Rebecca had only been there for ten months. So far, Ms. Parker was the one person at the center who made Rebecca the most nervous. She was a tall, thick, voluptuous African-American woman with clear skin the color of dark chocolate. Her nose was small, and she always had her hair done in some hip style. She had no problem asserting her authority and getting the girls to follow her every command. Rebecca wished she had one tenth of the assertiveness that Miss Parker had.

It didn't take the girls on the unit long to comply with Miss Parker's order. They lined up, but they still displayed their contempt for authority by talking in line and leaning against the walls with insolent looks on their faces.

"We can stand here all day ladies! We're not going anywhere until you get my line straight!" Miss Parker called out with authority.

"Yo dog! Chill out! You know Miss Parker don't play, she'll let the boys go first all weekend," one of the girls said to the ones making noise.

"Yo, why don't you shut the fuck up?!" Veronica said as she took a menacing step toward the girl who had spoken.

Rebecca jumped between them, and looked Veronica in the eyes as she told her, "You need to stop using profanity, and stop talking in line. You're already losing points."

"I don't give a *fuck* about those *damn* points!" Veronica spat out.

"Well, you should Veronica, because it's the only way you're going to get out of here," Rebecca said.

"Don't call me Veronica anymore!"

"Why not?" Rebecca asked confused. She was sure she had the right name.

"Just call me Ronnie Miss. Please?"

"Okay. Get in line and be quiet…Ronnie," Rebecca said quietly.

"If y'all are done talking… ladies give me a count so we can go to breakfast," Miss Parker said.

When Miss Parker passed by, Rebecca offered her a small smile, but she didn't seem to care. Rebecca's very presence seemed to be an irritant to her. Today was going to be a long day.

By Sunday night Rebecca felt exhausted from her back to back double shifts with the girls. She doubted she would feel like going out to run six miles in the morning, but she set her alarm for five a.m. anyway. She hadn't seen "David" since Wednesday morning when he'd run with her. Thursday she ran at the park, and Friday she'd done some cross training instead of running. Saturday and Sunday had been spent working. As she went to bed, she wondered if he would be there in the morning.

Monday morning was the coldest day of the season so far. By 5:30 the temperature was still in the upper thirties, and Rebecca really didn't feel like running in the cold. She dressed in long tights and a long sleeved, moisture wicking shirt to keep warm.

A slight dusting of frost covered the grass as a stark reminder that winter was just around the corner. Most of the trees were beginning to look barren and depressing, and the days were getting shorter. Rebecca ran the road-march route admiring the scenery and thinking about how beautiful the Tennessee hills looked first thing in the morning. The sky was almost clear, except for a few light wispy clouds that emphasized the brilliant light blue of the morning sky. She struggled up the first hill as she looked at nature and felt very small and insignificant in comparison. Today, the vastness of the outdoors made her feel as if each stride was inching her forward towards no real progress.

Her breath came out in short gasps, and after a short time her side began to hurt from the labored breathing pattern. Her lungs hurt from the cold air, her nose leaked, and her head ached as well. Today just wasn't her day for running.

She just kept telling herself that it would all be worth it when she crossed the finish line. She slowed down to a mere jog at times, and at others she had to constantly bargain with herself to keep her feet moving because she was so tired from working all weekend. As she neared the turnaround point she saw a lone figure running towards her in the distance. Instinctively she knew it was the same man she'd seen before. She turned around and hoped that he was running slow enough to stay behind today.

Now that she'd seen him, her feet seemed to move a little faster, and her stride was more purposeful. She wanted to make it back without being passed up by him again. She could sense his eyes on her as she ran, and it was nerve racking. Her entire body was on edge as she listened for any sign of approaching footsteps. She had gone less than half a mile when she heard him behind her. He ran so much faster than she did, she expected him to pass her up at any moment.

When he finally got to her side she felt an odd sense of relief mixed with trepidation. He ran beside her, but he didn't say anything. Rebecca glanced over at him and felt sudden irritation with herself for being so affected by his presence, and with him just for being there. How *dare* he run next to her as if he knew her?

She didn't know what was guiding the odd sense of perverseness that caused her to run faster. Heaven knew there was no way she could out run him, but she lengthened her stride anyway and picked up the pace. He did the same, except with a lot less effort. His breathing still sounded calm compared to hers.

She glanced at him again and ran a little faster. He ran a little faster as well... They were now coming up to the big hill that always gave Rebecca problems. She glanced at it uneasily, and then she glanced back at the man beside her. Her face set with determination and she ran even faster. He must have been surprised, because she managed to break away from him for a moment before he caught up and passed her.

Damn man! Rebecca thought as she broke into an all out sprint towards the top of the hill. All she wanted was to get to the top first. Her nostrils flared as she pumped out as much speed as possible from her tired body. Her legs moved so fast she actually felt like she was flying for a moment. Her focus remained fixed on the top of the hill. She would get there first, even if it killed her. The wind roared past her ears as she concentrated on her wild sprint, she barely noticed when the rubber band that had been holding her voluminous hair in a bun broke. Her hair was suddenly all over the place and in the way, but she continued to run with all her heart. The finish line was so close now, and suddenly he was right beside her with his longer more powerful stride. She didn't look at him; she stayed focused and they both reached the top at about the same time. It was impossible to tell who had won.

"A photo finish!" he said as they both slowed down to a jog. This time he actually sounded a little out of breath.

"What?" Rebecca huffed out in indignation. "I beat you!"

"It looked more like a tie to me," he countered.

Rebecca had to catch some more of her breath before she replied again. "Then we'll have to do a tie breaker."

"I'm game if you are," he managed to sound so arrogant she momentarily felt like punching him.

"Okay, once I get to the end of my run. I have about two miles left to go. We can sprint to the finish," she said between breaths as they continued to run at a slow pace.

"You mean I have to run this slow for two more miles?" he teased.

Rebecca narrowed her eyes and said, "I don't recall asking you to join me."

"Touché!" he smiled down at her. "I never did tell you my name last week... it's Norman."

"Nice to meet you Norman," Rebecca said, trying not to sound too out of breath.

"Aren't you going to tell me your name?" he asked.

"Rebecca," was her terse reply.

"Mind if I ask how old you are?"

"22," she really wished he would stop talking. Running was hard enough without adding conversation with the most attractive man she'd ever seen into the mix.

"You barely look old enough to be out here running by yourself all the time."

She didn't know what to say to that, so she didn't respond. He took the hint and they ran in silence the rest of the way. Rebecca kept wondering why he was running with her. Surely he must recognize her from her personals profile picture.

"You see that blue car up there?" she said when the end was near.

"Yeah," he answered.

"Whoever gets there first is the winner. On the count of three...you count."

He gave her a strange look before he said, "Okay. One...Two...Three."

And they were off again. This time he was the obvious victor. Rebecca came in a half step behind him despite giving it her best effort. Defeat rankled, especially because he didn't look like he'd given it his very best shot.

They both stood panting for a moment before he said, "We should walk for a while and stretch to cool down."

"Okay," Rebecca panted, unsure if she couldn't catch her breath due to the sprint or due to his electrifying presence.

So far she'd managed to avoid looking directly at his face. It had been easy because of his height. He was more than a foot taller than she was.

"So you're 22... you don't look it," he said as he walked beside her.

"Yeah, I hear that a lot."

"I'm not surprised. Why do you run out here every day? You're not in the army are you?" he asked.

"Nope."

"What do you do?"

"I work, and I go to school."

"You don't talk much, do you?" he observed.

"Not really."

"So what brings you out here every morning? Most women wouldn't choose the road-march path to run on... It's not exactly for the faint of heart." he said.

"I just want to get better at running," she told the half truth, because she had a feeling that if she admitted to wanting to run a marathon he would laugh at her.

"I could help you with that," he volunteered. He stopped walking and began to stretch. She still managed to avoid looking directly at him while they stretched their hamstrings, thighs, hips, and calves. Her legs trembled a little, and she hoped he didn't notice.

When they finished stretching he came to stand in front of her, virtually forcing her to look up at him or seem like a coward. He stood close enough for her to smell the raw, potent masculinity of his sweat mingled with deodorant and the scent of the crisp morning air. She shivered a little as she tore her eyes away from his chest and looked into his face. He looked at her with a stern expression that was very intimidating to say the least. At the moment his eyes looked more blue than gray.

"So what do you think? You want my help or not?" he sounded impatient.

"You sure you want to run with me? I run really slow," she said as she looked straight into his eyes.

A faint glimmer of a smile passed over his face, and he said, "I don't mind. It's nice to take it slow for a change."

"Okay then," she smiled and stuck out her hand. "Nice to meet you Norman."

"Nice meeting you too, Rebecca," he laughed a little as he shook her hand. His grasp was warm and firm and he held her hand for just a moment longer than necessary.

"Well I'll see you tomorrow then," she said quietly after he released her hand. She smiled and turned to walk back toward her car.

She was some distance away when he called out, "What time?!"

"Six!" she yelled back, and continued walking away.

Norman tried not to watch her walk away, but he kept glancing back at her. Rebecca... that was a pretty name. He wondered if anyone ever called her Becky. She didn't look like she would let anyone shorten her name. For such a young looking person, her gaze was very direct and assessing. While he'd been talking to her, he'd gotten the curious feeling that she could see directly into his soul without even trying that hard. It was irksome to feel so unnerved by a woman, especially one who was so much smaller than him and looked like a mere girl.

He had complained about her slow pace, but he honestly didn't mind too much. That surprised him, because most of the time slow runs got on his nerves. The race to the top of the hill had been the most exhilarating and spontaneous thing he'd done in a long time. As he ran beside her earlier he couldn't keep himself from glancing down and admiring her form. She wasn't the best runner he'd ever seen, but she did try harder than most.

He chuckled a little to himself thinking about how she'd tried to outrun him when they'd come to a hill. No one had ever tried that before, and he'd had a hard time not cracking up about it right in front of her. He also hadn't felt so alive in a long time.

Rebecca was determined to spend her Mondays relaxing, because it was her only day off all week. The first thing she did when she got home after her run was take a shower and wash her hair.

Norman. She couldn't believe that such an attractive man could have such a terrible name. Norman Bates the psycho came to mind, and then Norm from "Cheers" came next. Norman was one of those names that made her wonder what the victim's mother had been thinking to stick them with it. She hoped Norman's middle name wasn't something equally atrocious, like Edith. Lucky for him he was good looking.

She still couldn't believe he didn't recognize her from her personals profile. If he never did she certainly wouldn't bring it up. It would be better to spare herself the embarrassment. While she was thinking about it, she logged on and made her profile private so that he couldn't look at it again even if he wanted to.

Rebecca hadn't practiced on her keyboard for more than a week, and she really had the urge to play today. She'd had a few piano lessons when she was younger, but her mother had always been critical of the fact that she liked to waste too much time on frivolous things. Piano was considered frivolous by her mother's standards, but something about the sound of the piano had always stirred Rebecca's soul. Despite the fact that her mother had disapproved of her learning piano, Rebecca had found ways around her mother's condemnation. She'd often volunteered to help clean the church so she could play on a regular basis without her mother finding out. Her favorite music had always been classical piano, but few people knew that about her.

Rebecca's mother had actually been disapproving of many of her interests. She'd constantly lectured her on the importance of doing things that served a purpose, things like working, volunteering, and saving money. If Rebecca had wanted to spend her time practicing martial arts her mother would have been ecstatic, but her childhood pursuits had always been more academic than physical. Rebecca had grown up with more than a few interests her mother didn't know about. Her interest in the piano and classical music was the main one she'd kept secret.

She'd splurged on a keyboard that sounded very close to a real piano, and no one knew she played it. In her younger years she'd struggled learning the fingering techniques on her own, but now she was pretty good at it. Her main problem now was reading more complex pieces of music, but she was made steady improvements through practice.

She sat down and played Beethoven's "Fur Elise" several times to warm up her fingers. It was one of her favorites, because she'd found that in times of emotional stress the easy melody soothed her. As her fingers caressed the keys she completely lost herself in the music. Tension melted away, and she felt the calm begin to seep into her body. When the song ended she opened her eyes and began to struggle through the ridiculously difficult drills in her newest practice book.

Chapter 4

The next morning Rebecca arrived ten minutes early. From her days in the military she knew that if you weren't present ten minutes prior to the prescribed time you were late. The last thing she wanted to do was give Norman a reason to dislike her. Her new middle name was going to be punctual from now on.

She spotted a lone figure stretching in the distance as she parked her car. She recognized him instantly, and hoped that he wasn't impatiently waiting for her. She also hoped that he hadn't changed his mind.

He stared directly at her as she got out of her car and walked towards him. She felt as if she were walking up to a drill sergeant as he continued to assess her with his serious gaze. This morning his face looked as if it were set in granite that would crack if he smiled. By the time she got to him, Rebecca thought seriously about turning around and running alone.

"You're early," he said, sounding more curious than anything. His face was still inscrutable and stern.

"No I'm not. I'm right on time," Rebecca said quietly as she stood in front of him feeling like she was in the middle of an in-ranks inspection from the first sergeant.

"Ten minutes prior…" he smiled at her. As unexpected as it was, this smile seemed to lighten his face just a little bit. It wasn't like the grimace she remembered from his profile pictures.

"Yeah, I know how you military guys are about punctuality," she admitted ruefully.

"That doesn't apply to civilians, so I wouldn't have held it against you if you'd showed up right at six," he said brusquely.

"That's good to know." He didn't seem to want to chit chat anymore, so she began stretching.

"How far you plan on running today?" he asked as he watched her stretch.

"Three miles," she said expecting him to laugh at her. She glanced at him and caught him staring at her again. He looked so disapproving she had to fight the urge to check her appearance for flaws. She'd taken extra time to secure her thick hair properly this morning. She wanted to be absolutely sure it wouldn't come loose again while she ran. Her attire was decent and appropriate for the weather, and she didn't have any strange things growing on her face.... So, what was he staring at?

"I'm ready," she said when she finished stretching.

"Alright. I'll run at your pace until you warm up, and then we can do a fartlek run since we aren't going that far."

"Umm, what's a fartlek run?" Rebecca asked hesitantly. She was sure she'd heard of one before, but she couldn't remember the particulars.

"It'll help you run faster. All you have to do is run faster when I tell you to, and when you're not running faster we'll keep to an easy pace that you can handle," he explained.

"Okay, I can do that," Rebecca said as she started running.

Norman fell into step beside her and said, "Where do you normally run?"

"At the riverside park, and on a treadmill," Rebecca replied while trying to concentrate on her breathing pattern.

"This is quite a change for you then... Lots more hills on post," he observed.

"Yeah, tell me about it!"

He glanced at her and chuckled. Their breath was clearly visible in the chilly morning air, but their bodies were getting warm from their exertions. Soon they'd be sweating.

"You see that light pole over there?" he pointed ahead.

"Yeah," Rebecca said trying not to sound out of breath.

"Think you can pick up the pace until you get there, then go back to the pace you're running at now?" he asked.

"Yeah," she panted. She wasn't sure exactly how much faster she should run, so she lengthened her stride and ran fast enough to feel just outside her comfort zone. She looked up at him for some sign of approval, and was captivated by the sight of his handsome profile and magnificent upper body. He wasn't even breathing that hard... She had to wonder why he was running with her. He must be bored and tired of running alone. As soon as the thought crossed her mind, she latched onto it as a good excuse for such a handsome man to willingly spend time with her. She managed to relax some; he was just a lonely man who wanted some company. Loneliness was something that she could relate to, no matter how good looking he was.

The distance to the pole had seemed short when he'd pointed to it, but as she ran it seemed to extend as if by magic. When she finally reached it, Rebecca was ready to walk instead of just slow down.

"Remember to breathe," he advised her when he noticed her sporadic labored breathing.

She went back to telling herself, *in, in, out* as she ran. It worked. A few minutes later she felt as normal as she could while running.

"When you get to the next pole, do it again. We'll do the same for every other pole... Okay?" he said.

"Sure," she replied. She looked ahead at how far apart the blasted poles were, and all her motivation seemed to migrate towards her feet again.

"You can do it," he said as if reading her thoughts.

Rebecca didn't reply, because it was time for her to pick up the pace again.

By the end of the run her legs felt hot and uncomfortable, she was sweaty and disheveled, her hair was coming loose, and she couldn't remember feeling so proud of herself in a long time.

"Thanks Norman," she told him right after they stopped to walk.

"You did good," he said, sounding like he actually meant it.

She looked up at him and said, "Really?" Their eyes met for a moment, and her heart began to beat faster again.

"Yeah, I thought so. I see soldiers who fall out of the unit runs all the time. The important thing is that you kept trying. Half of the battle is mental. Whether you think you can or you think you can't, you're always right."

"I've heard that before somewhere," Rebecca said.

"I know; so have I," he said. "But I don't remember who said it," he admitted with a slight grin.

"And I was beginning to think you knew everything!" Rebecca quipped with a smile.

"Man... Someone should have told me to beware of the quiet ones," he laughed.

"What do you mean?" she asked.

Norman opened his mouth to respond, and was beset with the momentary urge to ask her out, but her raised eyebrow and discerning expression stopped him. "Just that you don't talk much, but when you do it usually has a kick to it," he said instead.

"I wasn't trying to be mean, I was just kidding!" Rebecca exclaimed. "Anyway, you barely know me," she added with less heat.

For a fleeting moment Norman felt like he knew her better than she thought. Something inside him had felt a connection with her the first time he'd seen her running alone so early in the morning. She'd been struggling up the hill and encouraging herself along the way, unaware that he had slowed down to listen to her. He'd wanted her to make it to the top; he'd wanted her to make it to the top of her hill just as much as he'd wanted to conquer every hill he'd encountered since he'd started running at ten years old. He understood her better than she thought he did. He even understood her desire to be alone, and he recognized the same loneliness in her expression that he often felt. They both kept it hidden well, but it was there. He was seeing it right now as he looked directly into her eyes.

"Then we're going to have to do something about that," he said. He looked at her expecting a reply, but she said nothing. "So, same time tomorrow?" he asked after a long silence.

"Yeah," she said. "Thanks again for helping me with my run. I really appreciate it."

"No problem, see you in the morning."

"Bye," she said and walked away.

Norman watched her walk off, and felt like a dumb ass. She hadn't even responded to his obvious attempt to get to know her on a more personal level. She must be a lesbian...maybe he should ask her tomorrow just to clear things up.

Wednesday morning Rebecca showed up right on time.

"What happened to ten minutes prior?" he asked.

"There was a long line of cars coming on post this morning," Rebecca yawned.

"I think 3rd Brigade had an alert this morning," he told her. When she didn't reply he cleared his throat and said, "Let's go ahead and stretch so we can get started." Was she always this difficult to talk to?

As they ran at a steady pace for five miles, Norman fought the urge to ask her a bunch of questions. He had a feeling she wouldn't answer more than half of them anyway. She didn't say one word to him the entire time they ran.

When they finally stopped to walk and cool down he'd had enough of the silence. He was a very social and friendly person, so it went against the grain to be so taciturn, especially with a woman he liked.

"Why are you so quiet?" he asked trying not to sound too irritated.

"I don't know," she admitted after thinking about it for a moment.

"I don't know that many quiet people."

"Neither do I," Rebecca said.

Norman stopped walking and chuckled.

Rebecca looked up at him and was once again arrested by how magnetic he was. His face had a slight sheen of perspiration, his eyes were crinkled with laugh lines at the corners, and his lips were turned up in an easy smile. Everything about him called out to her at that moment, and she quickly looked away before he saw the naked longing in her eyes.

"What's so funny?" she asked.

"You are!" he smiled at the top of her head. "So, why does your boyfriend let you run alone all the time?" he asked.

"I don't have one...and if I did he wouldn't tell me when and where I can run," she retorted.

"That's cool," he said. He had a feeling that she must be a lesbian. Asking couldn't hurt; she wasn't in the military, so "don't ask don't tell" didn't apply to her... "Can I ask you a personal question?" he said.

She gave him a suspicious look, and then said, "Yes."

"Do you have a girlfriend?" Now that he'd asked he felt a little silly.

She didn't answer right away; instead she burst into an uncontrollable fit of laughter. When she finally recovered enough to speak, she exclaimed, "What do you think?!"

He watched her laugh, and realized for the first time since meeting her that she was shy about her smile. The first thing she'd done was cover it up with her hands. He had the urge to hold her hands down with his so he could see her entire face.

"I think you should just answer the question," he said. He was almost holding his breath waiting for an answer.

"I'm not gay... I'm a shy individual who never goes out," she admitted as she looked him in the eye.

"Then we'll have to do something about that... What are you doing today?"

"Not much. Why?"

"I have the day off. I only got up this early because I promised to run with you. Let's have breakfast together," he said.

"Okay," she surprised herself by agreeing so quickly. Just a couple of weeks ago she'd been irritated at his rejection, and now she was acting like a school girl with a crush.

"Good. Let's go then, I'm parked a little ways up the road." He immediately started walking towards his truck before she changed her mind.

"Wait!" she said. "You want to go *now*? I'm all sweaty..."

"You look fine, and I'm hungry." This time he grabbed her hand before he started walking again, and pulled her along behind him.

"Are you always this forceful?" Rebecca demanded with slight smile in her voice. She sounded upset, but in truth she was m⸍ excited than anything else. He hadn't been rough at all when ⸍ taken hold of her hand, and her body temperature had gonꞙ practically freezing to overheated in the space of two secon⸍ hand completely engulfed hers, bringing some welcome waʳ the cold.

"Nope," he said. He hadn't even spared her a gⱡ kept walking with her hand in his as if he had every righ⸍

"I can walk on my own you know..."

"I know," he said, but he didn't let go. ⸍ like to go?" he asked.

"Let's go to the pancake house up the rꞓ

"Okay." He liked her choice, and thꞓ seven a.m. was good for him. It meant there to crowd the place.

They walked in companionable his truck. He hadn't thought to let g protested again. He hadn't held a woman's hand in a long time. Since his marriage had gone sour he hadn't even had the urge to hold anyone else's hand. He looked down at Rebecca and wondered what it was about her that made him want to hold her hand.

She was much shorter than the women he normally dated. Being such a tall guy had caused him to develop a preference for tall women. His ex-wife had been almost six feet tall. Standing next to Rebecca was almost like standing next to a kid. In addition to her smaller stature, she was also much more reserved and quiet than other women. Usually shy people irritated him... so why in the world did he like her? She was the opposite of everything he'd ever been attracted to in a woman. The only thing that didn't puzzle him about his attraction to her was her prettiness and her shape. He'd always liked pretty women with an hour glass figure. What guy didn't?

When they got to his truck she paused by the passenger side door and looked at him with one eyebrow raised. What now?

"I've never been in a truck this big. Why do you drive such a big truck?" she asked.

"There's a first time for everything... and look at me, what else would I fit in?" he said as he unlocked the door for her. "Hop in."

Rebecca climbed in thinking about how strange the morning was turning out. Not only was she going to breakfast with the very man who had rejected her, but she was excited to be doing so. Feeling a little like Alice falling down the rabbit hole, she decided to just go with the flow. For once in her life she was doing something spontaneous and...fun?

"So, Becky...can I call you Becky?...what do you do to relax?" Norman asked once they were on their way.

"You can call me Becky if I can call you Norm, and I read books to relax. You?"

He chuckled and said, "Rebecca it is! No one's gonna call me Norm." He glanced at her before he continued, "I like to run to unwind."

Rebecca didn't know how to reply to that. She hated running, would never see it as a relaxing activity. She didn't know what else to say but it seemed to be her turn to come up with something. "Neat," she said.

"I admire your enthusiasm," he laughed.

"I just can't believe you find running to be relaxing... of all the things to choose from why running?"

"I haven't really given it much thought... Part of the appeal is the feeling that I'm totally alone with my thoughts, especially when I run in places where there aren't many people," he answered.

Rebecca wondered why he chose to run with her if he valued privacy, but she didn't ask.

"I'm a very social person, and running has always been the only time I really have to myself. I started when I was a kid. I have six brothers and a sister, so I needed to do something on my own. Running was my thing," he told her.

Shortly after he stopped talking, they arrived at the pancake house. He came around, opened the door for her and helped her down.

"Thanks," she smiled up at him.

"No problem."

Once they were seated, Rebecca felt nervous again. He sat across from her and looked directly at her. She wondered what he was thinking. She looked down at the table most of the time, but every once in a while she glanced up at him to find his eyes still on her.

"Silence doesn't bother me... I could sit here and just look at you all morning, but I would rather talk about something," he said eventually.

"What do you want to talk about?" she asked.

"What do you do for a living? What are you going to school for?" he leaned forward and waited for her response.

"I'm working on a Master's in psychology, and I plan on having a career as a school psychologist. Right now I work as a counselor for teenage girls who live at a mental health facility."

"Wow, that's interesting. What kind of things do you do at work? Sit behind a desk and ask questions like, 'How do you feel about that?'" he half joked.

"Not at all. The therapists get to do that. My job is *way* more hands on than that. I have to monitor the kids, give them on the spot counseling when they need it to avoid trouble or some sort of emotional crisis. We write down everything they do, break up fights, and escort them everywhere they go...even the bathroom. The residential counselors are the most hated of all the staff because we are the ones these girls see all the time, so we are the ones they take all their anger, aggression, and frustration out on. It's a hard job to be honest with you. I hate having to restrain children, but I hate even more seeing them hurt themselves or anyone else."

"Sounds like you're a lot tougher than you look."

"Thanks…I think," she replied.

"I wasn't messing with you; I really meant it as a compliment." He gave her a serious look, and she believed him.

"What do you do?" she asked trying to keep things light.

"I'm in the army."

"I kind of figured that," she said. "What do you do in the army?"

"Nothing too interesting. I'd rather hear more about you."

"Okay. What do you want to know?" Rebecca asked.

"Why did you decide to improve your running? You don't even seem to like it much."

Rebecca looked down at her hands crossed in her lap, and decided to admit the truth. The worst he could do was laugh… "I want to run in the next Music City Marathon," she confessed.

Norman sat back and observed her with a thoughtful expression. He was about to say something when the server appeared with their breakfast. They ate in silence for a few minutes. Rebecca steadfastly stared at her plate, and Norman stared at her. He kept thinking about the day they'd raced up the hill. He could have easily won, but he'd been taken aback by the sight of her long dark hair falling down as she'd run. He looked at her now as she sat across from him eating her buttermilk pancakes. Her hair was tied up in a knot at the back of her head again. He wondered how she would wear it on a date.

"Do you ever wear your hair down?" he inquired.

"Not usually, but I have on rare occasions. Why do you ask?"

"No reason… just curious," he said then cleared his throat. "So, I was just thinking that since you want to run a marathon you might want to start a training program…if you haven't already. I can help you with that," he blurted out on impulse.

"But you already are helping me," Rebecca said hesitantly. She wasn't sure where he was going with this new offer, but her curiosity was piqued.

"Yeah I know, but that help is just with running. To run a marathon you'll need to do lots of physical training if you plan on finishing. You'll need to do more running, cross-training, and lots of strength training. You'll also have to eat right, and prepare yourself mentally, especially for the first one. This is your first, right?" He looked at her as he waited for a response.

"Yes it will be my first. I can't believe you're willing to help me out with all of that stuff. You barely know me," Rebecca replied. She was baffled by this man. He sat across from her looking attractive and stern, but at the same time he was making her an offer that seemed to be based on kindness. Maybe he wasn't quite as mean as he looked sometimes. He'd certainly been nice enough to her.

"It won't really be any trouble. I already run and work out all the time. I can just adjust my schedule to accommodate your training needs. Besides, I think it'll be kind of fun to help someone out with their first marathon," he shrugged.

"I'll let you think about it some more before I take you up on that offer," Rebecca said.

"Okay," Norman smiled. "You ready to go?"

"Yes," Rebecca said, and they stood up to leave.

That weekend at work Rebecca and Ms. Parker had to work together. Every other female staff member had called in with some sort of excuse. Thirty hostile girls had to spend all weekend together, and tension was always high around the facility.

Shirelle and Veronica, or Ronnie as she was now called, still hated each other. Rebecca made sure to keep an eye on them all weekend. At one point in the gym it seemed as if an all out riot was about to occur between the rival cliques, but a quick call to the shift supervisor promptly squashed the matter.

"Okay! Everybody on the wall! If you're not on the wall, you're going down to the floor!" Chuck yelled as he entered the gym to break up the melee.

As a supervisor, Chuck was perfect. He was huge and he had a big booming voice. Usually the girls quieted down as soon as he entered the room, and if he entered yelling they practically fell all over themselves to do his bidding. Today was no different. Ms. Parker and Rebecca had been yelling in vain and trying to gain control of the situation, but all it took to calm things down was Chuck's presence.

"If you move you're going to BLO!" Chuck yelled as the girls all ran towards the wall to sit down. Within moments the gym was silent.

"Chuck, you need to just go on ahead and start BLO!" Ms. Parker huffed as she stomped over towards him. "Shirelle and Veronica were at it again, but this time Veronica was trying to incite a riot. I got it all down on the points sheets."

"Do we need to do an incident report?" Chuck asked.

"No. Nobody was hurt, and there was no protective hold." Ms. Parker answered.

Miss Parker and Chuck stood talking and going over the points sheets for a few minutes while Rebecca silently watched the girls. They were all sitting against the walls of the gym with sullen looks on their faces. A few were crying, but most of them were glaring at each other.

"...so I told those girls that they don't need to get themselves in trouble to fight Shirelle's fights..." Ms. Parker was saying just when Rebecca noticed Shirelle and Veronica getting up.

It happened so fast, that Rebecca didn't even think to yell. She just took off running towards the two girls so that she could stop them before they hurt each other, but she forgot one crucial detail. They were both much bigger than she was.

Once she reached the other end of the gym where they were, they had already punched each other in the face several times. Veronica had Shirelle by the hair, and Shirelle had Veronica by the neck.

"Let go of each other, and stop it!" Rebecca yelled as she tried in vain to yank the girls apart. She managed to wedge herself between them a little and push them apart for a moment, but she got hit in the face several times while doing it. They were just about to come at each other again when Chuck and Ms. Parker reached them. Each of them grabbed one of the girls and slammed them onto the floor in the protective hold that all staff members had been required to learn.

"I dropped my radio!" Ms. Parker yelled as she held Shirelle down. "Ms. Rebecca, go call for the nurse!" she yelled as she struggled with Shirelle.

It took Rebecca a moment to realize that one of the girls was bleeding. Her head was still reeling from being punched and knocked around by Shirelle and Ronnie. She looked around for Ms. Parker's radio, and spotted it in the hands of one of the residents.

"Give me that radio!" she demanded as she walked up to Kanicker.

"I don't have it!" Kanicker yelled back.

"I saw you stick it behind your back," Rebecca snapped as she reached for it.

'Don't touch me again!" Kanicker sneered after Rebecca had taken the radio.

Rebecca ignored her and called for the nurse. Despite the fact that the gym was not that far from the main building, it still took almost five minutes for the nurse to arrive. In the meantime, Chuck and Ms. Parker had let Shirelle and Ronnie up off the floor. The girls were now each on opposite sides of the gym being verbally de-escalated by Rebecca and Ms. Parker. Chuck had taken control of the rest of the girls.

"I hate that bitch!" Shirelle cried as she held a paper towel to her bleeding nose. "I hate this fuckin place!" she continued to sob.

"Do you want to talk about what happened?" Rebecca asked her.

"I didn't do nothin' Miss. Those girls always startin' shit!" Shirelle sniffed.

Rebecca knew that part of the blame lay in Shirelle's court, but she didn't say so. At that moment the child just needed someone to talk to, not another finger pointing at her and telling her how wrong she was.

"Do you need another paper towel?" Rebecca asked gently.

Shirelle shook her head, and then she began to vent again. "None of you staff know how it feels to be in here. All day, every day I have to see these stupid little girls and listen to their stupid shit... Ronnie and Kanicker and Diamond and all of them like to talk shit about me. And every time something goes wrong the staff wants to blame *me* for it.

"I try my best to be mature and to tell myself to stay out of trouble, but those girls like to test me. Ronnie wants to run things around here, so she acts all hard around me because she knows that most of these girls on the unit do whatever I tell them to. She's just jealous because the only ones who listen to her are her dike-ass roommates." By the end of her tirade Shirelle had stopped crying and the bleeding in her nose had slowed down.

Rebecca waited patiently for her to finish talking.

"All these hoes care about is chasin' after them ol' sorry ass boys on the male unit. They were gonna pass a letter and get us all in trouble today, and they got mad because I wasn't going to do it for them like I always do. I ain't passin' no letters for Ronnie. I ain't goin' down for someone who ain't gonna ride for me." Shirelle said vehemently.

"Why does it upset you so much that they like boys?" Rebecca asked.

"I don't give a damn what those little girls do, but I ain't getting in trouble for no one but me," she replied.

Rebecca didn't push the matter, but she could tell that there was more to it than Shirelle was telling at the moment.

The rest of the day was relatively calm. Chuck started up BLO, which stood for Behavior Learning Opportunity. BLO simply meant that the girls would have to spend all day in the classroom without the privilege of talking or doing anything fun. They would have to face the wall and study packets prepared by their therapists on how to behave better. Rebecca hoped a week in BLO would have an effect on the girls; she didn't know if she could take another weekend like the one that just ended.

Chapter 5

When the alarm rang on Monday morning Rebecca pushed the snooze button….at least she thought she did. She realized she'd turned it off when she woke up almost an hour later.

"Crap!" she spat out as she jumped out of bed. Norman was probably long gone, but she still pictured him waiting for her impatiently. She imagined him pacing with a look of irritation on his face, and that thought made her dress as quickly as possible. She threw her running clothes on, shoved her feet into her socks and shoes, and dashed out the door. She didn't even bother to look in the mirror before rushing off.

When she reached her usual parking spot on post she noticed Norman's truck parked in the distance. She looked around and didn't see him anywhere, so she figured he must have started without her. Now that she was here, she felt a little foolish for rushing. Of course he wouldn't wait for her for almost an hour!

Disappointment mingled with relief settled over her as she started to stretch. She was so tired from work that she almost turned around and drove back home, but she figured she might as well run since she was already on post. There was no sense in wasting a trip.

Norman spotted Rebecca as soon as she pulled up and got out to stretch. It was already 6:50 am, but he'd decided to wait for her simply because he'd said he would be there. He hated to break his word, and he hated when someone broke their word to him without a good reason. He'd been sitting in his truck to stay warm wondering whether or not she was going to be able to go through with the training and the marathon itself. He hoped she had a better explanation other than the usual "my alarm didn't go off," excuse young soldiers used when they were late for morning formations.

He watched her until she was a few hundred feet from his truck, and then he got out so she could see him. As soon as she noticed him her steps faltered a little and she cast an uncomfortable look in his direction. He decided to give her a break and look away until she reached him. Shy people seemed so peculiar to him sometimes, but he understood how awkward it would be for her if he stared at her the entire time she ran towards him.

She stopped when she reached him.

He'd been standing with his back to her, and as he turned around to ask her why she was late the words froze in his mouth.

"What happened to your face?" he demanded instead.

"What?" Rebecca asked. Her hands instinctively flew to her face to feel what he was talking about. "Do I have something on me?" she asked in bewilderment.

"No, but you look like someone beat you up! What happened?" He looked so disapproving Rebecca was hesitant to tell him a couple of teenagers at work had done it. She hadn't seen the damage, but her face had been sore since the fight in the gym and she did have a bad headache.

"It's nothing I can assure you that I wasn't in a fight, and I'll be fine," she tried to sound reassuring and professional, but he didn't look totally convinced. He actually looked angry.

"I never would have thought you were one of those women who pretend like nothing is happening even when it's obvious something is... I can tell you right now that if I ever see the guy who did this he won't be able to do it again," Norman said as he took a closer at the bruises on her face.

"Look Norman," Rebecca said carefully. "I appreciate your concern, but you've got the wrong impression. I told you already that I don't have a man in my life, so no man could have done this. It happened yesterday at work. Two girls got into a fight, and I had a hard time breaking them up," she admitted ruefully.

A look of understanding dawned on Norman's face. "What kind of kids are in that place?" he asked as he gently grasped her chin and tilted her face up to get a better look at the damage.

"I told you already that they are teens who have been abused and neglected. Most of them have anger and aggression disorders, so they fight all the time. Not a day goes by that something doesn't happen, but staff doesn't usually get hurt." His warm hand on her face was so comforting she almost smiled up at him. For such a big man his touch was surprisingly tender.

"You don't look like you should be working in such a hostile place," he said quietly. His hand stroked the side of her cheek and he wrapped his other arm around her back and pulled her closer.

"You look like too nice of a person to have bruises messing up your pretty face," he continued as he watched her with his usual stern expression. His words were gentle, his touch was gentle, and the tone of his voice was gentle, but his face still looked as stern and inscrutable as ever.

Rebecca closed her eyes for a moment and enjoyed the feel of his hand on her cheek and his arm around her back. The morning was chilly, and his warmth was comforting on so many levels. She found herself swaying closer as if some sort of animal magnetism was pulling them together. For a minute he continued touching her face, and then he enfolded her in both of his arms and she rested her head against his chest. She told herself that it wouldn't hurt to give in to the urge to be closer to him for just one moment.

Norman stroked Rebecca's hair as she lifted her head off his chest to look up at him. She offered him a small, apologetic smile before she spoke.

"I'm sorry I was late this morning, but you know how it is when you accidentally press the off button instead of the snooze button," she said.

"Don't even worry about it!" he exclaimed. "You look like you should still be sleeping.... How does your head feel by the way?"

"It hurts, and my face is kind of sore," Rebecca admitted.

"I think you need to get some extra rest today. You look like you could use a break," he said as he pulled her close again.

Rebecca's heart began to beat rapidly inside her chest as his strong arms enfolded her again. She could hear his heart beating, and she wondered why he was suddenly being so nice to her. He seemed to be very concerned about the bruises... maybe they looked worse than they felt.

"I'm okay. I promise," she told him as he continued to hold her. Heaven help her, it felt so nice she didn't want him to stop.

"I believe you," he said, "but at least let me drive you back to your car."

"That's not necessary."

"I want to do it anyway. You have a headache and it's cold out here," he insisted.

"Alright." Had she always been this much of a push over?... she wondered briefly as she climbed into the warm interior of his truck.

The ride back to her car ended much too quickly for Rebecca. As he pulled into the parking spot next to hers, she prepared to exit his truck.

"Wait a minute!" his voice stopped her. "What's the rush?" he asked gently.

"Nothing, but don't you need to be going soon?"

"Yeah, but I have a few minutes," he told her.

When she sat back and looked at him without saying anything he chuckled. Her hair was untidy, she had bruises on her chin and her cheek, and her glasses were crooked, yet she somehow managed to look as poised and dignified as a duchess. She even raised one eyebrow as if to subtly inquire why he was making demands on her precious time.

"Don't look at me like that! I just wanted to give you my number in case you plan on being late again. That way you can call and warn me not to come too early," he half joked.

"If my face weren't so sore I'd frown at you..." she warned him, and then she ruined it by laughing. He noticed that she covered her smile with both hands again. He felt the urge to pull her hands away from her face, but he restrained himself.

"Seriously, give me a call if you need to," he said after she stopped laughing.

"Okay Norman. I'll see you tomorrow morning, and thanks for the ride," she replied before she got out.

After she left Norman remembered that he was going to ask her if she'd made up her mind about training with him. She hadn't seemed too enthusiastic about it when he'd first mentioned it, so he was really curious to hear her response. He wondered how serious she was about completing the marathon. Plenty of people could start such a task, but not all of them had the internal fortitude to finish it. He liked everything he knew about Rebecca so far, and he really hoped she wasn't one of those people who give up easily.

His memory of her racing up the hill encouraged him to believe that she would make it to the finish line, but he didn't know her well enough to believe in her without any doubts. Tomorrow would tell.

Rebecca showed up ten minutes early to find Norman sitting in his truck. He'd parked in the spot next to the one she usually parked in.

"Good morning," she smiled brightly as they both exited their vehicles.

"Hi," he said. "You're looking much better this morning. Did you get some rest?"

"Yeah I did. Mondays are always kind of tough for me," she admitted.

"Why?"

"Because I have to work 32 hours over the weekend. I do back to back double shifts at the youth center, so by Monday morning I'm usually beat," she told him.

"Why do you do cram in all those hours in two days?" he asked.

"Because I'm busy during the week with classes and volunteering at the elementary school."

"What do you do at the school?" he asked as she started stretching.

"I'm just a classroom volunteer. I take the kids who need extra help out into a quiet area away from the rest of the class and help them practice whatever skills they need to improve.... mostly reading and math," she explained.

"What did you say you're studying? I forgot..." As he awaited her reply he watched her with his usual unnerving and stern expression.

"Psychology with a concentration in child psychology and education. I'm less than a year from earning my Master's and working as a school psychologist," Rebecca said.

"What are you doing your graduate research on?" he asked.

"The correlation between the availability of SAFE certified nurses and the reporting of sexual assault and abuse."

"What's a SAFE certified nurse?"

"SAFE stands for Sexual Assault Forensic Examiner. A nurse who is certified has special training on how to handle victims of sexual assault. In most places, when a woman is assaulted she's treated just like any other emergency room patient. With SAFE centers there is a more compassionate level of care, and victims of sexual assault aren't made to wait for hours in the same room as everyone else. There's already some compelling evidence that more women would report the crime if the process of reporting it and being examined weren't so traumatic."

"Why did you decide to focus your research on that when your concentration is in child psychology?"

"Because it's relevant to my job. Almost all of the girls I work with have undergone some sort of sexual abuse or assault. A lot of them didn't report it when it happened because they thought no one would care. Imagine being young, scared, and even ashamed of something someone else did to you... and then having to go and sit for hours in the emergency room, trying to keep it together until they call you to the back. And then when you do get called to the back, they examine you and question you in one of those semi-private bays where almost everyone can hear what's going on," Rebecca explained.

"That sounds like very heavy research. How far are you from finishing?"

"I'm somewhere in the middle. I'm hoping that more cities will start training their emergency room nurses in the SAFE procedures." Rebecca sensed that the topic was probably too serious for a conversation with someone she barely knew. She stopped talking and went back to stretching. They stretched in silence for a few minutes, before she got up the nerve to ask Norman a question.

"What's your job like?" she asked him.

"It's actually pretty easy. I have an office job as a network administrator for my brigade. It has a lot to do with computers, information technology, and network security," he replied.

"Sounds.... Interesting," Rebecca said. She was actually thinking that it sounded complicated. Computers had always intimidated her a little, and although she wasn't in the Stone Age when it came to technology, she was far from a 'techno-geek.'

"Hmmm," he looked at her for a moment. "You don't look like you really think it's interesting."

"I just never would have thought you'd have a job like that. You look like some Airborne, Air Assault Ranger. People who work with computers are usually geeks who look like geeks. You don't even wear glasses..." she looked at his powerful arms and legs, and silently added that he was much too strong and handsome.

"I'll just take that as a compliment," he grinned. "You ready to start?" he asked brusquely.

"Yeah," Rebecca said. She was thrown off for a moment by his abrupt change in demeanor.

They set off at a quick pace and ran approximately three miles. Running with Norman turned out to be an enjoyable experience, except for the fact that he had decided to be a chatterbox. He'd explained more about his job, and asked her questions about hers as they'd run. Most of her answers had been panted out in a vastly irritated tone of voice, and Norman had chuckled at her a few times. It seemed the more she'd glared up at him the more his good mood had increased. By the time they finally stopped to walk Rebecca was almost livid with vexation.

"Something wrong?" he asked innocently.

"Do you always talk so much while you run?" she demanded.

"No, usually I run alone and I make it a point not to talk to myself...unlike some people I know," he chuckled.

"What's that supposed to mean?" she asked.

"You know exactly what I'm talking about. And why are you so grumpy right now anyway?" he asked.

"You were running too fast and talking too much. I had a hard time concentrating on breathing," she admitted. Now that they weren't running anymore her irritation was quickly disappearing.

"You could have just said so," Norman replied. He looked down at her and laughed at her expression. She reminded him of an irritated fuzzy bunny. It was hard to take her seriously.

"Just *what* is so funny?" she demanded.

"Nothing," he smiled.

Their eyes met for a moment, and a flash of intense awareness went through Rebecca. He was easily the most attractive man in the world. His blue eyes gazed into hers with a mixture of humor and some more complex emotion. It was that unknown emotion that caused her breath to stop somewhere in her throat as her other senses focused solely on him. His scent filled her nostrils, and she longed to reach out and touch him. Her entire body came alive and tingled in anticipation as he leaned a little closer.

"Are you still mad at me?" he asked as he reached out a hand to lightly touch the side of her face.

She couldn't seem to find her voice, so she slowly shook her head to say 'no.'

"That's too bad…" he said flippantly.

"Why?" she'd managed to find her voice after all, but it sounded oddly breathless and husky.

"Because, you're so cute when you're mad," he whispered right before he kissed her.

His hand stayed at her cheek as his warm lips covered hers. They stood in the cold for an endless moment with just that small point of contact, yet it seemed as if every nerve ending in her entire body were connected to her lips. Her eyes closed the moment his lips touched hers, shutting out everything but the sensations he evoked in her. Nothing beyond their lips touched, and the kiss amounted to nothing more than a simple, albeit prolonged, peck on the lips. But it felt like so much more than that. Rebecca's entire face was still hot as Norman pulled away to look at her.

Rebecca stared at her feet for almost a full minute before Norman finally spoke.

"I guess I shouldn't have done that," he said into the lengthy silence.

"No, I guess not," she replied.

"So…" he began awkwardly, "I've been meaning to tell you that I can't make it the rest of this week. I have to be at work early, so you'll be back on your own for awhile."

"No problem," she said a little too cheerfully as she offered him a bright smile.

"Well…" he let the word hang between them for a moment.

"Well… I guess I'll see you around," Rebecca finally said.

"Uh, yeah…well, I have to go now… Bye," and then he was gone.

As Rebecca watched his awkward and abrupt departure she wondered if kissing her had been as bad as he was making it out to be. Was she the only one who'd enjoyed it? Actually, enjoyed was an understatement. Her face felt hot just from thinking about it, and their lips hadn't even parted!

He must have left so suddenly because he'd found the kiss distasteful. It wouldn't be the first time she'd been rejected by him, but it still hurt. The past few weeks of running together off and on had lulled her into thinking he must like her, but apparently she was wrong. Maybe it would be better to just continue her training alone. She had no doubt that she could, and it would spare them anymore uncomfortable encounters with each other.

The rest of the week Rebecca concentrated on studying for an exam and finishing a few research papers that were due soon. She still managed to keep herself motivated on her early morning runs, but she had to admit that part of her missed Norman's stimulating presence. Her mind kept wondering back to the kiss. Why had he kissed her in the first place? Why hadn't he seemed to like it as she had? Maybe she should have kissed him back or something… or maybe she should have stopped him before his lips had touched hers. At least then she wouldn't keep thinking about how nice it had been.

By Friday night she'd almost worked up the nerve to call him and tell him that she didn't think training with him would work for her, but ultimately she put it off again. Working at the center all weekend was more than enough to deal with.

By Monday morning she still hadn't called him, so she decided to simply avoid him and hope that he would get the message. She decided to change her routine to the point where she didn't even run in the mornings anymore. She'd decided to simply switch to running at night; that way she could still have the benefit of running in the same place.

Chapter 6

Over the next few months, the situation at work grew more and more tense between Veronica and Shirelle. To make matters worse, several new girls had been admitted and they had already been forced to choose sides. The consequence of not choosing was to have threats coming in from both sides, and protection from neither. One could easily see why it was necessary to join a clique as soon as possible in such an environment.

Some staff members were trying to have both Ronnie and Shirelle removed from the center. At times Rebecca agreed with them, but she still felt that all Shirelle needed was help from the right source. She couldn't deny that Ronnie made her extremely uncomfortable. On a typical day Ronnie would intimidate anyone in her path, especially those who were smaller and weaker. She would spit on anyone who looked at her wrong, and most of the time she openly defied staff direction.

Shirelle on the other hand, was someone Rebecca could sympathize with. She at least tried to do her best, but she still had frequent temper tantrums involving Ronnie and several staff members whom she'd never liked. She was able to get some of her anger and hurt out during poetry hour. The weekend shift supervisor allowed the girls who'd behaved well enough to spend an hour every Sunday evening sharing their poetry with each other. Shirelle was a regular attendee, and her poetry was always among the most heart wrenching.

One Sunday after poetry hour was over, Shirelle approached Rebecca.

"Miss Rebecca, can I ask you something?" she requested with an uncharacteristic amount of timidity in her demeanor.

"Sure," Rebecca replied as she sat in the empty desk next to Shirelle.

"Would you read this poem and tell me what you think?" she pushed a crinkled sheet of notebook paper towards Rebecca. Obviously it had been written some time ago.

Shirelle silently continued working on a letter to one of her friends as Rebecca read the poem. It described her life back in the tough streets of Philadelphia with her father a drug addict. Details of spending nights alone and scared as a small child flowed from the pages in Rebecca's hands. There was even a verse about an unspeakable act committed by Shirelle's own father. He'd been too broke to afford his fix, so he'd started selling his own daughter to support his drug habit. Shirelle's poem seemed to scream out loud about all the hurt and pain she'd been through. From the tender age of ten, she'd been forcefully raped by a drug dealer every time her father wanted to get high. She still referred to him as 'Daddy' in her poem, but Rebecca couldn't understand why. Daddies didn't do things like that to their daughters.

When she finished, Rebecca looked up at Shirelle and asked, "Is this true?"

"Yeah, all that stuff really happened. That's why I'm in here," Shirelle whispered.

"It's a very well written poem, but why did you show me? Do you want to talk about it?"

"Sort of..." the child hedged.

"Would you like to talk out in the hall?"

"Sure," Shirelle said.

Rebecca wasn't sure what to say, so she waited patiently for Shirelle to speak first. After about ten minutes of silence, Shirelle finally spoke.

"It really makes me mad when these stupid little girls in here get themselves in trouble to pass letters to these stupid boys. I mean... they ain't about shit. Don't none of these boys up in here give a fuck about them. All they do is laugh at all the dumb stuff they write."

"Don't you write letters to boys too?" Rebecca asked.

"Yeah, but not like they do! You see them Miss.... Every time some ol' dumb boy passes by the window they practically break they neck just to look at 'em. I don't be writin' about how I'm gonna ride so-and-so's dick or nothin' like that. I ain't dumb like them other girls," she answered passionately.

"Why does it bother you so much when they get themselves in trouble? All you have to do is ignore them and distance yourself from the trouble," Rebecca pointed out.

"It's hard Miss. I can't do that. Too many of you staff members wanna accuse me of startin' anything that goes down on the unit. I can't deny that most of these girls in here listen to me, but that don't mean that every time they do somethin' wrong it's because I told them to..." she paused for a deep breath before continuing in the same angry tone.

"I'm sick and tired of bogus ass staff tryin' to accuse me of *everything*. I mean, I know I come across as mature and all, but I'm only 15. And now I feel like *I* have to make these girls act better."

"Have you talked to your therapist about the way you feel?" in staff training sessions, resident counselors were taught to simply listen, neither agreeing nor disagreeing with the complaints of the residents, but Rebecca found it hard not to express sympathy after reading Shirelle's poem.

"Yeah, and she always says the same thing, but I'm tired of being the only one who acts mature. Hell, I do a better job of controlling these dumb girls than a lot of you so called staff members. Even you can't control some of them," was Shirelle's testy reply.

"Why should I want to control you or anyone else in here when the main reason most of you are here is to learn *self* control? You wouldn't learn anything if all I did was use brute force and the power of my position to keep you 'under control.' What are you going to do once you get back out into the real world if you never even try to set limits for yourself?" Rebecca asked.

"I don't have a problem controlling myself! I was just saying that I'm tired of being expected to control all these other girls in here."

Rebecca thought carefully before she replied again. "No one expects you to control the other residents... I think that may be something you expect from yourself, and you project that onto the staff members because it's easier to point the finger than it is to look inside yourself and see what you need to change. And what makes you think they benefit from learning to be controlled by a peer? Do you think you benefit from exerting so much control over them? What's going to happen once you're not in an environment where you can readily control others the way you do here?"

"I don't know," Shirelle said quietly after a moment's thought. Before Rebecca got the chance to speak again the shift supervisor stepped into the hall.

"What's going on here?" he asked briskly.

"Chuck!" Shirelle smiled as she jumped up to greet the supervisor. As much as the girls fell all over themselves to sit down when he entered a room yelling, they were even more eager to greet him when he came around just to check on them. He'd endeared himself to them with his fairness, his easy command of any situations that arose, and his inspirational poetry hour.

"Whoa! Whoa! Back up, back up. Keep your hands off me! Ten feet! Ten feet now!" he boomed out playfully as he backed away from the child.

"You play too much!" Shirelle laughed.

"Who's playing? I'm not. Now why aren't you in the classroom with your group? Do I need to put you down as out of area?" he teased.

"No Chuck! I was just talking to Miss Rebecca about some stuff."

"Yeah," Rebecca chimed in. "She was doing fine. She just wanted to talk in private."

"So this isn't a time out?" Chuck asked.

"Not at all, in fact no one has been angry yet today," Rebecca was proud to say.

At that moment it seemed as if God himself must have wanted to prove Rebecca wrong, because the classroom suddenly erupted into chaos. A few girls got into a fight which set the tone for the rest of the weekend. Shirelle had turned sullen and taciturn soon after Rebecca, Miss Parker and Chuck broke up the fight. By the end of the weekend Rebecca was once again emotionally and physically drained by the time she reached home.

She was steadily getting better at her job. During one of her employee evaluations Chuck had told Rebecca that she had to be herself when dealing with the girls.

"They can tell when someone's being fake, and they hate that more than anything else," he'd said as he went over her performance sheet.

"What can I do better?" she'd asked.

"From what I can tell, you're doing a great job as it is. You get in there and restrain them when you need to, and you're one of the best at talking to them when they're upset. I noticed that none of them have tried to get you fired, and none of them talk bad about you... That means a lot. It means they think you're fair," he explained.

"Then why do they still give me such a hard time?" Rebecca asked in bewilderment.

"Because you're still new, and they want to test you. Also, because you're nice to them. They know Miss Parker will slam 'em down in a minute if they cut up, but they feel like they can manipulate you; you just have to stand your ground and let them know they can't," he advised her.

Now his words still reverberated in her mind as she clocked in every Saturday morning. *Stand my ground, and don't allow them to manipulate me...* she'd tell herself when they asked her to bend a couple of the rules for them.

Shirelle had begun to act like she expected Rebecca to take her side in any situations involving other residents because of the time they'd spent talking about deeply personal issues. Rebecca couldn't deny that she felt a bit more sympathy than she should for Shirelle, but at the same time she knew that she had to obey the rules and set limits on their rapport.

Chapter 7

It was early February, and the average daily high was still around freezing. Rebecca didn't miss running in the mornings at all. In fact, she felt sorry for all the soldiers who still had to get up at such an ungodly hour to face the frigid temperature and do physical training with their units. She remembered hating to run in the cold when she'd been a soldier; actually she remembered hating to run period. Now it felt like she was an old pro at it... sort of, anyway.

She'd managed to progress to twenty mile runs over the past few months. It had been no easy feat. There were days when she missed Norman's short-lived but influential encouragement. She hadn't seen him since the day he'd kissed her, but he was never far from her thoughts. Sometimes she even felt like calling him. A few times, she'd taken out his number and started to dial only to return to her senses and hang up before she'd put all his digits in. Part of her still longed for more of that one kiss he'd given her, but another part of her was glad they'd stopped talking. She had a feeling that her heart would have ended up broken anyway. Usually the strong, handsome type was so used to having any woman they wanted that they thought it was okay to have flings. Emotionally discriminating people like Rebecca on the other hand only let themselves get intimate if there was the possibility of more than just a casual fling. She didn't doubt for one second that Norman hadn't really been all that interested in her in a romantic way, but that didn't stop her from wanting to feel his arms around her again.

As she always did, Rebecca put such thoughts out of her mind so she could concentrate on work and school.

One day during her volunteer time with Ms. Martin's class she noticed that Peggy had bruises on her back. The only reason she happened to see them was because the child kept fidgeting, and her shirt slipped down a couple of times while Rebecca was helping her with her school work. When the students went out to lunch with the teacher's assistant Rebecca went in to talk to Ms. Martin instead of leaving as she always did.

"Ms. Martin, I need to speak with you for a moment about Peggy."

"Sure, what's going on?" Ms. Martin asked as she sat down at her desk with a sigh.

"I noticed some bruises on her back while we were out in the hall reading this morning," Rebecca stated without preamble.

Ms. Martin sat up straighter and demanded, "Really? Did you get a good look at them? Does it look like abuse?"

"I don't know, they are mostly under her shirt..."

"Can you stay late today? We'll have to notify the school nurse, and she's going to have to file a report with the Children's Protection Services. Peggy's mother is already assigned a case worker due to neglect, but this is the first evidence of any abuse."

"Do I need to do anything?" Rebecca asked concerned.

"I'm not sure, but I think you may have to sign a paper or be a witness since you saw the bruises first... Did you ask her about them at all?"

"No," Rebecca answered. "I wanted to tell you first since I'm just a volunteer."

"You did the right thing, you can relax. We'll have the nurse look at Peggy as soon as she's done with her lunch," Ms. Martin sighed.

"Okay," Rebecca said as she tried not to feel so out of place. Ms. Martin had always intimidated her a little. She was taller and she had bigger breasts. Rebecca felt so unwomanly in comparison, but Ms. Martin was a very nice person and she was excellent with children. She had bright red hair and kind grey eyes. There were laugh lines and crinkles at the corners of Ms. Martin's lovely eyes; she was obviously a person who loved to smile. She'd been teaching for more than ten years, and was in her late thirties. She looked good, not just good for a woman her age, but good period.

"So Rebecca, how much longer until you finish school?" she asked in a conversational tone.

"Less than a year Ms. Martin," Rebecca answered.

"Enough of that Ms. Martin stuff, please just call me Shelly. I feel old enough as it is..." she chuckled good-naturedly.

"Do you deal with this sort of thing very often?" Rebecca inquired.

"Unfortunately we do," Shelly said sadly. "You'd be surprised how many parents don't care for their children. It's not always just the abuse; the neglect can be just as appalling. I've seen kids who are so much brighter than average suffering academically because their parents wouldn't take care of them. At this early age there is no reason for a child to get behind...other than lack of support from their parents or problems at home."

"Sounds like you've been dealing with this for some time..." Rebecca said.

"Yeah, and let me tell you about Peggy. Her mother is a single parent now, but before she was married to a methamphetamine addict. Peggy's father ended up killing himself in their meth lab. It's all in her file. Now her mother is working two jobs and living pay check to pay check. It was easy to see how the neglect can occur in Peggy's situation, but the abuse is something that even I never suspected... I mean I've talked with her myself, and she seems to really love Peggy. They're all each other has, so I'm truly shocked about these bruises. Nothing like this has ever happened to Peggy before, but then again there's always a first time," Shelly said.

"I'm hoping that I'll be able to make a difference as a school psychologist," Rebecca interjected brightly.

Shelly gave her a peculiar look and then shook her head.

"What?" Rebecca asked.

"Oh, nothing really. I was just remembering when I began my career as a teacher. I remember thinking almost the exact same thing you just said, but I've learned a lot since then... If optimism and good intentions could change the world there would be no suffering, we wouldn't be at war right now, and Peggy wouldn't have bruises on her little back," Shelly said with a touch of sadness in her voice.

"I still think that as long as we can help at least one child in the course of our career we've done something worthwhile... My boss told me that most of the girls at the youth center where I work will end up back on the streets, either dead or in some kind of trouble with the law, but I still think it prudent to maintain a positive attitude and tell myself that I can help all of them if I try hard enough," Rebecca responded.

"Oh honey! If only you knew! You'll burn yourself out thinking like that... It takes way more than the effort of one person. You'll see that even when you're sacrificing yourself and doing more than one person could possibly do, there will always be another reason why a child couldn't be helped. When you start out you always see all the possibilities. You see the ones you want to help, and you envision yourself helping the ones you can. You never focus on the ones you can't help until you actually see with your own eyes just how many there are that can't be helped," Shelly replied earnestly.

"And I think that as long as I don't give up, even when it seems like nothing can be done, then there is still hope. It's the ones who keep trying even when it seems hopeless that make the biggest difference," Rebecca said as Shelly sat back and shook her head.

"I like you Rebecca and I would hate to see you get burnt out. Just remember that not everyone can be helped... no matter how hard you try."

"Thanks for the advice, Shelly."

"Do I detect a 'but' in there somewhere?" Shelly asked with a small laugh.

"I guess so; I still want to be an optimist..." Rebecca trailed off at the look on Shelly's face.

"I'll tell you what. Next time I make a home visit to Peggy's mother you can come along. Give me your number again so I can make sure to give you a call ahead of time," Shelly said.

"Okay," Rebecca said as she scrawled her cell number down on a post-it-note.

By the time she got home that night she was emotionally drained. After the nurse had examined Peggy's back and found a multitude of bruises, the school had contacted the Children's Protective Services. The visit to Peggy's apartment hadn't gone very well. The authorities had shown up to find Peggy's mother beaten so badly it was a miracle she'd survived. Peggy had no other suitable relatives willing to take her in, so she was now in state custody living in a home much like the one in which Rebecca worked. She'd be there until her mother recovered, or until a suitable foster family could take her into their home.

Rebecca went to bed that night with an inkling of what Shelly had told her in class earlier that day. Whereas before she felt good about being in Peggy's life and helping her with her school work, she now realized just how minimal her contribution had been. Now there was nothing she could do for the child other than pray that her mother makes a full recovery. She hugged her pillow and tried to think of all the things she could control before she drifted off into oblivion.

The following weekend at work Rebecca got to go on her first outing with the girls. Shirelle had behaved and earned enough points over the past few weeks to be included in a trip to a local recreation center. Fred, one of the other shift supervisors, came on the trip along with Rebecca and four of the girls. Shirelle was the oldest one, and she knew that she needed to set a good example for the other girls to follow. First, they went out to eat at a Chinese restaurant, and then to see a movie. The rec. center was their last stop before heading back for the evening, and the girls had behaved so beautifully Fred was already talking about the next outing.

As the girls dispersed to play different games, Rebecca noticed a piano standing alone in the far corner of one of the larger rooms in the center. It seemed like forever since she'd played on a real piano, and she suddenly wanted to so badly that her fingers fairly itched in anticipation.

"You look like you want to eat that piano over there!" Fred said suddenly beside her.

"What?" Rebecca laughed.

"Do you play?" he asked.

Rebecca opened her mouth to say 'no,' but Shirelle answered before she could get the word out.

"Yeah, she does. She told me all about it at quiet time one night... Play somethin' Miss Rebecca. You said you would one day," the child said.

"Yeah, play something," the other girls chimed in.

"Yeah, Miss Rebecca play something for us," Fred added mimicking the girls.

"It seems as if I'm outnumbered," Rebecca said as she took a seat at the piano bench. She didn't even know how to tell if it was out of tune... Hopefully it wasn't, and hopefully she wasn't about to make a complete fool of herself.

"I need to warm up first," she mumbled. A quick glance over her shoulder revealed that they were all still watching her. Her hands shook slightly as she placed them over the keys in the middle c position. She played a c major cadence using broken chords to make sure all the notes sounded right to her, and then she glanced over her shoulder again to find them still watching.

"You're doing good, Miss Rebecca," Shirelle smiled encouragingly.

For some reason Shirelle's simple, friendly smile set her at ease. All she had to do was play a simple song for a few people who weren't expecting her to play that well. It's not like she was in a concert hall with hundreds of people expecting her to play some difficult piece brilliantly.

She placed her fingers over the keys once again after a quick stretch and began to play "Blue Danube." She allowed herself to open up to the music as it reverberated throughout the room. Just as the melody flowed in a relaxing manner from her fingers, she began to relax in front of Shirelle and the other girls. When she finished she was surprised to hear light applause coming from the few people who'd come into the room when they heard the piano.

"Play one more!" Shirelle begged. "That was really pretty."

"Okay," Rebecca quickly agreed. "But just one," she added.

Then she did something that she never thought she'd do in a million years. She played one of her own personal compositions. The piece was mostly in the C minor and A melodic minor keys, and she'd been working on it in secret for several weeks.

As her fingers danced rapidly over the keys she once again lost herself in the song. It started out mainly on the lower octaves, but as the melody gained speed and intensity her fingers moved in quick succession all the way up to the very highest notes. She could feel the excitement coming from her small audience in tangible waves as the song built to a shattering climax. It ended on a quieter and more soothing note, but the ending melody was no less haunting than the exciting climax as she played the final c minor arpeggio.

Rebecca hadn't realized her eyes were closed until she finished to a fair amount of enthusiastic applause. She stood up and looked around to see that more than twenty people had come into the room to hear her play. Their looks of appreciation were a far cry from the looks her mother used to give her when she'd finished playing. Rather than feeling embarrassed, she was surprised that she actually felt proud of herself.

"Wow! Miss Rebecca, you play good!" Shirelle said in awe. "Was that classical music?"

"No, I wrote that last one myself," Rebecca admitted a bit sheepishly.

"I'm impressed! You shouldn't keep talent like that a secret," Fred was saying as he gazed at her with admiration in his eyes.

"Thank you," Rebecca found herself saying over and over again to all the compliments coming her way as she scurried from the room.

She spent the rest of the hour in the rec. center watching the girls have fun. She was so preoccupied with keeping track of them and chatting with Fred that she failed to notice Norman's presence at all.

After Rebecca, Fred, and the girls returned to the youth center Norman spent the rest of the evening trying to get her out of his thoughts.

He'd noticed her as soon as she'd entered the building, and his son Dylan had as well.

"Hey, it's Miss Rebecca!" Dylan had exclaimed in excitement. "Can we go say hi Dad? Can we?"

"She looks pretty busy at the moment..." Norman hedged as he tried to keep Dylan quiet. The last thing he wanted was for her to notice them.

"Come on Dad, please?" Dylan begged.

"How do you know her anyway?" Norman asked.

"She helps me with my reading at school in class."

"How come I never see her when I pick you up?" Norman asked. Out of all the classrooms in all the schools in town why did she have to be a volunteer in the one his son attended?

"Because she only comes in the mornings," Dylan explained with infinite patience in his little voice. His tone also implied that Norman should have already known that.

"Okay, well you'll see her in the morning then... we don't have to bother her right now."

It was then that Norman heard the piano music flowing from the room she'd entered moments ago. Some part of him recognized that she was playing. He'd probably never be able to explain how he knew, but somehow he just did. A few others in the area went in because she'd played an easily recognized piece so beautifully, and it wasn't often that one heard someone playing like that...especially in the rec. center. In fact, he'd never heard anyone play that piano in the corner in all the time he'd spent hanging out there with his kids.

And when she'd launched into the second song, absolutely nothing could have kept him from going in to watch her play. As a pretty young woman who'd wanted to run a marathon she'd been interesting, but now that he was glimpsing this new artistic, soulful side of her he was thoroughly fascinated. He watched her and wondered how many hours of practice it had taken her to learn such an exquisite piece. He'd been listening to classical and romantic piano music for a long time, and he'd never heard it.

Now he was lying in his bed with the melody playing over and over again in his head as he imagined the way she'd looked while she'd played. Her hair had been in its usual functional bun, and she'd been dressed modestly in jeans and a cotton t-shirt. Yet she'd still seemed like the most beautiful woman he'd ever seen as he'd watched her fingers glide over the keys. Something about her posture had reminded him of his mother. His mother had died when he was a small child, but he did remember watching her play the piano in the mornings. In fact those were some of the fondest and most cherished memories of his entire life. His mother had been a gifted player, much like Rebecca seemed to be. He wondered if he'd ever get her out of his mind now... Out of all the recreation centers in all the towns in the world, why did she have to show up at his?

"The doctors at Vanderbilt are saying that Peggy's mom should make a full recovery... physically anyway," Shelly told Rebecca one day after lunch.

"That's good news," Rebecca sighed. "Did they ever catch the boyfriend?"

"I don't think so," Shelly said thoughtfully.

It had been more than a week since Peggy's mother had been found half dead in her small apartment. She'd been in a heavily sedated state for a few days with no family to care for her, so Shelly and Rebecca had made a few trips to the hospital to visit and just sit with her for moral support.

When Mrs. Bellefonte had started talking again she'd told authorities all about her ex-boyfriend. Apparently, she'd discovered that he was molesting Peggy. When she confronted him about it he'd taken off after a nasty fight between them. During the fight Peggy had tried to intervene, only to be thrown against the wall. Mrs. Bellefonte hadn't realized how bad the damage had been until Shelly, Rebecca, and her case worker from the state social work service had talked to her about it. She'd broken down as she looked at the pictures of the bruises on Peggy's back.

"Oh my God!" she wailed in a pathetically thin and sickly voice. "You have to catch that bastard! Oh God, what have I done?"

"Mrs. Bellefonte, we need you to calm down for Peggy's sake. Can you give us a description, and tell us what happened?" one of the agents asked.

"I don't know," she moaned. "I thought he was gone when I put Peggy on the school bus…she didn't have any bruises then. Then I went back inside to clean up, because I was supposed to have a visit from my case worker…" she seemed to struggle to remember for a few minutes before relaxing again with a sad look. "The next thing I remember is waking up in here while the nurse was checking me," she'd sighed in resignation.

Mrs. Bellefonte was lucky to be alive. She'd suffered from a moderate concussion, multiple bruises and abrasions, several broken ribs, a punctured lung that had collapsed and nearly ended her life, and a broken foot. She'd been a pathetic sight to behold as Shelly had sat holding her hand during the visit.

"You can just come with me on another home visit. That situation is much worse than normal…" Shelly's kind voice interrupted Rebecca's reverie.

"Sure," Rebecca replied still a little distracted with thoughts of Peggy and her pitiful mother. "When will this one be?"

"Tonight, I'm going to see Dylan's parents. He's been in the tutoring program for reading long enough to have a second assessment. What we do is visit the parents before the program starts, and after each assessment to discuss the child's progress. He's been doing well enough that they may decide to take him out of the program to make room for another child who could use the service," Shelly explained.

"What time should I meet you?" Rebecca asked.

"Be here around 4:15. You can ride with me, that way I don't have to worry about giving you bad directions… I'm terrible with directions," Shelly said.

"Alright, see you at four fifteen then," Rebecca smiled as she left.

She spent the remainder of her free time finishing some homework that was due in her 7:00 class and playing through more scales from her practice book. She also went for a quick run, because she'd spent so much time on the keyboard it was all she had time for. By 4:00 she was quickly throwing on some clothes and berating herself about managing her time more effectively. She barely made it to the school on time.

"Hey!" Shelly greeted Rebecca as she jogged up to the main entrance. "I'm parked in the teacher's lot."

"Sorry I'm late..." Rebecca began, only to be interrupted.

"You're not late, you're right on time. And calm down! You look like a deer in the headlights. Dylan's parents aren't nearly as bad as Peggy's. They're divorced, but they are both still involved in his life. He doesn't see his father as much as he wants because of the deployments and all..." Shelly continued giving Rebecca background information about the visit as she drove off.

Rebecca thought about Norman as Shelly talked about the deployments to Iraq. He'd been one of the many soldiers who had to miss more than a year of their child's life. Maybe Dylan hadn't been doing well simply because he missed his father, and on top of that his parents were divorced. Those factors could cause any kid to need some extra help. An even clearer picture of Shelly's advice from a few weeks ago began to take shape in Rebecca's mind. There was absolutely nothing she could do about deployments and divorced parents, no matter how much she wished there was.

"This year has just been something else," Shelly sighed as she knocked on the door.

It was a nice house. It looked like the sort of place where you would find a housewife inside wearing an apron, making pies, and tending to flowers. It was a simple two story brown brick house with a dark blue door; there was even a cute little kid sized porch swing next to some wicker furniture.

"I guess Mrs. Gregory must have forgotten about this appointment," Shelly frowned. She'd knocked more than four times, and if anyone had been home they surely would have answered by then.

"Dylan's father picked him up from school today, and he said he'd remind her about the appointment... I guess he couldn't reach her," Shelly said. She pulled out her cell phone and began to dial.

As she dialed, Shelly accidentally dropped the papers she'd been holding. It was a cold blustery day so she and Rebecca both made a mad dive to gather them up before they blew away. Shelly was wearing high heels, so Rebecca leaped off the porch to go after the ones that landed in the yard... and as luck would have it, it was just then that someone pulled into the driveway.

Rebecca focused on collecting the papers as quickly as she could, and she paid no attention to the man who got out of the car. It wasn't until they were both reaching for the last of the runaway documents that she noticed him.

At first she was confused. He must be a figment of her imagination... her brain didn't want to accept the fact that after months of no sight of him he was suddenly right there. And at the worst possible moment! Her hair was all over the place because of the wind and the fact that she'd been whirling around like a mad dervish trying to catch the papers before they flew away. And there he stood in his uniform looking neat and professional, and *laughing* at her.

"Hi Miss Rebecca!" Dylan chirped happily.

"Hi there Dylan." She deliberately didn't look at Norman again, and she could have kicked herself for not knowing that Dylan was the same little boy in the pictures she'd spent so much time looking at online the night she'd first viewed Norman's profile. He looked older, but now that she knew it was him she could clearly see the resemblance to his younger self and to his father.

"Nor- Mr. Gregory!" Shelly smiled from the porch. "It's good to see you! I think perhaps Dylan's mom must have forgotten about our appointment," she said. Rebecca looked up at her, and silently cursed her for looking so calm, collected, and statuesque. Her height and vivid coloring caused her to stand out like some Greek goddess, and next to her Rebecca felt childlike and insignificant. She didn't even want to glance at Norman to see the admiration in his eyes.

Norman glanced at Rebecca for a moment before clearing his throat and saying to Shelly, "Her spa appointment took longer than she thought it would, so she gave me the keys to let you guys in. I'll stay until she shows up."

Rebecca noticed the slight catch in his voice, and felt a strange sort of longing in her heart. Apparently Shelly's beauty made him nervous, and Rebecca couldn't stop the jealousy from welling up in her. *Focus!* She told herself as she made her legs carry her up the steps behind Norman.

Shelly smiled graciously as she stuck out her hand to pat Norman's arm. "Well, I'm glad you and Dylan showed up," she said easily. Then she indicated Rebecca, "And this is one of my classroom volunteers, Rebecca Graves. She's helped Dylan with his reading since school started, and I've been bringing her along on some of my home visits because she's an aspiring school psychologist. I'm sure any school will be glad to have her once she's done with her education. She's basically here to observe like we talked about earlier."

"Alright," Norman smiled. "I guess I should let us in since I have the key," he added with a chuckle.

The only accurate way to describe that meeting was awkward...simply awkward. Norman and Shelly discussed Dylan's progress for about fifteen minutes, Norman signed some papers, and Norman and Shelly both seemed totally unaware of Rebecca's presence. Other than the occasional peculiar glance sent her way, they might as well have not even looked at Rebecca. Not that she wanted them to pay any attention to her... She'd been too busy trying not to gaze at Norman like a teenager with massive a crush, and she'd also been trying not to let them hear her pounding heart. It was so loud to her that at times it drowned out the sound of them talking, and she barely absorbed a word of what they were saying.

All she could think about was how his overwhelming physical presence filled the entire room, and how she could feel as well as hear the reverberations of his deep voice. And her mind kept wondering back to that one kiss he'd given her all those months ago. He probably didn't even remember it, and that thought made her feel all the more pathetic for allowing herself to be so consumed by it.

Too quickly it seemed, Shelly was standing and saying, "Thank you for your time, and I'm sure Dylan will continue to progress in school. Becky and I will make sure of that."

Norman looked askance at Rebecca after Shelly called her 'Becky.'

Rebecca looked right back and raised her eyebrow, prompting a deep chuckle from him.

On her way to the car she heard Norman call out, "Bye Ms. Martin, bye *Becky!*" It couldn't have been her imagination that he'd deliberately over emphasized the nickname. The man was actually teasing her!

She glanced back and said, "Bye Norm." She'd said it so quietly she wasn't even sure he'd heard her until he laughed.

"What was that about?" Shelly asked as soon as they were in the car.

"Uh... nothing really... Norman and I kind of know each other," Rebecca hedged.

"Oh?" Shelly said with her voice full of unasked questions.

"Yeah, we used to run together in the mornings sometimes... I never even knew Dylan was his son! That shows how well we knew each other. We just ran a little, that's all," Rebecca stopped talking abruptly when she realized she was on the verge of rambling.

"Well, you could have talked more. Why did you ignore him? He asked you several questions," Shelly sounded puzzled.

Shocked, Rebecca exclaimed, "I didn't hear him ask me anything!"

"Yeah you were off in La-La Land somewhere. He just asked how you were doing, and he said it was good to see that your face was back to normal... whatever that means."

"Okay... enough about Norman. He actually kind of gets on my nerves," Rebecca interjected at that point.

Shelly regarded her with a discerning look, but she said no more on the subject. They rode the rest of the way back to the school in silence.

The rest of the week Rebecca couldn't stop herself from thinking about him. He'd been right there! Close enough for her to reach out and touch him, yet he'd barely noticed her presence the entire time she'd been there. She groaned aloud at the mental image of herself running around grabbing all the papers. What a fool she was!

Friday night came, and she declined an invitation to go to dinner with Shelly and her little brother. She just wanted to relax and mentally prepare herself for the upcoming weekend. She had high hopes after the weekend at the rec. center. Shirelle had been steadily improving her behavior, but Ronnie had shown no signs of improvement. Tension was still high, but Rebecca no longer felt that Shirelle was about to get herself in trouble. She seemed to be making a valiant effort to keep Ronnie's taunts and antagonism from getting to her.

Shirelle had shown Rebecca more of her poems. Their new ritual was that at quiet time Rebecca would spend a few minutes listening to one of Shirelle's poems. The child blossomed under the positive attention.

The phone rang and interrupted Rebecca's thoughts just as she was starting to drift off to sleep. It both startled her and irritated her at the same time. She almost didn't answer because the caller i.d. said 'private caller.'

"Hello."

"Is this R. Graves?" a deep male voice asked.

"Yes," Rebecca replied. "Who is this?" she added with slight irritation.

"Now I'm hurt... surely you recognize my voice....*Becky.*"

"Norman?" Rebecca practically squeaked. The oxygen supply to her brain suddenly froze as the bottom fell out of her stomach... not literally, but it sure felt like it.

"How have you been?" he asked after a lengthy silence.

"Fine. You?" Rebecca said.

"I can't complain. You sound like something's wrong," he said.

"I'm just surprised to hear from you," she admitted. "It's been months since we've seen each other, and we never even talked all that much in the first place..."

"No, *you* never talked all that much and it hasn't been months. We just saw each other a few days ago."

"But that was different...anyway, how did you get my number?" she suddenly demanded.

"You are on my son's class roster," he drawled out. "I have your number, Shelly's number, and the full time aide's number. But you're the only one who goes by only your last name and first initial... on the roster anyway. I just realized that R. Graves and the Rebecca I know are the same person, otherwise I would have called sooner. "

"What difference does it make?" Rebecca asked. She didn't miss the fact that he'd referred to Ms. Martin as 'Shelly.' They must be closer than either of them had let on in front of her. Jealousy did not sit well with Rebecca, but she wasn't about to ask either of them about their relationship.

"It makes a lot of difference from where I'm standing. I thought you wanted me to help you train, and then I never see or hear from you again! You must have lost my number or something, and you certainly never gave me yours. I've been wondering what happened to you, and I didn't even know your entire name," the emotion behind his words blindsided Rebecca. She couldn't miss the glaring fact that he was angry with her.

"Calm down," she began. "First of all I thought maybe you'd changed your mind because you said you couldn't make it the rest of the week after that day we...you...umm...well, you know! The day the incident happened. It sounded like an excuse because you didn't want to see me again, so I decided to make things easy for you and leave you alone." She was extremely flustered by the end of her statement.

"Well that was nice of you," he said sarcastically.

"Anyway, why did you call me?" she asked in a small voice. "We barely know each other…"

"Maybe because I believe in finishing what I start, and I did promise to train with you," he said. *And maybe because I like you*, he added silently.

"So it bothers you that you didn't get to help me with my training, and you want the chance to finish what you started?" Rebecca asked for clarification.

"Yes, and I'll apologize for 'the incident' as you call it. You won't have to worry about me trying to take advantage of you if you decide you want to run with me again," he tried his best to sound reassuring.

"Okay, I'll think about it," Rebecca said.

"That's what you said last time."

"I'm done thinking about it… Is six o'clock on Tuesday morning good for you?" she said.

"Yeah, that's perfect" he said, obviously nonplussed by her sudden acceptance.

"Well, I have to get up early for work. Remember I do back to back doubles on the weekend, so I'll need some sleep. It was nice talking to you," Rebecca said sleepily.

"I didn't mean to keep you up late. See you Tuesday."

Rebecca fell asleep wondering what had just happened. Why did he want to run with her? Did he just want to be her friend? Why had he apologized for kissing her? Why were men so difficult to understand?

Chapter 8

The next day, Rebecca arrived at the center to find that some major changes had taken place. Shirelle and Ronnie were now roommates. The treatment team had decided that it was best for all the girls on the unit so that they would no longer feel they had to take sides. Rebecca wondered how Ronnie and Shirelle felt about the arrangement.

While the girls were standing in line waiting for breakfast, Rebecca approached Miss Parker.

"Morning," she said, trying her best to keep the nerves from showing in her voice.

"Morning," Ms Parker responded with a sidelong glance filled with derision.

"Were you at the morning meeting when treatment team decided to put Veronica and Shirelle in the same room?" Rebecca asked.

"Nope," was the terse reply.

"It just doesn't make much sense to me," Rebecca continued, despite getting the distinct feeling that Ms Parker didn't want to talk to her.

No response from Ms Parker, other than another scornful glance.

"They can't stand each other, and it just seems like there's going to be trouble," Rebecca didn't want to take the hint.

"They've been getting along fine all week," Ms Parker said.

"Oh?" Rebecca said. "That's good."

"Why don't you go in the day room and watch the ones who are finished with their breakfast," Ms Parker responded as she turned and walked away.

Rebecca stared after her for a moment before complying. She ended up feeling like a fool every time she had any interaction with Ms Parker.

While she was in the day room, Fred came in to talk to her.

"Hey Ms Rebecca, how're you doing today?" he asked politely.

"Good. How are you?" Rebecca responded.

"It's a great day to be alive, but not a great day to be here," he joked.

"The kids getting on your nerves already?" Rebecca smiled.

"Nah, but you know how it is some days..."

Rebecca nodded. She was having one of those days right now. She glanced into the cafeteria. Ms Parker was sitting at the staff table talking to another staff member. Her entire demeanor was different when Rebecca wasn't around; she actually smiled and seemed friendly.

"How come Chuck isn't here today?" Rebecca asked.

"They switched him to the weekday supervisor position. I'm doing the weekends now."

"Why'd they do that?" Rebecca frowned.

"Because the other supervisor left and I can't come in all week. We were going to split it, but Chuck would have missed his day off and had to work for seven days straight indefinitely if he came in all weekend too," Fred explained.

"The girls are going to be disappointed about Sunday evening. That's when Chuck and I usually do poetry hour."

"Yeah, he told me about that. He said he'd come in every Sunday for poetry."

"That's nice of him," Rebecca smiled. Poetry hour was one of the only weekend activities for most of the girls, because they couldn't all go on the outings to the recreation center, movies, and college ball games.

"The girls are still going to miss seeing him all weekend though," she added.

"They'll be alright. See you later."

"Have a good day," Rebecca said as he went into the cafeteria to talk to Ms Parker.

Rebecca watched them talk for a few minutes, and wondered why Ms Parker didn't seem to want to be civil to her.

Norman felt a little tense by the time Tuesday morning rolled around. He shouldn't have gotten slightly drunk on Friday night before he'd called Rebecca. His intention had only been to talk to her and show her that he wanted to be on friendly terms with her. He hadn't planned to irritate her and badger her about running with him again. When she'd agreed so quickly he'd been surprised, and now he was just nervous. Something about her set him on edge, and he felt like if he didn't at least try to be her friend he'd be missing out on something…maybe even something big. Perhaps if he'd never seen her playing the piano he could have stopped thinking about her by now, but ever since that day he just couldn't seem to get her out of his head. Maybe one day she would play for him.

She was already stretching when he pulled up, and she glanced up at him for a moment between stretches. Her hair was still in the same bun she'd always worn. For some reason it irritated him today.

"Morning," he said as he walked up to her.

"Good morning Norman," she said with a quick glance in his direction. Was that a smile on her face? He wasn't sure.

"So, what's the plan for today?" he asked.

She stopped stretching and looked up at him. It was nice to see something other than the top of her head for a change. "Today is a short quick run day. I do five on Tuesdays, Thursdays, and Fridays; and on Wednesdays I do ten or more at this point. Sunday morning is when I do my long run. This week I have a 20 miler coming up."

"You've been moving right along… That's really great," he smiled. "You're already doing exactly what you need to be doing to succeed. When is the big day?"

"Next month on the 26th," she answered.

"Well, I guess I should stretch so we can get going."

"Hurry up, it's cold out here," Rebecca urged him. She started jogging in place to warm up, but she doubted it would help. She hadn't run this early in months, and she'd gotten used to the warmer evening temperatures.

"It's not too bad today," Norman said. He couldn't help but notice a new firmness in her body. She'd also lost a little weight since he last ran with her. He missed the slight curviness she'd had before, but she still looked really good to him. The last few weeks before a big race his own body fat percentage tended to drop due to the intensified training, so he knew she wouldn't stay this thin too long...hopefully.

"You ready?" she asked.

"Yeah," he said, embarrassed because hadn't realized he'd been staring at her until she'd spoken.

They set out at such a quick pace Norman thought she didn't know how to pace herself. He almost told her she should slow down some, but he decided to keep quiet today and let her run the show. During the run she managed to keep to the pace she'd set. She ran somewhere between a six and seven minute mile. Obviously she'd been working hard on her own.

"You've improved a lot since November," he said somewhere towards the middle of the run.

"Thanks," she huffed out sounding irritated.

"Still don't like to talk while you run I see," he teased.

She didn't respond.

He wasn't surprised.

He restrained himself from talking for the remainder of the run, but he couldn't resist saying a few things once they were done.

"I'm really impressed," he said. "You're pace is way better than it used to be, and you attacked that hill you used to hate... That was an awesome run!" he smiled.

"Thanks Norman," she said.

"Hey, you want to go get breakfast? With me?" he thought it wouldn't hurt to give it a shot.

"Sure, I'll meet you at the pancake house in an hour," she said after consulting her watch.

"Cool, see you there!" he hopped in his truck and left before she changed her mind.

Over the next month, Norman and Rebecca spent most of their mornings together running and doing strength training for the upcoming marathon. He'd kept to his promise. He hadn't tried to kiss her or get too friendly at all. Not once.

They ate breakfast together almost every morning, and they'd gotten to know each other a lot better. He found it increasingly difficult to run with her, and sit across from her so often and not feel something beyond friendship for her. He kept thinking about the way she played the piano, but she never mentioned it, and he was reluctant to bring it up because they were getting along so well as friends. Also he had a feeling that it was a sensitive issue for her. She shared so little about her private life and where she'd come from, always dodging his personal questions by giving out replies rather than actual answers. She thought he didn't notice, but he did.

He could tell she was lonely. It was written all over her face at times. She had a difficult job that would be hard enough to handle on its own, but she also balanced it with school, training, and volunteer work. He sometimes wondered if she worked so much just to stave off the loneliness. He often did that very thing himself. He stayed late in the office to finish work that most often could wait until the next day. He always told himself that he was staying on top of things, but he was really just trying to fill up as much time working as he could so he wouldn't have to face the fact that he was tired of going home to an empty house and an empty bed every night.

He sometimes thought about his ex-wife when he was with Rebecca. There was no comparison between the two of them. His ex-wife Juliana was exceptionally beautiful, so beautiful that he'd been blinded to almost every fault she had. Over the years, her selfish disdain for everyone other than herself had tainted her in his eyes. Despite her flaws, he'd still loved her. His love for her didn't die until she'd betrayed him in the worst way. She'd had a long standing affair with a co-worker of his. Even now, despite the fact that they'd been divorced for years, he still felt humiliated at the thought of his wife sleeping with one of his subordinates.

The differences between Rebecca and his ex-wife were like night and day. He'd never known someone as genuinely nice and caring as Rebecca was. Her face lit up whenever she talked about the girls she worked with in the mental health facility, and he could tell that her heart was in her work. She seemed to care more about the girls in the facility than she did about herself, often shrugging off the late nights and the emotional upheaval from working in such an environment. In every area where his ex had given him problems, Rebecca had shown uncommon strength of character. The only problem Norman had with Rebecca was her complete lack of interest in him as a man. He hoped someday she would see him as more than just a friend and running buddy.

On the Thursday before the marathon, they had just finished a short run when he decided to press his luck with her.

"Will you go out with me tonight?" he asked without preamble.

Rebecca was surprised, but she tried not to let it show. Her heart raced as she considered her answer carefully. She couldn't imagine why he'd asked her out; she could be his little sister for all the interest he'd showed in her over the past month.

"I might," she said. "What's the occasion?"

"The marathon is coming up in a few days, and I just want to have a good time for one evening. We've been training hard... you deserve it." He cleared his throat and waited for her answer.

"I do have a class from four to seven fifteen, but if you don't mind waiting 'till after I'll be glad to," she smiled.

"Great, I'll pick you up at your place at seven forty-five," he said. "If that's alright?" he added as an afterthought.

When a knock sounded at her door at precisely 7:45 Rebecca shook her head. He'd taken punctuality to a new extreme, and she wasn't ready yet. In fact she'd just gotten out of the shower.

"I'm so sorry!" she said after answering the door in her bathrobe. "Just give me ten minutes... Class ran a little late tonight, and I thought I had enough time to take a quick shower, and I wasn't expecting you to come right on time, and I got stuck in traffic on my way home after class, and-"

"It's okay, I can wait a few minutes," he cut her off. He'd never heard her ramble on like that before, and he'd just had a powerful urge to kiss her so she'd stop talking so fast.

"I'll be right back," she called out as she dashed down the hall.

He didn't mind waiting. Some things about women were the same universally; they all took extra time to get ready for an evening out.

He wasn't sure what he'd been expecting her to wear, but when she reappeared fifteen minutes later he was disappointed that her appearance didn't give any clues as to how she felt about going out with him. She still had her hair tied down at the back of her head, and she was dressed as modestly as a school teacher. Her attire seemed to be an indication that she wasn't interested in anything beyond friendship with him. What made him think that she might try to dress up for him? He hadn't actually called this outing a date, but that's what it was.

"What?" she demanded with a stricken look on her face. "You look like something's wrong."

"Nothing... I'm just really hungry," he lied.

They had dinner at an artsy restaurant near the Austen Peay State University campus in Clarksville. Various paintings from local artists hung on display in the dining room, and each lighting fixtures was unique, giving the place an eclectic feel. The food was pretty distinctive, but he barely noticed it as he sat across from her. In the soft lighting she looked ever prettier than normal, and his mind wandered back to the one kiss they'd shared all those months ago. Tonight she really looked like she needed another one.

"You know, I think you have beautiful hair. Why do you always wear it tied down like that?" he asked.

"Because it takes forever to do anything with it, and I don't have time for the salon," she said.

"If you'll let your hair down just for tonight, I'll show you something really interesting that you probably haven't seen before," Norman said. He looked into her eyes, and held her gaze. There was nothing friendly about the way he looked at her just then, and the air between them practically sizzled until she cast her gaze downward again.

"What is it?" she asked.

"It's a surprise," he said. "But I guarantee you'll love it." He reached across the table and placed his hand over hers.

"Well then, if I'll love it then of course I'll wear my hair down. I'll let it down as soon as we leave here," she smiled.

Norman smiled back and asked, "What do you like to do besides stay busy all the time? There must be lots of stuff I don't know about you yet."

"Not really. You know just about everything. There isn't much to know about me..." Rebecca hedged. Then after a moment's thought she said, "You should tell me more about you!"

"Okay Becky, what do you want to know?" he asked.

"Where did you grow up? What was your family like? How was your childhood?"

"Very good questions," he chuckled. "My childhood was normal, as normal as it could be with seven siblings. I'm the youngest of eight, and my mother died when I was six. She was one of the most beautiful women I've ever seen. She and my father were both uncommonly tall, which is why I'm tall. Actually, everyone in my family is tall. Even my sister is somewhere around six feet tall without heels. My sister is the only one I'm close to, because we're only two years apart and we played together a lot as kids. The rest of my brothers are all older than I am. My parents married young, and they really loved each other."

Rebecca restrained herself from asking how his mother had died, but her heart went out to him. Her foot accidentally bumped his under the table, but he didn't seem to notice as he went on.

"I'm actually from around here. I know a lot of military people come to Ft. Campbell from all over the United States, but I'm a true Tennessean," he said with a grin.

"How come you don't have the accent?" Rebecca teased.

"Because I've been in the military for so many years… After so many duty stations you begin to lose a little bit of where you came from," he explained.

"You didn't answer all my questions Norman," Rebecca said when he didn't say anything for a few moments.

"I know, I'm getting to it," he said before continuing. "As a kid I always had too much energy to be allowed in the house too often. My mother used to make us go straight outside after school every day, and we always stayed busy until dark. We lived on a horse ranch, so there was always plenty of room to run around, and plenty of chores to do. I never took to the ranching thing. I preferred running to riding, but my sister is an excellent equestrian. My oldest brother took over the ranch after my father passed, and all my other brothers do various things. Only my oldest brother, my sister, and I live around here. One of my brothers is a doctor in Chicago, one is in the military like me, one is a butcher, one is a baker, and one is a candle stick maker. That's my childhood in a nutshell," he smiled when he finished.

When she didn't say anything he prompted her, "Now it's your turn."

"What do you want to know?"

"Come on don't tease me! The same stuff I just told you."

"Jeez, I wouldn't know where to begin…"

"Why don't you start by telling my about your parents?"

"There isn't really much to tell about them," she said with a glance down at the table.

"I don't want to pry… but I've been curious about your background for a while now. Are you mixed or interracial?" he asked.

Her eyes shot up to look at him in discomfort. "What makes you think I'm mixed?" she asked.

"Well," he cleared his throat and met her gaze head on. "From your skin tone I would guess that you're African American, but your hair and facial features seem like something else. Am I wrong? Are both of your parents African American?"

Rebecca was silent for so long he added, "I hope I haven't offended you…I was just curious."

"No, I'm not offended. I just don't know what to tell you. My mother and father never married, and I have no idea who he is or even what he looks like. I'm not sure about my mother's ethnic background either. She says she's African American, but her skin is a lot lighter than mine."

Norman sensed her growing discomfort with the subject, so he smiled and said, "It doesn't really matter one way or the other… I was just curious. So, what is the rest of your family like? Probably not as big as mine, I'll bet."

"My entire family is my mother. She's worked in the same bakery for as long as I can remember. She decorates cakes for special occasions. I had an identical twin sister, but she died when we were both small. A car hit her one day. I barely remember her. So, basically I grew up as an only child. I wanted some adventure, so I joined the army straight out of high school. I've been an adult since I left home at seventeen, and my mother and I aren't very close."

"Why aren't you close? You're all each other has…" he was genuinely concerned as he observed the distant look that appeared in her eyes when she mentioned her mother.

"I don't really know," Rebecca admitted. "We've never been close, not even when I was little."

His gave her hand a gentle squeeze. He couldn't imagine having grown up without the love and support from his parents and all his siblings.

When they got up to leave he reminded her about her promise to let her hair down. When they got back in his truck he felt his self control start to slip a little. The close quarters, the fact that he could feel her body heat, and the enticing way her lips looked all combined to make him want to get as close as possible to her.

"Let me help you with your hair." He reached across the seat toward her.

Rebecca turned and presented him with the back of her head, so that he could remove the rubber bands holding her hair in place.

"Ouch!" she said as he tugged a little too hard and pulled her hair. "I'll take the rubber bands out while you drive, but thanks for trying to help."

"Okay," he was slightly embarrassed. He'd imagined that taking her hair down would be sort of romantic...

"Tell me about the surprise," she said after a few minutes of silence.

"Now that I can't do, but you're going to love it... at least I hope so."

By the time they arrived at their destination, Rebecca had managed to take her hair down and run her fingers through it so that it looked presentable.

He parked and hastened to open the passenger door for her.

"Where are we?" she asked as she huddled inside her jacket to ward off the excessively chilly night air.

"We're at my house."

When they got inside Rebecca was pleased to find his home warm and comfortable. He had a small sitting area next to a glass wall that overlooked a deck with an exquisite panoramic view of a clearing just down the hill. The entire scene was lit up by the silvery moon. Next to the window stood a large cylindrical white object that Rebecca couldn't identify.

"What's that?" she asked.

"That's the surprise," he whispered in her ear.

She still had no idea what it was.

He turned on a light, and she could suddenly see the main theme of his sitting room. It was actually quite fascinating, and Rebecca got the feeling that she could spend hours just looking at all the interesting pictures and artifacts. The walls were lined with pictures of distant galaxies, planets, stars, and other cosmological images taken with the Hubble Telescope. She walked up to one that caught her eye, because it looked so much like what she'd imagined heaven itself must look like when she was a child.

"What's this?" she asked as she pointed to the large framed picture.

"That's an enhanced image of Crab Nebula taken with the Hubble Telescope."

"What's a nebula?" Rebecca queried as she continued to look around.

"I'm glad you asked," Norman smiled as he came to stand next to her. "That's part of the surprise."

His arm brushed against hers as he indicated the cylindrical object Rebecca had first noticed.

"That is a telescope, and tonight is an excellent night for looking at nebulae through it. I think you'll be amazed at what even an amateur can see these days." There was obvious excitement and pride in his voice as he walked to the telescope.

"I've seen telescopes before, and that one looks nothing like the ones I've seen," Rebecca said.

"That's because you've probably seen either a refractor design, which uses a lens to gather light; or a reflector which uses mirrors to reflect light to enhance the image. This baby is a hybrid that uses elements from both, and it's known as a compound telescope." He smiled at her as she briefly examined it.

"And what's this for?" she pointed to a cable and a small mount that was sticking out of the side of it next the eyepiece.

"That's what I use to take pictures with my digital camera."

"You mean you can take pictures of the things you see through the telescope, and they'll actually come out good?" Rebecca asked in disbelief.

"Yep. It just takes practice, but I've been doing it for years." He walked over to the wall with all the amazing photos and pointed at several pictures of the moon at different phases, and several planets. "I took these," he said.

"Wow! I'm impressed," Rebecca said.

"You ready to see something spectacular?" he asked.

"Yes," Rebecca replied in anticipation.

"Do you mind going outside in the cold again?"

"Not really," she replied.

"Okay, give me a few minutes to set it up." Then he opened the sliding glass door and wheeled the telescope outside onto the deck.

Rebecca spent the next few minutes looking around in appreciation. He had all sorts of pictures. There were galaxies, planets, stars, star clusters, and many detailed pictures of the moon. He also had a book shelf filled with references, and many books about the universe. Rebecca never thought about the stars much herself, but she could see how Norman found them fascinating.

She picked up one book written by a New York University theoretical physicist and began to thumb through it. It was all about the possibilities of higher dimensions, parallel worlds, and time travel. Norman had a very interesting hobby.

Norman came back in while she was looking at his books.

"Have you read all of these?" she asked.

"Most of them," he said.

"When do you have time to read so many books, and take so many pictures of space?" Rebecca teased.

"Actually I read most of those on deployments, during any downtime I had. And taking the pictures isn't as hands on as you think it is. My telescope has a motorized mount that tracks the trajectory of whatever I'm taking pictures of as the Earth continues to rotate. All I have to do is set it up properly and capture several exposures over a period of time to get the picture," he explained.

"Cool," Rebecca replied. She knew nothing about telescopes, and now she wanted to learn more about them.

"We can go out in about thirty minutes. I have to let the telescope adjust to the outside temperature so we'll get a clear image…meanwhile we can just hang out in here."

Rebecca sat down on the end of the couch closest to the book shelf. She continued to look at all the titles for a few minutes while he went to the kitchen. A few minutes later he returned with two mugs of hot chocolate. There was a companionable silence between them while she sipped her cocoa and looked at one book that had lots of high resolution pictures of galaxies.

While she looked at the books Norman made no pretense about looking at her. He drank in the sight of her beautiful hair in slight disarray down her back, and no matter how many times he looked away his eyes kept returning to her lips. He'd tasted them once, and the more he thought about it the more he realized that once could never be enough. When she glanced up at him with a look of admiration in her beautiful brown eyes he felt his resolve to keep his hands to himself slipping even more.

He sat down beside her so close that their legs were pressed together, and she didn't seem to mind.

"You want to know what I think is the most beautiful thing in here?" he asked as set their empty mugs on the tray.

Rebecca couldn't stop herself from leaning closer to Norman's warm body. She could feel his every breath as she looked around briefly to try and guess which picture was his favorite.

The largest one was of the moon, so she took a wild guess and pointed to it saying, "It must be that picture of the moon right there."

"You're way off," he said. He touched a lock of her hair before he spoke again. "*You* are the most beautiful thing that has ever been in this room."

He looked at her with his usual stern expression, but this time his eyes roamed hungrily over her face. She knew that he was telling the truth, because at that moment his eyes were telling her that she was the most beautiful woman in the world.

Rebecca leaned slightly closer, but the kiss her body was expecting never came. Instead, Norman continued to play with her hair as if he were fascinated by the feel of it. She relaxed and allowed herself to lean closer to him. He wrapped his arms around her and pulled her against his chest. She closed her eyes and enjoyed the feel of his hand in her hair, his arm around her, and the sound of his steady heartbeat. She didn't even think to analyze why they were cuddling or what it could lead to; she simply enjoyed being close to him. She wasn't sure how much time passed until he spoke again

"You're not sleep, are you?" he murmured against her hair.

"No. Why?" she responded.

"Because the telescope should be ready now."

Rebecca reluctantly pulled away from his warm embrace to follow him outside.

"Take a look through this," he said pointing at the eyepiece that stuck out of the side of the telescope.

Rebecca didn't know what she'd been expecting to see, but she wasn't prepared to see a detailed image of an entire galaxy. It was spectacular to be able look into the eyepiece and know that she was seeing something that existed millions of miles away.

"Wow! That is probably the coolest thing I've ever seen," she said honestly.

"That's the Andromeda Galaxy. You can't see it that well with anything less than an eight inch aperture," he informed her.

"Can you take a picture of it?" she asked.

"Yeah, I already set up the camera... it's still taking exposures. It needs to continue for another hour at least if you want a good picture."

Rebecca looked back into the eyepiece and marveled at the tiny galaxy before her eyes. If it hadn't been so cold outside she would have been content to stare indefinitely, but as it was she started to shiver.

Norman noticed and came to stand behind her. Then when he put his arms around her she forgot all about the galaxy.

"If you're too cold we can look at the stars another night," he whispered against her hair.

"I'm okay," she whispered back. She didn't want to spoil the relaxed and majestic quietude that surrounded them tonight. She looked up at the multitude of stars that shone in the night sky and wondered why on earth she'd never taken the time to notice them before.

"I'll be right back," Norman said after she shivered again. He jogged into the house and returned a short time later with a soft fleece blanket.

"You didn't have to get me a blanket, but thanks," Rebecca said as he draped it around her shoulders.

"I want you to be comfortable." He sat down on a large padded wicker chair and patted his lap. "I'll keep you warm," he smiled.

She approached him with caution and sat gingerly on the edge of his knees as if she were afraid her weight would crush him. However, before she settled completely he wrapped his arms around her and pulled her closer. She allowed her head to rest against his shoulder and looked up at the sky again.

They gazed at the stars for some time without speaking. Norman's warm hands held Rebecca's cocooned in his, and every once in a while they tightened almost imperceptibly.

When a cold north wind started to blow Norman suggested they go back inside. She looked through the telescope once more as he stood silently behind her.

She turned around to tell him something, and then all thoughts abruptly left her head when he kissed her.

This kiss wasn't like the first one at all. This was the kiss of a man who was hungry for more. His arms went around her back to press her up against him as his tongue gently explored hers. When she responded with some exploration of her own he groaned and pulled her even closer.

Reality was suspended for a magical moment as they kissed and caressed each other. Even the cold didn't seem so bad to Rebecca while she was enfolded in his warmth. She enjoyed the feel of his hard masculine strength pressed firmly against her smaller, softer and more feminine curves. She enjoyed the sound of his ragged breathing, and she enjoyed knowing that she was the cause of it.

When they finally separated enough to catch their breath Norman found himself in a quandary. He wanted much, much more than just a few kisses from her, but at the same time he also wanted to take things slow. He'd rushed headlong into his previous marriage, and he owed it to himself and his children to take more time before rushing into any future relationships. Perhaps he shouldn't have brought her to his house. The mere fact that she was there, with his bed so close by, was turning the direction of his thoughts farther and farther away from what he should do. As he looked down at her he knew exactly what he should do, but he did what he wanted to do instead.

He kissed her again.

Rebecca shivered as Norman's lips met hers again. Whether it was from cold or from the sheer physical joy of being this close to him, she wasn't sure... Norman must have assumed she was just cold, because he promptly picked her up and carried her inside still pausing to kiss her lips even as he walked with her in his arms.

Rebecca's arms went around his neck to hold on. She even sighed a little as she thought of how romantic it was to be carried in his arms.

He took her down a long hallway that led to his bedroom, and placed her directly upon his bed. His heart was beating fast, and he felt almost as if he'd just thrown down a challenge. He looked in her eyes to see if she would accept him this time, and the uncertainty in her eyes almost undid him...almost. If not for the way she'd responded to his earlier kisses he would have left her alone, but he had a feeling that she looked uncertain for the same reasons he felt unsure... not because she was actually afraid of him.

"Norman," she spoke in a low voice. "What exactly do you want from me?" she asked.

She'd wasted no time putting him on the spot, and suddenly he felt even more unsure. How could he tell her what he wanted, when he couldn't even figure that out for himself? He decided to go with complete honesty.

"I don't know," he said as he knelt in front of her and took her hands in his. He kissed each of her fingers before continuing, "But I do know that the more I find out about you the more I want to know... and I do know that I want to kiss you again."

It seemed like an eternity before she replied. She didn't actually speak, but she did allow her forehead to rest against his for a moment of silent communication. Then she kissed him on the forehead.

He laughed.

"What's so funny?" she asked.

"I think that's probably the only time you'll ever be able to reach my forehead to do that," he said still chuckling.

She laughed a little as she hugged him and kissed his forehead again. Then she made a small trail of gentle kisses that led to his lips. Once she got there, she gave him a lingering, heartfelt kiss filled with all the longing she'd felt for him over the past months. As he kissed her back, Norman felt a curious tightening in his chest. It affected him very strongly and made him want to pull her as close as possible and get rid of all the barriers between them.

When the kiss ended, he looked up at her for a moment and tried to guess what she was thinking. She looked way too serious for his peace of mind.

"Do you want me to take you home?" he asked as he stood up beside her.

She remained seated and said, "No."

"Good, because I might have refused if you'd said yes," he joked. He didn't immediately speak again; instead he turned on his stereo.

Rebecca's face lit up in surprise when she heard classical piano music flow from the speakers.

Norman carefully observed her as he asked, "Do you like this sort of music?"

"I do...quite a lot actually," she admitted, but she didn't elaborate.

"My mother was an exceptional pianist. She used to play music like this for me all the time when I was a little boy."

"I have a little trouble believing that," Rebecca said.

"Why? My mother was really good, everyone thought so."

"Not that... I'm having trouble believing the part about you being a little boy, there's no way you could have been little," she joked. She laughed at the expression on his face, and covered her smile with her hands.

Norman took that opportunity to touch her again. He gently grasped her hands and lowered them saying, "You shouldn't cover up such a lovely smile."

And just like that, Rebecca's heart was racing again as she looked up into his stern features.

When she didn't reply, Norman pulled her to her feet and began to sway back and forth to the music with her in his arms. They didn't talk for a while, but their hands continuously stroked each other. Rebecca let her fingers trace the outline of his shoulders, his neck, and his face as they held each other. His hands played in her hair and caressed her waist and her back...and they kept pressing her closer to him. He was using his body very subtly to set her at ease and bring her closer, and it was working like magic. By the end of the song they were kissing again.

Somehow they ended up back on the bed with Rebecca lying on top of Norman as he continued to kiss her. His hands were all over her gently kneading, caressing, and lighting fires wherever they touched her. For the first time ever she wasn't hesitant about touching him, and he felt his resolve to take it slow cease to exist completely when she proceeded to undo the buttons on his shirt.

From the moment Norman started kissing her, Rebecca had felt as if a secret compartment in her heart had been opened for the first time. She was no longer the shy outcast ignored by almost everyone, including her own mother; tonight she was a goddess who wanted to love and be loved. The look in his eyes as she glanced up at him made her feel like the most desirable woman in the world, and she'd never even felt the least bit desirable before.

She smiled and kissed him again. Her attention then returned to his bare chest. She'd fantasized about kissing him like this, and it almost felt like a dream... except that the sensations caused by his hands were very, very real.

She straddled him as she finished unbuttoning his shirt. After every button she'd paused to kiss his chest until she got all the way to his navel.

Her trail of kisses left him almost breathless in anticipation. His whole state of awareness was heightened beyond anything he'd ever felt before. Even the feel of her hair gliding across his chest made his skin tingle. He didn't know how much longer he could lie still and allow her to torture him with her gentle, almost hesitant caresses. He wanted to see her completely naked with her hair spread out all around her as he thoroughly explored every inch of her body, yet at the same time he completely enjoyed every second of her gentle, sensual exploration of his body.

"I can't believe I'm doing this," Rebecca whispered as she gazed at Norman's half naked body in appreciation.

"I can't either," he smiled as he played with her hair. "The first time I kissed you, you didn't seem to like it much."

"*I* didn't seem to like it?!" Rebecca exclaimed. "You acted like you couldn't wait to leave, and then you told me you didn't want to run with me anymore that week... *you* didn't seem to like it much. And all you did was give me a peck on the lips... I figured if you'd liked kissing me it would have been more... you know....more like tonight," she explained.

"Apparently we need to talk," Norman said as he sat up. He leaned against the head of the bed and wrapped his arms around her as she sat still straddling his lap. "Is that why you stopped running in the mornings and avoided me for months? You thought I didn't want to see you anymore?" he asked.

"Yes."

"I'm going to let you in on a little secret about us men... When we kiss a woman, and she stares at her feet and doesn't say anything we feel awkward. I was just reacting to your response at the time, and I didn't want to avoid you, I just wanted to avoid the awkward feeling I had at the moment. I loved kissing you, but I didn't want to hurt you. You still had bruises from work at the time. And I thought that maybe I'd overstepped the boundary," he explained.

"Well in that case you were very considerate, and I'm sorry I made you feel awkward," Rebecca laughed against his chest.

"I'm glad you see the humor in the situation," Norman said dryly.

"Why don't you show me now how you would have kissed me if I hadn't had bruises that day," Rebecca whispered provocatively as she ran her fingers down the side of his face.

In the space of seconds Norman's body was fully aroused again, and his mouth hungrily covered hers for a searing kiss. This time he was the one doing most of the touching, and it seemed like his hands were suddenly everywhere at once. He unbuttoned her shirt so fast she didn't realize it was coming off until she felt the cool air on her back. She shivered as he kissed her neck and shoulders.

"Do you have any idea how beautiful you are?" he breathed as he paused to look at her.

"Not until tonight," Rebecca answered honestly.

"Then I'm going to have to make sure you never forget it."

"You look pretty good yourself you know," Rebecca replied.

"Yeah, I work out quite a bit with this gorgeous young woman I know," he smiled at her before he proceeded to finish undressing her. He thoroughly enjoyed kissing every inch of her bare skin until she was begging him for more.

"Oh Norman," she breathed as he teased her breasts with his tongue.

"You like that?" he asked.

"Yes." She arched her back as his mouth returned to her breasts.

"What else do you like?" he asked as he lightly touched her between her thighs.

"You touching me, kissing me, putting your arms around me...you on top of me," she said boldly.

"Rebecca, what are you trying to do to me?" he whispered against her neck. They were both lying naked in the shadows of his darkened room. The more he'd touched her and tasted her, the harder it had been for him not to pounce on her like a madman. Now her words aroused him almost to the point of pain.

She opened her legs wide to accommodate Norman's weight and felt her first twinge of hesitation. He was so much bigger than she was, and she felt she had to get some reassurance.

"Norman," she said hesitantly.

The tone of her voice got his immediate attention. "What's wrong? You're not having second thoughts *now*, are you?" he sounded like he was in physical pain.

"No, it's just that..."

"What?" he prompted when she didn't continue.

She hid her face in his shoulder as she said, "It's just that I've never done this before, and you're so...just don't hurt me... Okay?"

For a moment Norman cursed his rotten luck. How did he manage to find a woman so desirable and sexy, only to discover that she's a virgin? His resolve to take things slow suddenly strengthened again as he looked down at her. He saw naked vulnerability in her eyes, and he didn't want to push her too far. He wanted her to be completely comfortable with him before he made love to her, and there was not a doubt in his mind that they would get around to it... it just wouldn't be tonight. Her words had been like a bucket of cold water being thrown on his overheated body, but they'd also caused a curious feeling in his heart. He felt like he'd been given a precious gift, and he also felt a bit of possessiveness because he was the only man who'd ever been intimate with her.

"I'd never intentionally hurt you, but I do know that the first time can be painful," Norman said. He got off of her and pulled her into his arms. "Don't think that I don't like you... I just wasn't prepared for this. I've never been with a virgin before, and I don't want to cause you any pain tonight...besides, you have a marathon to run in a few days." He kissed the back of her neck and hugged her close to his chest.

"Are you disappointed?" Rebecca asked after a few minutes of silence.

"Give me twenty minutes and I won't feel too disappointed anymore," he joked. "We can just lie here and talk if you like."

"You mean you want me to stay?" Rebecca asked in shock. She was sure he'd want to take her home after her big announcement.

"I don't know what type of guy you think I am, but I like you. I didn't invite you over just to have sex with you. Don't get me wrong, sex would have been great, but that's not what I was after... I really did just want to show you the heavens with my telescope. The rest just happened."

"Thanks for tonight. I enjoyed it... all of it," Rebecca replied.

"No problem. You should come over again."

Norman lay on his side pressed up against Rebecca's back and tried to go to sleep, but every time she moved his body responded to the point where he was just short of arousal. It was torturous to lay next to her naked and not make love to her, but he didn't want to let her go. He listened to her deep even breathing for a while as he tried to fall asleep, but her round bottom pressed up against him kept distracting him.

He moved her hair aside and kissed the back of her neck, and then he kissed her shoulder and her back. He just couldn't seem to keep his hands or his lips off her. He lightly traced his finger over her arm and caressed her fingers as he thought about the way she'd played the piano. He wondered why she never mentioned the fact that she played, especially after tonight. Why would she want to hide such a talent from him?

The first thing Rebecca became aware of the next morning was the fact that she was completely naked and uncovered. The second thing she noticed were the hands playing in her hair. For one disoriented moment she had no idea where she was or how she got there, but then memories from the previous night quickly replaced her bewilderment with embarrassment. She'd behaved like a wanton hussy, and Norman still hadn't been able to bring himself to do anything besides kiss her.

"Good morning Becky," the subject of her turbulent thoughts said gently.

"Good morning," Rebecca said with a wealth of uncertainty in her voice. She hadn't looked at him yet, but she did quickly grab the sheet to cover her nakedness. How long had he been awake?

He chuckled at her. "I've been staring at you long enough to memorize what you look like naked, so covering up won't make much difference," he said unabashedly.

"Why were you looking?" Rebecca demanded.

"The same reason any other man would stare at a beautiful, naked woman he happened to find in his bed…because I just couldn't resist. As soon as I opened my eyes this morning I felt as if I'd woken up next to an angel."

Rebecca turned to look at him, and was immediately arrested by the sight of his naked chest. Last night in the dim light she hadn't noticed how well defined his muscles were. He had wide well built shoulders and an incredible physique. Eventually her eyes made it up to his face to find an odd expression that she couldn't even begin to recognize.

"How long has it been since you've had a woman in your bed? It must have been awhile if you think I'm beautiful," Rebecca said wryly.

"Are you kidding?" Norman asked. "I've been around enough women to know what's beautiful and what's not, so please don't put yourself down when you're with me."

"I'm not putting myself down; I'm just stating the facts," Rebecca countered. "I've lived in this body for twenty-two years, so I think I know better than anyone else about how beautiful I'm not. You're the first man who's ever paid the least bit of attention to me, and I'm sure it's not because you think I'm so irresistible. It's probably because we've been running together, and you're too busy to find someone else to socialize with. You think I don't know that? Nobody picks me out of a crowd... I might as well be an insignificant pebble in a pile of millions of pebbles. I also know that as soon as someone prettier, smarter, and more interesting comes along you'll pretend like you never met me."

Norman just stared at her for a minute before replying. "You're wrong about me if you think I could do that to you, and you're wrong about yourself. I can't answer for any other men, but you didn't make it easy for me to talk to you on a personal level. I'll bet there are plenty of guys interested in you, but you just don't notice...or you just don't give them the chance to show it," he finished with a gentle kiss to her cheek.

"I never thought of it that way," Rebecca said quietly.

Norman sighed as he pulled her close and started kissing her again. "You women never do," he observed.

Chapter 9

By Sunday Rebecca was filled with such nervous anticipation it was a wonder she hadn't thrown up several times. She'd thought of scarcely anything else besides the race and the one wonderful night she'd spent in Norman's arms. As the start time drew nearer, the race became her most prevalent concern.

She had no designs on winning; she just wanted to finish with a respectable time. After months of training she was finally going to see the fruits of her labor, and all she wanted to do was vomit. She was in the last corral of runners, and she'd heard at least twenty different people talking about the previous marathons they'd run and how they'd give anything to finish one in under three hours. Previous records were discussed and hopes for future records were discussed as they waited.

Rebecca just listened to them in silence. She didn't fail to notice that there were plenty of other people in her position; this was their first marathon, and they didn't want to talk about it. Maybe the nerves were getting to them as well.

At what seemed like long length the race finally started for Rebecca. She walked right up until she crossed the start line, and then she took off at a very modest pace. Despite the slow pace, she was still aware of her heart slamming into her chest much like it did the day she'd raced Norman up the hill. The sheer volume of runners was enough to intimidate anyone, and first timers like Rebecca were doubly affected. At first she felt a bit conspicuous because so many people were passing her, but after awhile she stopped noticing everyone else and concentrated on her own pace and breathing. *You will get through this*, she told herself over and over again as she ran... and she did.

Rebecca had wanted to appear relaxed for her finish line photo, but when she did finally arrive at the finish line all the anguish and toil of the past 26.2 miles clearly showed on her face. Her teeth were bared in a hideous grimacing expression, her hair was untidy because her rubber band had broken during the last mile, and she was soaked through with sweat mingled with tears. Whether they were tears of joy or tears of pain she could hardly distinguish as she slowed to a walk and looked around at all the other finishers.

After a few minutes of walking around reflecting on her accomplishment Rebecca ran into Norman.

"Rebecca! How do you feel?" he greeted her warmly.

"How do you think I feel," she retorted as she eyed him in his running clothes. He looked way to calm and relaxed for having just run a marathon. "Anyway, how come you didn't tell me you were going to enter the race?" she demanded.

"I decided at the last minute, and I didn't think it mattered one way or the other," he answered.

"It doesn't really, I was just surprised. You don't even look tired."

"I'm not," he grinned.

"Well I am," Rebecca muttered under her breath.

"Do you ever congratulate yourself? You just did something that only a fraction of Americans even think about attempting, and you finished with a damn good time, especially for a first timer. For once in your life just give yourself a pat on the back."

Norman's impassioned speech was met with stony silence.

"Say something," he prodded.

"I'm happy I finished, but running always irritates me... I hate running." Rebecca said grudgingly.

"Then why did you push yourself so far? Most people do something of this magnitude because they feel some sort of passion for the sport."

"You wouldn't understand my motivation."

"How do you know?" he asked.

"I just know, and I don't want to have to explain when you'll probably laugh anyway."

"You're a tough nut to crack... You could at least give me the opportunity to understand; you'll never know unless you try."

"Giving out too many opportunities only leads to pain and heartache," Rebecca said flippantly.

"You sound like you're joking, but you're not. I know you a lot better than you think I do Becky," Norman said as he grasped her chin and forced her to look up at him.

Rebecca met his intense gaze, and for the first time in her life she felt that she could trust somebody with her deepest secrets and maybe even her heart. The fact that that somebody just happened to be the most drop dead gorgeous man she'd ever laid eyes on probably contributed to loosening her tongue, but she wasn't ready to analyze that part of herself just yet. It was foolish to trust a man because he was handsome and charming, but she couldn't help the way she felt at that moment.

"I just wanted to prove to myself that I could do it. I believe that doing productive things that are hard, that you don't want to do, is a good way to build strength and character. I've always felt this overwhelming need to prove to myself and everyone else how smart I am, how tough I am, and how capable I am. Other women have charm, grace, sex appeal, and beauty, but I have character and capability," *and you'd better not laugh*, she added silently to herself.

"That explains a lot," Norman said thoughtfully.

An image of her disapproving mother flashed up before Rebecca. She hadn't mentioned her aspirations of running a marathon, because she'd wanted to be able to come to her mother with actual results rather than intentions. Now that she'd done it she probably wouldn't tell her mother; Rebecca had learned after years of trying that it was nearly impossible to make her mother proud of anything she did.

"Well Norman, it was nice talking to you, but I have to go now. I'll see you around sometime." She started to walk away and he stared at her in puzzlement, her parting words ringing in his ears.

"Wait a minute!" he stopped her. "What was that all about? 'I'll see you around sometime?' You sound like you don't want to see me again at all..."

"I didn't say that, but I'm not going to be running as much anymore for awhile and I'll probably be doing it in the evening when I do. Am I mistaken that you're unavailable in the evenings?" Rebecca said.

"Yes you are mistaken. And what about the other night? Are you saying that you don't want to see me unless we're running together? I thought we were friends," he said.

"We are friends, but I don't want you to feel obligated to spend time with me."

"Obligated?!" he practically choked out. "Rebecca, I *like* you. I want to spend time with you as more than just your friend... What did you think Thursday night was about? I like you, and I was under the impression that you like me too."

"I do," Rebecca said.

"Then stop acting like you're trying to escape from me," he said.

"Okay. Give me a call sometime then," she smiled before she walked away. The crowd quickly swallowed her up, making it impossible for Norman to catch up to her again without stomping all over people. More than anything else she wanted to go home, shower, and lie down before she collapsed. She didn't want Norman to see just how exhausted she really was, so she made a hasty retreat.

Once Rebecca made it home she soaked in a warm, relaxing bubble bath for almost an hour before she could bring herself to get out. Memories from her night with Norman clouded her head as she got dressed. She could feel all the danger of allowing herself to care too deeply for such a man. He'd said he liked her, not that he was interested in a serious relationship with her, and she just wasn't a casual sex type of woman. That's why her own behavior both frightened and surprised her. She'd been totally willing to go all the way with him if he hadn't stopped, and she knew that meant her feelings must be stronger than she'd admit even to herself.

She didn't love him, but she could certainly see herself falling in deep if she wasn't careful. She didn't want to be in love with a man who saw her as a plaything. According to her mother men only wanted one thing from women, and Norman was a man. Another part of her wanted to throw caution to the wind and abandon herself to the adventure taking each moment as it came. Maybe it would be worse to miss out on being in a relationship with him, even a casual one, than it would be to get her heart broken in the long run. There were just too many sides to the issue, and Rebecca's experience with men and relationships was limited at best. Her mother was the only one who'd ever given her any advice on the subject, and her mother's advice had been clear...no matter how nice they seem at first, men were not to be trusted.

Eventually she found herself at the keyboard pouring her emotions out in an impromptu piece that reverberated throughout her small apartment. Norman was uppermost in her thoughts, second only to her mother. For the first time in years she had the urge ask her mother why she didn't like her. Norman had said they were all each other had at dinner, and Rebecca couldn't get that statement out of her mind. It was true; she had not one other living relative that she knew about other than her mother. Her mother had always barely tolerated her, and after years of simply accepting it as a fact of life she now wanted to know why…she *needed* to know why.

She played on as she imagined that magical night she'd spent with Norman, and she wondered where it would lead. All she could see at the moment was potential heartbreak and more loneliness and dejection for her. This wasn't the right time in her life to engage in any relationships, especially not potentially heartbreaking relationships. Norman had insisted that he liked her, but liking someone wasn't enough to build anything substantial. Rebecca had a feeling that she might not be able to settle for anything less 'substantial' when it came to engaging Norman's affection.

Rebecca was so deep into the music that she failed to notice the tears that streamed down her cheeks, and she almost didn't hear the knock at her door. As soon as she realized someone was knocking she quickly dried her face and opened the door. To her surprise Norman was standing there with a beautiful flower arrangement.

"Hi," he smiled. "I hope this isn't a bad time."

"Not at all," she lied. He looked so good she had the momentary urge to throw herself into his arms and tell him all about her troubles.

"I brought you some flowers…"

"Oh, thank you! Those are beautiful, and so is the vase. You want to come in?" she said as she slowly came back to her senses. It was difficult to keep her wits about her when he was in such close proximity. "I'll take those," she said as an afterthought when he stepped inside.

"How come you never told me you play?" Norman asked her as he eyed her keyboard. It was still on, so she couldn't deny using it.

"I don't… not really," Rebecca hedged.

"I could hear you from outside."

"You could?! How much did you hear?" she demanded.

"I was out there for a few minutes. I hated to interrupt you, but your neighbor started to give me some strange looks," he admitted a bit sheepishly. "You play exceptionally well."

"Thanks," Rebecca's heart raced from his modest praise. She could see the sincerity in his eyes as he looked at her admiringly.

"What were you playing? I don't think I've heard it before," he said as he sat right next to her on the tiny sofa.

"It was nothing," Rebecca said. She'd be extremely embarrassed to tell him that she came up with her own music most of the time.

"Don't do that to me. That sounded way too good to be called nothing. If for no other reason than out of respect to the composer you shouldn't call it nothing. It's okay if you don't know where the piece came from... I could help you find out if you like."

"I know exactly where it came from, and trust me, the 'composer' wouldn't be offended at me calling it nothing," Rebecca laughed.

Norman looked into her eyes for an uncomfortable moment before saying, "Even though you're the composer you should still respect your own work."

Rebecca opened her mouth to deny it, but he brought his finger to her lips before she could speak.

"I know you wrote that, and I was there that day you played for those kids at the rec. center. I think you play like an angel, so please don't say anything else negative about your talent, especially not while I'm around." With that statement he'd managed to shock her into complete silence.

He then took advantage of her silence by kissing her. The moment their lips touched they were immersed in a fantasy world, and he wondered if that would happen every time they kissed. Her response to his gentle kisses was honest and all-consuming, and he loved every second of it. His ex-wife had never gotten the dreamy eyed look that Rebecca was now giving him. Juliana had been a much more sophisticated lover, always just passionate enough to get him going. He'd never felt this all out surrender before, and for the first time in his life he felt unsure of what to do next with a woman who was clearly into him.

He wanted her more than he'd ever thought it was possible to want a woman. Maybe it was the fact that he'd gone almost a year without being with a woman, or maybe it was the fact that he'd fantasized about this particular woman for months. He didn't know what it was about her, but he definitely wanted to experience everything with her. On the other hand, he felt the most overwhelming need to practice restraint. She was like a delicately carved little Faberge egg, exquisite and endlessly fascinating, but also easily broken if he wasn't careful. He didn't want to hurt her in any way, and if he was honest with himself he wasn't sure he wanted to hurt himself. She was on the verge of forging her own path in life, and he already had an established military career that could, and often did, take him many places in the world. Part of him felt like he'd have a much more difficult time letting her go if they made love.

All of these doubts and emotions surfaced from a single look in her eyes, and Norman didn't even want to analyze his other urges where she was concerned. Like the urge to listen as she played piano in his house every night, or the urge to have her in his bed every night. He even had the urge, the powerful urge, to make a baby with her.

Somehow he ended up slightly reclined on her small sofa with her cradled in his lap. Their passionate kissing had given way to an occasional light caress as he held her in his arms. She yawned a few times, obviously tired from running her first marathon that day.

"Rebecca," Norman said quietly as he stroked her arms.

"What's up?" she murmured sleepily.

"Is it safe to say we're more than just friends now?" he asked.

When she didn't answer he looked down to find that she'd fallen asleep. He stayed quiet and held her, listening to her deep even breathing.

As he sat with her, Norman couldn't help thinking about a future with her in it. He certainly wanted to be more than her friend, and he wondered if she saw him as the man in her life. He certainly hoped she did, because as far as he was concerned other women didn't even exist anymore.

Eventually he carried her to her bed and tucked her in. She was so exhausted she didn't even stir. She had trained intensely for the marathon, and it was possible that she overdid it a little.

"Becky," he shook her lightly.

"Huh?" she barely responded.

"Do you want me to leave? Do you have a spare key I can lock your door with?" he asked.

"Don't go," she murmured.

That was all the encouragement he needed to crawl into bed to take a nap with her. She snuggled up next to his chest like she'd always belonged there. Norman thought she fit perfectly as he embraced her small frame and settled with his nose in her hair.

"Sleep tight honey," he whispered against her neck as he shut his eyes.

Rebecca awoke a few hours later to the sound of Norman's quiet snoring. He was lying on his back with his arm flung over his eyes, and his magnificent chest rose and fell hypnotically with each breath. Rebecca had never felt at liberty to stare at him before, but now she took advantage of the fact that he didn't know she was looking. He seemed way too good to be true as he lay in her bed. Eventually she was able to tear her eyes away from his upper body, and when she saw his feet hanging off the edge of her bed she couldn't suppress the surprised laughter that burst forth.

"What are you laughing at?" he asked. He rubbed his eyes and looked over at her.

"Your feet... I'm surprised you fell asleep; that doesn't look very comfortable," Rebecca admitted with a little smile.

"I'm okay," he grunted as he sat up. "Come here gorgeous," he reached out and pulled her onto his lap. His superior strength made it seem effortless for him to lift her, and she was incredibly turned on by that.

"Don't you have to go soon? Don't you work tomorrow?" Rebecca asked as she sat atop him in the dimly lit bedroom.

"Didn't we just have a talk about you trying to get rid of me all the time?" Norman half joked.

"Maybe I was asking because I don't want you to have to go just yet," Rebecca countered.

"Well, I do not have to work tomorrow Miss Graves. Does that suit you?"

"Yes it does Mr. Gregory," she responded in kind. "I would invite you to stay all night, but your feet would hang off the bed."

"Honey, that wouldn't stop me from spending a night in *your* bed."

How could mere words have the power to make her feel so much? Rebecca's entire body felt flush as Norman held her gaze. This must be that mysterious chemistry she'd heard so much about yet experienced so little of, until she'd met him. He just had to be too good to be true.

"Norman, maybe we shouldn't do this..." Rebecca said. Right after the words left her mouth she wanted to take them back. If she rejected a casual relationship with this man perhaps that was the same as rejecting the chance that he might eventually want more.

"You know, I've given this a lot of thought myself, and I understand what you mean," he said carefully. "You and I could never be 'friends with benefits,' so please don't worry that all I want is a stupid little fling. That could never be enough, not with you. At the same time, I don't want to ask too much of you. I realize you are in the middle of school, and you're trying to make a career for yourself. I respect that. I also respect the fact that you are so dedicated to your chosen path, and I realize that a divorced man with a kid and a military career may not fit into your life right now. All I'm asking is that you don't just shut me out completely. I think we may have something special here, and I want to see where it leads. If we end up as friends or more that'll be great, and if we don't... at least we won't always wonder what would have happened."

Not one word was spoken about love. As if by tacit agreement they both acknowledged silently to themselves that love was what they sought, yet they gave each other the benefit of being able to take each step as it came along. As long as the words weren't spoken aloud neither could be accused of giving the other false hope.

"I've never done anything like this before. I mean, you're the only guy who's ever even kissed me, and I can't seem to think straight when you're around... I just don't want to jump into everything too soon," Rebecca said.

"And by 'everything' I'm assuming you mean sex."

"Yes."

"I promise not to pressure you about that. After the other night, I completely understand. When you're ready all you have to do is let me know... but, please tell me you don't object to kissing me," he whispered against her lips.

"Not at all," she breathed.

After that night Rebecca stopped analyzing Norman's motives for being with her; she simply accepted the fact that he was there. They continued to run together most mornings, but their new morning routine involved a parting kiss and hug.

Chapter 10

Once their relationship had moved out of the friend zone, they spent a lot of time together learning more about each other. Rebecca even opened up to the point where she frequently played for him. He spent many evenings in her small apartment listening to her play. Most of what she played sounded sad, and one night she seemed so down he finally commented about it.

"Becky, do you ever play anything that doesn't sound so sad?" he asked after she finished playing a particularly heart wrenching piece. She turned to face him, and he thought he detected unshed tears in her eyes.

"I usually just play how I feel," she said.

"Is there anything I can do to cheer you up?" he asked.

"Not this time superman. I talked to my mother today, and she hurt me pretty bad."

"What happened?"

"I asked her about my father, and she called me the devil's spawn and hung up on me. I don't understand. I've never done anything to give her grief, yet she has always shut me out. At first I thought maybe it was because she preferred Sarah to me. Perhaps my twin sister had been her favorite and she'd have been happier if I had been the one to die. But when I think back to before the accident it was apparent even then that she disliked us both."

"Come here Sweetie," Norman held her as she cried on his chest. He'd never understand why her mother didn't like her, and in his opinion Rebecca was way too nice about it. He often wished she could stand up to her mother and get to the root of the problem.

"Becky, you've got to stop letting your mother walk all over your feelings. I know she's your mother, but that doesn't give her the right to belittle you like that."

"You're right," Rebecca said after a moment of reflection. "I'm not going to let her get away with talking to me like that. I'm calling her back right now. I'm tired of feeling so alone all the time; besides her I have no one else."

"Rebecca, you have me. Even if things don't go well with your mother you'll always have me," Norman said. He didn't miss the significance of making such a statement. He'd said always, and he knew exactly what that implied. He'd been thinking a lot about what always implied every time he looked at her lately. This was just the first time he'd voiced any of those thoughts.

"I'll be back in a few minutes," she squeezed his hand briefly before she disappeared down the hall to call her mother.

"Hello," her mother answered after two rings.

"Mom it's me."

"What do you want now?" her mother grumbled.

"Mom, I called because of what happened earlier. I think we should talk about it."

"Rebecca, stop pushing. I've been telling you for years that your father is worthless. I'm not going to tell you who he is, so don't ask again," her mother slurred with barely disguised venom in her voice. She'd been drinking that day, and she was always hostile when she'd been drinking.

Perhaps she should have dropped it and left her mother alone, but this time she just couldn't.

"I think I have the right to decide for myself whether he's worthless or not. Just because things didn't work out between the two of you doesn't automatically mean he's a terrible person. I work with kids whose parents do that to each other after they split up; they bad mouth each other, the kids have to take sides and the result is a child with only one parent when there could be two. I know I'm an adult now, but I still think I have the right to at least know something about my father. *You* certainly never seemed to love me, so maybe he will at least tolerate me and give me the chance that you never did." Rebecca's chest was heaving by the time she finished talking. She'd never confronted her mother before, and doing so now felt wonderfully liberating and incredibly frightening at the same time.

"Whatever's gotten into you, you're going to regret it if you don't leave me alone about this. I did right by you! I sheltered you and clothed you for seventeen years! I owe you nothing," her mother spat out with disgust in her voice.

"You're my mother! That's what you were supposed to do. Would it have killed you to treat me like you wanted me at least a little?" Rebecca demanded.

"Yes it would have killed me. Sometimes I wished you'd both been killed. If I'd known I was pregnant in time to do something about it you wouldn't even *exist*! You ruined my entire life," her mother sobbed.

Rebecca was momentarily stunned into silence. She'd never been attacked with such naked hatred before, and the fact that it was coming from her own mother made it twice as corrosive.

Eventually she collected herself enough to say, "Well mother, it is *your* fault you didn't use birth control, so don't you dare blame *me* for ruining your life. That was *your* mistake, *not* mine." She was about to hang up when her mother's sudden crazed half sob half shout stopped her.

"You don't know a fucking thing! Your father was a real piece of work alright. I have no idea who he is because he *raped* me! He was that stranger that comes out of the dark and takes what he wants because he has a gun and I don't. He almost killed me, and he left me you and your sister as a parting gift. I know nothing about him other than the size of the damn dick he shoved up in me. He didn't give a damn how much it hurt or that I was just a child, and I *begged* him to stop. How do you think it felt when I found out I was too far along to get rid of you? I felt like the devil himself must have impregnated me! And don't you ever, *ever*, EVER call me mom again…"

Rebecca's ears rang for almost a full minute after her mother slammed the phone down. She felt as if her entire world had just entered a black hole, and she was being crushed by the force of its darkness. A small part of her ceased to exist as the images her mother's words evoked invaded her head. Not only did her mother hate her, but she had a good reason. Her father was a violent rapist. She had the genes of a violent rapist in her blood. Her skin crawled with self loathing and disgust as she imagined how her mother must have felt when she'd insisted it was her fault for not using protection.

If only she'd had some inkling beforehand Rebecca could have tempered her confrontation with her mother. She would have been more patient and understanding rather than impatient and demanding. All of the thoughts swirling in Rebecca's head centered around her mother and the suffering she must have gone through to want to inflict that kind of pain on her own daughter. She didn't know how it was possible, but once she knew the cause she'd instantly forgiven her mother for being distant for most of her life. So many things from the past suddenly made sense that Rebecca was momentarily overwhelmed with sadness for herself, her mother, and her deceased sister.

One thing was certain; Rebecca still loved her mother despite the fact that she'd just told her how much she hated her. Rebecca knew that had been the alcohol talking, and all her mother needed was some time to cool down.

Cece stared down at the phone after she hung up on Rebecca. Tears streamed down her face and her heart hammered relentlessly at her chest while she considered calling her daughter back to apologize. She reached for the phone, but stopped herself. Rebecca was better off without her.

Rebecca had always been too sweet and soft-spoken, two traits which Cece had never been able to understand. Even when Cece had attempted to teach her some basic self-defense techniques, she'd balked at the idea of hitting anyone. Tonight's conversation was the first time Rebecca had ever stood up to Cece about anything; she'd just picked the wrong thing to stand up for. Cece's hands shook as she thought about Rebecca's "father," the nameless, faceless thing that had taken so much from her.

She took another drink from her bottle of discount liquor and sat down in the corner between her bed and the wall. She tucked her head between her knees to keep the nausea at bay, but eventually it overpowered her like it always did. She ran to the bathroom, toppling over the bottle and bumping into her nightstand on the way. His voice repeated in her head as she collapsed down by the toilet to be sick.

Afterward, she washed up in the sink, careful to avoid her own reflection. She couldn't stand to look at herself, especially not after the way she'd just attacked her daughter. When she finished washing her face she accidentally caught a glimpse of her reflection in the mirror and was reminded again of cold, grey steel. Many times over the years she'd wanted to gouge out her own eyes just so she wouldn't be reminded of those mocking, derisive chips of ice that had laughed at her pain over and over again. The face in the mirror staring back at her ceased to be her own for a moment, and she attacked it with both fists, shattering the mirror.

The medicine cabinet came open and several bottles of pills fell into the sink with the shards of the mirror. Cece picked one up and looked at it for a long time. She stumbled out of the bathroom, taking the bottle with her and resuming her post in the corner beside the bed. She picked up the liquor bottle and took another drink of what remained. All her life, she'd been nothing but a problem, a problem to her mother, a problem to herself, and now a problem to her daughter. She looked down at the bottles in her hands. In one hand the bottle of liquor and in the other the bottle of sleeping pills that sometimes helped her sleep. They could do more than help her sleep tonight. There was only one solution to the problem between her and her daughter, and she was staring at it right now. Rebecca would be better off without her.

"Becky, are you okay?" Norman asked as he opened her door. "You've been back here for half an hour. How did it go?"

"Not good," Rebecca barely got out before she burst into uncontrollable sobs. These were not the pretty sobs of a woman crying for a man's attention. They were the ugly, all consuming, soul racking sobs of a person in pain too deep for words. Years of heartache that she'd held in for her mother's sake suddenly came pouring out of her. Every year her mother had gone on a two day drinking binge around the same time. It had only happened once a year and it had never made any sense before today. That must be the way she'd coped with memories of the event on each anniversary. As an aspiring psychologist, Rebecca knew that it wasn't uncommon for victims of trauma to cope in such a way.

Norman had never seen her act like this, and he was unsure how to handle it. He now felt like his happiness was linked to hers, and watching her in such a state actually caused him pain.

"Honey, just let me know what I can do," he said as he enfolded her in his arms on the bed. "I'm here, just let me help," he whispered as he continued to hold her through her tears.

Eventually, when the whole front of his shirt was wet and she'd used almost an entire box of tissue she seemed calm enough to talk.

"I was so mean to her, and I accused her of being irresponsible," she wailed against his chest.

"Shhh, it's okay. Maybe you were right, and she just didn't want to hear it," he pointed out.

Rebecca shook her head. "I was wrong! Oh God I wish I had left her alone. I feel so bad now. She was raped when she was thirteen. That's how she got pregnant. The man almost killed her, and she figured out she was pregnant after it was too late to have an abortion. She hates me... it doesn't matter what I do for the rest of my life, she'll still hate me."

Norman's arms tightened around Rebecca. She felt his support and his willingness to listen to her, but she couldn't bring herself to say anymore. She couldn't look into his face to see how he took the news that she was the child of a violent rapist.

"I know it's asking a lot, but could you please just be honest about how you feel about me now? If you'd rather not know me anymore I'll understand. Right now I don't even want to know myself... please don't try to be nice to me if you'd rather not stay," Rebecca whispered haltingly against his chest.

Despite all the bravado of her words, the fact that she still clung almost helplessly to him made him even more determined to protect her. He didn't speak immediately because he recognized the magnitude of this new obstacle. She'd just found out that her mother hated her, and her father was a rapist, so it was no wonder she'd jump to the conclusion that everyone else would reject her as well. The trouble with that theory was that he wasn't like everyone else, and the only way she'd learn that was if he showed her.

"Rebecca, you are the nicest and most adorable woman I've ever known, and there is no way I'm walking out on you over something you had absolutely no control over." He had no intention of leaving her alone that night. It was clear that she needed him, and he'd just promised he'd always be there for her.

She still didn't lift her face away from his soggy shirt, but he felt her small body relax slightly. He continued to hold her and think about what had just happened. He couldn't even begin imagine how he would feel in the same situation. His parents had always been loving and supportive. They had obviously loved each other a great deal, and that love had extended to all their kids. He had never in his life felt rejected by any member of his immediate family, especially not his mother. That's not to say that his parents were permissive. Norman and his siblings had not been spoiled by any means. They'd gotten their share of punishments and grueling ranch chores over the years, but no matter how much trouble he'd been in as a child he'd never had a reason to doubt his parents' love.

Eventually she stopped crying altogether and they went back out to her living room. It was almost dark outside, but the weather was nice. Late spring was a beautiful time of year in Middle Tennessee, so they decided to take advantage of the mild climate by going for a walk.

They frequently went on evening walks, holding hands and discussing the events of the day. Tonight, Norman thought a walk was the only acceptable way to get Rebecca's mind off of her troubles. The only other way that came to mind was still off limits for him, no matter how much he would have preferred making love to her rather than taking her walking.

"How far along are you on your thesis now?" Norman asked as they kept to a slow steady pace.

"I'm almost done. Right now I'm writing my conclusions. I've already analyzed all the data, and typed up the results in tables."

"So you'll have your Masters in a couple of months?"

"Yeah."

"Have you been applying for full time positions yet?"

"I have, but I think I might just stay at the youth center. Once a therapist position opens up I'll be qualified to fill it because of my work experience and degree. I'll have an edge because I already work there, and the pay increase would be substantial," she informed him.

"I thought you wanted to work as a school psychologist," Norman said.

"I do, but I would need at least a few years of experience as a clinical therapist before a school would look at hiring me."

"So you plan on working at the youth center for a few more years?" Norman asked in concern.

"If that's what I need to do, then yes," Rebecca said decisively.

Norman squeezed her hand. Sometimes he hated her job because of the toll it took on her. He'd seen her come home exhausted and bruised more than enough in the past few months, but he realized he had no right to ask her to change her lifestyle for his peace of mind. If they were in a more permanent relationship he wouldn't hesitate to talk to her about the possibility of taking a different job; a job that didn't cause him so much concern for her safety.

"How are you feeling now?" he changed the subject.

"I hardly know," she admitted in a slightly husky slightly tearful tone.

"I know it's got to be hard for you, but please don't ever for one second think that this changes things between us. It doesn't matter to me who your father is. Other than the fact that I care because it causes you pain I don't think it matters at all."

"Thanks Norman."

"Rebecca, you don't ever have to thank me for caring about you; you're always welcome." He hoped his meaning sunk in. He was not going to leave her unless she assured him that his leaving would make her happier.

When she looked down at their clasped hands he had a powerful feeling that his hand on hers was important. He knew that the physical contact between them served as a concrete assurance that he was there for her now, and that he would always be there. He raised her hand to his lips and kissed it.

Chapter 11

Norman was greeted by the news of an impending deployment order first thing Monday morning. The aviation brigade he was assigned to was scheduled to deploy to Afghanistan in just under three months, and his battalion had just received the warning order. His first thought was of Rebecca and his kids. He'd been on deployments before, but he always thought of how it would affect the people he cared about each time a new one came up. This time was no different, except for the fact that this time he would be leaving behind a woman he had no legal ties to. He and his ex-wife had been married for almost five uninterrupted years before their first separation due to deployment, so he'd felt secure in the knowledge that she would be there when he returned.

He did not have that luxury with Rebecca. She was only a woman with whom he was romantically linked; she never even referred to him as her boyfriend. He definitely did not have a secure feeling about leaving her. He had no idea if she would be willing to put her love life on hold for an entire year for him when there was no guarantee of a future together. He wasn't even sure if he wanted to ask her to put her life on hold for him; it would be incredibly unfair to her. At the same time he had other thoughts that involved making their relationship more permanent before he left. He'd been having an increasingly difficult time coming up with reasons why they should continue to take things slow and easy, but he hadn't put any pressure on her. The last thing he wanted to do was scare her away, but now that he was faced with the real possibility losing her, he decided to go with what his heart had been whispering almost since he'd met her. Maybe some things were just meant to happen quickly.

Rebecca frequently felt like she was making real progress with the girls at the youth center, but sometimes a setback would put things off kilter again. This time the setback involved a co-worker... none other than Ms. Parker. Rebecca had applied for a job as a therapist, and she was assured of the reasonable possibility of her getting it in less than two months. Another therapist had requested a transfer to a different facility because her husband was moving to a better paying job, and Rebecca was almost a shoo-in for her spot. At least she was until Ms. Parker filed a complaint against her, citing that she refused to restrain certain kids when they needed it.

The accusation really angered Rebecca, because she'd always seen Ms. Parker as overbearing and too quick to restrain kids when it wasn't necessary. Rebecca knew that the root of the complaint lay in the fact that Shirelle had come to trust her, and as a result of this trust she tended to follow directions best if they were given by her and no one else. Rebecca refused to see that as a problem. Ms. Parker refused to see it as a sign that the child was responsive to cognitive reasoning as opposed to brute force and pain compliance.

Rebecca was still likely to get the job, but the attempted sabotage really rankled. When it was time for her quarterly performance review she made sure to address the issue with her supervisor.

"Did you see the complaint Ms. Parker wrote against me?" she asked as soon as Fred sat down.

"Yeah I did." He looked uncomfortable.

"What was that all about? Do you think she has a point? How will this affect my prospects as a therapist?" she asked.

"Calm down there Miss! First of all, no one agrees with her. No one else has ever complained about you, and she's had several against her over the years. I think she's jealous."

"Of *what*?" Rebecca demanded in surprise.

"Think about it... She has to get physical with the girls to get results. They only respect her now because they know she'll slam 'em on the floor in a minute if they cut up. When she's not around they cut up anyway. You on the other hand, they listen to because you have a way of talking to them that makes them want to do better all the time for their own benefit. Treatment team has been talking about Shirelle's new behavior. It's nothing drastic, but there have been some noticeable improvements. And not just when you're around, but all the time. She does act best when you're here, but still better overall. Ms. Parker hasn't had that effect on one kid since she started working here. I think she's just jealous that you have a smarter way of dealing with these girls. Not that she isn't a valuable employee… She can get them under control pretty good because they fear her, but maybe she'd rather be respected for another reason." Fred explained.

Rebecca had never been more thankful for her training in the education field. She knew that the courses she'd taken and the time she spent as a school volunteer helped her to deal with the girls at the center in an authoritative way rather than an authoritarian way. There was a clear difference between the two discipline styles.

"So how has my performance been this quarter?" Rebecca changed the subject.

"Still room for improvement when it comes to standing your ground. A lot of the girls on the unit think they can get away with more when you're around because you're so nice to them. Other than that you're good. The only area you didn't get excellent is maintaining control of the unit, but nobody gets that consistently. The girls are still acting out because they're testing you."

The rest of the meeting went well, and Rebecca came out of it feeling a little disappointed. She'd been trying hard to be a good employee and a good person, but with this job the two seemed to conflict sometimes. A good employee would be way tougher on the residents than she was, but a good person recognized that inflicting more pain on an already hurting person tended to make things worse.

Instead of going home as she normally did, Rebecca decided to go to the school to talk to Shelly. She knew Shelly would have some valuable insight into the conflict she felt about her job.

Of course, she wasn't exactly sure what to say. She could begin with "I'm not the type of person who likes to slam emotionally troubled kids on the floor every time they commit the least infraction, but my co-workers think I should so that the kids will learn to fear me and never step out of line," but that seemed like a bit much.

The door to Shelly's room was already open, so Rebecca walked right in expecting to see her seated at her desk working on her lesson plan as she normally did after school. Instead, she saw Norman embracing her in a very familiar manner. Rebecca's first instinct was to simply back out the door and avoid Norman without ever confronting him about his relationship with Shelly. Maybe he'd been in love with her for years and she was just now starting to reciprocate... Rebecca could certainly see why he would choose Shelly over her. Shelly was gorgeous, she was tall, she was an awesome person, and she was older and much more sophisticated.

Just when she was about to turn around and walk out, an image of her mother rose up before her and stopped her cold. All her life she'd faded into the background, and she was tired of always being okay with whatever wrongs were done to her. She squelched her first instinct to slink quietly away, and decided to confront them just as she'd confronted her mother. She may not like the outcome, but at least she could say she hadn't run like a coward. So there she stood, feeling heartbroken, as she watched the woman whom she'd thought was her friend embrace the man whom she'd fallen completely in love with. Rebecca didn't know why seeing him in the arms of another woman finally forced her to admit her true feelings to herself, but for whatever reason it did.

After what seemed like both a brief moment and an agonizing eternity Norman noticed her standing there. His expression registered shock, but he didn't immediately push Shelly away. He slowly took his arms from around her, and when she turned around Rebecca saw that Shelly had tears in her eyes. *She* looked absolutely startled to see Rebecca.

"Becky! How long have you been standing there?" she demanded.

No answer. Rebecca couldn't find her voice after all. The confrontation would have to wait. She simply turned around and started to walk out before her tears began to show.

"What's wrong? Didn't you tell her yet?" Rebecca heard Shelly say to Norman in a scolding tone as she walked down the hallway. "Are you just going to let her walk out of here? Go stop her!"

"Becky," she heard Norman say at her back. Apparently she hadn't been walking fast enough. "I have something to tell you."

Those words stopped her in her tracks. Even as she turned to face him she couldn't believe what a pushover she was. Any other woman would have kept on walking.

"What Norman?" she asked in a monotone.

He reached out to take her hand and she snatched it back and crossed her arms defensively in front of her.

"What? Do you just *have* to tell me to my face that you're with Shelly now, so I'm out? I could clearly see *that* without you having to explain. I'm sorry I ever trusted you, and I'm glad we never slept together. You are hands down the most deceptive man in the world! What was all that talk about you always being there for me? Is this what you call being my friend? I don't even know why I'm standing here like a fool still talking to you."

As she talked Norman first looked confused, then surprised, then relieved, and Rebecca wanted to slap the relief right off his face. Instead she shoved her way past him and walked away.

He grunted because it was unexpected, but he was otherwise unaffected. Rebecca's hands smarted a little as she stomped down the hall and out the main entrance.

She didn't get more than ten feet from the door before Norman was suddenly picking her up and slinging her over his shoulder.

"Put me down *NOW!*" she screamed.

"No, not until you listen to me," he said.

"Listen to *what*? You jackass!" Rebecca stormed.

He didn't talk again until he'd carried her around the side of the school to the deserted playground.

"Will you calm down?" he asked as he put her down.

She immediately walked off again.

His answer to that was to grab her about the waist from behind and haul her against his chest. She struggled briefly as he walked over to a nearby bench and sat down, but his superior size and strength made her exertions seem comically futile.

She sat breathing heavily for a few minutes as his arms kept her pinned to his lap like bands of steel. She didn't want to cry in front of him, so she tried to hang on to her anger for as long as possible. The trouble with that plan was that his breath against her neck, his heartbeat, and the fact that she felt totally surrounded by his warmth all combined to suck the anger right out of her. How could he have that effect even after what she'd just witnessed? Was she that weak?

"Rebecca, Honey," he began.

"Don't call me Honey!" she interrupted.

"Good grief woman! Will you just listen? Shelly is my older sister. I was talking to her about a deployment order I got the other day. My unit is going to Afghanistan in less than three months, and Shelly got all emotional because her husband was killed in action over there a few years ago. She's worried about me going back, and I've been trying to think of a way to tell *you* that I'm leaving soon."

After a long uncomfortable silence, Rebecca finally said, "I'm sorry I hit you," in a very small and contrite voice. And then in the next breath she hit him and demanded, "Why on Earth didn't either of you mention the fact that you're related? Do you have any idea how weird that is?"

Norman looked embarrassed and said, "I was going to get around to it soon."

When his face just continued to achieve even brighter shades of red, Rebecca cut him some slack and changed the subject for the time being. She could always come back to it later. "How long will you be gone?" she asked.

"A year," he sighed.

Rebecca couldn't think of anything else to say. She hoped this wasn't going to be good bye. She wasn't ready to let go yet.

"What are you thinking?" he asked.

"I'm thinking you better write to me and call me every chance you get," she said.

His response was a fierce kiss that made her completely forget herself until she heard Shelly say, "I guess this means you two worked things out."

The next evening Shelly stopped by to visit Rebecca.

"Norman tells me you play very well," she said when they sat down to chat.

"That's nice of him, but he doesn't know that I've hardly had any lessons."

"Really?" Shelly sounded intrigued. "How did you learn to play so well?"

"I mostly learned on my own. I've always loved the piano, even when I was very young. Before my twin sister died we used to play together. After she died it was the only way for me to feel close to her, and it sort of took off from there. I can play almost anything by ear," Rebecca admitted.

"No wonder Norman's been spending so much time listening to you play."

"He told you about that?"

"Sometimes it's all he talks about, but he says you're really shy about it. I used to be shy about singing, so I understand, but it's nice when you can share your talent with others. I'd love to hear you play sometime."

"Do you ever sing for an audience?" Rebecca asked.

"Do you ever play for an audience, besides my little brother?" Shelly countered.

"Oh," Rebecca smiled. "I see where this is going... you'll sing for me if I'll play for you?" she asked.

"No Becky. What I was getting at is that you and I are very similar in that way. From what Norman says you have an incredible talent. I understand what it is like to be gifted with something incredible; yet not want to share it with a large audience. I'm not an exhibitionist, and I don't think you are either," Shelly explained.

"You're right. I never even told Norman how I love to play, he found out by accident," Rebecca said.

"The last time I sang for an audience was at my late husband's funeral. I sang 'Amazing Grace' and I remember feeling that my entire aching soul had been bared for everyone to see as I was singing. I understand the power of expressing your deepest emotions through music, and I know it touches people in a way nothing else can."

"Shelly I'm sorry about your loss. I can't even begin to imagine how you dealt with it," Rebecca told her when she saw the tears in her eyes.

"Deal," Shelly said. "You can begin to imagine how I deal with it, because to this day I am still dealing with it."

Rebecca wanted to hug Shelly, but she held back, unsure how to go about it. Her upbringing had been almost completely devoid of affection and unnecessary physical contact, so giving it didn't come natural.

"Are you okay," she asked hesitantly.

"Yeah. I just wanted to talk to you about something we had in common. It's rare to find a friend who understands such a secret part of oneself, but I know you understand because you are very similar. If I know you like I think I do, you'll deal with Norman's deployment by pouring your emotions through your music. I just want you to know that you can also talk to me if you want. When my husband died I cut myself off from people for a while, and music was my only consolation. I just don't want to see you do that when things get hard. I want you to know that you can call me up to talk or go out and do something."

"Thanks Shelly, but why are you offering? Is it because of what happened yesterday?" Rebecca couldn't stop herself from asking.

"Partly. It isn't hard to see how you and Norman feel about each other, and besides that I really do like you," she smiled just a bit as she reached out for Rebecca's hand.

"About yesterday... why didn't you ever mention the fact that Norman is your brother?" Rebecca asked.

Shelly's face got a little red as she considered her answer. "Norman didn't want me to tell you. As soon as he figured out that you were a volunteer in my classroom he practically beat my door down to beg me for your number, but when I refused to give it to him he started pestering me to find out more about you. He thought you'd be more comfortable opening up to me if you didn't know we were related... I didn't tell him anything of course. I actually told him over and over again how silly he was being. So anyway, that day I brought you with me on Dylan's home visit was all Norman's idea. He was supposed to 'bump into' you and ask you out while I met with Dylan's mother Juliana, but her extended spa day kind of ruined that plan. He just didn't want to make it obvious that he was still so into you after you ditched him with no explanation. I think he was a little intimidated by you."

"Intimidated by me?" Rebecca echoed.

"Well, you're one of those independent people who don't need someone to 'complete' them. A lot of guys don't know how to handle a woman like that."

"But I'm the least intimidating person I know. You two should have just been honest with me. The only reason I avoided him is because I didn't want to get my feelings hurt."

"Then why did you tell me that he got on your nerves the day I took you with me for Dylan's home visit?" Shelly asked. "I think that one might have hurt his feelings when I told him."

"You *told* him I said that?"

"Yes, that's about all I told him, but apparently he didn't listen. He pursued you anyway."

"I didn't mean it. I only said it because I was jealous. I could tell you two were closer than you were pretending to be in front of me."

Shelly sighed and looked down at Rebecca with a cryptic little smile. "My little brother has been through a lot Rebecca. He thought he needed my help to win you over, and I didn't have the heart to ruin his convoluted little plan. That's all there is to it. Be gentle with him."

Shelly squeezed Rebecca's hand again, and they both giggled at the situation.

There had been a slight awkwardness to the encounter, but Rebecca and Shelly both came away from it with a feeling that their bond had just grown much stronger than either of them had ever thought possible.

On her way out Shelly told Rebecca that Norman was getting promoted the following week, and invited her to watch the promotion ceremony with her.

It seemed so much like an afterthought that Rebecca had no idea it had been the main reason for Shelly's visit. Norman had put her in charge of making sure Rebecca would be there.

Chapter 12

The day of Norman's promotion ceremony Shelly encouraged Rebecca to dress extremely nice, and fussed over her hair as she helped her get ready. For the most part Rebecca felt a little affronted at all of Shelly's well meaning advice regarding her appearance, but when she saw the final result she felt nothing but shock and gratitude.

Her hair flowed down her back in soft alluring curls, because Shelly had taken the time to instruct her on the use of a flat iron. She'd been stunned to find out that Rebecca didn't even own one, and she made a special trip to the beauty supply store to rectify the situation.

The dress was the main thing Rebecca was grateful for. Shelly had helped her pick it out over the weekend, and Rebecca had to admit that she'd never felt prettier in her life.

She wore a simple little emerald green dress with an empire waist which accentuated her bust paired with some cute, low heeled brown leather shoes. It wasn't a flashy outfit, but wearing it made her feel absolutely beautiful.

"Norman's going to fall all over himself when he sees you today," Shelly smiled as they both took one last look in the mirror before heading out to Ft. Campbell.

There were a lot more people than Rebecca had expected to see. During her short stint in the army she'd seen soldiers get promoted in a company formation which usually consisted of no more than 130 soldiers. Apparently, when an officer got promoted to Lieutenant

Colonel the entire battalion had to witness the event. There were over five hundred soldiers standing in formation for the ceremony.

Norman wasn't the only soldier being promoted that day, but he was the highest ranking. About fifteen other soldiers had their new rank pinned on by the commander before they finally got to Norman. As the battalion secretary read Norman's promotion orders Shelly took Rebecca by the hand and squeezed it. Obviously, she was very excited for her little brother and also very proud of him. Rebecca looked at her and smiled as the brigade commander and the battalion commander removed Norman's old rank and pinned on his Lieutenant Colonel rank. When they finished the task he saluted smartly and then returned to the position of attention.

While Rebecca was busy staring at Norman with admiring eyes she missed the almost imperceptible nod that the battalion commander directed at Shelly. She did, however, notice when Shelly started walking to the front of the formation while still holding her hand. Not sure what was going on and not wanting to make a scene, Rebecca didn't protest. She suddenly found herself standing in front of the over five hundred pairs of eyes with the two imposing commanders facing her. Shelly finally let go of her hand at that point and took a discreet step back. Unsure what to do in front of so many people Rebecca glanced at Norman for reassurance.

Then, just when she thought the promotion ceremony was over, the battalion secretary said, "I'm sorry, we're not done just yet. I have another matter to attend to. It seems that the new Lieutenant Colonel Gregory is requesting another promotion."

Cheering erupted as Norman got down on one knee in front of Rebecca and pulled a small jewelry box out of his pocket.

As he kneeled, the battalion secretary had gone on in the same loud, authoritative voice she'd used to read all of the promotion orders, "Miss Graves, he's requesting that, as commander in chief of his heart, you'll promote him from mere boyfriend to fiancé."

Suddenly, the five hundred pairs of eyes didn't exist anymore as Rebecca looked at Norman. "Becky, I love you, and I can't stand the thought of being without you. Will you marry me?" he said.

"Yes," she breathed without hesitation as everyone looked on eagerly awaiting her response. Norman was the only one who heard her whisper, but then again he was also the only one who needed to hear it.

He slid the ring on her finger and then he stood up and kissed her to the sound of applause from his entire battalion.

After the formation was dismissed and all the congratulations were over Norman, Shelly and Rebecca had a moment alone to talk.

The first words out of Norman's mouth were, "My God, you look stunning! Your hair is absolutely beautiful and you look adorable in that dress."

"You can thank Shelly. She helped me embrace femininity a bit more than I have in the past," Rebecca quipped.

He hadn't let go of her hand since he'd put the ring on her finger, and he gave it a gentle squeeze.

"Becky, you should've seen your face," Shelly said cheerfully. "That was priceless!"

"Did you know about this the entire time?" Rebecca asked her.

"Of course! Why do you think I was so forceful about getting you dressed up?" Shelly laughed.

"Well, I was certainly surprised." Rebecca looked at Norman again, and felt her entire body almost go up in flames from the look he was giving her.

"Congratulations again little brother and soon to be little sister-in-law. I'll be going now. I'm sure you don't mind getting a ride home from your future husband," and with a jaunty little wave Shelly was gone, leaving Norman and Rebecca alone.

The proposal hadn't really sunk in until Shelly had referred to Norman as her 'future husband.' She looked up at his incredible face as the heady realization hit her, and she felt like the luckiest woman in the world.

"I just love it when you look at me like that," Norman said as their eyes met.

She glanced down at her ring again. His love was still a new and unexplored area for her, so she was a little unsure of how she should act at this point. She wanted to throw herself into his arms and kiss him like the world was ending, but she didn't think that an 'I love you' was a free pass to suddenly smother him with too much affection.

So she tamped down her feelings and said, "And I love it when you surprise me like that."

"And I love that you accepted the surprise." He held her close and whispered in her ear, "but I love you best of all."

"I love you too," she replied feeling almost light headed with giddiness.

"I'm through with work for the day. Will you come over to my house for a while?" Now that he'd declared his love for her he had no more scruples about consummating their relationship, and the way she looked at the moment made him eager to get to it as soon as possible.

"Sure, I guess now is as good a time as any to talk about setting a date and all that other stuff that comes with an engagement," Rebecca replied.

Norman did not disabuse her of the notion that he just wanted to talk. He saw no reason why they couldn't talk after they'd made love a few times.

Rebecca noticed his rush to get to his house, but thought nothing of it until they were there. As soon as the door shut his hands were suddenly all over her as he hauled her against him and kissed her like a starving man. Her knees turned weak, and if he hadn't picked her up for easier access to her lips she probably would have melted into a puddle of hypersensitivity right on the floor of his foyer.

Somehow her legs ended up wrapped around his waist as she clung to him for dear life. His passion was surprising, exhilarating, and incredibly sensual all at once. He kissed her lips, her neck, and her chest as her head tipped back in near ecstasy. When his large hands gripped her hips and pressed her against him there was no mistaking his arousal.

"Norman," she breathed his name as he continued kissing her.

"You have no idea how bad I've wanted to do this," he said fiercely against her neck.

"Do what?" she asked.

"Make love to you," he rasped as he pressed her against his arousal again.

"Wait, we can't do that *now*," Rebecca said as she rapidly returned to her senses.

"And why not?" he breathed as he continued nuzzling her neck.

"I'd like to wait until after we're married. It's important to me."

Norman could tell from her tone that she was being sincere, and his disappointment was swift and acute. He couldn't manage to relinquish his hold on her though. He leaned against the wall and slid down to the floor while holding her to him.

"You sure know how to torture me," he said as he looked at her face. Her lips were still slightly swollen from his kisses and her hair fell in slight disarray that just begged to be touched. He looked into her eyes and felt that there was no request she could make of him that would be too hard, as long as she continued to look at him like he was her personal superman. "How is it that you manage to get more beautiful every time I look at you?" he whispered as he tenderly traced the outline of her lips with his fingers.

"You don't mind waiting?" she asked as he continued to lovingly study her face.

The look he gave her clearly said that was a stupid question, but he said, "Not as long as you don't want to have a long engagement while you plan the wedding of the century," he said emphatically.

"We don't even have to have a wedding if you don't want to. We can just get married at the county clerk's office with two witnesses," Rebecca said.

"Honey, don't take what I said the wrong way. I do want it to be special. It's your wedding day, and you deserve to have a nice one. I want you to be happy, and I won't settle for anything less. I love you," he said.

"I think something small and romantic would be best. I've always wanted an intimate ceremony with just close family and a small dinner afterward instead of a big reception. Oh, and I also want it to be formal. I don't think the most important day of my life should be a casual event."

"That sounds wonderful," Norman told her. He was vastly relieved that she didn't want to put on some grand production. His first wedding had boggled the imagination. The guest list had included over three hundred people, many of whom he didn't even know. The decorations in the church and the reception hall had cost over thirty thousand dollars, and his wife had demanded that everything be perfect. During the last few weeks of their engagement she'd morphed into a real bridezilla, and when all was said and done they had enjoyed their wedding day only half as much as they should have because of her complaining and whining about every little thing that wasn't exactly how she'd envisioned it. The wedding planner had been brought to tears at one point. Looking back, Norman realized that it had been one of the most stressful days of his life. By the end of the day he just remembered feeling glad it was all over rather than elated to have taken a wife.

"I've always thought it would be cool to get married in the Garden Conservatory at the Gaylord Opry Land resort. I saw a ceremony there once, and it looked so sweet," she informed him.

"That's what we'll do then."

"There are only three people I want to invite; my mother and a couple of my supervisors from work," Rebecca told him.

"That's all?" he asked surprised. "You don't have any other friends or family?"

"No. My mother is truly the only relative I have. She told me a long time ago that her parents kicked her out when she got pregnant, so I've never met them. I don't even know their names or if they're even alive. My only sister died when we were small, and I've been so busy with school and work that you, Shelly and a couple of my co-workers are my only friends," Rebecca explained matter-of-factly.

"You know," he said thoughtfully. "I could take care of everything. You need to finish your thesis, so you won't have time to plan anything. I promise you it will be what you want," Norman said.

"If we wait until I'm finished with school you won't have to go through all that trouble," Rebecca replied.

"I'd like to get married as soon as possible, because I'm deploying soon. I don't think I can wait until I get back from Afghanistan to make you my wife," he said gently.

As the word wife sunk in, Rebecca tried to calm her beating heart. "Wow, we're really going to do this," she said.

"Yes. I know it may be hard for you to accept, but I believe I've been in love with you almost since that day you raced me up the hill. I didn't realize what it was at the time, and by the time I acknowledged it to myself I was already in too deep to think of a future without you in it. I feel like I've finally found the one woman who was truly meant to be with me, and when you realize you've found someone special to spend the rest of your life with it's best to get on with it as soon as possible." He sealed his words with another kiss that left her in breathless wonder.

"We could go get the marriage certificate today if you want, that way we can get around to the wedding night as soon as possible," she whispered when he finished kissing her.

Chapter 13

The wedding arrangements came together quicker than Norman could have hoped for. Less than a month after proposing, he was lying awake in his bed in nervous anticipation of his wedding day. It was hard to believe that in less than twenty four hours Rebecca Graves would be Rebecca Gregory. His heart skipped a beat as he thought about the wedding night. He admitted to himself that if she hadn't been a virgin there was no way he would have been okay with waiting until after the marriage to make love to her. He would have tried harder to persuade her to make love with him. His first wife hadn't been innocent, and they had been having a sexual relationship for almost a year prior to getting married. Norman felt like he was in all new territory when it came to the wedding night with Rebecca.

He knew it would be special for him because it would be his first time making love to her, but it would be so much more special to her because it would be her first time making love ever. That knowledge put an enormous amount of pressure on him to get it right. He'd been concerned enough about it to ask his sister for advice. An embarrassed blush crept up his neck as he remembered the look Shelly had given him when he'd told her about Rebecca's virginity. The scene replayed in his mind as he lay in bed.

"She's a what?" Shelly asked.

He cleared his throat and said, "I believe you heard me the first time."

"Why are you telling *me*?" she asked.

"Because we'll be married soon, and I've never been with a virgin before. I know you were one once, so maybe you can give me a little advice. I really want the wedding night to be special for her," he said with a blush.

Shelly's eyes got misty as she laughed at her brother.

"The only thing I can tell you is that my first time was embarrassing and awkward like almost everybody else's. I was seventeen and Johnny was eighteen. He was over eager, and that made me feel nervous. The worst thing to do to a woman at a time like that is to freak her out with how fast you want to get in her pants. If you relax and take it slow things should just fall into place. I had been sexually active for years before I had my first orgasm, and the reason was something so simple I could kick myself. I was too shy in bed to tell my partner what I liked and what felt good, and what didn't. It wasn't until I was with Jake that things changed. He helped me feel relaxed enough to tell him what I liked and he paid attention to me. I think that was the most important part. Pay attention to what she likes, because at this point she's probably not going to tell you on her own. Just be her prince charming."

When Shelly finished talking Norman felt like he'd just been enlightened. His first wife had been a very sexually assertive woman, and she'd had no problem telling him exactly what she liked. She'd actually been pretty bossy about it, something he'd found arousing, because it got them to the end result quicker, but not very romantic.

He thought back to the day he'd proposed about how he'd pounced on Rebecca as soon as they were alone. He groaned a little as Shelly's words about over eagerness echoed in his head. He'd probably scared her. How in the world was he going to get through tomorrow? Just the thought of what they were going to do had him fully aroused in seconds. He'd been celibate for too long; no man should be expected to wait a year to make love to the woman of his dreams and maintain his patience, or his sanity for that matter.

Rebecca's thoughts were centered around Norman as she tried to sleep. Although she'd had an entire month to let the reality of the situation sink in, she still had a hard time believing that a man as wonderful as Norman was totally in love with her. He was caring, sensitive, strong both physically and emotionally, he was fun to be with, he was intelligent, he was successful, and they had incredible chemistry. What more could a woman want in a husband?

They hadn't been spending much time together in the past few weeks, because they'd both been busy preparing for the big day. Norman had lots of extra work to do because of the upcoming deployment, and Rebecca had been working hard on finishing up the requirements for her master's degree. They hadn't spent an evening relaxing together or a morning running together since before Norman proposed to her. It seemed corny to miss a man whom she saw at least once a week, but Rebecca missed Norman with an intensity that took her by surprise.

Her only regret was that her mother hadn't responded to her invitation, so Fred and Chuck would be the only friends she had to attend her wedding. She had no idea how many other people would be there, but she knew there wouldn't be very many.

The day of Rebecca and Norman's wedding dawned bright and sunny, and as she opened her eyes the first thing she saw was her wedding dress lit up by blazing morning sun that shone in her window. As she lay in bed and reflected on what today was she could hear birds singing a happy little tune outside her window. She got up to look out her window and the little copse of trees down the hill behind her apartment had never looked more beautiful than they did bathed in the magical golden glow of the morning sun on her wedding day.

A knock on her door reminded her that she had a busy day ahead. Shelly had offered to help her get ready for the big event.

"Good morning Becky!" Shelly squealed as soon as Rebecca opened her door. "How are you feeling today?"

"Like this is going to be the best day of my life," Rebecca answered honestly.

"I'm sure it is. Listen I made an appointment for you to see my personal stylist. It would be a shame if all your beautiful hair didn't look absolutely perfect today. I wish I had a thick head of hair like that," Shelly finished with a sigh.

"Oh, I was just going to flat iron it again like you showed me. I don't really want to spend the money to pay a professional. They usually charge me more because I have so much hair," Rebecca said.

"That won't be an issue today, so let's get you looking gorgeous," Shelly went on, undeterred by Rebecca's reluctance.

By the time they arrived at the Garden Conservatory Rebecca felt like she'd been primped and preened for hours. Shelly's appointment with the hairdresser had turned into an all out spa treatment. Rebecca had been waxed, tweezed, buffed and shined to a fine polish. When she finally slipped on her wedding dress she felt like a pampered princess.

The ceremony was performed by the battalion chaplain. It was very simple and traditional. There was no long procession up some grand aisle. Instead Norman and Rebecca took their spots in front of his family and vowed to love, honor, and cherish each other until death parted them. Norman slipped a wedding band on her finger to accompany her engagement ring, and his hands were warm and steady as she watched. When it was her turn to put his wedding band on her hands were shaking.

By the time the chaplain declared them husband and wife Rebecca's hands had stopped shaking so much. Norman and Rebecca's first kiss as husband and wife was much like the first kiss they'd ever shared. It was just a peck on the lips, but Norman's overheated body overreacted to an almost embarrassing degree.

He'd been fighting to control his carnal urges as soon as he saw her walk in with his sister. Her hair was done in some fancy up do that framed her face just right, and she wore a knee length white wedding dress. The style of the dress was very simple, but on her it looked magnificent. It had a fitted bodice and it flared out gently at the waist and fell gracefully around her legs in delicate flounces. The best thing about it was the way it sparkled slightly when it caught the light.

Now that she was his wife, all his thoughts turned to the wedding night and stayed firmly on that subject for the rest of the evening. He'd never in his life wanted his family to eat faster and stop telling him how happy they were for him more than he did tonight.

He'd managed to secure a small, luxurious banquet room for the reception. His sister and his six brothers and their wives were the only ones he invited out of respect for Rebecca's wish to have an intimate wedding. He'd hired a pianist to play for a couple of hours and a photographer to take pictures, but other than that he was related to almost everyone else in the room.

Rebecca sent a slightly panicked look at Norman as all of his brothers converged on them at once to be introduced. They were all just as tall as Norman; a couple of them were even taller. She felt like she was surrounded by giants. She might get a cramp in her neck from looking up at all of them all evening.

"Would you believe that Norman told me nothing about you until I received an invitation to the wedding?" one of them said playfully as he shook her hand.

"He's been really busy, I guess," Rebecca responded.

"My name is Oliver by the way, and this is my wife Ruthie," he said.

"Nice to meet you both," Rebecca said as she stuck out her hand.

She was surprised when Ruthie ignored her hand and hugged her instead.

"We're family now," Ruthie said by way of explanation.

"Keep it moving Ollie," someone said from behind them. "We want to see her too!"

"Hey Rebecca, this is my brother George. He must have forgotten his manners back in Chicago. He's the doctor of the family," Norman said after Ruthie and Oliver walked off.

"Hello George, it's nice to meet you," Rebecca said as they shook hands.

"Well, I can't believe Norman got so lucky... What do you see in him anyway?" George joked.

Rebecca just smiled in response.

Right behind George another couple stepped up to say hi. Their names were Ronald and Anna. Ronald was the only brother with red hair the same color as Shelly's, and his wife was a sweet looking blond lady with a bosom so large it was a wonder she could walk upright.

Brent was the only one of Norman's brothers who had blond hair, and he was a lawyer who lived right there in Nashville. Shane and Edward were the last two to be introduced. Edward was the oldest, and Shane was six years older than Norman.

"I'm surprised Norman hasn't invited you out to the ranch yet. Do you ride?" Edward asked.

"No, I've never been on a horse in my life," Rebecca admitted.

"Well, we'll have to do something about that. You're welcome to come out anytime, so don't be shy about it after Norman leaves for the desert."

"I won't be a stranger," Rebecca promised.

After dinner was over, and Norman and Rebecca had fed each other a piece of the single tiered wedding cake they took the small dance floor for their first dance as husband and wife. It was well into the evening and Norman was eager for the small party to wind down, but he thoroughly enjoyed their first dance as husband and wife. Shelly surprised the newlyweds with a heartfelt rendition of "At Last." Everyone looked on as they twirled around the dance floor in each other's arms. When it was over Norman looked down at her, and couldn't stop the sappy grin from spreading across his face. She looked just as happy as he felt, and she smiled up at him with admiration in her beautiful brown eyes. He felt like he could do anything when she looked at him like that.

"You're so beautiful," he whispered, and for that moment they were the only two people in the room. He picked her up in a bear hug and spun her around till her feet flew out behind her and she shrieked in exhilaration. When he set her down his entire family was staring at him.

"What's with Norman?" Shane asked Shelly when she sat back down.

"He's in love Shane," Shelly replied in exasperation.

"Yeah, but I've never seen him act like this before... it's disgusting. He must just be whipped," Shane said derisively. "I hope he has a good pre-nup like last time. I love him, but watching him fawn all over her like this is kind of scary. Have you forgotten how bad things got with Julie?"

Shelly laughed outright at Shane's comment.

"What's so funny?" he demanded.

"First of all, Rebecca is nothing like Julie. Furthermore, there's no way he can be whipped. Rebecca is a virgin," Shelly informed her brother with barely contained relish.

Before Norman and Rebecca retired to their honeymoon suite the news had been whispered throughout the room, and everyone was giving Rebecca special looks when she and Norman finally told them good night and departed.

"Your family is pretty nice," Rebecca said while they made their way through the romantically lit atrium to their room.

"I'm glad you like them. We don't get together like this very often, but we have fun when we do," he replied.

"Do you think they liked me?" Rebecca asked.

"Of course they did," Norman reassured her. "I'm sorry your mother didn't come. I was hoping that she'd be talking to you again by now."

"Me too."

"If you're not ready to go to the room yet we don't have to," Norman said as he hugged her to his chest. "We could walk around and explore a bit if you want to."

"This place is awesome, but I'd like to be alone with my husband now." She slipped her arms around his neck and pulled him down for a kiss that quickly turned the direction of his thoughts.

"That can be arranged Mrs. Gregory," he whispered against her lips.

When they got to the door of their suite Norman's heart started beating a rapid tattoo inside his chest as he thought about making love to his wife for the first time.

"Close your eyes, I have a special surprise for you," he said, and then he picked her up to carry her into their room. As soon as he touched her again blood started going to places other than his brain. *Calm down*, he told himself as he walked into the suite with her. "Okay, you can open them now," he said once he was standing directly in front of the bed.

Rebecca opened her eyes to see a present sitting right in the middle of the bed. Next she noticed all the rose petals scattered about the bed. When Norman finally put her down she took in the scene with no little wonder. The room turned out to be a deluxe suite that was bigger than her entire apartment. She'd heard of luxurious hotel rooms like this one, but she'd never been in one. The other cause for her amazement was the way the room had been romantically set up for them. There were fresh flowers all over the place, and a bottle of champagne on ice on a table near the bed. She'd never been surrounded by so many gorgeous flowers before, and they smelled heavenly. She closed her eyes again and took in a deep breath.

"Aren't you going to open your gift," Norman asked after she'd taken a moment to look around.

"Yes." She perched on the edge of the bed, almost afraid to touch anything because it all looked so perfect.

The gift turned out to be a small, wooden music box that Norman had purchased for her. It featured an intricately carved design around the edges of the wood, and her full married name was carved into the top in fancy script letters. What made it so special was the fact that it played the main melody from one of her personal compositions.

"That's the song you played at the rec. center that day you took the kids from your job. It's permanently stuck in my head. I think

I realized I was falling in love with you while I watched you play that day. You reminded me so much of my mother," he told her.

"How did you have this made though? I don't even remember all the notes to that song," Rebecca said.

"I just remembered it accurately, and my brother Shane owns a florist shop that also sells specialty personalized gifts. He makes keepsakes like this, and sells them for ridiculously high prices," Norman informed her.

"This is the sweetest thing anyone's ever done for me," Rebecca told him. "Thank you," she leaned forward and kissed his cheek.

"There's something else for you in the bathroom," he said. "Take all the time you need."

Rebecca wondered at his cryptic remark until she saw what the second surprise was. It was lingerie. She slipped out of her wedding dress and took a few minutes to freshen up in private. The event she'd been anxious about for so long was finally here. She was going to make love for the first time in her life to the most incredible man imaginable. She spent extra time preening in the mirror and trying to calm her racing heart. Her mother had never talked to her about sex, other than to warn her that it was horrible, mostly enjoyable to the man only, and a good way to ruin her life. She was nervous to say the least, but she also trusted that Norman wouldn't do anything to hurt her. He'd already proven time and time again how caring and considerate he was, and she didn't expect him to be any different on their wedding night.

By the time she emerged from the bathroom Norman had removed his dress uniform and poured two glasses of champagne. He had also lit candles and turned on some music to give the room a more romantic ambiance. He had to restrain himself from pouncing on her when he noticed her standing in the doorway watching him. The bright bathroom light behind her shone through the sheer fabric of her nightgown, giving him an unimpeded view of her silhouette. She looked ravishing.

He walked over to her and handed her a glass of champagne.

"Is it pink?" she asked as she studied it more closely in the dimly lit room.

"Yes. I thought you might like that," he said. He was surprised how normal his voice sounded given the nature of his thoughts.

"I do," she said.

"Rebecca honey, your hair looks absolutely gorgeous, but do you mind if I take it down while you drink your champagne?" he asked.

"Not at all," she replied as she scurried over to the bed.

Norman marveled at the thickness and length of it as he removed all the decorative pearl hair pins that held her style in place. Once he got it all loose he brushed it with a pretty silver hair brush that he'd bought as another present for his new wife. As he ran the brush through her hair he could feel her relaxing more and more. Shelly's advice was uppermost in his mind as he thought about what he was doing. He was trying to subtly seduce a woman who already knew that he had every intention of making love to her.

"How long did it take you to grow your hair this long?" he asked.

"I've never had a big haircut, I just keep it trimmed and neat," Rebecca replied. Her voice had that dreamy quality that drove him wild.

"I love your hair," he said as he continued brushing.

"Thanks," she glanced over her shoulder at him and the small strap on her lingerie slipped off of her shoulder. He pushed it back up for her and gently caressed her arm before resuming his brushing.

"Tonight was my first time having champagne," she said. "It was good, but I don't think I want anymore. I'm starting to feel a little too warm."

Norman had been burning up since they'd said "I do."

When she reached over to set her glass on the table her strap slipped down again. This time Norman didn't push it back up for her; this time he bent down and kissed her shoulder.

"Oh Norman," she breathed. "I've never felt so special before."

Those simple words were his undoing; his plan to move slowly flew right out of his head and he pulled her into his arms. He hugged her against his chest and looked down at her face in the candle light. She was the most awesome person he'd ever known, not to mention the most beautiful, and her own mother hadn't bothered to attend her wedding.

"You're going to have to get used to feeling special when I'm around," he whispered against her neck. Her skin was so silky smooth that he felt he could easily lose himself in her. She watched him with a calm, steady gaze as he undressed her and kissed each new area of skin that he bared. He didn't miss an inch of her; even her toes felt the magic of his kisses.

When she shied away and tried to cover her nakedness Norman whispered, "Don't hide yourself from me honey. You are the most beautiful woman I've ever seen in my life."

He then proceeded to show her just how beautiful she was. His gentle caresses worked magic, and eventually she transitioned from shy to relaxed to incredibly aroused. Norman was fascinated with every stage of the change, and knowing that he caused it was the most powerful aphrodisiac of all.

Rebecca tried her best be calm. She'd wanted to impress Norman with at least a modicum of sophistication. In preparation for the wedding night she'd read a few articles in popular magazines that were all about how men preferred experienced, sophisticated women. Rebecca felt that she was at a disadvantage and wanted to avoid doing anything gauche. But when he started kissing her body she felt totally lost. A feeling like liquid heat spiraled downward into the juncture between her thighs as Norman flicked his tongue across her hardened nipples.

Her breathing deepened and her hips moved of their own accord. If she'd had any room in her head for coherent thoughts she might have been a little embarrassed about her wanton body language, but she was too lost in the sensual pleasure of fore play to think much. Everything about him turned her on, from the texture and warmth of his skin to the subtle scent of his cologne.

Norman made a trail of kisses all the way down to the most intimate part of her anatomy while she squirmed against him and ran her fingers through his hair. When she felt the velvet caress of his tongue between her legs she experienced a moment of shock that he would wish to kiss her *there*.

"Norman?" she whispered uncertainly.

"Shhh. Just relax Honey," he said as he grasped her hips and pulled her towards him.

The next few minutes proved to Rebecca just how wonderful her new husband truly was. He used his mouth to bring her to the very edge of her sanity. While his tongue caressed her she clung to him, and the pleasure he gave her increased to an almost unbearable agony. She felt that something explosive was just over some invisible horizon and his tongue was the match that lit the flame.

"Oh Norman," she panted over and over again as she got closer and closer. "Whatever you're doing, *don't stop.*"

In the next instant she felt the most blissful pulsations as her entire body shuddered at her powerful release. Her legs clamped around Norman's head and her hips rocked rhythmically against him as she slowly floated back down to Earth.

"Did you like that?" he grinned at her. She was lying with her limbs flailed every which way and a look of supreme satisfaction on her face.

"Yes, but you don't have to do it again unless you want to," Rebecca assured him.

"Of course I want to do that again. You taste great," he said as he came between her still trembling legs.

She wrapped her legs around his back as he dipped his head down to kiss her. He sucked gently on her bottom lip and his hand came between their bodies to touch her inner thigh. He stroked her sensitive spots until her breathing came in short gasps indicating her arousal. She was no passive partner, and he was delighted by the feel of her hands caressing his naked chest, shoulders and back with an almost feverish anticipation. His arousal pressed slightly against her already slick entrance, and he felt his control slip away completely when she wrapped her smooth fingers around him and gently squeezed.

"Norman, I want to feel you inside me," she whispered against his neck.

Elated, Norman carefully eased himself inside of her. He felt a small barrier, but he pushed through and was rewarded with the most delicious feeling of completeness he'd ever felt in his life.

"Oh my God," she breathed when he was fully inside of her.

"What's wrong? Did I hurt you?" he asked concerned.

"No," she said in wonder. "It feels amazing. Even my toes are tingling," she giggled.

"Thank God!" he fairly growled as he began to move inside of her.

"Norman, this feels so good," Rebecca breathed as her hips moved with his. The intensity of their lovemaking built until he felt her second orgasm of the evening surround him with soul shattering pulsations that sent him over the edge. Once their breathing returned to normal she placed an affectionate hand on his cheek and whispered, "Thank you Norman. This has been the most perfect day of my life." The honest vulnerability in her voice made him smile.

Norman looked down at his little wife and thought that tonight had been well worth the wait. He'd never forget this moment as long as he lived.

He rolled onto his side and pulled her into his arms. She snuggled against him with a contented little sigh and fell fast asleep in a matter of moments. Norman thought it was funny that her first night of lovemaking had proved to be so tiring, but part of him was a bit relieved that she'd fallen asleep so quickly. The thought of having to leave her behind so soon brought tears to his eyes, and he didn't want her to see them. He picked rose petals out of her hair as he watched her sleep.

Norman woke up long before Rebecca, and he slipped quietly out of bed so as not to disturb her. He looked down at her with a great deal of satisfaction, and a strong desire to please her in every way possible. He'd made up his mind to talk to her mother on her behalf, because he couldn't bear the thought of her being so coldly cast aside by the only living relative she had. He wondered why she didn't make more of a fuss about it; it would certainly be understandable if she did. The image of her struggling up the hill encouraging herself made him think she didn't know how to deal with hardships by asking for help. Maybe standing alone was the only thing she knew how to do. She'd just have to learn that it was okay to admit she needed help sometimes.

After a quick shower he stepped quietly into the bedroom to find her sitting up in bed with a pensive look on her face.

"How are you this morning?" he asked her.

"Wonderful," she grinned.

"That's always good to hear from one's wife after a night of lovemaking," Norman quipped.

"Are we going to do it again sometime soon?"

Before she'd said that Norman had had every intention of taking her out to do something fun rather than monopolizing her in bed all day to fulfill his physical urges, but those plans changed in the blink of an eye.

They ended up monopolizing each other from the rest of the world for the better part of the day.

Chapter 14

In just two short days the honeymoon was over, and Norman found himself worrying about the state of his house. Rebecca had only been inside twice, and both of those times she'd seen only a limited area. Now that she was to see the entire thing he was extremely nervous about her reaction. Only his bedroom, Dylan's room, and the sitting room were furnished; the rest of it he liked to think of as a blank canvas waiting for the right artist to give it life. He also had another surprise for her, and he was especially eager to see her face light up when she saw it.

"Well, here we are," he said with a great deal of apprehension when they got to the driveway. Instead of just parking in the front as he usually did he drove down the circle drive to the garage on the side of the house.

From the side perspective it was easy to see that the house was not just a house. It was at least five times larger than it seemed from the modest front perspective. The garage alone was larger than the average home.

Rebecca's eyes widened in surprise, but she didn't ask how he could afford such a house. Maybe lieutenant colonels got paid more than she'd previously thought.

"I've got to warn you… It's not furnished, so we're going to have to do some shopping if I have time before I leave," Norman said.

"Okay," Rebecca said.

"So, I'll give you the grand tour now that it's your home too," he said.

'The tour' began with the laundry room which was almost the size of Rebecca's old bedroom. Next they moved on to a kitchen that looked like it could have graced the cover of an architectural magazine. There were five bedrooms, each of them a small suite with a walk in closet and its own bathroom. One of them was the one Norman used.

"This one," he said as they came to a set of double doors, "is the master bedroom. I decided not to use it because it's too big for just me, but now that we'll be sharing you'll probably prefer to use this one."

When the doors opened Rebecca's heart skipped a beat and she fell instantly in love with the room. It had a fireplace in the corner of a cozy little sitting area and lovely molding throughout, but the feature that caught Rebecca's eye was the pair of huge bay windows that faced west, overlooking the backyard and the wooded area just down the hill. The view was spectacular.

"That looks so pretty," she said as she looked down the steep hill at the woods beyond the house.

"This place sits on ten acres…it's mostly woods though," he put his arms around her from behind and kissed her neck. "So, what do you think?"

"It's a great house," she replied politely.

"We're not done yet. There's more."

In the next few minutes He showed her the dining room, his small sitting room again, the great room which featured a wet bar, a normal sized room with lots of windows that he planned to use as an office and a few other rooms with no names. By the end of the tour she was overwhelmed by the size and beautiful architecture of the place. The kitchen had granite counter tops, the bathroom in the master suite had a double vanity made of Italian marble, and every inch of the house was obviously of the highest quality. All Rebecca could think about was the astronomical house payment he must have each month. Having been raised by a miserly mother, Rebecca was used to living well below her means. She could have afforded to buy a nice house on her own, but she'd chosen to live in a small apartment so she could save money. She didn't want to hurt his male pride so early on by asking, but she was dying to know how he could afford the place.

"What's wrong?" he asked when he saw her face. "That's not an encouraging look…."

"We can talk about it later," Rebecca hedged.

"What? Are you worried about buying furniture? If that's what it is I completely understand. Why do you think I have only what I need? I thought about hiring a decorator, but I've been too busy to go through with it. We could hire someone if you'd rather not take this on all by yourself." He sounded so reassuring that Rebecca wanted to believe things would be fine.

"Come on I have one more room to show you," he took her by the hand and led her back to the area of the house where the great room and dining room were located. He stopped at another set of double doors and whispered in her ear, "This room is all yours."

When she looked at him with questioning eyes he said, "Go ahead, and open them."

She opened the doors to a lovely oval shaped room. The walls were painted a soft lilac color that contrasted nicely against the pristine white molding. The ceiling was covered in molding as well, but it had an intricate pattern that started at the edges of the walls and expanded all the way to the center of the room. And there in the center of the room sat a baby grand piano with a giant yellow bow on top. It was quite a surprise.

Norman didn't have to ask what she thought; it was written all ever her face as she slowly walked into the room and looked around at everything. She circled the piano several times before speaking again.

"This is the prettiest room I've ever seen in my life," she said honestly. "I could stare at the ceiling for hours." She looked up at the intricate designs in the molding and then back at her husband, "Thank you so much."

"You're welcome," he smiled. "Actually this room was built to be a music room. The ceiling and walls were designed with the acoustics in mind," he informed her.

"And is this the end of the tour?" she asked.

He burst out laughing at the hopeful note in her tone. "Yes, now we can get started on dinner."

"Before we do that, we need to talk."

"You sound too serious. What's up?" he asked.

"I make less than thirty thousand a year, but when I get a better job soon I'll still only be making about forty," she took a deep breath before continuing. "How in the world can we afford to live in a place like this? You have a good job, but frankly after seeing this house I'm a little worried about money... I mean, you do know how important it is to save," she said quickly all in one breath.

"Do you like this house?" he asked carefully. "Or is it too much for just us?"

"Who wouldn't love this house? Especially the music room... And someday there won't be just two of us anymore, but how are you, we, paying for it?" Rebecca asked.

"Is *that* why you've been looking like a deer in the headlights since we got here?" he demanded.

"Yes," she replied in exasperation.

"Rebecca, I own this house. It's already been paid for in full, and the taxes aren't as high as you'd think they'd be for a house this size."

The rest of the evening she looked pensive, and he repeatedly caught her gazing at him in a strange way. It didn't upset him, but it did make him wonder until she finally spoke about what was on her mind.

"Norman, what was your first wife like? I mean before the drinking and the jealousy," she asked.

"Why are you asking me about her all of a sudden?" Norman asked. This was an extremely uncomfortable subject to be discussing with his wife of less than one week.

"Because I've been thinking all day that there is any number of things I could do to make you want to leave me. I'm not perfect, and I don't know how well I'll fit into your life."

Norman bolted upright and looked at her like she'd lost her mind. "Are you serious?" he demanded.

"Yes!" she snapped undeterred by his body language. "Your first wife wasn't good enough after awhile, and she's not here right now, so how secure do you think I feel now?"

"Wait just a minute!" Norman exploded. "First of all I wouldn't call extreme jealousy and a drinking problem just 'not good enough.'"

"She's human. Those are things that could've been overcome if you'd wanted to be with her. If you want to be with someone and you truly love them, flaws and all, you don't divorce them when they go through a rough time. You rushed into things with me, and you barely know me... What happens when I have a rough time Norman? What happens when you get to know me better and you suddenly decide I don't fit into your lifestyle? What happens when I get a little jealous of all the women who fawn all over you? What happens then?" she demanded.

"Rebecca, I did not divorce her just because she had a drinking problem. I always wanted her to go to AA and get some help, but she hated taking any advice from me. She only went after we were already divorced, because I offered to buy her a house if she did it for the kids' sake," he raked a hand through his hair in agitation before continuing. "The day I filed for divorce was the day I found out that she'd been sleeping with one of my co-workers, and that the little girl I'd thought was my daughter actually isn't. I still have pictures of her because I was her father for a few years, but she isn't mine. Julie was so proud to be able to hang that over my head. It was just another way to hurt me. I divorced her because she's not a nice person, and she did two unforgivable things, so unless you plan on sleeping around and deliberately having another man's child while you're married to me the last thing you have to worry about is being good enough."

Rebecca instantly regretted giving Norman such a hard time. "I'm sorry, I had no idea about your daughter, or any of the other stuff," she said.

"I know how hard it is for you to understand that you're worth something to me, but when I said I love you I meant it. Look, we're married; I want you to stop questioning the permanency of it and just accept that it is. You are my wife, and as far as not fitting in goes...I grew up on a horse ranch, Honey. I'm still the same Norman you seemed to like yesterday. This house may look like it cost a fortune, but when I bought it it was a distressed property. No one else would touch it because it needed so much work, and do you know what I did? I bought it anyway because I saw the potential. I've spent the last three years scrounging for nice things in salvage yards and fixing it up in my spare time. I'm not the sort of man who would love you one day, and then just give up on you the next."

"Would you like it if I slept on the couch tonight?" Rebecca asked. She was surprised he wasn't calling for an annulment, and she just knew that at any moment he was going to start regretting the fact that he married her.

"Well, I'm not sleeping on the couch, and you're sleeping where I sleep so I guess that means you're not sleeping on the couch either," was his testy reply.

Rebecca's heart warmed but she didn't let it show, instead she changed the subject to the other thing that had been on her mind all day.

"I wish you didn't have to leave me alone in this big house so soon," she said quietly.

"Do you really Honey?" he asked as he wrapped his arms around her. "Don't think of it as me voluntarily leaving you behind, just think of it as a soldier doing his duty just like any other good soldier would."

"I understand," she sighed.

"You know I'll be able to call you often. That is one advantage of my rank. I get to use a phone almost anytime I want, and I can email you every day. Snail mail takes forever, so email is the best way to keep in touch while I'm gone. Oh, and I forgot to tell you that I might get to come back for two weeks of leave after a few months. The commander's policy is to allow all the lower enlisted soldiers to take leave first. It's based on a points system, so married soldiers with kids are most likely to go first. At my rank I don't count, but if there are enough slots I might just get one... I promise I'll try."

As he talked Rebecca tried to hide the fact that she was crying. Unfortunately he noticed. He didn't have to ask why.

"Honey, please don't cry. I will come home to you, I promise," he kissed her tears away while he tried to reassure her.

"You can't promise me something like that," she said sensibly. "How many dead soldiers do you think told their wives the exact same thing? Don't you think Shelly's husband Jake said the exact same thing to her before his last deployment? How many do you think go over there expecting to die? I know you want to come home, but in a lot of ways it isn't up to you. Whether or not you encounter some roadside bomb is just a mixture of chance and divine intervention, and I have every right to be scared for you right now. And you have every right to be scared for yourself. So please don't make impossible promises... just promise me that you'll be careful and you'll think of me in your spare time."

"Rebecca, it's not as dangerous as you think it is right now. A few years have made a big difference in the number of casualties. Deaths are on the decline," he said.

"Don't waste your breath. There's still a chance, and that's all it takes for me to have sleepless nights while you're gone. Also, consider the fact that we're still newlyweds. I'm not even going to get used to having you around before you'll be gone."

"Rebecca, I'm here now, and I'll be here every night for a month," he said firmly.

"But you'll be gone soon," she said sadly.

"I know... so why give yourself a hard time dwelling on it? I'm here right now, so why not just be here with me?"

He was right. Why waste precious time with her husband thinking about what was to come? She'd have all the time she needed to miss him when he left; there was no sense missing him while he was right there with his arms wrapped around her.

The time for talking ended as soon as Rebecca pulled Norman's head down for a passionate kiss. It was her way of letting him know that she was living in the moment, and it was a great moment to be living in.

"Norman, does it always feel so wonderful?" Rebecca asked in the afterglow of their lovemaking.

"Why do you ask?"

"Because I feel like I'm living a romantic movie when I'm with you. I always thought that the real thing could never be quite as good as a fantasy, so I came into this marriage with realistic expectations about the physical part of our relationship. I do have a master's in psychology, so I know the importance of seeing you as a real person. It would be unfair of me to project all my romantic ideals of what a man should be onto you. Anyway, the point is that making love with you feels way better than I could've dreamed, and I just wonder if it's like that for a lot of people. Is that how it was with your first wife?" she asked.

"I cannot believe you had the nerve to ask me that," Norman chuckled.

"Never mind, you don't have to answer that. I don't want to put you in the position of feeling like you have to lie to spare my feelings. It's none of my business," she said brusquely. She should have put more thought into that question.

"It's okay, I can answer honestly and not hurt your feelings. There is no comparison between you two. Julie's personality in the bedroom was much the same as it was any other time. She was bossy and demanding because her parents spoiled her rotten. She thinks that everyone was put on earth to please her, especially me. She always had a way of looking at me like she expected more, and sometimes she even told me how inadequate I was," Norman admitted.

"Ouch. That's pretty mean," Rebecca said.

"I know," Norman continued. "No one wants to hear things like that from their significant other. Honestly it made me feel like less of a man, especially after I found out about her affairs."

Rebecca's head was resting against his chest, and she lifted herself up to kiss him just then. "I'm glad I never slept with anyone else before I met you."

"To answer your question, no it is not like this for everyone. I've never felt even remotely close to the way I feel with you. I feel like I can never get enough of you. We are very lucky that we happen to be totally in love with each other and have great physical chemistry, because I think that with a lot of couples it's one or the other."

Eventually conversation gave way to the sweet slumber that can only be found in the arms of a dear one. With each precious moment counting down to Norman's departure, both wanted to spend as much time as possible in each other's arms.

The next morning Norman awoke to an empty bed. He was surprised that he hadn't noticed Rebecca leaving his side, and when he didn't find her in the bathroom, the kitchen, or the sitting room he began to worry. When it finally occurred to him that she might be in the music room he felt incredibly stupid for thinking that she might have left him.

He approached the doors quietly because he could hear her as she cautiously pressed the keys on her new piano. He listened as the notes she played grew bolder, and when she started to play an actual song he smiled to himself. She played even more brilliantly when she thought she was alone, and Norman listened in rapt fascination as she proceeded through Mozart's Piano Sonata No. 15, Sonata Semplice. Before that moment he hadn't known she could play any Mozart.

When she finished he opened the doors and allowed her to see him standing there. She briefly acknowledged his presence with a sweet little smile, and then she started playing again. His heart gladdened at this small indication that she was learning to trust him more. She didn't mind if he watched her play her new piano. He took a seat on the floor and watched her play while the sun came up in the window behind her. Her hair was loose and she still wore her night gown, and she looked so ethereally beautiful in the morning light that he found himself mentally comparing her to a little fairy that would disappear if he tried to reach out and touch her. He was transfixed by the way she played and the way she looked. He was really going to miss her.

At the end of the next piece she didn't immediately get up, instead she sat with her head down as she played an A minor arpeggio over and over again with her right hand.

Norman came to stand behind her. He stroked her hair as the notes reverberated throughout the room.

"What time is it?" she whispered when he bent down to kiss her neck.

"Six," he said. "Do you mind if I sit with you?"

"Not at all," she replied making room on the bench.

He ignored the space she made for him and pulled her astride his lap as he sat down. Through her thin nightgown there was no mistaking his arousal. His boxers allowed him to quickly free himself as she straddled his lap. All he had to do was look at her, and kiss her neck once and she began to feel that new pulse beat that only he could bring to life.

"Do you want to go back to bed?" she asked. She had a special look in her eyes that he was coming to know and love.

Norman's answer was to make love with her right there on the piano bench. He held her and guided her hips as she rode them both to repletion.

"That was... wow!" Norman panted after a swift and intense climax.

"Thanks for the piano," she said as she clung to his naked chest.

"You're welcome sweetie," he replied. He really liked her way of saying thanks, and he vowed at that moment to give her as many reasons as possible to thank him in the future.

Over the next month the newlyweds never spoke of Norman's impending deployment, except when it was necessary to take care of certain perfunctory issues such as obtaining a will and powers of attorney, and filling out emergency notification forms. Once the Friday before the deployment arrived, Norman caught Rebecca off guard with some bad news. He came home and told her that he would have to spend the weekend on lockdown in the personnel holding area with the rest of his unit.

"Why?" she demanded immediately.

"Because the commander's policy is to prevent any young soldiers from going AWOL before the deployment. You wouldn't believe how many of them make stupid choices in the last forty-eight hours before a deployment… We all have to be there, but it's mostly a preventative measure aimed to help the lower enlisted soldiers stay out of trouble," he explained.

Rebecca could tell he was upset, so she tempered her own response. "When do you have to go?" she asked.

"I have to be there by ten pm tonight. I was able to get away with a few extra hours; almost everyone else has to be there by six," he said in a flat toneless voice.

Rebecca felt as if she'd just stepped into a deep hole where she'd been expecting solid ground. She was shocked, disoriented, and more than a little hurt.

"It's too soon," her voice sounded far off and strange even to her own ears.

"I know Honey, I know."

"So when does the plane actually leave?" she felt proud of how brave and strong her voice sounded that time.

"Monday afternoon at one," he said.

"How can the commander do that to us? That's two extra days we could be together. It's just not right," she said sadly, and then she ruined all of her previous bravado by breaking into tears. "I thought I had more time, but we just have this evening. Just tonight, and not even all of it. I just wasn't prepared for this. I was prepared for Monday, but not this…"

"Calm down Sweetie, you'll get to come to the airfield on Monday and say goodbye right before we get on the plane. We'll get to spend two more hours together. The commander is calling it 'family time,'" he smiled. "Anyway, the FRG will give you a call about where to be sometime tomorrow. All the wives are upset, so maybe you could talk to some of them. You know, the FRG is something that I think you would benefit from while I'm away," he advised her.

The image Rebecca had of the Family Readiness Group was of a bunch of military wives hanging around crying because their husbands were gone. She did not think she would benefit from crying with them; she preferred to cry alone.

"It's something to think about," Norman said when he saw the look on her face.

They spent the rest of the evening doing routine things, as if they could simply ignore that this would be their last night together for a long time. Rebecca's mind repeatedly shut out the thought that it could be last evening she ever spent with her husband. Despite her many attempted smiles, Norman knew what she was thinking and he staunchly refused to acknowledge the possibility of his death.

Rebecca's eyes kept returning to Norman's uniform hanging near the door and his gear piled up on the floor beneath it. His boots, his Kevlar helmet, his load bearing vest, and his Kevlar vest all served as reminders that he would spend the next twelve months in a dangerous place.

Finally nine o'clock rolled around and Rebecca had the pleasure and the agony of watching her husband of less than two months don his uniform. As she watched him through her unshed tears she admired the very maleness of his body while he pulled on his trousers and tucked in his shirt. He sat next to her on the edge of the bed to pull on his boots. When, at last, he put on his jacket he looked every inch the soldier he was.

The heavy feeling that had settled in Rebecca's chest intensified while she drank in the sight of him standing in all his military gear. He looked huge and imposing, and he looked ready to go.

When they arrived on post she parked and walked with him to the gate of the personnel holding area. He grabbed her for a long intense hug as the gate guard discretely turned away. His hard vest pressed up against her chest in a painful way, but she still clung to him as tightly as she could for that brief moment.

"I'll see you Monday," he said tenderly as he brushed her silent tears away. "Please don't stand here looking at me like that. It'll be much easier if you go get back in the car instead of watching me walk away," he said to her.

"Okay," she sniffed as she turned away from him.

When he started walking toward the gate she covertly stopped to watch anyway.

The soldier on guard snapped to attention and saluted him as he approached. "Air Assault!" the soldier called out in a loud crisp voice as he held his salute up. Norman returned it and the soldier opened the gate. Rebecca continued watching until he glanced back at her once, and then disappeared into the dark shadow of the building.

She went home and sat in the kitchen staring at the refrigerator for almost two hours before she finally went to bed.

Her first night alone in the house was far from relaxing. She did the typical thing that army wives do when their husbands leave; she hugged his pillow and cried until she was too exhausted to think. Sleep eluded her because of her stuffy nose, swollen eyes, and pounding headache, so she lay in bed into the long hours of the night wondering at every little sound she heard.

When morning finally came Rebecca felt slightly better, until she thought again about the sad look Norman had given her when he'd caught her standing there despite his wishes. She got through the weekend by telling herself that at least she would get to spend two more hours with him on Monday. In a way she was also dreading Monday, because having to say an emotional goodbye all over again would just prolong her pain.

Chapter 15

By Monday morning Rebecca had managed to stop crying every time she thought about her husband. She'd spent the weekend chastising herself for being so emotional about an event that she'd known was coming for months now. She kept telling herself that she *was* prepared for it and she *could* deal with it, but then she'd picture Norman's face as he'd caught her staring after him Friday night and tears would threaten to come out again.

It was five in the morning, and she was still lying in bed staring up at the ceiling with Norman's pillow tucked under her arm. She felt like she hadn't slept in days, but even in her exhaustion her body was like a tightly wound coil holding an incredible amount of tension. Shelly had told her that the first deployment was always the hardest, and that she would get used to it, but even Shelly had looked like she didn't believe those words as they came out of her mouth. How could anyone get used to sending someone they love off to a place where they could be killed or seriously injured? Rebecca couldn't begin to fathom how other military spouses handled the emotional upheaval of deployments, but she figured that if millions of other women had gotten through it over the years then she could too.

She was about to turn over and try to get at least a little sleep when the phone rang. She scrambled to table to answer it, half expecting Norman to be on the line. Her spirits sank again when she heard her supervisor's voice instead of her husband's.

"Sorry to bother you Miss Rebecca, but one of the female staff members quit, and I can't get a hold of any other female workers. Do you mind coming in today?" he asked.

"Actually I do. My husband's plane leaves at one today, and I want to be there to tell him goodbye," she said. Ordinarily she had no problem covering an extra shift if a staff member quit, because she knew that if no one voluntarily came in one of the night shift workers would be in the position of having to work for twenty four hours strait.

Half an hour later Fred called back, "Miss Rebecca, I hate to ask again, but we can't afford to have low staff. The state would have to shut us down for that type of violation. I need someone to come in right now, and Miss Green can't be here until ten. Can you come in just until ten?" he practically pleaded.

"Okay," she agreed after a moment. At least going to work would give her something to keep her mind off of Norman's departure for the desert.

"Thank you so much," Fred said fervently before he hung up.

By six thirty she was being greeted by the austere sight of the youth center complex. For some reason it looked even more depressing than usual today. Everything seemed to have lost its luster since Friday night.

Fred was in the break room when Rebecca went to clock in.

"Who quit this time?" she asked him with a yawn.

"Ms. Jackson," he answered.

"Really? That's weird; she's been here for a while. Why did she quit?" Rebecca asked in surprise. Ms. Jackson had been one of the most solid workers on the staff.

"That girl Diamond attacked her last night, and the other staff members didn't help much. Shirelle and Ronnie had an argument and Ronnie lost all her points for the hour. I guess Diamond thought she needed to teach Ms. Jackson a lesson about taking her home-girl's points. I still don't know why these kids get in trouble for each other. I mean Ronnie wouldn't give Diamond the time of day back on the block," Fred said.

They talked for a while about the status of all the girls on the female unit before the rest of the day shift counselors arrived for the 6:45 morning meeting. Ms. Parker was among them, and she gave Rebecca a look that clearly said she was not happy to see her.

"Did you change shifts?" Ms. Parker asked. If her voice had been any more frigid the entire room would have frozen over.

"No, I'm just here until ten today because Ms. Jackson quit last night," Rebecca replied.

"What?" Ms. Parker said in disbelief.

"Yeah," Fred chimed in. "She got attacked by a resident and staff didn't have her back."

"I know how that feels," Ms. Parker said derisively with a sidelong glance in Rebecca's direction.

Irritation instantly blossomed as Rebecca returned Ms. Parker's look. Ten o'clock couldn't come soon enough.

"Let's take the floor," Fred said as soon as the nurse's briefing was over. Waking up the girls usually went pretty slow, and today was no different. No one wanted to get up and get dressed for breakfast. Then once they made it to breakfast no one wanted to stand in line. Everyone had an attitude, and Rebecca got the feeling that they were all skating on thin ice. From the staff to the residents the entire mood was just bad in general.

"Ladies!" Ms. Parker called out after breakfast. "No gym time this morning, instead we're going to go back on the female unit because those rooms are tore up!" she announced in a loud voice.

Complaints were swift and numerous.

"And if you don't get quiet and get in line now, you'll be on silence all morning while you clean," she added. By nine o'clock they were all back in their rooms cleaning. Ms. Parker and Rebecca were the only two staff members on the unit, so they each took a section of the circular hall to watch over. Rebecca's section included Ronnie and Shirelle's room. She walked back and forth and peered into her three rooms periodically to make sure all the girls were working.

"Miss Rebecca," Shirelle called out after a few minutes. "Will you check my room? I'm done," she said.

"Looks good, but you have to stay in here until everyone is finished," Rebecca said after a quick inspection.

"Can I sit at my desk and write?" Shirelle asked.

"Sure you can," Rebecca smiled at the child. She was always glad to encourage Shirelle's talent for writing.

Rebecca heard Ronnie let out a contemptuous snicker as she left the room to check on the other girls.

Not five minutes later Rebecca ended up back in Shirelle's room under completely different circumstances. She'd just cleared another room when she heard Ronnie shout, "What you gonna do about it *bitch*!" in a tone that clearly spelled trouble.

She ran down the hall to the room just in time to see Shirelle hurl a chair across the room at Ronnie. It soared clear over the bed and slammed full force into Ronnie's head causing it to bounce off the brick wall with a sickening crack. Ronnie slumped to the floor and lay motionless while Rebecca stared in mute shock.

When Shirelle bolted across the room and tried to kick Ronnie in the head Rebecca snapped out of her shock and leapt forward to restrain her. She struggled to get her down on the floor as she called for a nurse on her radio. Immediately she heard rushing footsteps, but they were those of the other residents coming to see who was fighting. What they saw stunned them and incited Ronnie's crew to violence.

Diamond ran over and attacked Shirelle as Rebecca restrained her on the floor. They were both getting kicked and punched by various girls as Rebecca tried to keep Shirelle subdued. Shirelle was completely crazed and it took all of Rebecca's strength to hold onto her arms as she screamed, "Get off me! Get off me! I'll kill him! I'll kill him! Get off me you fuckin ho! I hate you! Ahhhhhh!"

Then there was Diamond punching both Rebecca and Shirelle as she screamed at Shirelle, "What did you do?" over and over again.

"We need a nurse to room nine!" Rebecca screamed repeatedly. One of the girls had smashed her radio against the wall, and she was frantic for help to arrive before someone else was seriously injured. She was still trying to keep Shirelle from pouncing on Ronnie, but all the other girls were making the task extremely difficult. The crying, jeering, and screaming reached an almost unbearable pitch as Rebecca shielded Shirelle's head from the repeated blows coming from the melee. Attempting to shield the child and restrain her at the same time proved to be a nearly impossible task.

After what seemed like an eternity, Ms. Parker entered the room.

"I'm sorry, I was in the break room," she choked out as she yanked Diamond away, and herded the other screaming girls out of the room. The fact that she was bigger than most of them combined with her tough reputation worked to get most of them to back up, but Ms. Parker still had to send a distress call on her radio for any available staff members to come to the female unit.

Rebecca could still barely contain Shirelle, and out of the corner of her eye she saw a growing puddle of blood forming around Ronnie's head. The vivid red clashed against the dingy white tile floor, and the puddle was so smooth and undisturbed that the reflection of light coming from the window was nearly perfect, as if it were reflecting off of a liquid crimson mirror. The puddle was so smooth because Ronnie hadn't moved an inch since falling to the floor. Even preoccupied as she was with Shirelle still screaming and flailing in her arms, Rebecca knew that Ronnie wasn't going to be okay. The perfectly smooth puddle continued to spread across the floor toward Rebecca and Shirelle, and the closer it got the more the sense of foreboding in Rebecca's stomach grew. The nurse shuffled in slowly, and then immediately called a code blue on her radio after checking Ronnie's vitals. Within seconds all the nurses rushed in and attempted to contain the bleeding and revive the child while they waited for an ambulance to arrive.

By the time the nurses took over the room, Ms. Parker had returned to help Rebecca. Somehow the two of them managed to drag a still kicking and screaming Shirelle into the time out room. They left a smeared trail of blood behind, but Shirelle didn't seem to notice. The sight of so much blood did nothing to bring her back to her senses. Despite the gravity of the situation, nothing they said or did helped.

It took several male staff members helping out to calm all the girls on the unit and take them to the classrooms in the education building, so that they wouldn't have to witness the scene that stretched from Shirelle and Ronnie's room through the hall to the time out room near the nurses' station.

When the paramedics finally arrived they were unable to revive Ronnie. They rushed her to the hospital where she was pronounced dead on arrival. She'd suffered a massive skull fracture from Shirelle's assault, and the police wasted no time coming to the center for Shirelle.

When the police entered the building, Shirelle was still furiously struggling against Rebecca and Ms. Parker's attempts to calm her. She thrashed her head repeatedly against the mat on the floor even as she attempted to bite them several times. She spat in Rebecca's face, and continued to kick and convulse in a manner so wild it was almost inhuman. Yet, as soon as the police came into the timeout room Shirelle calmed down to an almost eerie degree of quietude and looked Rebecca directly in the eye.

"Please don't let them take me away Miss. I didn't mean to do it," she said in a near whisper.

"But Shirelle, I saw you," Rebecca replied tiredly.

"No, Miss," she said in growing desperation. *"Please* help me! You know I didn't mean it! *Please* help me!" she screamed as the police cuffed her. Suddenly she looked very much like a child again as she lay on the floor with handcuffs around her boney wrists and a puddle of blood tinged spit near her mouth. "Please..." she whimpered again. The two policemen had to lift her by the arms to take her off the floor, because her body had gone limp with exhaustion and the realization that this situation was not going to go away just because she'd calmed down.

Once the police actually started dragging her from the building she began to wail again. "Please! Miss Rebecca, you know I didn't mean to do it!.... please don't let them take me away! Please.... Please..... Tell them it was an accident," she pleaded to Rebecca as the policemen struggled to get her through the open doorway. She stiffened her legs and kicked at the door frame as she cried and pleaded, but once they got her out the door her entire body slumped again in resignation. Rebecca watched in silence feeling very much like she was watching a part of the child die, and feeling very much like a part of herself died with it.

Shirelle's words rang in Rebecca's ears as she recounted the ordeal for more than two hours afterward. The police questioned her, and she gave several statements, including a sworn statement for the police, a statement for the nurse's incident report, and a statement for the supervisor to present to treatment team. By the time she finished Norman's plane was long gone, so she went straight home to hide from the demands of the world.

Norman and his unit were allowed two hours of family time in the old hangar on the day of their departure. Two hours in which to embrace their loved ones and try not to cry. The soldiers always managed to look brave for their wives. They kept the stiff upper lip as they faced down the tears in their spouses' eyes. He'd seen it time and time again before deployments, and he knew that those same brave men who told their wives not to worry would get on the plane and need a moment alone to shed a private tear.

On the all day flight across the ocean there was nothing but time, time to think about the ones who were being left behind. The female soldiers who had to say goodbye to their civilian husbands were rare, but they were no less affected than the other soldiers. There was even an added pressure on them not to cry, because women were known to be more emotional, but women soldiers were expected to be able to control it.

When the first busload of family members arrived at the hangar Norman went outside and watched for some sign of Rebecca. When she wasn't on the first bus he was slightly disappointed, but he told himself that at least she would be there soon. An hour and a half later, when there were no more buses arriving and it was almost time for the soldiers to get into formation and march out to the plane he felt absolutely crushed.

He'd watched bus after bus, and hungrily scanned the faces of those getting off hoping for some sight of his wife. Each time his disappointment increased exponentially. He tried calling home several times, and he got no answer. Where was she?

Finally in the last half hour one more bus came with some family members who'd arrived late. Norman rushed outside with a few other hopeful soldiers when he heard the announcement, and he was never more disappointed in his life to see his sister step off the bus. Where was his wife?

"Norman!" she said as she rushed over to give him a hug. "I would have come earlier, but I wanted to give you and Rebecca a little time alone," she said.

"She's not here," Norman informed her.

"Why not?" Shelly asked.

"I don't know," he said. "I'm hoping nothing has happened to her. I didn't even get an answer when I tried calling home," he said.

"Norman, maybe this was just too much for her. She's been really upset all weekend," Shelly said. "I remember the last time Jake left. I didn't watch his plane leave either," the old sadness had crept back into her face as she spoke. "If I'd known he wasn't coming back I would have been there," she added nostalgically.

"But she said she would come," Norman said. He was dangerously close to shedding a tear.

"I'll go talk to her Norman. She's probably hurting right now, and she didn't know what to do," Shelly said in Rebecca's defense. "When will you get the chance to call again?" she asked.

"I'm not sure. It could be anywhere between two days and two weeks," he said. "Shit! I have to go. They're already in formation. Take care of yourself big sis," and the next moment he was blending into the sea of camouflage uniforms marching out to the plane.

Shelly stood outside in the summer heat and watched as the hundreds of soldiers walked up the steps onto the plane. She watched the plane take off into the clouds and sent a silent prayer with all of them.

"Lord, please bring them all home," her lips whispered even as her heart whispered that she was setting herself up for disappointment. They never all came home, there were always a few who were lost along the way.

Always the dutiful big sister, Shelly drove all the way out to Norman's house to talk to Rebecca. It was almost three in the afternoon by the time she arrived, and she spotted Rebecca going inside as she came up the long private drive.

Shelly wasted no time. She got out and pounded on the front door and rang the bell so there was no chance that she wouldn't be heard.

Rebecca answered almost immediately with a frightened look on her face. When she saw it was just Shelly she slumped against the doorframe in intense relief.

Shelly took in her appearance, and decided not to question her about why she'd left Norman alone today. Her arm was in a splint, her face was swollen and bruised, with one eye almost completely shut, and she still had a small trickle of blood coming out of her nose.

"I didn't get to tell Norman goodbye," she said in a tragic, broken voice when she saw Shelly standing there. "I just wanted to see him one more time, but I couldn't."

"Rebecca, what in the world happened to you?" Shelly stepped inside and asked.

That was when the floodgates opened. Rebecca completely broke down in tears and sank down to the floor of the foyer. Shelly closed the door and sat beside her sister in law, afraid to touch her for fear that she would cause pain, yet not wanting to leave her alone in such a state.

When the hysterics finally subsided Rebecca said more calmly than she felt, "When you came banging on the door like that I thought you were the police coming to question me some more," she explained. "I was called in to work this morning, because somebody quit, and I was supposed to be off by ten this morning. But that girl Shirelle that I told you about killed her roommate. I was right there and I couldn't stop it, and the other girls tried to jump her while I tried to keep her from attacking Ronnie again. They beat us both pretty badly, and

Ronnie was on the floor across the room with all this blood. It was the worst thing I ever saw in my life Shelly. Ronnie died today, and Shirelle is now in police custody. I've already been grilled about it for most of the day, and I was so afraid that you were the police. Oh God!" she ended with a sob. "I cannot believe this happened, and of all days why today?"

For the first time in a long time Shelly had no idea what to say. Everything that immediately came to mind she quickly dismissed as trite and placating. How could she tell her that it would be okay? That would be the nice thing to say, but it wouldn't necessarily be true.

"It all happened so fast," Rebecca continued. "It was like watching something in slow motion, and you're moving in super slow motion. It happened so slowly that I noticed every single detail, yet it went by so fast that there was nothing I could do to stop it," she explained. "She just threw the chair so hard."

"When do you have to go back to work?" Shelly asked gently.

"I don't know. Since my wrist is broken I can't be on duty as a resident counselor. But if I get the therapist job I applied for I should still be able to work with a broken wrist," she explained.

"Aren't you going to take any time off due to the emotional stress?" Shelly asked.

"I don't know if I can," Rebecca answered. "We're short on staff as it is."

"Well, you can't go in until you can at least see out of both eyes," Shelly said firmly.

"I hadn't thought of that," Rebecca said. "Does it look real bad?" she asked after trying to open her eye a little wider.

"It looks terrible. I'm actually glad Norman didn't have to see you like this before he left. It would have made him crazy," Shelly said with a halfhearted attempt at a smile.

Rebecca chuckled a little unwillingly as she recalled the day Norman had seen a few bruises from work and thought her boyfriend must have done it. She told Shelly about that day, and Shelly smiled and said fondly, "That sounds just like my little brother. Once when he was a company commander this soldier punched his wife in the head, and Norman picked that little bully up clear off the floor and shook him as he read the article fifteen to him. I didn't get to see it, but according to the first sergeant it was hilarious to see a grown man intimidated so easily," Shelly said.

They shared a brief moment of respite from the weight of the world, and it helped Rebecca regain her spirits enough to at least get up off the floor. She yawned heavily, and her one good eye looked at Shelly pleadingly.

"I'd rather not tell Norman about this, he'll have enough to worry about for the next year," she said.

"Rebecca, he can handle it. I don't think he'd like you keeping something this big from him," Shelly responded.

"I'd still rather not tell him."

"Why don't you go lie down before you fall over?" Shelly said when Rebecca yawned at her again. Her exhaustion was painfully obvious. It was definitely a good thing Norman hadn't seen his wife looking like this. "I'll make something for supper since you only have one eye and one hand to work with. Just go lie down for a while," Shelly insisted when Rebecca looked like she was about to protest.

"Yeah, I should. I took some strong pain pills the doctor at work prescribed this morning, and my brain is just about to shut down," Rebecca admitted. "Been up since four," she muttered on her way down the hall.

Shelly watched and shook her head sadly. She knew exactly how Rebecca was feeling about Norman's deployment, and she could only imagine what toll today's fiasco at her job was taking on her.

About an hour after Rebecca lay down the phone rang. Shelly grabbed it before it woke her up.

"Hello," she said not recognizing the number.

"Shelly, have you talked to Rebecca?" Norman asked.

"Hey, I thought you couldn't call for two days!" Shelly exclaimed.

"I decided to use the expensive airplane phone. It just dawned on me that I can afford it," Norman said satirically. "Where's my wife?"

"About that," Shelly began carefully. She didn't want to break Rebecca's confidence, but she felt her brother deserved an explanation. "She's sleeping right now, and I don't think it would be very nice to wake her up," she said.

"Why not?" Norman stormed. "I want to talk to her."

"Let me explain why she's sleeping… She had an incident at work today, and she's kind of hurt," Shelly said.

"What do you mean kind of hurt?" Norman demanded in alarm.

"Her wrist is broken, one of her eyes is swollen shut, and she's pretty banged up. She took some pain medication, and she's really tired, but she's okay. I'll stay with her to help out at least until she can see properly," Shelly said.

After a long moment of silence Norman finally gritted out, "What happened?"

"Take a deep breath Norman, and calm down. You can't be angry at her for having a job you don't approve of when you just got on a plane to a war zone today," Shelly admonished him.

"I'm not angry at her. Will you just tell me what happened?" he tried to sound calm when he was anything but.

"From what I understand two girls got in a fight, and one of them ended up killing the other. Rebecca was hurt because she had to hold one of the girls off of the injured one while some of the other girls rushed in the room to attack her and the one she was trying to subdue," Shelly explained.

"So she was attacked while keeping the killer from attacking the victim again?" Norman asked for clarification.

"Yes, I think that's what happened. She was pretty upset about it when I asked, so I didn't catch everything she said," Shelly said.

"Jeez!" Norman said. "So a kid was killed today?"

"Yes, it happened this morning around ten, and the police kept all the employees for questioning, especially your wife since she's the only one who saw the whole thing."

"She was in there *alone*?!"

Shelly flinched at his tone. "Yes, that's how she managed to get hurt. When the other workers got there they pulled the girls off of her," Shelly was uncomfortable because she'd already said way more than she'd planned on saying. "Like I said, she's pretty upset and I'd rather not wake her up. I think she went in around five this morning, and it's been a rough day for her."

"You're right… I can call her again another time. You'll stay with her until she's okay?" he asked.

"Yeah, she's just hurt right now. Give her a few days and she'll feel better," Shelly said.

"Stop trying to make me feel better when you and I both know that it isn't going to happen. I know she's not going to feel better in a couple of days after what happened. You wouldn't be okay if some kid killed another kid in front of you and a bunch of them jumped on you and kicked your ass, so don't tell me she'll be okay in a couple of days. I just really wish I could be there with her instead of on a damn plane to the other side of the world right now. Please tell me she's not going back to work there?"

"She was talking about how short staffed they are, and I think that if her eye wasn't swollen shut she'd probably be there now," Shelly said with a little too much pride in her voice for Norman's liking.

"That's not funny," he said flatly.

"I wasn't trying to be funny. Do you think Juliana would've lasted for one minute in an environment where everyone's not bowing down to kiss her rear end? I'll never pretend that I don't like Rebecca's grit," was Shelly's forceful reply.

"I'm happy you like her, but jeez! That's my *wife* who could've been killed by some punk ass kid today," Norman said angrily.

"She'll be fine Norman," Shelly insisted.

"Will you stay with her for a few days?" Norman asked again.

"I already told you I would," Shelly replied gently. There was no mistaking the vulnerability in her little brother's ordinarily strong voice.

"Even if she acts like she doesn't need you?" Norman continued.

"Yes," she assured him. "I remember what you told me about her mother, and even though *she* thinks she has no one *you* can be assured that she has *me* as a sister. I don't turn my back on family."

"Thanks Shelly, you don't know how much this means to me," Norman sighed before hanging up the phone.

Rebecca slept straight through until morning, and the first thing she did when she woke up was get dressed for work. Shelly was still asleep on the couch, so Rebecca left her a hastily scrawled note on her way out the door.

Chapter 16

Driving with a broken wrist and only one good eye proved to be much more difficult than Rebecca had thought it would be. By the time she made it to the youth center she had serious doubts as to how she would make the drive in the dark. She would just have to ask her supervisor if she could leave early when she came to work her actual shift on Saturday.

She proceeded slowly up the long drive to see a gaggle of television news reporters surrounding the front entrance. In an attempt to escape their notice, she drove around back to park, but there were more in the back.

"Ma'am, were you injured during yesterday's incident?" one lady asked before she was even out of her car.

"Yes," Rebecca answered without thinking.

"What can you tell us about the child who was killed in that incident?" the lady went on.

Rebecca didn't respond that time. There were several cameras aimed at her by now, and she just wanted to get inside as quickly as possible.

"Ma'am, can you tell us anything more?" the first lady asked just as three other reporters came up and began questioning her.

"Ma'am!"

"Excuse me Miss!"

"Can you tell us how the incident occurred?!"

"Have any charges been filed?!"

Questions were fired rapidly from every angle until she managed to open the door with her electronic key card and step inside.

Ms. Jackson was the first person she saw.

"I thought you quit last night," Rebecca said immediately.

"I did, but after I heard what happened I had to come back," Ms. Jackson said. "Are you alright?"

"Yeah. Don't I look alright?" Rebecca tried to joke, but it fell flat.

"Fred told me about it yesterday after you went home... I don't get it. Why were you back there all alone with all of the girls, especially with the way they'd acted last night?" Ms. Jackson demanded with concern in her voice.

"Ms. Parker was in the break room, but she didn't tell me she was going. I didn't know I was alone until after it happened."

"That's not like Ms. Parker. Usually she never leaves another staff member alone unless it's some kind of emergency," Ms. Jackson said thoughtfully.

"She can't stand me," Rebecca stated with certainty.

"Let's not jump to conclusions," Ms. Jackson admonished her.

"It's true. She probably thought something would happen and that I'd get fired for not handling it properly. She just didn't expect the something to be that bad," Rebecca said in a bitter voice. "Not that having her around would have helped much anyway. It all happened way too fast. By the time I ran to the room to see what the yelling was about Shirelle had already thrown the chair. It was too late," Rebecca's voice shook as she spoke about the incident.

"How did you get so beat up? Was it Shirelle?" she asked.

"No," Rebecca answered. "Veronica's crew, including Diamond did it. They were trying to get at Shirelle while I restrained her."

"Did they hurt her pretty bad?" Ms. Jackson asked.

"Diamond kicked her in the head once. She got me once in the eye with her sharp little shoes."

"Fred was talking to me earlier about pressing charges for last night, and I think that's what I'm going to do. You should too. Just look what they did to you," Ms. Jackson said as she looked at Rebecca's hideously swollen eye.

"I think I already told the police yesterday that I didn't want to press charges. Diamond is only thirteen and she saw her friend lying on the floor in a puddle of blood. She was just upset at the time," Rebecca answered carefully.

"She ain't got no excuse for last night," Ms. Jackson said.

Just then Ms. Parker walked in. "You decided to come back?" were the first words out of her mouth.

"Yeah, I heard about what happened yesterday," Ms. Jackson told her.

At the mention of the incident, Ms. Parker glanced uncomfortably in Rebecca's direction. She was taken aback by her battered appearance, because when she'd left yesterday to talk to the police she hadn't looked nearly that bad.

"They broke your arm Miss Rebecca?" she asked with uncharacteristic normalcy in her voice.

"No, just my wrist. I have an appointment with the orthopedic surgeon to get a cast put on tomorrow. It's a compound fracture," Rebecca replied.

Miss Parker looked down at the floor when Rebecca met her gaze. "Is your eye going to be okay?" she asked.

"Eventually," Rebecca said coldly.

There was a long uncomfortable silence as they all avoided looking at each other. Fred was supposed to come in and talk to them soon, but he was about ten minutes late. They just sat in silence as they waited. Miss Parker looked uncomfortable and Rebecca grew angrier by the minute as she thought about yesterday. After all the complaining Miss Parker had done about her, Rebecca couldn't believe she'd had the nerve to go on break and not even tell her.

"Why were you in the break room yesterday?" Rebecca's voice suddenly broke the oppressive silence.

Miss Parker didn't answer.

"Isn't that one of the things you aren't supposed to do?" Rebecca went on undeterred.

Still no answer from Miss Parker.

"I can't believe you had the nerve to submit a complaint against me when you are so far from perfect it's ridiculous," Rebecca snapped. "I was alone back there! And I was getting attacked for at least a full minute before you showed up! All that talk about staff not having *your* back... and you do that to me," she pressed on relentlessly.

"That wasn't the same, and you know it," Miss Parker finally spoke.

"Why not? I've *never* left you alone. I might not restrain them every time they look at me wrong like you do, but I have *never* left a staff member alone without telling them." Rebecca's voice had grown louder and stronger with each word aimed at Ms. Parker.

"Do you think Diamond would've attacked me?" Miss Parker responded with heat. "Those girls know they can't get away with *shit* while I'm around, and they think they can walk all over you because you're too nice to them! So *what* if I put them on the floor for talking?! What? All it means is that they know I mean business!" Miss Parker snapped.

"No it doesn't!" Rebecca shouted. "All it means is that you've proved you can exert physical control over them, just like the parents who abused them, and any other bully from back on the block who ever pressured them into doing something they didn't want to do. The only difference between you and them is that you're self-righteous about it because you get *paid*!"

"Fuck you!" Miss Parker shouted with tears in her eyes.

"I'm not finished yet, so you better listen," Rebecca ground out in a steely cold voice. "You think I don't know that Shirelle was a major influence over these girls? I had nothing to prove to anyone in this place by using brute force to control that child. She'd already been controlled all her life, and she needed to learn how to deal with life. Her father the drug addict sold her to a dealer when she was ten so he could get his fix! All she knows is how to be controlled by those who are stronger and how to control those who are weaker. Maybe, you should try to see that the same approach doesn't work for every case. I don't have a problem restraining any of them when it is necessary, but I was not going to restrain Shirelle over stupid little stuff when she has a background like that. And I think that anyone who would is an insensitive moron."

"Do you know how long it takes to get these girls to respect you if you don't get tough with them from day one?" Miss Parker demanded.

"Since when is the focus of this job gaining respect? This is a mental health facility. These children are here for treatment! They are not here so you can prove to them how far beneath you they are," Rebecca said, her voice dripping with scorn and derision.

By the time she stopped talking Fred and several members of the treatment team had come quietly into the room. They were giving her strange looks, and she just knew that her job was on the line because of her emotional display. She glanced briefly at each of them before she spoke again.

"If you think that hiring people like her is going to help these kids, then I can't work in a place like this. Shirelle didn't throw that chair at Ronnie because she didn't get *restrained* enough. There was obviously a deeper reason that probably has to do with the fact that Ronnie was a violent bully, and Shirelle couldn't stand being bullied anymore. I've always thought it was a stupid idea to put those two in the room together, so now you can give yourselves a big pat on the back. You managed to get rid of the two worst ones just like you've been wanting to for months. I quit."

No one spoke a word as she walked back out into the horde of reporters and drove home.

Shelly went back to Rebecca and Norman's house after packing a few days worth of clothes that evening. Rebecca was already home when she let herself in with the spare key. She was in the kitchen trying to cook with one hand, and it was going surprisingly well.

"I thought you might need a hand with things since your right arm is in a splint, but I guess you must be left handed. I swear I thought you were right handed though," Shelly said.

Rebecca looked at her and smiled briefly. "Most of the time I write with my right hand," she said, "but I'm actually ambidextrous."

"Oh, so you really don't need much help, do you?" Shelly asked.

"Not really, so you don't have to stay. I don't want you going to any trouble for me," Rebecca said in a monotone.

"Well, I already drove all the way out here, so I might as well just crash here," Shelly responded. "If you don't mind," she added as an afterthought.

"I don't mind."

Rebecca hardly talked all evening, and Shelly didn't press her to make conversation. They just sat around Norman's sitting room alternately looking in books and watching television.

When the evening news came on Shelly saw a clip of Rebecca walking into the youth center when a story about the death aired. She looked at Rebecca expecting her to be upset, but there was no sign of emotion on her face. A short time later she simply told Shelly she was going to bed.

That night Rebecca had decided not to take her pain pills, so she lay in bed with an aching head and a throbbing wrist. She struggled into the wee hours of the night to keep her good eye open, because every time she closed it images of Ronnie and Shirelle flashed in her head. She couldn't get the blood off her mind, nor could she forget for a moment the way Shirelle had pleaded for her help. The darkness and solitude had a way of magnifying all her troubles into monstrous, insurmountable obstacles.

She tried hard to think of something in her life that wouldn't give her pain just so she could fall asleep, but every direction her thoughts took included heartache. What was Norman doing at this moment? Was he okay? Was he upset with her for not showing up to say goodbye? When was her mother going to talk to her again? What was going to happen to Shirelle? Why did Shirelle throw the chair? Why couldn't she have gone into the room just one minute sooner? Why did the corner of the chair have to smash right into Ronnie's head? Why couldn't it have hit her shoulder?

She tossed and turned with these thoughts circulating and gaining speed in her head until she had a massive headache. Sleep eluded her until the predawn minutes of the morning.

It took about two weeks for Rebecca's eye to return to normal, and during that time she spent most of her time hiding from the world. The death at the center had caused a local media frenzy, and public calls were made for the center to be investigated or shut down. Shelly came over once a day to check on her, but Rebecca wished she wouldn't. She was beginning to feel like a burden. And she still hadn't heard from Norman yet.

The head of the FRG had called her to let her know that the soldiers had arrived safely at their undisclosed destination, but other than that Rebecca was in the dark about her husband. She felt like she hadn't slept in months, and she wished Norman were there so she could feel his warm arms around her at night.

Nights were the hardest time of day for Rebecca. Images of Ronnie's death and Shirelle's pleading eyes peppered all her dreams to the point where just closing her eyes was distressing. Yet still she talked to no one about her thoughts.

One night as she lay in bed listening to a thunderstorm through her drowsiness she suddenly saw Norman standing beside the bed.

"How did you come back?" she whispered when he leaned down to kiss her.

The lightening lit up the room behind him, and she could see the silhouette of his uniform and all his battle gear. "They let me take leave so I could be with you," he said tenderly. He leaned down and kissed her lips with warmth and the smell of masculinity clinging to him.

"I miss you so much," she said as tears streamed down her face.

He brushed them away and said, "I'll never leave you again Honey, I swear."

She closed her eyes to enjoy the feel of his hand against her cheek, and when she opened them again it was to discover the sunlight streaming into the room. He hadn't been there after all; it was just a dream that had lulled her to sleep. Sadness and disappointment were swift and Rebecca cursed herself for waking up.

It was a beautiful day, but she closed the curtains, determined to be alone. A sense of depression began to settle about her when she got back into bed. She had no job, and she wasn't currently volunteering at the school because summer break hadn't ended yet. Her days seemed like they had no point anymore. Even her research project had been defended and turned in to the psychology department at the university. By the end of the summer semester she'd officially have her master's degree, yet she felt little satisfaction about the accomplishment.

Her days were filled with thoughts of Ronnie's death, and no matter how much she analyzed the incident she just couldn't make sense of the tragedy. Fred had called her a few days after she'd quit to inform her that she could keep her job if she still wanted it. Apparently the treatment team and the head psychiatrist had agreed with her about Miss Parker. Following a thorough review of the surveillance tapes from the past few weeks, Miss Parker had been fired.

The youth center's policy had been to review the tapes only if there was an incident, but they saved them in an archive for six weeks before recording over them. When they reviewed the ones from the past they saw that Miss Parker had been in clear violation of the company policy. She had restrained residents for slight offenses that would have normally warranted a trip to the time out room. After watching the tapes they'd been quick to get rid of her in an attempt to improve their public image. Rebecca knew Miss Parker's method was wrong, but she also felt that the center was wrong for using her as a scapegoat. Her methods were widespread among the staff members because several supervisors approved of, and even encouraged, the use of pain compliance to keep the residents under strict control.

News of Miss Parker's dismissal still hadn't been enough to make Rebecca want to return to work at the center. Fred had given her a few weeks to think about it, and the general manager had also called to let her know that she had an interview for the therapist position she'd applied for. That had been last week, and she hadn't gotten back to them with a decision yet. She closed her eyes and tried to shut out all her turbulent thoughts and focus on something positive, but nothing came to mind.

Chapter 17

"Rebecca, you have to get out of this house," Shelly said as soon as she opened the door. "You haven't been anywhere for over a month, and you're starting to look like a skeleton," she continued as she barged into the house. "How's your wrist?" she added as an afterthought.

"Itchy," Rebecca yawned.

"How long do you have to be in that cast?" she inquired.

"A few months. Look Shelly, I appreciate you coming all the way over here every day to say hi, but you really don't have to. I'm fine," Rebecca insisted.

"I'm not here to say hi," Shelly pressed on, undeterred by Rebecca's dismissive attitude. "I'm here to take you out."

"I don't want to go out," Rebecca grouched as she followed Shelly into the kitchen. "What are you looking for?" she asked as Shelly opened all the cabinet doors and looked inside the refrigerator.

"No wonder you're wasting away, there's no food here," Shelly said without looking at her sister-in-law.

"Shelly," Rebecca began only to be cut off.

"You need to go grocery shopping. Go get dressed. I'll come with you," Shelly commanded imperiously.

"I don't need any help to get groceries," Rebecca groused.

Shelly raised an eyebrow and indicated the empty fridge with a flick of her wrist.

Several hours later Rebecca looked at her new sister-in-law and realized that she was a force to be reckoned with. Shelly refused to take no for an answer, and she'd managed to drag Rebecca all over town. On the way to the grocery store Shelly had stopped by a furniture store. When Rebecca perked up slightly it was all the encouragement Shelly needed to turn the impulse stop into an all out shopping expedition.

By the time they returned to the house Rebecca had ideas of how she wanted to decorate and furnish the master suite before Norman's return. He had said he wanted her to furnish the house however she wanted, so she felt no compunction about getting started on it soon. It was funny how a simple thing like shopping with Shelly had helped to lift her mood.

Shelly stayed for a while to help put away groceries and talk about the decorating scheme while they made dinner together. Rebecca actually found herself looking forward to the next day, because she now had something to occupy her time. She had the monumental task of turning this huge empty house into a grand home before Norman's return.

Long into the evening hours Shelly finally left. As soon as she walked out the door the atmosphere in the house felt flat and lifeless once more. Rebecca spent yet another night lying awake in bed waiting for dawn to chase away some of the darkness.

When morning came Rebecca called the youth center and asked if the therapist position was still open. Chuck was the supervisor on duty that day, and he informed her that the manager wanted to conduct the interview as soon as possible. She scheduled an appointment for that very afternoon. She no longer felt so conspicuous about being seen, because the only physical trace she had left from the incident was the cast on her right arm.

"Miss Graves," the manager greeted her as soon as she stepped into his office.

"Good afternoon Mr. Garcia," Rebecca responded.

"You're looking much better I see. How's the arm?" he asked.

"It actually doesn't hurt at all anymore, but I'll be in the cast for about two more months," she answered.

They took seats and Mr. Garcia launched immediately into interview mode. "Why do you think you'll make a good therapist here?" he asked.

"Well, I feel that the kids in this facility are unique, and I've had the opportunity to learn a lot more about them as a counselor than I would have learned if I'd started out as a therapist. I think that gives me an advantage when it comes to their individual treatment," she answered.

"It might also present a conflict of interest since you've worked with all of the girls. Some of them might think that those who get assigned to your case load are getting preferential treatment," Mr. Garcia answered thoughtfully. "What do you have to say about that?" he asked.

"I still feel that there are more benefits to hiring me as opposed to getting someone completely new. I've already been through all the initial training and I've become accustomed to this environment, so you can at least be assured that I won't quit because I can't handle the pressure."

"I was there when you walked out last month," he returned in a serious tone.

"I'd just seen a child die, and I was upset about the way certain other workers did their jobs. Miss Parker did not follow the rules in the company policy, and I know of several others who are the same way. I do not approve of their actions, and I didn't want to be part of a company that condones those actions," Rebecca replied just as seriously. Then she thought it prudent to add, "I wouldn't be here now if I hadn't heard of some of the changes being made to make this facility better, and I know I can contribute to those improvements."

"There is a ratio of staff to residents that we have to maintain, and if we go firing everybody we'll be in violation of state law. I don't always approve either, but the alternative is to shut the facility down or turn away patients," he said.

"Is that the same approach you take with therapist? Will you keep substandard therapists because there is a shortage of good ones?" she asked quietly.

Mr. Garcia gave her an odd look before answering carefully. "It's not the same with the therapists, because they don't have to spend as much hands on time with the residents. Also, the kids never give therapists a hard time. Only the counselors have it that bad. But to answer your question, the center is already trying to hire new counselors to replace those who can't do the job right. It's hard to find workers in this industry who won't engage in power struggles with the patients."

"I can't stay on as a resident counselor anymore, but I'd love to work as a therapist. I just finished with my master's in psychology."

Rebecca handed Mr. Garcia a typed letter from the university stating that she'd finished all the requirements for the degree.

"So, you meet all the requirements for the job, but it isn't entirely up to me," he said. He then cleared his throat before continuing, "I saw the tape, and I want you to know that what happened that day wasn't your fault. You did your job, and that was all we could ask. I know that a lot of staff around here feel guilty because they didn't prevent it, but the truth is that some things cannot be avoided. Even if they hadn't been roommates those two would've found a way to hurt each other. Shirelle was a victim of repeated violent rapes, and Ronnie was convicted of armed robbery and assault. All she knew was how to be a bully, and her entire personality was a trigger for Shirelle. Treatment team has gone over and over the tape from their room, and we've discussed it with the police. The psychiatrist is going to testify at her hearing. Doc thinks that Shirelle might be able to use the temporary insanity legal defense, because it's clear from the tape that Ronnie had said something to her to make her snap that day."

"Can I see the tape?" Rebecca asked thinking she might be able to clarify some things and help Shirelle.

"The police have it now," Mr. Garcia said. "But I can tell you what happened right before Shirelle threw the chair..."

"What happened?" Rebecca asked in anticipation.

"Shirelle was sitting at her desk writing, and Ronnie came up and snatched a paper from her and started saying something. Shirelle tried to get it back, and Ronnie backed away and grabbed her crotch. That's when Shirelle went back to the desk to sit back down. She had her head in her hands and she was rocking back and forth like Jenny used to do when she had flashbacks about the day her father shot her mother. Ronnie grabbed her crotch again and said something else, and Shirelle looked up at her and said something. That's when Ronnie yelled and you came running to see Shirelle throw the chair."

"Does anyone have any idea what Ronnie said to her? Did she tell anyone?" Rebecca asked.

"She claims she doesn't remember most of what happened, but we do have a copy of the paper Ronnie was holding when Shirelle threw the chair. The police kept the original as evidence," he explained. He went into a filing cabinet, and pulled out Shirelle's file. "Here it is," he said before thrusting it into her face.

Rebecca's heart skipped a beat. She recognized it instantly as the poem Shirelle had showed her the first time she'd talked to her about the rapes. "I've seen this before," she said. "Shirelle told me that she wrote this to get out all the hurt and anger she felt at her father, and she used to read it to herself a lot when she felt bad," Rebecca informed him. "I can't imagine how it felt to have Ronnie making fun of her about it."

"That's something her therapist would know more about," said Mr. Garcia.

"Thanks for showing me."

"No problem. We need to set up a time for you to have your second interview with Doc. All of the therapists have to get through me first, and you just did. What time next week is good for you?"

"First thing Monday," Rebecca answered quickly.

"See you then," he dismissed her with a smile.

The interview on Monday was mostly geared towards salary negotiation. The combined advantage of Rebecca's outstanding quarterly reviews and her performance on tape were actually more instrumental in getting her the job than her interview with the doctor was. The salary was a little less than she'd hoped, but it was decent. She would now be working Monday thru Friday from nine to three, and she would be on call one weekend a month. Compared to her previous hours the new ones seemed like a dream come true.

Shelly was ecstatic for Rebecca when she heard the good news.

"You won't be able to be a classroom volunteer any more... I'm sure the kids will miss you," Shelly said kindly.

"They probably won't even remember me," Rebecca said. The only kids she'd had extended contact with were Dylan and Peggy. "How is Peggy?"

"She's back with her mother now," Shelly answered.

"Did they ever catch the boyfriend?" Rebecca asked.

"Not yet. He's considered armed and dangerous though. He was caught on video robbing a convenience store at knife point."

"When did that happen?" Rebecca demanded in alarm.

"Just a few weeks ago over near Knoxville. He might have friends over there that he's hiding with," Shelly informed her.

"That's awful," Rebecca said. "I hope he doesn't try anything else with Peggy or her mother.

"At least this time Sharon knows what he is," Shelly replied.

They were sitting in a restaurant having lunch, and most of the midday crowd was waning by now. Rebecca took a sip of her drink, and when she looked back at Shelly she saw a strange expression on her face.

"What's wrong?" she asked.

Shelly didn't get the chance to answer before Rebecca heard Dylan saying from somewhere behind her, "Hi Aunt Shelly!"

Rebecca turned to greet the child, because she hadn't seen him in over a month, and she was immediately caught off guard by the sight of his mother. For the first time she was seeing Norman's ex-wife in the flesh, and it was quite a sight.

Shelly stood up and said, "Hi Julie, how are you these days?"

Julie smiled and said, "Just fine. And you?" in a cloying voice that instantly grated on Rebecca's nerves. "And who's your little friend here?" she pointed at Rebecca as if she were a child needing Shelly's permission to be introduced.

Rebecca opened her mouth to introduce herself, but Dylan beat her to it.

"That's Miss Rebecca. She helps me with my reading," he chirped.

"Well! I'm sure you won't mind if we join you then," Juliana said as she took a seat without waiting for a response.

"Where's Abigail?" Shelly asked.

"She's with her father. He's getting deployed soon, so he took leave to go see his family back in California. Abby went with him, but I couldn't go. I would have loved to get some of that California sun though," she sighed a bit dramatically.

Rebecca listened to Juliana and Shelly as they talked amongst themselves. Juliana had summarily dismissed her as unimportant in the blink of an eye. She even managed to keep the conversation totally centered on herself, ignoring Shelly's many polite attempts to change the subject.

It wasn't hard to see why Norman must have married her. She was a drop dead gorgeous woman. She was the epitome of the ideal classic beauty that western civilization seemed bound and determined to impress upon the entire world. Juliana's face could have graced the cover of Vogue, Cosmopolitan, Rolling Stone, or any other popular magazine.

Her honey blond hair caught the light just right, and Julie sure knew how to flip it in such a way as to make every man in the restaurant take notice. Her eyes were a pure light blue that stood out against her tanned skin. Her body was toned and feminine and she knew how to flatter her already perfect figure with the perfect clothes. There was nothing dowdy, mousy, or mismatched about her appearance, and she knew it. Juliana fairly glowed with the sexiness that only a truly confident woman can exude.

"So I've got an appointment with the tanning salon in about an hour, and I thought since I ran into you that you might be able to watch Dylan for me. He hates having to wait," Julie said. Rebecca sat at the table and silently reflected on what a knockout her husband's ex was.

"I actually have plans for this afternoon," Shelly began only to be interrupted.

"It'll only take about an hour, and I'll pick him up as soon as I'm done this time. I'm not going to the spa...just the tanning salon," Juliana pleaded with a pretty pout.

"Why don't you just reschedule?" Shelly suggested sensibly.

Julie looked at her like she must have lost her mind. Rebecca had to suppress a chuckle at Julie's look.

"You know, I always liked you Shelly, and when Norman and I get back together I'll be sure not to mention that you'd rather not spend time with your own nephew..." she said sweetly.

"Aren't you with Abigail's father now?" Shelly demanded in outrage.

"Mom, I need to go to the bathroom," Dylan interjected at that point.

"Go on Honey," Julie said in an even tone as her eyes shot daggers in Shelly's direction. As soon as Dylan was out of earshot she hissed, "That's not your business," in a venomous voice.

"There is no way in hell Norman's going to give you the time of day when he gets back from Afghanistan," Shelly said.

"We'll just have to see about that? Won't we?" Julie said as she flipped her hair again. "Things have changed. He called me last night, and I can always tell when a man wants me back," Julie boasted.

Rebecca was stunned. How could he have called his ex-wife before he called her? She hadn't heard from him at all, and she'd had only the memory of him walking into the shadows the night she'd dropped him off. It had been more than a month, and he hadn't called her. But he had called his ex-wife?

"That's not true and you know it," Shelly said. "My brother just got remarried, so there's no way he'd call to try and patch things up with you.   He doesn't even like you anymore," she continued forcefully.

"He's *what*?!" Julie demanded in disbelief.

"I guess your invitation to the wedding got lost in the mail. This is Rebecca Gregory. In addition to being a licensed, clinical therapist, she's also Norman's wife. We were celebrating her new job when you showed up," Shelly informed her with barely contained relish.

To Rebecca's credit she did not flinch or look away when she met with Julie's astonished gaze. She was however, painfully aware of the other woman's perusal. She knew that all Julie saw was a short woman dressed very plainly. In fact, Julie so discounted Rebecca's presence after the first glance at her that she seemed to have forgotten she was even sitting there.

"You expect me to believe he married her?"   Julie said scathingly.

"It's true," Rebecca said with an awkward smile.

"Talk about a step down," she muttered as she looked down her perfect nose at Rebecca. She managed to maintain her disdainful expression until her eyes alit on the huge diamond engagement ring twinkling on Rebecca's finger. Rebecca knew that it was way bigger than the one he'd given Julie when he'd been a mere sergeant. He'd told her about how he'd saved up for months to get Julie's ring, only to have her chastise him about the size of the diamond. Jealousy crept into Julie's expression as she stared at it.

"You know, maybe it is a good idea for me to take Dylan for the afternoon. That way he can start getting to know his new stepmom," Shelly said mercilessly as Julie sat transfixed by the ring on Rebecca's finger.

"No, I'll just take him with me," Julie said as she stood up to leave. She briefly looked around in confusion.

"He's still in the restroom," Shelly informed her in an arid voice.

"I knew that," Julie snapped as she walked off. Men turned to stare as she passed by with her hips swaying, and her large breasts bouncing to some inaudible beat.

Rebecca and Shelly simply looked at each other, but that single look spoke volumes.

"Why do you think Norman called her and not me?" Rebecca finally asked.

"Don't believe a word she said. If Norman hasn't called you yet, he hasn't had the chance. He hasn't talked to me or Dylan since the day he left and there is no way he called her and no one else," Shelly insisted. "Furthermore, she's a pathological liar. She's still with Abby's father, who she cheated on my brother with, and that poor sap is still enthralled with her looks. She and I have never liked each other, and the only reason she came over here was to foist Dylan off on me so she could go pamper herself...as if she needed more pampering," Shelly gritted out in sheer exasperation.

"It's okay, Shelly. Really," Rebecca tried to console her sister-in-law.

"How can you sit there and say that after the way that woman just insulted you?" Shelly said.

"Well, she had a point...look at me. I can't believe Norman took a second look at me. Juliana is way better looking than I am," Rebecca said.

"You shouldn't be so down on yourself," Shelly admonished her. "The only reason everyone else thinks Julie is so beautiful is because she thinks she's all that. If you walked around like you were queen of the world men would look at you exactly the same way."

Rebecca didn't even attempt to make a response.

Later that night Rebecca stood in her huge closet surveying her meager wardrobe. Her clothes took up less than one tenth of the space available, and there were very few items that could be considered fashionable. The nicest things she owned were the green dress she'd worn the day Norman proposed and her wedding dress. Shelly had helped her pick both of them.

She tried on a few of her clothes and sized up her reflection, not liking what she saw. Suddenly the phone interrupted her fashion show, and she ran to answer it hoping it was her husband.

"Hello," she said in breathless anticipation.

"Hi Rebecca," her mother's voice said.

Cece sat on the edge of her bed and twisted the phone cord round and round her finger while she tried to come up with something to say to her daughter.

"Hi Mom... I mean, hi there," Rebecca said hesitantly.

"You can call me mom," Cece said, remembering the last time they talked. Had she really screamed at her own daughter not to call her mom ever again? How could she ever make up for that? "I'm sorry I didn't come to your wedding," Cece said quietly. She wanted to apologize for so much more, but she just didn't know where to begin.

"Don't even worry about it. You can meet Norman when he gets back from his deployment," Rebecca replied.

"I didn't miss it because I didn't want to come." Cece thought about what she'd done after their last conversation. She'd taken the entire bottle of pills, intending to end her own life. If her long time employer Mrs. Lee hadn't thought to check on her when she failed to show up for work for the first time in more than twenty years, she wouldn't be alive right now. Following a lengthy stay in a mental hospital she'd found an invitation to Rebecca's wedding in her mail, but the wedding date had already come and gone by then.

"It's okay Mom... really. How have things been for you lately? Have there been any more big fights for you or Karen?"

Karen was Cece's only friend, and she too was a fighter like Cece. The difference was that Karen was a famous full-time mixed martial arts fighter, and Cece only did Judo and Muay Thai style kickboxing on a part-time basis when she wasn't working at the bakery. "Yeah, Karen has one coming up pretty soon. It's going to be on pay-per-view in a few weeks. She'll be defending her title out in Vegas, but I'm not going to that one," Cece informed her.

"How's everything else?" Rebecca asked with a great deal of concern in her voice.

"Just fine," Cece hedged. "Why do you ask?" she said despite the fact that she knew Rebecca wanted to know more about the secret Cece had let slip the last time they'd talked.

"I care about you... and last time we talked you got pretty upset. I don't blame you for any of those things you said. I understand how you could feel that having kids ruined your life. I'm sorry I gave you such a hard time when I was asking you all those questions. You know, if you ever wanted to talk about what happened to you I would be glad to."

"How can you be so understanding? I've never been able to comprehend that about you," Cece whispered as tears came to her eyes. She'd never been all that nice, yet she'd somehow given birth to a daughter who took kindness and understanding to extremes that she herself could never identify with.

"One of the girls I worked with is in jail on a homicide charge right now because her roommate said the wrong thing to her. When she was ten her father started letting a drug dealer rape her so that he could get his drugs for free. This girl is an awesome person, but certain things triggered her to act in an ugly way. She just needs some time to heal, and I understand that you need some time to heal too."

Rebecca's gentle willingness to listen encouraged Cece to open up some. "I've always just pushed it to the back of my mind, so I could get through the daily business of survival. I guess I never realized how much it was eating me on the inside. Sometimes I feel as if there's almost nothing left... You know when you're a single parent you can't afford to be depressed or hurt, so I put it out of my mind so I could work and train harder. And look what good it's done for me. I have a daughter who I barely know, and all I know how to do is bake cakes and cookies. Can you believe that I used to want to be a doctor?"

"You can still be a doctor," Rebecca said encouragingly.

"I'm thirty seven years old, and I don't even have a GED. I feel like I've wasted so much of my life working and fighting just to distract myself," was Cece's sad reply.

"How come you never went back to school when we were younger?" Rebecca asked.

"At first I couldn't. I had two new babies and no place of my own to live, so I had to hang on to the job I had until I'd saved enough to get a place. I had a job and I didn't want to jeopardize it by asking my boss for time off to go to school. By the time you and your sister were old enough to go to school I thought it was too late. I thought that nineteen was too old to go back to school to earn a GED, so I just kept working... and then I met Karen and started training with her all the time. I made so much prize money from the tournaments I entered, I forgot all about going back to school. Now when I think about it I feel so foolish. If I had just gone back then, I could have a college degree like you right now. And you'd be proud of me instead of afraid of me. Now that I have more responsibility I love my job, but when I first started Mrs. Lee wouldn't let me touch the cakes. All I did was scrub the floors for years."

As she told Rebecca about her feelings, Cece allowed the tears to flow unchecked down her face, but she gave no indication in her voice that she was crying. She didn't like the idea of anyone seeing her cry, ever, not even her daughter. Right now she really wished she felt as okay as she wanted Rebecca to believe. In truth, she was struggling through a deep depression. She'd never been able to get over what happened to her, and now she fully recognized just how damaging her own private pain had been to her daughter. She never should have told Rebecca she hated her. Those words had been an outright lie meant to push her away so she would stop asking so many difficult and painful questions. Even while in the hospital after her suicide attempt, Cece hadn't told the therapists or the psychiatrist the truth. She'd only told them what they needed to hear to let her go home.

"Mom, I'm so sorry about what happened to you. I just wish you had talked to me about it sooner. That's too much to deal with alone. I may be young, but I understand a lot better than you think I do. I care... I love you."

I love you too, Cece's heart whispered, but she couldn't get the words to come out of her mouth. "You take care of yourself," she said in a gruff voice that didn't betray her secret tears. Her daughter really deserved better, and she hoped that whoever she'd married truly deserved her.

Chapter 18

Rebecca's first week at work went nothing liked she'd expected. She'd just assumed that she would have teenage girls on her case load, but on her first day she found out different. She was the new therapist for the boys aged six through twelve. Currently there were only seven of them living at the center, and Rebecca had never worked with them. She'd only ever seen them in passing, and she knew none of their names.

She spent an entire day going through each of their files before she set up their initial appointments. What she saw was heart wrenching. One little boy had been sexually assaulted and sodomized by his own father, and he now had a tendency to attack other kids. Sometimes without warning he would attempt to strangle his roommates. Most of the time he had to be within arm's length of a resident counselor to protect him and the other young boys. Two other boys were there because they had no parents and were waiting for a suitable foster family. They all needed therapy to deal with their past and present issues.

Rebecca wanted to be as thorough as possible in her new position, so she even took extra time to analyze the daily behavior sheets from the past month for each boy. What she saw was very disturbing. The resident counselors who spent all day with these little boys had recorded more than ten restraints in the past month. She was now in the position to ask why, and expect an answer rather than an argument. She also had the authority to recommend that certain children on her caseload be exempt from restraints. That knowledge kept her in a good mood long into the night that night.

The next weekend Rebecca attended her first FRG meeting. At first she'd told herself that she was only going to find out why Norman hadn't called yet, but when she got there she admitted she was also curious to see what some of the other soldiers' spouses were like. She'd been told that her husband would be able to call after a couple of weeks, but it had been more than two months. She really wanted to know what was up with that.

During the meeting it became apparent that she wasn't the only one who wanted answers. So many women were demanding answers from the FRG leader that the poor woman actually broke down in tears in front of them.

"I'm waiting to hear from my soldier as well ladies," she said tearfully. "Please don't think that this is an oversight on my part. When they call is completely out of my hands, but I did get a report from the commander via email that suggested they were in a communication blackout due to some imminent threat in their area. As soon as they are allowed they will call home," Christine Worthington said.

Rebecca felt deep sympathy for Christine as she sat in the alternately hostile and tearful group. Christine had a huge load on her shoulders from the look of things.

When the meeting was over, Rebecca stepped out of her comfort zone and introduced herself to Christine.

"Hi," Christine said a bit warily.

"Hi there," Rebecca began with what she hoped was a friendly smile. "I just came over to introduce myself. I'm not a formal member of the FRG, because I just got married a month before my husband left... I'm afraid I don't know anybody, and I just wanted to rectify that. My name is Rebecca."

"I'm pleased to meet you Rebecca. As you know, I'm Christine but everyone calls me Christie. I'm the head of the company FRG. The company commander Captain Worthington is my husband," she said.

"My husband mentioned that sometimes the FRG does activities, but he didn't say what kind. I was wondering if I could sign up to volunteer to help out with some of those," Rebecca said.

"We mostly just do meetings and potlucks, and we keep track of those who have special needs and do whatever we can to help and support each other," Christie said with some hesitancy in her voice. "About once a year we have a series of self defense classes, but those are getting harder to schedule because of all the spouses needing child care. Other than that we don't do many activities that the younger wives like yourself think are fun. I'm always open to suggestions though, so feel free to leave a note in the suggestion box or email me or whatever."

"Okay I'll do that," Rebecca smiled. She clearly recognized that she'd been dismissed as unimportant. Christie had given her a look that bordered on disdainful when she'd mentioned helping out.

Usually the younger wives tended not to get too involved in the FRG, and Christie was in her thirties and used to seeing spouses who looked more like herself joining the volunteer path. During first deployments lots of young wives said they were going to help out, but then they never did. The wives of young soldiers on their first deployment also tended to call her at all hours of the night wanting to know what was happening with their husbands and expecting her to have all the answers. Christie was too used to that sort of disappointment to get her hopes up about Rebecca.

"Is that all?" Christie asked dismissively.

"Yeah, that's all," Rebecca said as she signed her name on the volunteer list. She looked surprised to see only three other names.

When she started to walk away Christie glanced down at the list and her heart skipped a beat as she recognized the last name. She'd just been borderline rude to a superior officer's wife, and experience had taught her long ago what a bad move that was.

"Mrs. Gregory!" she called out as she scrambled after Rebecca. "I just remembered that we're going to be scheduling video teleconferences for next month, if you want you could help out with that," this time she injected a lot more kindness into her tone.

"What all will I have to do?" Rebecca asked.

"Just send emails to everyone on the list with the attachment giving details, and when they respond schedule them in an open time slot. I'll have to turn in the list by next Wednesday so that their soldiers can be scheduled accordingly, but I have no idea if they'll actually be able to go through with them. I wish I knew when they are going to call, but I don't," Christie ended with a sigh.

"I can handle that," Rebecca assured her. "Where's the list?"

Christie let out a pent up sigh of relief at Rebecca's smile. Maybe Rebecca wasn't as bad as some of the officer's wives Christie had met over the years, but she still didn't want to get her hopes up.

Before bed that night Rebecca sent out emails to over a hundred people on the list about the VTC. After a full week at work, and what felt like a productive start as an army wife she fell asleep a little easier than she had previously. She still lay awake for a while wondering what Norman was doing, and how Shirelle was holding up in her jail cell. Nothing could take away her concerns, but she felt some peace knowing that she could do something to make small differences in her world.

When the gray morning light of an overcast day shone gently in her window the next morning, she opened her eyes still feeling eerily tired. She struggled to get out of bed despite the early hour and the fact that she had the day off. She didn't know why she couldn't just lie down and go back to sleep. It was as if some unknown force compelled her to start the day early.

Once in the kitchen she turned on a pot of coffee as she gazed out the window to the front drive. The sky held an almost winter-like grayness to it. There was no semblance of autumn outside her window.

While the coffee brewed she noticed a dark car pulling into the front part of the circular drive. It had tinted windows, and it definitely wasn't anybody she knew. It sat there for a few minutes as Rebecca stared out the window in curiosity. As she thought about the fact that she hadn't heard from her husband in almost three months, her curiosity slowly turned into dread.

With a sick feeling, she watched the doors all open at the same time and the occupants step out. Norman's words rang in her ears as she recognized the faces coming to her front door.

"Rebecca, if anything happened to me you would be the first one notified," he told her when they'd filled out the emergency notification form. "Whoever you put on this paper will come with two officers of the same rank as me or higher... oh, and a chaplain will be with them. If you don't see those people at the door, then please don't worry about me," he'd said.

Now she was standing in her robe and nightgown staring at a chaplain, two colonels and Shelly, the person she'd put on the form, all walking somberly to her door. She knew something had happened, and all she could think as she watched Shelly's stoic face approaching the door was, "Oh God, please don't let him be dead."

She ran to the door and opened it before they even knocked, and the look on Shelly's face said it all.

"Mrs. Gregory your husband made the ultimate sacrifice for his country last night," the chaplain said right after Rebecca let them inside.

Although she already knew, hearing the words still impacted her. She sank down to the floor in deep despair and there was a loud ringing in her ears as the two stony faced colonels and Shelly reached out to catch her.

She could hear her own voice as if from far away saying, "No, this can't be happening," over and over again as the ringing in her ears grew louder and more persistent.

A moment after the darkness engulfed her she groggily became aware that there really was a ringing. It was the phone waking her up from a terrible dream.

She sat up in bed and grabbed the phone, relieved that it wasn't actually morning and she wasn't actually getting news of her husband's death.

Rebecca wiped her tears away as she said, "Hello," into the receiver.

"Becky," Norman's voice greeted her. It was the only voice in the world that could have consoled her after such a harrowing dream.

"Norman! I'm so glad to hear your voice!" she exclaimed in intense relief. "You have no idea how good your timing is. You just woke me up from having the worst dream of my life," she told him.

"How are you?" he asked.

"I'm doing great. I took your advice and joined the FRG, and I got that therapist job I'd applied for a few months ago. What's going on with you? How come you couldn't call sooner?"

"We just got our own equipment set up, and before that we were living in tent city with access to only a few phones that could be used for personal calls. The average time spent waiting in line for a five minute phone call was two hours. I was busy or I would have called. I really, really wanted to call you sweetie," Norman replied.

"Do you only have five minutes to talk now?" Rebecca asked.

"No, we can talk as long as you want," Norman said.

"How is it over there?" she asked.

"Hot, crowded, and lonely without you," Norman answered succinctly.

"Are all the other soldiers in the company going to get a chance to call home soon?" Rebecca asked.

"Yeah, I think most of them did earlier," Norman informed her.

When she didn't immediately say anything he asked, "Are you okay?"

"Yes," she lied. "Other than missing you, things are going pretty good. I'm really enjoying the piano you gave me, and Shelly and I have gone shopping for furniture a few times. My new job is super great, and the hours and the pay are ten times better than before... Oh! And my mom is talking to me again now," she said with a bit of false cheer. What she'd really wanted to say probably would have bothered him. She didn't want to bother him with how much she missed him, and how hard it was to sleep since he's been away, and how after Ronnie's death she really needed a strong, broad set of shoulders like his to lean on.

"How are you enjoying your piano?" he asked.

"Very much."

"No, how is it possible with a broken wrist?" he clarified.

"Oh.... So you know about that?" Rebecca asked with a sinking feeling.

"Yeah, I saw a story about it on the local news via the internet. I saw a clip of you walking into the building looking like someone tried to kill you," he said mildly.

"So, if you saw the story then you know all about why I missed seeing you before you left," Rebecca said quietly.

"I know about that, but what I want to know now is, are you okay?" the concern in his voice made her want to break down and cry and tell him just how far from okay she felt sometimes.

"I'm doing fine," she lied instead.

"Then why do you sound like you're about to cry?" he asked gently.

After that it was impossible for her not to open up to him a little bit. "Because I miss you, and what happened at work was extremely hard on me. I think I allowed myself to get much too attached to Shirelle, and it hurts that her life may be over because of one terrible mistake. I also can't get the image of Ronnie's head busted open and surrounded by blood out of my mind. I have so much trouble sleeping now that I hardly feel like myself anymore...."

"I wish I could be there with you right now Honey. You know I love you," he said even as he felt all the frustration of being unable to give her physical comfort rather than just words.

"Thanks Norman. I love you too, and I promise I'll be fine. Things are still raw right now, but maybe after a few more weeks I'll feel much better," she tried to assure him.

"No one's going to think any less of you for being hurt over this. You don't have to be so brave all the time," Norman admonished gently.

"Shelly's been incredibly nice since you left," Rebecca changed the subject.

"That's good. She really likes you a lot, you know…"

"Well, she comes over almost every day, so I figured she must enjoy my company. We did a bit of furniture shopping together, and I'm going to start with the master bedroom."

"I'm glad to hear it," Norman responded. He wanted her to cry on his shoulder and tell him all about her troubles, because he knew she was deeply disturbed by the recent traumatic events in her life. She just seemed so reluctant lean on him.

"You know, we can talk about what happened if you want," he offered carefully.

"It's all I think about lately, especially at night, but I'd rather not bring you down talking about it. You have enough to worry about right now," she sighed.

"Rebecca I love you. You are my wife, and I'll always have room in my life for your concerns. I want you to lean on me. I'm strong enough to handle it honey. Is there anything I can do for you?"

"There is something I've been thinking about," she said hesitantly.

"Whatever it is the answer is yes," he said fervently.

"You haven't heard the request yet… it's actually kind of expensive," she said.

"I'll still say yes, so go ahead and tell me. I won't think any less of you for wanting a new car or whatever. Things like that make lots of people feel better when they're going through a tough time."

Rebecca hesitated for a fraction of a second before she said, "I want to ask my mother to come stay for a while so she can start college, and so we can spend some more time together. I don't think it's a good idea for her to live alone right now." It wasn't what she'd really wanted to ask, but she'd changed her mind at the last second.

"I really appreciate the fact that you asked, but that's not something that you ever had to ask for. If I'd known she didn't have a

degree I would have suggested it myself," Norman said in surprise. "Was that all you wanted?"
"Yeah, that's it.   There's nothing that I really need," she sighed.

Her words made him feel the beginnings of guilt because he wasn't there with her now. Maybe she couldn't recognize the vulnerability in her own voice, but he definitely did. She did not sound like the same Rebecca who was able to talk herself up the big hill. Instead she sounded like she was just going through the motions of encouraging herself. Her tone lacked conviction, so she probably didn't really believe that things would get better soon. That was a dangerous state of mind for any woman to be in, especially a woman whose husband was in a war zone.

"Rebecca will you promise me that you'll tell me if you need anything. There's always something, even if you haven't thought of it yet," Norman said.

"I promise," she replied.

"What else has been going on since I left?" he asked after a few moments of silence.

"I met Juliana," she chuckled.

"Really.... When did that happen?"

"A week or so ago. She's very beautiful."

"She's just superficial. You are beautiful. You're at least ten times prettier than she is," Norman felt it prudent to say.

"She was going on about how you want to get back together with her, and then Shelly told her we were married. It was hilarious. At first she didn't believe you would marry someone like me, she called it a step down. Then she got all huffy and left," Rebecca recounted the incident with a great deal of humor.

"That sounds just like her. She's been saying we're getting back together since she got bored with old what's his name. It *is not* going to happen," he stated emphatically.

"I know... You have me now," Rebecca quipped.

"While you're joking about it, I'll just tell you that it's true. You're my ultimate fantasy girl, and Julie has absolutely no chance of getting me back. If you ever left me, I'd spend the rest of my life alone begging you to come back to me," Norman joked. When he heard the difference in her voice he made an extra effort to keep her laughing. He looked around his drab and cramped quarters as he held the phone to his ear. Her laughter was the best sound he'd heard in a few months and he smiled to himself as he imagined her face.

When they got off the phone Norman put on his protective gear and grabbed his weapon as he went back to work. He was leaving to go on a convoy to help another unit with a network security issue they were having. He had a lingering smile on his face that stayed in place for the remainder of the day, and that night he fell into the first peaceful sleep he'd had in months.

The first phone conversation was the one that boosted his spirits the most, but the subsequent nightly talks with his wife were the food for his soul that kept him from missing her too badly as the months dragged on.

Chapter 19

"I still can't believe the self defense classes were cancelled," Christine said to Rebecca shortly before the FRG meeting was scheduled to start. They had both worked hard to schedule classes for almost fifty women including free child care for those who needed it, and at the last minute the instructor had cancelled with no explanation.

"He didn't give any reason at all?" Rebecca asked.

"Nope. And this is the most people we've had sign up for anything in a long time. They're going to be pretty disappointed..." apparently Christie was dreading tonight's meeting. Her brows were furrowed and she kept pressing her lips together.

Rebecca wanted to tell her that it wouldn't be that bad, but she realized that she had no right to try placating her. Maybe it *would* be that bad. She couldn't forget how dramatic the first meeting she'd attended had been.

She found out twenty minutes later that the situation was that bad. Besides the outright anger that was directed at Christie, the looks from the wives who were just disappointed were pretty guilt inspiring. Many of the young wives who were stay at home moms had two or more small children and didn't often get the opportunity to take time for themselves and have someone watch the children for free. To them the cancellation of self defense classes was doubly disappointing.

"Ladies, I'm so sorry...." Christie repeated over and over again during the course of the meeting. The ladies were going to have to find another way to occupy their Saturday afternoons for the next few months.

"You want to go get coffee with me?" Rebecca asked when the meeting was over. "I'm meeting my sister-in-law at that new coffee shop that just opened up on Wilma Rudolph Boulevard. I'm sure she'd love to meet you."

"Sure," Christie said. One thing she knew as an officer's wife was that you do not refuse an invitation from the wife of a superior officer.

Rebecca and Christie were discussing the disastrous meeting when Shelly walked up to join them.

After the introductions Shelly sat down and said, "Have you two considered asking someone else to teach the classes instead?"

Christie seemed intrigued by the suggestion.

"The only problem with that is that I don't know anyone else who can teach self defense classes for free... I'd scheduled classes before with the same guy for self defense, because he works as a martial arts instructor at the Y. He does it as a hobby and doesn't need money, I don't know any other instructors like that," Christie explained.

"Rebecca might," Shelly offered.

"Oh? Really?" Christie asked hopefully. She looked to Rebecca for an answer, but Rebecca was too busy eyeballing Shelly to give her one.

Since she and Shelly had been spending so much time together, Rebecca had gotten into the habit of talking about her mother. Less than a week ago, she'd told Shelly a little bit about her mother's background as a kick boxer. She'd fought in amateur tournaments when Rebecca had been too young to know what was going on, but after she'd gone pro she no longer attempted to hide her secret passion for fighting. She'd even attempted to teach Rebecca the fundamentals of the sport. Rebecca had been a sore disappointment to her mother though; she wouldn't have hurt a fly back then. She still winced when she remembered some of the things her mother had yelled at her during those grueling training sessions.

"You're never going to get anywhere in life if you keep acting like such a damn wimp!" Cece had yelled as Rebecca started crying during one of her training sessions. "Keep your hands up!"

"Yes ma'am," Rebecca had sniffed as she'd attempted to block yet another barrage of attacks from her mother. Cece had been going way easier on Rebecca than she ever did on her opponents in the ring, but that hadn't made it any less traumatic for her. At the end of those matches Rebecca had often walked straight home so she could cry alone and wonder why her mother seemed to hate her so much sometimes.

"I bet she'll do it. All you have to do is ask her... The worst she'll say is no," Shelly prodded, interrupting Rebecca's thoughts.

Rebecca pulled out her cell phone, but she looked at Shelly one more time before making the call, "Are you sure *you* don't know anyone?"

Shelly shrugged, "I sure don't."

Rebecca bit her lip in consternation. Her mother may be talking to her again, and attempting to get closer to her, but that didn't change the fact that she wasn't exactly a sweet person. She was actually incredibly intimidating, and she had impossibly high standards, especially when it came to her martial arts training. Rebecca imagined her mother would be frightening to a class full of *nice* women; she'd probably treat them the same way drill sergeants treated new privates in basic training. It had the potential to be a disastrous situation. "That's not the worst she can say," Rebecca mumbled under her breath as all those thoughts passed through her head, but she made the call anyway.

After Rebecca stepped out to talk to her mother, Christie turned to Shelly and asked, "Who is she calling?"

"She's calling her mother."

"Rebecca's mother can teach self defense?" Christie demanded in surprise.

Shelly smiled and said, "She can do a lot more than that... she actually has a fourth degree black belt in Judo, and she's a professional kick boxer."

"*Rebecca's* mom? Rebecca is so sweet and timid I can't imagine her mother being a professional fighter... have I ever heard of her?" she asked.

"Her name is Cece Graves...She's not real well known. According to Becky she likes to keep a low profile; she's been working in a bakery making cakes for more than twenty years now, I guess she doesn't want to lose her day job," Shelly told Christie.

Christie was about to ask even more questions when Rebecca returned.

Rebecca sat down with a stunned look on her face and said, "She'll do it."

"Why do you look so surprised?" Christie asked.

"She lives in Nashville, and she works every day, but she didn't have any problem driving down here when she gets off work every Saturday. She actually seemed excited about doing this. She just needs directions to the Y," Rebecca smiled.

"About that...." Christie said with a grimace. "The venue was cancelled as well. We were going to do it at the Y, but since the instructor cancelled they already scheduled the next few months of aerobics classes in the room we were going to use," she explained.

"This can still work out," Shelly insisted with a pointed look in Rebecca's direction.

Rebecca didn't immediately get the hint.

"I know there might be someone who has extra room that they're not using..." Shelly continued as she nudged Rebecca's foot under the table.

"Yeah, I'm sure I could find someone," Rebecca said hesitantly.

By this time Christie was giving them strange looks, and probably wondering what she was getting herself into.

"It's okay if this doesn't work out. I'm sure I can schedule something else that the ladies will like, it's just that the self defense has always been the most popular activity," Christie said.

Shelly shot Rebecca an apologetic look before she said, "Rebecca has a huge room in her house just perfect for these classes."

"Oh! Right... Of course I do. I actually have a few of those, because we don't have furniture yet. Yeah, we can use my house. Parking won't be a problem, but I will have to print out some maps for directions. It's kind of out there," Rebecca was quick to respond.

After Christie left, the first words out of Shelly's mouth were, "You are so dense sometimes." Her warm smile and playful tone took the sting out the words.

"What made you think of my mother?" Rebecca demanded.

"She knows Judo, and isn't that one of those martial arts that's mostly about self defense?"

"Yeah, but..."

"But what?"

"I don't know. I just wouldn't have thought of her if you hadn't suggested it."

"Well, I don't know why not... from what you've told me about her she seems like a very interesting person, and I also suggested it because I'd kind of like to meet her," Shelly admitted.

"My mother isn't all that interesting. She does the same thing every day. Her routine has never changed, not in more than twenty years... she is a good fighter though."

The following Saturday Cece arrived at Rebecca's house for the first self-defense class. Cece had never seen the house before, and as Rebecca let her in she looked around with wide eyes taking in the expansive home.

"Why in the world would you choose to live in a house this size? Didn't I teach you anything about being wasteful?"

Rebecca looked up at her mother and smiled. It felt like forever since she'd seen her, and she didn't want the visit to start on a bad note. "You did Mom, but Norman bought this house before he ever met me. Someday I'll convince him to move into something smaller and more economical." By now she knew just what to say to take the wind out of her mother's sails...most of the time anyway. She escorted her mother to the kitchen and gave her a bottle of water. They sat in silence for so long Rebecca started to get restless.

"Thanks again Mom, for doing this," she said just to fill the silence.

"It's no big deal," Cece said. And then they were silent again.

Rebecca released a sigh of relief when she saw Christie's car coming up the long drive.

Christie stepped out of her car looking like she was expecting the worst. Rebecca opened the door and invited her inside.

"Well, there's certainly enough room..." Christie said in awe as she stepped into the grand two story foyer. "This place doesn't look nearly this size from the front," she continued as Rebecca led her down the hall to the kitchen.

"I know. Norman said that's one of the things he loves so much about this property," Rebecca responded.

Over the next fifteen minutes all the other ladies showed up and were escorted to the kitchen, where they stood around drinking bottled water and talking. The class didn't begin until four o'clock. By then everyone had had the chance to mingle and get to know her mother a little.

Rebecca had never had any type of social interactions with her mother, and she saw for the first time ever that Cece could be nice and likeable. Everyone in the house seemed to find her fascinating, and they looked at her with obvious admiration. They were all shocked that Cece was her mother, but Rebecca was used to that reaction from people. She and her mother looked nothing alike. Cece was about half a foot taller, she had lighter skin, strikingly gorgeous facial features, and a very athletic body. There was a time when Rebecca would have given anything to have people look at her the way they looked at her beautiful mother; Cece was certainly not the type of person you could ignore. In comparison to her mother Rebecca had always felt bland and insignificant. She stayed in the back of the room behind everyone else as her mother took command and showed the ladies one of the basic fighting stances in martial arts.

That night after everyone else left, Cece and Rebecca retired to Norman's sitting room. They spent some time catching up on the significant events they'd missed in each other's lives. Rebecca showed her the wedding album, and the finish line photo she'd received after running in the Music City Marathon. Cece barely gave the pictures in a wedding album more than a polite, sparing glance... but she did seem to be impressed by the marathon photo.

"I didn't know you had it in you," Cece smiled at Rebecca.

"I didn't either, until I tried," Rebecca admitted.

She and Cece sat in silence for a long time. There seemed to be so much to say, yet neither of them could find the right words. Rebecca was on call that weekend, so she wasn't planning on going to bed. She usually just dozed on the couch when she was on call. Cece reclined on the couch and watched television while Rebecca stretched out and fell asleep next to her. Rebecca was in the middle of a sound sleep when the phone rang. As she jumped up to answer it she noticed that her mother had left while she was sleeping. The call was from the nurses' station at work. There was a problem on the teenage girls' unit, and since she was the on-call therapist, she had to deal with it. She hadn't been on the girls' unit since the day Ronnie had been killed.

"What's going on?" she asked Fred as soon as she stepped into the building.

"Diamond and Kanicker jumped on Jenny, and now the other girls are threatening them," Fred answered.

"That's quite a change... I thought they ran things around here," Rebecca commented in surprise.

"That was before Ronnie died. Now they kind of stay to themselves..."

"Thanks," Rebecca said on her way down the hall.

She found Diamond crying in one timeout room and Kanicker sitting silently on the floor of the other. She decided to talk to Diamond first.

"What do you want?" Diamond asked as soon as Rebecca entered the small six by six foot room.

"I want to know why you and Kanicker jumped on Jenny," Rebecca got right to the point.

"Because she said she was glad Ronnie got her head busted open," Diamond said. She looked at Rebecca with a piercing red eyed stare before continuing, "You're glad too, aren't you?"

"No!" Rebecca was quick to reassure the child. "Of course I'm not happy about that."

"She's the only person who ever loved me, and no one likes me now. I hate this place, and I want to go home," Diamond sobbed as she banged her head against the wall.

Rebecca grabbed her shoulders and said, "Don't do that unless you want to end up in a restraint."

Diamond continued to sob, and her attempts to slam her head against the wall grew more violent. Rebecca had no choice but to initiate a restraint.

Her trip to the youth center hadn't yielded any tangible results. Diamond and Kanicker were still deeply depressed, and Rebecca had placed them on suicide watch. She'd also placed them in protective custody to keep them safe from the other girls on the unit. They had to sleep in the infirmary right next to the nurses' station, and they weren't allowed to have any shoestrings or personal items with which they could attempt to harm themselves. She stayed about an hour in her office filling out the proper paperwork, and typing a briefing for the treatment team to read during the morning meeting first thing Monday.

As the on call therapist she'd been able to diffuse the immediate danger to the girls, but she knew that the real root of the problem was too deep for just one person to solve. Shelly's words of advice from the day they'd discovered the bruises on Peggy's back replayed in Rebecca's head as she drove home. So far she hadn't truly helped one child at the youth center, but she wasn't ready to admit defeat and fall into the rut of simply doing the same job day after day whether it yielded results or not. That refusal to be a cog in a machine was the very thing that Shelly thought would burn her out eventually.

Chapter 20

As winter drew closer Rebecca stepped up her running. She wanted to run in the Nashville marathon again in the spring, so she put herself back on the same training schedule she'd used last year. She ran early in the mornings before work each day, and she did her long run for the week every Saturday afternoon while her mother taught the self-defense class. She told herself that she didn't chose to run on Saturdays just to avoid her mother, but no matter how many times she told herself it never rang true. Seeing her mother being so nice to all those other women when she'd been so cold and demanding to her struck a raw nerve. How could Cece be normal with everyone else except her own daughter? Even as the thought passed through her head Rebecca felt guilty, because she already knew the answer. Of course her mother couldn't stand her...would probably never be able to stand her. She was a living reminder of the rape. It didn't matter if she were the greatest daughter who ever lived; she'd never be able to overcome the circumstances surrounding her conception.

She stopped to walk when she got to her private drive. From the highway she had to walk almost another mile uphill to get to her house. The sun had set just moments before, and the temperature dropped quickly as darkness descended. Usually by the time she got home all of the women were gone, and her mother was on the way out the door.

She wiped sweat from her face as she stepped into the garage entrance at the side of the house. Her mother's car was still parked out front, and Rebecca called out for her as she made her way to the kitchen.

She made a beeline straight for the sink to grab a glass of water, and was caught off guard by a cake sitting on the counter. It was a small cake, but it was exceptionally beautiful. It looked like one of the cakes that her mother frequently decorated for special occasions and weddings.

The cake was covered with a flawless layer of pastel yellow rolled fondant, and decorated with a multitude of hand-made gum paste flowers. Cece always made perfect cakes, and Rebecca had admired them for years... but this was the first one she'd ever made for her daughter. Rebecca looked down at the cake and smiled. This was the first birthday gift she'd ever received in her life.

"Mom, this cake is awesome!" she called out, but Cece didn't answer. Rebecca was about to call out again when she caught a glimpse her mother's tail lights disappearing down her driveway through the kitchen window. She sat down on one of the stools surrounding the island and stared at the cake. Most of the flowers where various shades of lilac, her favorite color.

When she finally got up for a knife to cut a piece she noticed the envelope tucked under the edge of the cake board. It contained a birthday card with a note from her mother. The note read:

Dear Rebecca,
I know you haven't had very many happy birthdays with me, but I hope this one is good and I hope they continue to get better as the years pass.

Rebecca read through the note several times before it sank in; it was so at odds with the way her mother normally treated her. This was the first time her mother had ever made a nice gesture towards her. Growing up, Rebecca's relationship with her mother had been very perfunctory. There was never an over abundance of kisses, hugs, or other forms of affection. Cece looked down on anything frivolous, and that included gifts and birthday parties. There had never been any sort of celebrations, not birthdays, not Easter, not Independence Day, not even Thanksgiving or Christmas. At the bakery all she did was make specialty celebration cakes and treat customers like they were her best friend as she took their orders, but at home she'd lived a sparse and regimented life with her daughter, unable to engage in the more nurturing side of parenting. She'd been almost like two different people. Rebecca cut into the cake. It was a moist, delicious raspberry filled confection that melted in her mouth. She enjoyed every bite.

By the time the self-defense classes ended, winter was upon them. As the days grew shorter and colder Rebecca couldn't keep her thoughts off of her husband. Just last February their relationship had started in earnest, and this February she really missed him. He'd be home again in six months, but six months seemed like a lifetime away.

The winter months took the longest to drag by, but by late spring Rebecca had made progress in many areas of her life. After the self defense classes ended her mother still came and spent Saturday afternoons with her. Neither of them spoke much during those visits, but there was a significant amount of communication that went on in ways that weren't so obvious. Cece helped Rebecca with housework, and even went running with her sometimes.

Even the monumental task of furnishing her home was almost complete; she'd finally broken down and hired a decorator after what seemed like her and Shelly's millionth trip to the furniture stores.

If she had done it all herself Norman would have ended up with an overly feminine house, and Rebecca was nothing if not fair. The only room Rebecca had insisted on doing herself was the master suite. By late spring the house looked nothing like it had when Norman first left for Afghanistan.

"It looks so awesome," Shelly assured Rebecca as she walked around the house with her in what the decorator called the final walk through.

"Do you think Norman will like it?" Rebecca asked. She was a bit apprehensive because he would be home in about three months, and he had no idea what to expect. She'd offered to send him pictures of all the samples so he could have some input, but he'd told her he wanted to be surprised.

"I think he's going to love it," Shelly replied warmly. "I especially like what you've had done to his sitting room. I think he'll be pleasantly surprised."

Rebecca hoped Shelly was right. She'd had Norman's small sitting room completely redone. She'd had the walls painted a deep indigo color that matched the color of the midnight sky, and she'd also taken the liberty of having all of his photos framed and hung on the walls in artistic groupings. The main change she'd made was to have a creative light design applied to the ceiling. In dim lighting the ceiling appeared to be a replica of the night sky complete with stars that twinkled and a few shooting stars that left glittering trails of light in their wake.

When the decorator left Shelly and Rebecca went into the master suite.

"I wanted to show you this one in private," Rebecca explained. No one had set foot in the room since she'd finished it.

As soon as Rebecca opened the door her eyes flew to Shelly's face to gage her reaction to the room.

"Compared to the rest of the house it looks so simple... but I think I like this room the best," Shelly said as she looked around.

"I did this one myself... the painting, the molding, and I even installed the wall speakers without help," Rebecca said.

"I don't see any speakers on the wall," Shelly said as she looked around in puzzlement.

"I know! It's so cool isn't it? They're the kind that you put inside the wall, and then cover them up so you can't tell," she explained.

"It looks very relaxing... you know? I think Norman will like it."

"Good, because I didn't want to have a bunch of elaborate decorations in here spoiling my favorite thing about this room," Rebecca admitted.

"What's that?" Shelly asked.

Rebecca walked over to the bay windows and drew back the drapes to reveal the remarkable view of the woods behind the house.

"That is a nice view."

"I know. I stare at it every morning. I especially liked watching the new leaves start to bud," Rebecca said as she sat down on the edge of the perfectly made bed. Tears came to her eyes as she imagined enjoying this room for the first time with Norman. She hadn't seen him in so long he seemed almost like a romantic dream she'd had long ago. She didn't have any snapshots of him to remind her of how he looked on a daily basis. All she had was the photo album from their wedding. In those pictures he looked like a fantasy man, almost too good to be true.

Shelly sat next to Rebecca and put an arm around her small shoulders.

"You miss him don't you? But at the same time you're so nervous about his return that you don't know what to think... I felt the same way when it was time for Jake to come home from his first deployment," Shelly said.

"I just don't know if this is right... I feel like he rushed into things with me because of this deployment. You know, a few of the other women in the FRG talked about how their boyfriends got all romantic and proposed before the deployment. We even had a class about it," Rebecca sighed before she continued in a worried tone of voice.

"Apparently, Norman's proposal is nothing out of the ordinary for a man who is about to be deployed. We were even warned not to expect the same type of 'overly romantic' treatment when our husbands return. I think maybe the pressure of the deployment got to him, and he was too hasty in marrying me."

"Why would you think that?" Shelly asked.

"He never said he loved me before he got those deployment orders. He always used the word like. How would you feel in my shoes? Especially with the gorgeous Juliana wanting to get back with him..." Rebecca said.

"I can see why you'd feel some doubts, but the fact that he actually married you, not just proposed but actually made it official, speaks volumes about his feelings. He wouldn't have married you unless he'd already been thinking about it for some time, and I happen to know for sure that he had been thinking about it," Shelly informed her.

"How do you know?" Rebecca asked.

"Because he tells me everything.... You have no idea do you?" Shelly said with a touch of humor.

"About what?" Rebecca asked.

"My brother has been in love with you since he first kissed you." At Rebecca's look of pure disbelief she elaborated, "Yeah, he actually fell that fast and that hard. You should have seen him the day after he saw you playing the piano in the rec. center. He'd told me all about this mystery woman who he liked, but she disappeared on him when he kissed her... he meant you. Remember when we talked about how he acted once he found out you worked as a volunteer in my classroom? He was practically beating down my door to find out more about you. He told me he was falling for you right around the time you two started running together again. I think he did rush things a little, but only because he didn't want you to get away. Anyway, if he ever thought of leaving you to get back with that viper ex of his I'd slap him myself," Shelly said.

Rebecca chuckled and hugged Shelly.

"Thanks," she said after they both stood up.

"I'm serious Becky. Too many good relationships end because of unnecessary doubts and fears. Don't be one of those insecure women who drives a good man away because she never gets it... He respects you, he trusts you, he adores you, and he wants you in his life. That's all you need to know to ease your mind."

The next month went by in a whirl wind of activity and preparations. Rebecca and Shelly kept busy planning a welcome home party for Norman. The guest list was to include their entire extended family, plenty of friends, and even Rebecca's mother.

Cece and Rebecca managed to learn much more about each other than they knew before. Rebecca often reflected on how it was possible to live with someone for 17 years and know all of their personal habits, yet know so little about who they are as a person. Before, she'd seen her mother as simply cold and overbearing, but now she was coming to see her in a different light. Rebecca still wasn't sure if her mother actually liked her now, or if she was just being nice because she still felt guilty for having been so mean before. Either way, she had to admit that there was a noticeable difference in the way they interacted.

One of the biggest changes occurred the first time Cece had set foot in the music room. Rebecca had followed her in and watched as she'd looked around the room. When she'd finally noticed Rebecca standing in the doorway she'd asked, "You still like to play around with the piano?"

Rebecca almost lied and said that the piano belonged to Norman. She didn't want to hear the disapproval that she'd grown up with, so she froze. There was a tense moment of silence before Cece said, "Do you mind playing something? I haven't heard you play anything for a long time... I remember how you and Sarah used to play with the piano in the church while I was there cleaning."

Rebecca sat down at the piano bench, and for the first time in more than ten years she played something for her mother. At first she wasn't sure what she should play, but then she remembered the one piano piece that her mother did like. It was a piece she'd memorized long ago. As soon as she played through the first measure of Franz

List's Hungarian Rhapsody Cece's face lit up in recognition. She sat in one of the chairs and stared at Rebecca as she played flawlessly for the next fifteen minutes. When the private performance ended Cece had only one thing to say.

"I had no idea you could play like that. I'm sorry I gave you such a hard time about it when you were younger."

Rebecca wanted to ask why she'd been so vehemently against allowing her to take lessons, especially since they could have easily afforded them, but she didn't want to ruin the moment. She simply smiled and said, "Thanks," instead.

With about a month left before Norman's unit was scheduled to return Rebecca often found herself filled with excess energy. She needed something to keep her mind off of Norman's huge welcome home party, so she hung out with Shelly most of the time. Shelly spent many of her evenings visiting and helping out young single mothers in the community who needed a friend. Some of them she'd met through school, and some of them she'd met at play dates scheduled by the local social work services.

Sharon Bellefonte and Peggy were among the families that Shelly and Rebecca visited frequently. They had been doing much better since Sharon's recovery. They'd moved into a nice apartment in a better neighborhood, and Sharon had landed a job as a secretary after she received some vocational training. Peggy even had some nice clothes to wear to school that year. Peggy was no longer a student of Shelly's, but Shelly kept in contact because Sharon had requested it. Shelly had managed to become something of a mentor for the struggling single mother.

"I'm going over to Sharon's this evening," Shelly announced one Friday while she and Rebecca were having lunch.

"You've been going over there a lot lately. How's the new job working out for her?" Rebecca asked.

"She just got her first raise and she wants to celebrate, so I thought it would be nice if we all took her out for dinner someplace nice," Shelly replied.

"That sounds like a great idea, but my mom was supposed to come over tonight. What time did you want to meet up? Maybe I can have dinner with you guys before she gets here," Rebecca said.

Shelly rolled her eyes and said, "You're so funny sometimes! I wanted us all to go out together, especially your mother. I've been wanting the two of them to meet ever since you told me all about how she started over all by herself after her parents threw her out. Sharon has been down a lot lately, and I think it might help to see someone successful who had a rough start like she did."

"I never thought of my mother as an inspiration... at least not to anyone other than me."

"Well you should. Look at everything she's done," Shelly said.

"Okay then," Rebecca said brusquely. "What time and where are we meeting up?"

"You sound so businesslike.... Just swing by my place and pick me up after your mom makes it to your house. No point in wasting gas, right?" Shelly smiled.

"Is Peggy coming along to?"

"Yeah, it's going to be like a girls' night out except we have to be home before bedtime." Shelly's mood was incredibly light because it was almost time for the soldiers to return. The entire town had an atmosphere of nervous anticipation and restrained delight. "Man, this party for Norman is really going to be something. Too bad Julie has to come. I feel like she's got some sort of tricks up her sleeve.... There's no way she really thinks Dylan won't feel comfortable there without her. She is such a snake."

"We'll deal with that when the time comes," Rebecca changed the subject. "I'll see you later."

The ride to Sharon's apartment was peaceful and quiet. Shelly was content to stare out the passenger side window with a slight smile on her face as she thought about her brother's homecoming. A part of her rejoiced on Rebecca's behalf while another part of her ached. She still remembered the homecoming from the year her husband Jake had been killed in action. His death had occurred only two months into the deployment, and she'd thought she'd made remarkable progress in dealing with it during the many months that followed... But when the rest of his unit had returned to the joyous cries of their spouses and family members she'd felt the pain of loss all over again.

Rebecca's thoughts were of a similar nature in that she too was thinking of her husband, but her thoughts strayed into the realm of trepidation. She was in no way looking forward to the big gathering that she and Shelly had been planning. And she was absolutely dreading the fact that Norman's gorgeous ex-wife was to attend.

"I wonder why her door is open," Shelly's voice interrupted Rebecca's thoughts as they parked.

"She probably saw us pull up, and wants us to come right in," Cece volunteered.

"Sharon! We're here!" Shelly called out as the three of them approached the door. There was no answer, so Shelly pushed the door open and walked in.

Rebecca and Cece followed only to find themselves staring down the barrel of a gun as the door slammed shut behind them. Shelly stood still, frozen in shock as she gawked at the man who'd been hiding behind the door.

Chapter 21

The three of them stood motionless for what seemed like an eternity before the man spoke.

"Sit down and shut up," he snapped.

Shelly and Rebecca quickly complied, but Cece passed out in a dead faint. They both jumped to their feet to go to her aide, but the man shouted, "I said sit DOWN!" as he aimed the gun in their direction.

Rebecca trembled in fear, but she didn't sit down again and neither did Shelly. Instead they clung to each other as they gaped at Cece's small form crumpled on the floor.

The man then stomped over and delivered a vicious kick to Cece's stomach. When she grunted and started gasping for air he said, "She's alright."

He looked back at Shelly and Rebecca and let out an eerie sort of laugh. It was a half maniacal, half nervous sort of sound that revealed ugly brown teeth and terrible breath. His appearance was incredibly disturbing. His hair was long, greasy, and matted to his head, and he had scars and a multitude of bloody scabs on his arms and his head. At best he looked haggard and infectious.

"What's going on?" Cece asked as she gingerly lifted herself to a sitting position on the floor.

"What's going on?" the man mimicked in a falsetto voice as he made a threatening motion as if he were going to strike Cece across the face with the gun. While he appeared to be making up his mind as to whether or not he would hit her, a sound from behind the couch stopped him.

Shelly, Rebecca, and Cece all turned in unison when they heard someone moaning in obvious pain. A bloody blanket covered someone who was apparently now just waking up. When retching sounds started coming out of the blanket the man walked over and yanked it off to reveal a severely battered Sharon. She was tied up, gagged, and obviously choking on her own vomit.

"Take that thing out of her mouth before you kill her!" Shelly commanded.

The man did as Shelly instructed and seemed to ignore the rest of them for a while. He knelt down by Sharon. "You okay baby?" he asked in a cloying voice once the retching had subsided.

Sharon turned her head away from him. He then grabbed her chin and forced her head back towards him. "Why do you always provoke me? You know I don't like havin' to do this! You know I don't! All you had to do is come with me so we could be happy baby," he crooned out in the intimate tones of a lover.

"I just want you and Peggy to be happy. I just want us to be happy baby."

Sharon started crying again and her face contorted in obvious anguish, but she looked him straight in the eye as she choked out, "Where's Peggy?"

"Now sugar," he crooned as he kissed her on the lips. "You know I wouldn't hurt her. She's up in her room."

Sharon moaned again in disgust, but she didn't turn away from his kiss. She seemed completely powerless to the terror that gripped her. Her eyes grew wide and wild like those of a frightened animal until she looked up and noticed Rebecca, Shelly and Cece.

"Oh God..." she whispered. "What have you done Earl?"

"I was just gettin' ready to take you and Peggy home when they came bustin' up in here like they own the place. Now I need some time to think. No one was supposed to see us."

"Earl, I ain't goin' nowhere with you!" Sharon screamed. "Help!" she shouted. "Help!"

Earl jumped up and grabbed Shelly's hair. "Shut up! Before I kill her!"

Shelly cringed and squeezed her eyes shut as Earl thrust the gun into her temple.

"Oh God!" Shelly sobbed. He held onto her for what seemed like an eternity before Sharon stopped screaming.

"That's better," Earl gritted out as he shoved Shelly back towards Rebecca. "Now be quiet so I can think!"

Shelly, Rebecca and Cece sat quietly on the couch as he paced the room muttering to himself for several hours. Anytime one of them moved too much he would point his gun at someone's head and tell them to be quiet so he could think.

Once darkness descended, Peggy came to the top of the stairs. "Mommy, I'm scared," she called out into the almost pitch blackness of the apartment.

"Can I come downstairs with you?" she pleaded.

"Fuckin' brat," Earl muttered as he turned on a small table lamp.

After sitting in the dark for hours, all the women had to shield their eyes from the painful brightness.

Peggy didn't wait for permission. She plodded the stairs and ran over to her mother. Surprisingly, the child didn't have any visible bruises.

Sharon and Peggy sat on the floor looking gaunt and drawn as Earl approached them. Peggy shrank from his touch when he reached out a hand to ruffle her hair.

"What exactly are you trying to do Earl?" Cece suddenly asked. "You know you can't keep us all here forever. Eventually someone's going to notice we're missing."

"Mom... shhhh." Rebecca hissed in her mother's ear, fearful that Earl would become enraged again. He was a known meth addict, and he was apparently in some sort of extended drug induced mania right now. It could be days before he got tired enough to make a mistake or let them go.

"Maybe I'll just kill you all."

Cece didn't talk again for a few hours.

The night dragged on into eternity as Earl alternately paced and tried talking to Sharon. She remained bound on the floor in her uncomfortable corner with what looked like a broken nose and quite a few bruises on her body, yet she steadfastly refused to respond to anything Earl said.

As the night dragged on and his aggravation mounted he switched to making threats and waving his gun around more.

"Why can't you just talk to me baby?" he'd plead. Then in the next minute he'd bark out, "I oughtta kill you, you stupid bitch!"

Peggy clung wordlessly to her mother through most of the ordeal.

For most of the night, Shelly, Rebecca, and Cece also sat in silence, until Earl finally reached his breaking point.

"You're gonna talk to me Sherri. I'm not lettin' you see Peggy again until you do." Then he snatched Peggy up, and dragged her dangling by one arm to a chair across the room.

Peggy screamed in pain, and Earl slapped her hard across the face with his gun. Everyone watched in mute horror as blood trickled out of a small cut across the child's pale, bruised cheek.

Rebecca and Shelly subconsciously rose halfway out of their seats, but then Earl aimed the gun at Peggy's head and said, "Sit... down....," in a steely voice.

They slowly sat back down, and Earl took the gun away from Peggy's head.

"You call yourself a man? Hitting a poor defenseless child like that?" Cece said in a low shaking voice.

"Shut up lady!" Earl said as his grip on Peggy tightened.

"Why don't you just let her little girl go?" Cece pleaded in earnest.

"Shut *up* lady," Earl repeated.

"Why don't you just let Peggy come sit over here with us? We'll keep her quiet."

"Shut up!" he screamed at the top of his lungs as Peggy sat in frozen terror on his lap.

"Mommy," Peggy whined. "Mommy, his thing is poking me."

"You get your damn hands off her! You child molester!" Sharon screamed at that point.

An ugly sneer spread across Earl's face as he said, "You wanna watch don't you? My last girl liked to watch too."

"If you touch her again I'll kill you!" Sharon screamed as she began furiously kicking and struggling against her restraints. Her head slammed against the wall several times as she tried to wriggle her way towards Earl and Peggy.

Rebecca reached toward Sharon when it became apparent that she was about to injure herself further, but Earl vaulted forward and slammed the gun into Rebecca's skull with a sickening thud that sent her to her knees. Sharon continued to kick and struggle as Rebecca knelt stunned on the floor with blood dripping from her head.

"You wanna talk shit and give me trouble?" Earl shouted directly in Cece's ear as he butted her in the face with the gun. He then did the same thing to Shelly.

"You wanna talk shit?!" he continued to taunt them as he grabbed Peggy and roughly yanked at her pants. "Talk shit now!"

Rebecca and Shelly watched on in dizzy horror as Earl started to touch Peggy.

"We have to do something," Shelly said.

"What can we do? He has a gun, and we can all end up dead.... including Peggy..." was Rebecca's pragmatic reply.

"Mommy?" Peggy whispered. Earl reached for his belt buckle and started unbuckling his pants.

"Talk shit now..." he taunted as he fought to maintain his grip on Peggy, his pants, and his gun.

Peggy almost managed to break free from his grip, and when he turned his back for a second to get a tighter grip on her his gun was momentarily pointed away from the child. Cece capitalized on that small opportunity and lunged at him. She made a mad grab for his gun hand, and a second later Rebecca and Shelly dizzily followed her lead. He relinquished his hold on Peggy in an attempt to fend them off. Peggy scrambled over to her mother, curled up into a ball and closed her eyes.

During the brief struggle that ensued Earl ended up on the bottom of the pile. He still had a solid grip on the gun, but Cece had managed to get a grip on his gun hand. She was straining to keep him from pointing it at any of them when it went off.

The sound was oddly muffled, and not nearly as loud as Rebecca would have imagined it would sound in the small apartment. No one screamed, but there was an ungodly, deafening silence that settled suddenly over the room. Earl went completely still, and his eyes grew wild again as he shot a terrified look around the room.

When Cece attempted to stand up a bright red bloodstain was visible on the front of Earl's shirt, but instead of staying down and waiting for help he jumped up and dashed out the front door. Rebecca sprinted after him and managed to tackle him to the ground. She brought him down with the same protective hold that she'd learned from working at the youth center, and she felt sheer elation when she was able to hold him. The adrenaline rush from the brief scuffle had given her strength she didn't know she had.

"What's going on out here?" a male voice shouted from the apartment next door.

"Call the police!" Rebecca panted as she struggled against Earl.

"I already did!" the man shouted back as he rushed to her aid. "Did this guy hurt you?" he asked. Earl continued to struggle, and when he almost broke free the man slammed his knees into Earl's back.

"Yeah, but he's been shot..." Rebecca said. "He was holding us hostage all night and he tried to kidnap your neighbor and her daughter."

"He sure don't act like he's hurt," the man grunted as Earl continued to struggle against his knees.

Earl let out another sickening, maniacal cackle. "I ain't," he panted, "I shot that bitch though!"

Rebecca glanced down at him in confusion, until it occurred to her who he was referring to. "No..." she breathed as she turned and ran back inside.

Shelly was kneeling on the floor next to her mother, and there was a growing blood stain completely covering her mother's abdomen. Cece's face had taken on a sickly grayish color that turned Rebecca's stomach, and she was shaking almost uncontrollably as she reached out her hand towards Rebecca.

"Don't move," Shelly chided as she wrapped a towel she'd found around Cece's wound.

Blood gushed out at such an alarming rate that Rebecca felt a sick, dizzy sensation in the pit of her stomach. She reached for her cell phone and dialed 9-1-1.

"I already called the ambulance," Shelly informed her. "They're on the way."

Rebecca dropped the cell phone and dropped to her knees beside her mother. She had to fight the absolute panic that threatened to engulf her as she took her mother's bloody hand. She looked into her mother's eyes partly because she knew that if she stared at the injury she would lose her mind.

Peggy and Sharon were still lying on the floor trembling and in tears.

"I'm so sorry about all this," Sharon kept saying as if the words and the sentiment could make the situation go away. She kept apologizing for the actions of her crazed ex boyfriend, but for the moment her apologies fell on deaf ears.

The police arrived within minutes, but the wait for the ambulance seemed like days. By the time the paramedics loaded Cece's nearly lifeless body into the ambulance the sky showed tinges of dawn, and the bloody scene inside the apartment looked all the more grotesque in the golden glow of the early morning sun.

Rebecca rushed off to the hospital to be with her mother while Shelly initially stayed behind to talk to the police. After a full account of the night's events an officer gave her a ride to the hospital. When she got there, however, she found that Cece had been taken by helicopter to the nearest level one trauma center in critical condition.

"She's still in surgery," were the first words out of Rebecca's mouth when Shelly walked into the waiting room several hours after Cece had first been picked up by the ambulance.

Shelly plopped down next to her and made no attempt at conversation. They were both too traumatized to try to rationalize the events or even how they felt at the moment. For the time being there were no tears, nor was there any relief. There was simply the deceptively blissful feeling of emotional numbness mingled with physical exhaustion.

The next day Rebecca found herself staring down at her mother in the intensive care unit of the hospital. The doctors had warned her that her mother's condition was extremely unstable, so there was still a significant possibility that she would die. They gave her a list of so many things that could go wrong that she scarcely allowed herself to hope on her mother's behalf.

She spent most of the day simply sitting beside her mother's bedside and holding her hand. She tried not to look at all the tubes, wires, and medical equipment surrounding her mother, but it was a difficult task. The rhythmic sound of the ventilator hooked up to the patient in the next bay managed to put her to sleep for a while. When she woke again she sat caressing her mother's hand and whispering soothing words in her ear. The doctors had put her in a drug induced coma, but Rebecca talked to her anyway.

Rebecca had always seen her mother as something of a super hero. She'd always been so strong, so capable and it was shocking to see her in such a vulnerable position now. Rebecca had never even seen her mother down from a cold before, and it broke her heart to see her mother lying in the hospital bed barely clinging to life. Cece didn't look fearsome or intimidating at all right now; she looked so small and damaged it was scary.

Childhood memories that she didn't know she had surfaced all day during the course of her vigil, and years of resentment melted away under the weight of the present situation. Now that she was faced with the imminent possibility of losing her mother, she realized just how much she loved her. She thought about the nights immediately following her twin sister's death and about how her mother had slept with her. She thought about how she'd woken up many nights to find her mother's arms around her, and how she'd been able to go back to sleep with a secure feeling. Her mother had been there for her in so many ways that she'd failed to notice until now.

Rebecca allowed her mind to drift back to the day she'd graduated from high school. Cece hadn't talked to Rebecca once about how she should pay for college, and Rebecca, thinking that they were poor, had joined the military partly for the college money bonus. She'd lied and told her mother that she wanted some adventure, but she had really been worried about asking her mother to help her pay for college. In fact Rebecca had been reluctant to ask her mother for anything back then.

"I have something for you," Cece had said matter-of-factly as she'd reached into her pocket and pulled out an envelope.

Rebecca had expected to see a card with a check for a small amount included, instead there had been a bank statement to an account in her name. She'd looked at the balance in pure disbelief.

'Where did you get so much money from?" she'd asked in wide eyed wonder.

"Have you ever seen me spend money on something we didn't need?" Cece had replied.

Rebecca had looked down at the balance again, and then she'd looked back up at her mother's impassive face. There had been no smile nor had there been any warmth in her eyes. She'd just handed her daughter almost a half million dollars, and she hadn't even looked the least bit excited about the reaction.

"Now you have no reason to fail," Cece had said as she'd turned and started walking home. Rebecca had silently followed her mother, and not another word had ever been spoken about the money.

The sight of Shelly standing at the foot of the bed snapped her back to the present.

"Becky, you need to get some sleep. You've been up for almost three days straight, and you still have on those dirty clothes," she said gently.

Shelly had cleaned up and had the wound on her head from Earl's gun stitched and bandaged. For the first time ever she actually looked a bit haggard. The previous night's events had obviously taken a toll on her. Rebecca briefly wondered if she looked as bad as Shelly did. She looked down and felt her stomach lurch at the sight of the copious amount of dried blood on her clothing….her mother's blood.

Tears fell unchecked down her cheeks as she said in a barely audible voice, "I can't leave her like this… She wouldn't leave me."

"You don't have to go far… I've got a hotel room that's close by, and I'll stay with her and call you immediately if anything changes."

After a bit more convincing Shelly managed to get Rebecca into a waiting car and on her way to a bit of respite from the hospital.

When Rebecca returned feeling somewhat refreshed she found that Shelly had been true to her word. She was sitting with Cece's hand against her cheek and her eyes closed. Rebecca was momentarily taken aback by the familiarity of Shelly's position, but she was also touched at the same time.

By the third day of Cece's hospitalization the doctors gave Rebecca more reason to hope. They said that she was still in critical condition but they also said that she was stabilized. The risk of infection was one of their main concerns for the immediate future.

As Rebecca stared at the tube coming out of her mother's chest and the bloody incision that the doctors had made to save her collapsed lung she thought about the incident with Earl. Shelly had learned from the police that Earl had only had one bullet in his gun. Only one bullet was all it took to destroy multiple lives, and the irony of it was not lost on Rebecca. Perhaps if they had all known he had only one bullet they would have handled the situation much differently.

It also turned out that Earl had been on the most wanted list because of the store he had robbed months earlier, and there had been a $20,000 reward for his capture. Money itself was a small consolation for what had happened to her mother, but the knowledge that the money was going to substantially better Sharon and Peggy Bellefonte's lives did put a bit of a silver lining on it.

Rebecca was holding onto her mother's hand lost in her thoughts when the sound of footsteps made her look up. She expected to see Shelly, but Norman stood before her instead.

She didn't ask him why he was home a month early, she didn't ask him how his trip was, she didn't even say hello; she just rushed into his arms and accepted all the comfort that he could give her at that moment. He pressed her to him almost painfully and she barely noticed the sound of the ventilator as he held her.

"It's okay to lean on me. That's what I'm here for," his deep voice soothed her.

Rebecca hadn't realized that she'd been crying until he'd spoken. Her emotional numbness wore off quickly in the safety of her husband's embrace. Her knees went weak and she started shaking as the shock of what they had been through set in. She was trembling and in tears as she choked out, "It hurts to see her like this. Oh God, it hurts so bad."

"I know sweetie. Shelly told me everything.... You don't have to talk about it until you feel ready." He sat down on the large chair beside the bed and held her in his lap. After she cried for a while exhaustion took over and she fell asleep on his shoulder.

Norman sat as still as he could. He was afraid that any little movement would wake his wife or disturb his mother in law. At first he looked at the wall and the floor... at anything other than the woman in the hospital bed. Every time he looked at Cece's face with the tube coming out of her mouth his arms tightened ever so slightly around Rebecca. His heart skipped a beat as he thought of how easily she could have been taken from him.

The days and nights that followed were of the long, difficult variety. Conversation was scarce because no one wanted to rehash the terrible events that had put Cece in the hospital, yet any other topic seemed trite and placating in light of what had happened. By the second week the doctors were optimistic enough to tell Rebecca that her mother was likely to recover, but not likely to walk again. After cutting a path of destruction through Cece's organs the bullet had come to a stop close enough to her spine to cause a shock to her spinal cord. The extent of the damage was difficult to assess, because of all the swelling in the area. The doctor wouldn't know how serious it was until the swelling went down.

Norman and Rebecca hadn't really talked at all since his return. She'd chosen to remain silent through most of the ordeal, and he had no idea how to deal with her unnatural stoicism. He could handle her tears, but he couldn't handle the dead look that had settled in her eyes and remained firmly in place since her initial tears.

He was standing just outside her mother's hospital room watching her as she watched her mother. There were slightly less wires and tubes than there had been when he'd first walked into the room two weeks ago. She looked up and caught his eyes with a hint of a smile, and his heart skipped a beat. There must have been some good news during his short absence.

"What's new?" he asked as he walked into the room.

"She opened her eyes a few minutes ago," Rebecca said in an almost normal tone with a note of hope and a note of sustained concern all rolled into one.

"Does the doctor know?" Norman asked.

"Yeah, he said that they're bringing down her dose so she'll start waking up."

Just then Cece's eyes fluttered open for a moment and she groaned a little as Rebecca looked down at her.

Nothing else happened for the rest of the day, but Rebecca vigilantly watched her mother for signs of consciousness. Norman stayed with her hoping and praying for a miraculous recovery.

Once visiting hours were over Norman had to leave the hospital to drive back home. He'd only been allowed to take two weeks of leave, and he needed to check with his unit about extending it so that he could be with his wife.

He hadn't been to his house at all since his return to the states, and the thought of spending the night alone in his comfortable bed while his wife slept in an uncomfortable hospital chair did not appeal to him at all. Instead, he spent the night on the couch in the staff duty office while the soldier on duty watched him with trepidation. He was used to intimidating the young soldiers, so he paid no attention to the soldier's discomfort.

"Just pretend I'm not here," he said as he shut his eyes.

After a night of restless dreams, Norman awoke to the sun streaming into the small window above him and the brigade rear detachment commander staring down at him in disapproval.

"What are you doing here? Don't you have your own bed?" she demanded.

"I don't have the keys to my house," Norman lied as he sat up.

"How's your mother-in-law?" she asked.

"She's going to live."

"Good. You look a little better than you did when you signed in. What are you doing here?" she asked again.

"My leave is up, and I came to beg for more."

"You didn't have to come in for that. You know you're high ranking enough to call in and extend leave over the phone," she said as she eyed him shrewdly.

Colonel Higgins was a six foot tall robust Hispanic woman. She'd had to stay behind during this deployment because she had been pregnant when they'd received the order. She'd had her baby already, but she still wouldn't be deployable again until the child was four months old. She'd known Norman for a few years, and worked with him off and on.

"Get out of here. I'll sign you in so you don't have to waste your leave, and your assignment is to get your wife some flowers. Call in every morning to give me a status report, and come back to work when you can. The main body won't be back for three more weeks, and the rear detachment doesn't need an extra lieutenant colonel hanging around... I can handle things here." She paused for a beat as her work hardened features softened into an uncharacteristically sympathetic look. Then it was gone quickly as she said, "And for the love of God, go shave!" on her way out the door.

The soldier on duty was struggling to hide a smile as Norman got up and left the building. He felt properly chastised because he hadn't thought to bring flowers once in the past two weeks. One of the things he remembered most about the weeks before his mother died was the fact that her hospital room had been filled with flowers. When he'd been allowed to visit he'd marveled at all the beautiful blooms, and his spirits had been comforted slightly by the fact that so many people had cared for his mother. Cece's room had no flowers.

When Norman got back to the hospital he was relieved to find Cece sitting up slightly and talking to Rebecca. He backed quietly out of the room to give them some privacy.

He walked down to the nurses' station and smiled at the nurse at the desk.

"How long ago did Miss Graves wake up?" he asked.

The nurse smiled the special smile that women typically gave him when they found him attractive and said, "She started waking up last night, and this morning she was sitting up and talking when we went in to change her bandaging. She's in a lot of pain, but she's handling it pretty well. The doctor is supposed to come for his rounds in a few minutes if you want to talk to him."

"Thanks," Norman said with a friendly smile, and then he turned and walked back toward his mother-in-law's room

He tapped on the door and waited until Rebecca told him to come in. Then he proceeded into one of the most awkward introductions of his life. Rebecca seemed to be in a better mood, but she was obviously exhausted. She'd lost weight over the past two weeks, and her clothes hung off her small frame in a way that tugged at his heart. She looked like she needed a big stack of pancakes and a steak.

Her mother looked way worse. Cece looked downright wary when he approached the bed, and he had no idea why.

"Mom, this is Norman," Rebecca said as they sized each other up.

Norman saw a woman who looked way younger than her age. He knew she was a year older than he was, but she looked young. At least she looked young until he made eye contact with her. He was completely taken aback by brilliant, clear grey eyes that mesmerized him for a few seconds. The depth of character in her expression was nothing short of fascinating, and he found himself feeling much like a child in her presence. It was easy to see why Rebecca had always described her as intimidating. There was hardness around her eyes and a sense of general mistrust in her expression which made it obvious that she'd experienced some painful things in her life. Norman felt intense relief when her eyes allowed him to look away.

Cece looked at Norman and tried to see what Rebecca loved about him. At first glance he looked every inch the military man he was. His face was set with stern angles, and he had an intimidating physique. The room fairly crackled with his masculine presence once he'd arrived, and she'd felt the same discomfort that she always felt in a man's presence. Only this time it was more mortifying, because she really didn't want to dislike her son-in-law. She wanted him to leave her room.

"Why don't you two go spend some time together? Don't hang around the hospital all day on my account," she croaked out painfully. She leaned back and closed her eyes and hoped they would go away.

When she felt Rebecca kiss her cheek and whisper, "I'll be back later," she relaxed in relief. The doctor came in shortly after they left and gave her the good news... and the bad. It seemed she was going to need a wheelchair until she learned to walk again... but she *would* walk again. The doctor had said there was a small chance, and she knew that a chance was all she needed to make it happen. There wasn't a doubt in her mind about her ability to recover. She was glad her daughter hadn't been around to see her cry.

Chapter 22

Cece lay in the hospital bed, unable to eat because of her intestinal injuries, unable to move her legs, and unable to fathom why such things happened. The crazy little man at the apartment had not really scared her all that much. He had been depraved and sick and a discredit to the human race, but his gun had been powerful...powerful like the gun from her childhood had been. She thought back to that long ago event and tried not to relive it as she'd done many times before. She tried her best not to remember the feel of the cold gun metal pressing painfully into her skin as he had tied her down. She tried to shut out the memories of the thickly matted chest hair scraping against her tender skin as she'd struggled against her restraints and against the repeated invasion of her body. She closed her eyes tightly against the memories, but found that the images in the dark recesses of her mind were far worse. Her eyes opened again, but the unwanted images continued to fill her vision.

Tears came as she fought through the panic that threatened to send her over the edge. A powerful gun had almost taken her life on two separate occasions, and now she lay powerless and unable to defend herself at all. She fixated on the door as she strained to move her legs. She told herself that she could do it by willpower if she just tried hard enough. She had to move before someone else got the opportunity to hurt her. Her desperation to move was so overwhelming she didn't hear the quiet, polite knock that sounded at the door, nor did she feel the searing pain in her abdomen as she strained her stitches.

When the knob turned, the blind panic she'd been fighting engulfed her and she clawed at the side of the bed trying to get away from *him*. Her legs still wouldn't move, but she managed to flop herself out of the bed as a strange man entered the room. She screamed out both in pain and in terror as a fresh blood stain started to grow on her hospital gown. The stranger put something down and rushed towards her, but she clung to the tangled sheets and wires and tried desperately to defend herself against him. When the nurses hurried into the room she collapsed in relief and exhaustion.

"From what we could see in the surgery, it seems like the infection started in her lower intestine. Her fall turned into a blessing in disguise, because if we hadn't had to fix the stitches we might not have caught it until it was too late. In addition to the intestine we removed in surgery, she's also had a dose of broad spectrum antibiotics, and we think it's best to keep her sedated for at least a few more days. Whatever is going on in her mind right now is causing her to fight too much to heal properly."

The doctor's words seemed to go in one ear and out the other as Rebecca stared down at her mother. Her mother was once again in the intensive care unit as she recovered from yet another surgery. This had been the third since she'd been hospitalized.

Norman stood with his arm around her and didn't say anything. He was solid, so she leaned on him and allowed him to hold her close. His comforting embrace was a strange place to be at that time. He didn't seem much like the same Norman she had married. He'd come back from his deployment looking more formidable than ever before, he talked less, and he smiled not at all. But his arm had been a constant fixture surrounding her with strength and warmth when she needed it.

"Let's step outside for a moment," he whispered in her ear before she realized she was shaking again. It happened so often these days that she failed to take notice anymore.

They walked the short distance to the outside seating area in silence.

"Honey, you can't keep doing this to yourself," he said as soon as they were alone. "You've got to get some sleep if you want to be strong for your mother. She's fine for tonight, and she won't even know you weren't there all night. The doctors said she's stable now," he reasoned with her as he rubbed her upper arms.

Rebecca looked up at him and shook her head. "You saw what happened when I left her alone today," she said.

"Honey, that was not your fault," he said emphatically. "And the doctor told me to take you away until tomorrow, because you're starting to look like you need to be a patient here," he added gently.

"Can't argue with the doctor," she sighed in resignation.

During the hour long drive home Rebecca fell fast asleep, leaving Norman alone with his thoughts. He hadn't slept with his wife since he'd returned, and the selfish part of him was glad he was going to be able to comfort her away from the hospital... for a little while at least.

When they got home, they went immediately into the master bedroom and slipped into bed, barely pausing to take off their clothes. In their exhaustion they didn't even bother to turn on the light to see what they were doing.

"I know it may not seem like it now, but things will get better," Norman said as he settled with his arms around her.

"I'm okay Norman. It's my mother that I'm worried about," she returned in a sensible tone.

It seemed like she wasn't ready to talk about it, so he kissed the back of her neck and let her rest. After a few minutes he felt her tears on his arm, and he wanted the power to make everything right for her. He felt all the frustration of knowing that the physical comfort he gave her paled in comparison to the comfort of knowing that her world would make sense again.

The following morning Norman awoke to find his wife staring down at him with a stricken look upon her face. He immediately sat up in concern.

"Did something happen with your mother?" he asked.

"No, but what happened right here?" she asked as she reached out and touched the jagged scar that ran across one side of his chest. He had hoped to avoid this confrontation for at least a little longer.

"Why didn't you tell me you were injured?" she asked.

"Because you had so much going on, and I didn't want you to worry about me. Do you remember how upset you were when I left? Imagine if you'd known about this.... It would have made your life even more stressful," he explained.

"What happened?" she persisted.

"It was a mortar attack that struck near the sleeping tents one night when we first arrived. There were a few injuries, but no one was killed," he said as he reached out to hold her hand. It felt cold and lifeless as it lay curled inside his hands.

"Is that why you didn't call me for so long when you first left?" she asked.

He hadn't really expected her to figure that out, but he was honest with her, "Yes. I was in the field hospital for awhile, and I didn't want to have to lie to you."

As he sat holding her hand he thought back to the night of the attack. He'd been lying awake in his cot thinking about all the upcoming work to be done when he'd heard the unmistakable wail of the sirens. He got up to run towards the bunker with the other occupants of the tent when the mortar hit. He'd been momentarily knocked off his feet by the force that shook the ground and the sudden explosion of pain in his chest. The company commander had been running right beside him, and he'd been hit in the leg. Norman had rushed over to him to help him up before he realized how serious his own wound was, and although he had initially assisted Captain Worthington it was the captain who was supporting him when they finally took cover at the bunker. He'd lost so much blood he was beginning to lose consciousness.

"Norman, just lie still until the medic comes. You'll be fine man," the captain said to him.

"Don't tell my wife about this," was the last thing Norman said before he slipped into unconsciousness.

Luckily the mortar attack hadn't lasted long, and he'd been rushed to the field hospital in time to get a life saving blood transfusion. It had also helped that he had the most common blood type. He'd never tell his wife how close he'd actually come to bleeding to death.

She was staring at his scar now, and he had no idea what she was thinking. He'd expected anger; he'd hoped for anger, but the look of hurt that was in her eyes when she finally did look at him caused a guilty knot in his gut.

"We've both been through so much this past year I feel like we're not even the same people anymore," she finally said into the silence.

"We're not," he said as he caressed her hand. "Our experiences cause us to change and grow every day. I think this past year has made us both stronger people, but that was a strength that helps us to deal with life without each other. Now we need to grow stronger together. That mortar attack is just a memory now, but it still affects me. Sometimes I wake up in a cold sweat terrified it will happen again, so I know how it feels to go through a painful experience. Trust me to understand what you're going through right now... talk to me about it."

He brought her hand to his lips and kissed her palm as he held her gaze with his. When she closed her eyes and leaned towards him to kiss the scar on his chest he felt his body come alive in response to her gentle touch. This was what he had been longing for during these past twelve months without her. He'd spent months in a harsh land dealing with the worst part of humanity. He'd kept his feelings in check while doing his job, but while he'd slept he'd often dreamt about the profound pleasure that can be found in a gentle touch or a simple kiss. Now that his wife was in his arms rather than just his dreams he felt as if his body and soul were experiencing healing on a whole new level.

She gently pushed him back until he was lying down, and she knelt beside him and massaged his chest as if assuring herself that he was still whole. Her hesitance seemed born of a reluctance to hurt him, and he smiled a little as he watched her. She rubbed his shoulders, his neck, and his temples until he felt incredibly relaxed and incredibly aroused at the same time.

When she leaned down to kiss his chest again he finally just pulled her into his embrace for a searing kiss that let her know exactly what direction his thoughts had taken. She wrapped her arms around his neck and kissed him back with the same intensity.

He rolled her over so that he was now the one on top giving out the gentle massage. It was as much for his benefit as it was for hers. His fingers touched every inch of her skin, warming her, calming her, and causing all her sensitive areas to long for more. When he finally did move between her legs she was so aroused that she had her first climax almost as soon as he entered her. He kissed her deeply as the pulsations surrounded him, and he began to move when she calmed down. He made love to her slowly after that. Watching the changing expressions on her face as the tension built within her after each thrust. When he felt his own orgasm nearing his entire body tingled as their rhythm became faster and more intensely carnal. Sensations had taken over, and he could barely think as he felt the explosion of a year worth of pent up sexual tension nearing. He couldn't control his reaction as the wave finally crashed over him, causing him to thrust deep one final time and call out her name as he held her tightly to him.

After their lovemaking was over he still felt intense pleasure just lying next to her. They held each other without speaking for almost an hour. Eventually he looked down at her to suggest they go eat some breakfast, and she smiled up at him. It was the first time she had smiled like that in a long time. He kissed her tenderly, and proceeded to give her something else to smile about.

By the time the sun was fully up they were both satiated and lying in each other's arms with the sheets tangled around them.

"I suppose we should get out of bed sometime soon," Norman yawned as his arms tightened around her.

"Yeah we probably should," she agreed, but neither of them made a move.

The sound of the phone suddenly interrupted the relaxed silence, and they both tensed as Norman answered the call. Rebecca got up and went into her closet to get dressed.

"You need to gain a little weight," Norman said as he came into the closet with her a short time later.

Rebecca ignored his comment and asked, "Who was on the phone?"

"It was my brother Shane. He's in town for a visit, and wanted to know when's a good time to stop by," he said as he stepped into his pants and zipped them. "He's on his way over right now."

When Shane arrived he was carrying flowers, and he had a strange look in his eyes. He avoided looking in Rebecca's direction.

"These are for you little sis," he said.

While Rebecca went to put the flowers away, Norman and Shane had a conversation regarding Cece's fall from her hospital bed.

After his talk with Norman, Shane left without saying much to Rebecca. He decided to go to Shelly's house to see if she needed anything. The first night of Cecilia's hospitalization Shelly had stayed the night in his guest room. She'd obviously needed comfort from a family member to help her come to terms with her harrowing experience. That night, for the first time in years, he and Shelly had a heart to heart talk. A large part of that talk had been about Rebecca and her mother. In the days since, Shane had looked forward to updates on Cecilia's condition.

He supposed he'd been hoping for a reason to meet the woman who had given free self defense lessons to over fifty women and taken a bullet for the little girl. When Norman had called him about flowers he'd jumped on that excuse to go to the hospital. He'd told himself that he was just trying to be thoughtful by delivering them himself, but he'd also been trying to appease his almost overwhelming curiosity. The last thing he'd expected to see was Cecilia falling from the bed as he walked into the room. He'd had no idea what was wrong, so he'd rushed forward to help her right after he pushed the call button for the nurse to come.

She'd held one hand up in a defensive posture and said, "Don't hurt me," in a chilling little whisper. He'd never seen someone in such a blind panic for no apparent reason before, so he'd backed quietly out of the room right after the nurses entered. He had then watched from a distance as she was rushed down the hall to surgery. He prayed that she would survive whatever new damage had been done, just as he had been praying for her since the night Shelly had come to his house in tears.

Last night he'd tossed and turned and tried to banish that sobering image of Cecilia attempting to drag her broken body across the hospital floor. According to Shelly, Cecilia had been a fascinating, healthy, and vibrant person before being shot. It was sad to see the amount of damage just one crazy person with a gun could do to so many lives.

Chapter 23

When Cece opened her eyes again she was comforted by the sight of just her daughter beside the bed. There was no trace of the dark haired stranger who had entered her room last time she was alone. Keeping her eyes open seemed a nearly impossible task at that moment, so she allowed them to drift shut again. It took her several attempts to wake up completely, but when she did she looked around the room and blinked several times to make sure she wasn't dreaming. She'd never received flowers in her life, not even when Rebecca's twin sister Sarah had died, and now she found herself in the midst of a room filled with them.

She took in a deep breath and allowed the fragrance to fill her nostrils. "Where did all these flowers come from?" she asked.

"From your secret admirer," Rebecca joked. For some reason the bright flowers and the lightness of her daughter's mood comforted her more than anything else she could imagine at that moment. She suddenly had the feeling that she was going to be alright.

She looked at Rebecca's smiling face, and for the first time in a long time she didn't have the feeling that she was staring directly into the face of someone who had violated her. Rebecca looked nothing like her, she had a darker skin tone, smaller bone structure, and completely different facial features. Cece had always known Rebecca must look a lot like her father, and she'd never realized how much she'd held that against her until now.

"Thanks Honey, they're beautiful," Cece said as she reached out for her daughter's hand.

Cece was grateful for her daughter's constant presence during her long, painful recovery. She'd never had to lean on someone so completely before, and she was thankful that it was her daughter who was giving her the most support. It gave her the opportunity to see Rebecca in a completely different light. Cece had always thought of her as something of a weakling in need of protection. She was a small person, and she was nice to everyone it was easy to mistake her kindness as weakness.

She rarely had to see her daughter's husband, and she was just fine with that. He was huge and he looked like he could kill someone with his bare hands without even breaking a sweat. She often wondered what Rebecca saw in him. Cece's experience with men had been limited to a few failed attempts at dating. She'd never counted what happened to her as a teenager as experience with men. She'd always tried to pretend that her nightmarish experience hadn't really happened, and sometimes it actually worked. Then there were the times when denying it didn't work... this was one of those times.

Towards the end of her hospital stay Cece was lying in bed alone thinking about the vast changes in her life. Her spirits had been kept up by two things, her daughter's constant reassuring presence, and the fresh, beautiful flowers that appeared in her room every few days. She'd stopped asking where they came from, but her curiosity hadn't gone away. Rebecca didn't know either; at least if she did she was great at hiding it. Today's new flower arrangement was a lovely combination of pink and purple blooms. She stared at it absent mindedly as she waited for the physical therapist to come.

When the day of her release finally arrived Cece had mixed feelings. She didn't want to go home with Rebecca now that her husband was there too, but she was glad to be leaving the sterile hospital environment. And for the first time in her life she was actually thinking of the future with hope and optimism rather than the jaded cynicism that had ruled her for most of her adult life.

Norman expected Rebecca to take more time off work, so he was completely blindsided when she went back to work the day after Cece was released.

"Where are you going?" he asked when she was about to walk out the door at four in the morning.

"Back to work," she answered matter-of-factly.

Norman quickly rubbed the sleep out of his eyes as he sprung up to follow her out of the room. "When were you going to tell me about this?"

"I wasn't."

"Why not?" he demanded.

"Because I know you don't like my job, and I don't want to argue about it with you," Rebecca said in a voice almost devoid of emotion.

"We still should have talked about it."

"I'll be home by noon. Can we talk then?" Rebecca asked.

Norman tilted her chin up so she couldn't avoid his gaze. He did not look pleased. "Yes," he said.

Norman spent the day doing yard work and trying to pretend that he wasn't angry with his wife. He started as soon as it was light outside, and he didn't even consider stopping until he heard Rebecca's car enter the garage. It was well past noon when she got home; it was almost dark.

He marched into the garage prepared to grill her about being late, but he stopped abruptly when he saw that she was sitting in the car with her head resting on her drawn up knees hugging herself. She appeared to be sobbing.

Eventually she looked up and noticed him watching her. She wiped her eyes and got out. "How long have you been standing there?" she asked.

"Long enough," he said.

"I'm sorry I'm late. Today was much harder than I expected it to be." She looked up at him and he could tell instantly that she was hiding something.

"Was there another big incident at work today?" he asked.

"No, not at all," she hedged.

"Then what's wrong?"

"Nothing specific really, I just need to relax... How was your day?"

The look he gave her should have sent her up in flames. He made no attempt to hide his displeasure with her.

"I spent the last six hours wondering where you were.... What happened to being home by noon?" he asked.

"There was something that really needed to be done before I came home."

He waited for her to tell him the rest, but when she didn't he prompted, "And?"

"And I don't want to talk about it right now."

Much to Norman's chagrin, this was the way things were between them for quite some time.

He went back to work immediately after she did, and Cece spent her days in physical therapy learning to walk again, and her evenings shut up in one of the guest rooms. Norman and Rebecca settled into a predictable routine. She would get home late and exhausted every day, and she never wanted to talk about what was obviously bothering her. When Dylan was staying with them, she was warm and engaging, but when it came to allowing Norman to support her she became cold and stiff as if she thought she could carry the weight of the world all on her own. After six months of this, Norman was seriously concerned about the situation.

Every morning she was out the door by four thirty, and she didn't get home until well after eight pm most nights. She'd said she was supposed to have weekends off, yet she frequently got called in to work on Saturdays. Nothing in her demeanor was suspicious, but her actions just didn't add up. As much as Norman wanted to trust his wife, he knew she was hiding something big from him. He just hoped to God she wasn't having an affair. He'd never forget the pain and humiliation of finding out that Juliana had knowingly had another man's child while pretending to be a wife to him.

He was waiting for her at the door when she got home from work one Saturday. She appeared totally exhausted as usual, and he felt like a jerk for wanting to confront her.

"Norman!" she exclaimed as he hugged her from behind. After she hung her jacket in the closet he kissed the back of her neck and gave her a squeeze.

"How was work?' he asked as he held her against him.

"Same as usual. Today we got a new case in from Memphis. It's so sad what some of these kids go through…. I'm glad to finally be home," she sighed.

At times like this Norman felt bad for doubting her, but that didn't make the doubts go away.

Rebecca walked into the dining room and stopped short when she saw that he'd taken out the candles and the dishes that Shelly had given them as a wedding present.

"I know it's late, but I wanted us to have dinner together tonight, so I waited for you," Norman said as he wrapped his arms around her and pulled her close again.

She closed her eyes for a moment and soaked in the feel of her warm strong husband at her back. It seemed like they hadn't spent time together in months, but she couldn't afford to take it easy lately.

That evening he was more attentive than usual. He insisted on cleaning up after the meal, and he even ran her bath water for her and placed scented candles beside the tub for her.

"What's with you tonight?" she asked as she relaxed into the warm soapy water.

"Does something have to be up for me to want to spend an evening with my wife?' he asked as he kissed her cheek. Her hair was pinned up, and he sat admiring the delicate arch of her back as she relaxed in the water.

"No, but usually when I get home you're busy doing something else. I hate coming into your office when you are working on army stuff; I always feel like I'm disturbing something really important." Her eyes were closed, so she didn't see the frown that appeared on his face.

"Is that why you always go straight to bed? I thought maybe you were avoiding me."

"Well, not exactly…Most of the time I'm just exhausted from work, but I'd rather have you in the bed with me," she explained.

They continued talking as she bathed and readied herself for bed, and Norman thought she was telling the truth, but he also felt like she was keeping something from him. He was reluctant to confront her about it because they hadn't spent time together in so long. He just didn't want to taint the evening with unreasonable suspicions.

When they went into the bedroom he sat in the large chair beside the window with her in his lap and watched the fireflies as they lit up the trees below. The view was incredibly romantic, and he leaned down to give Rebecca a kiss only to find that she had fallen fast asleep. That had been happening a lot lately, and as usual he didn't have the heart to wake her up. They hadn't made love for almost a month.

On Monday Norman decided to surprise Rebecca at work by bringing lunch for them to share. He didn't tell her he had the day off. He stopped by a sandwich shop and picked up her favorite before driving all the way out to her job. When he got there he was stunned to learn that she wasn't at work that day. She'd gotten up at four as she did everyday and told him she'd see him after work. Obviously she'd lied. According to the woman at the front desk, she hadn't been scheduled to work on a weekend, or past 2pm since she'd returned to work after her mother's hospitalization.

One thing Norman had learned from his first marriage is that you never confront a liar until you have evidence stacked up against them. He knew that if he confronted her on mere suspicions she would be able to cover up whatever she was hiding from him. He was shocked, hurt, and undoubtedly angrier than he had been in a long time.

When she got home that night she looked absolutely exhausted as usual. He almost softened toward her, until he remembered the humiliation of finding out that Julie had been lying to him and sleeping around for years. He didn't want to believe that Rebecca would do the same thing. He had more faith and trust in Rebecca than he ever had in his first wife and the fact that she betrayed him hurt more than anything else she could have done.

He went into his office and closed the door. With the door closed she wouldn't want to disturb him. He sat staring at the wall until he heard her quiet knock at the door.

"Come in," he said in a neutral tone.

"Hi Norman," she peeked around the door at him. She had dark shadows under her eyes. "I just wanted to let you know I'm home from work."

She walked in and sat on his lap, wrapping her arms around his neck and kissing him on the lips. She leaned her head on his shoulder and started telling him about someone she'd had trouble with that day. He knew it was a lie, and he felt his anger rise as he listened.

It took her a minute to realize he hadn't kissed her back, and that he hadn't hugged her.

"I'm sorry... I didn't realize I was disturbing you. I thought maybe you weren't busy right now," she said as she stood up to leave.

If he hadn't known she'd been lying to him for months, he would have felt extremely guilty for causing the hurt and vulnerable look that she was now giving him.

He didn't come to bed at all that night. Instead he slept on the couch in his office, and pretended like he had been working all night when she found him in the morning. He didn't miss the unshed tears in her eyes as she walked out the door. He almost felt bad for her.

By Saturday Rebecca knew Norman was seriously angry with her. He had slept in his office all week, and he hadn't kissed her once since Monday. Maybe it was time to tell him about her second job, and hope that he would understand her reasons. As she drove out to the women's detention facility where Shirelle was now serving a ten year sentence for Ronnie's death, she thought about what she was doing.

She kept telling herself that she was doing it for women everywhere who had been violated and left to fend for themselves at a young age. She kept telling herself that she was working so hard for Shirelle, and for her own mother, and for Sharon and for Peggy; but part of her whispered that she was also doing it so that she could ease the guilt she'd lived with since Ronnie's death.

She hadn't talked to Norman once about the incident because he'd assumed that all of her recent tears had stemmed from the night her mother had been shot. The truth was that she felt like Ronnie's death was largely her fault. She'd examined that day over and over again in her head and come up with about a million things she could have done differently.

Shirelle had told her she wanted to be a lawyer someday, but now that dream seemed to be shattered. Although nothing similar had ever happened to her, Rebecca understood the intricacies of what Shirelle was going through. Rebecca had been raised by a mother who had seen her own dreams slip away at a young age, and she knew that it wasn't something that one could recover from easily. Rebecca wanted to make sure that Shirelle would be given a chance once she was free, so she'd decided to do whatever it took to make it happen.

She'd been working two jobs and saving every cent she made so that she could invest it all in a scholarship fund specifically for women in situations like Shirelle's, Sharon's and Cece's. The idea had come to her the same day Ronnie died, but she'd told no one except the investment manager who had been giving her advice over the past eighteen months. She'd made more than enough money to get the scholarship fund off to a good start. She smiled slightly as she thought about the 150,000 dollars she'd managed to accumulate on her own during the past year and a half.

Part of it had come from the money her mother had given her, a large portion had come from her salary at the youth center, and the rest was from her part time job at an adult detention facility. She'd managed to save so much because she hadn't spent a dime of the money she'd made at both jobs. She made a mental note to thank Norman, because without his support it wouldn't have been possible for her to save up such a substantial sum. Now she felt like she had the power to help more people.

Rebecca visited Shirelle one Saturday a month, and today she was really looking forward to telling her the good news. She'd met with the advisory committee at the university to go over the guidelines for her scholarship, and everything had been approved. All she had to do now was sign some papers and hand over a cashier's check this afternoon after her visit with Shirelle. Now she could tell Shirelle with confidence that there would be a college education waiting for her when she got out.

Rebecca got home that night to find that Norman wasn't there. Cece informed her that he had been gone since early that morning. Rebecca didn't worry much about his absence until later that night. When midnight came and went with no word from her husband, she began to worry. She called Shelly and his brothers, but nobody had seen or heard from him that day. She was nearing her breaking point and getting ready to call the police when she finally found the half written note he'd left in his desk drawer. She read it with tears in her eyes and a feeling of rising panic in her chest.

"Rebecca, I don't know what has changed between us, but I feel like I can't trust you anymore. I do believe that married couples should talk about these things, but every time I've tried to talk to you in the past six months you refuse to let me in. I don't know what to say to you anymore."

She lay in bed in emotional agony all night. The note was not clear about his intentions for the future. He hadn't said he wanted a divorce, but the tone of the note suggested he had given up on her.

Chapter 24

Norman spent the day following Rebecca around because he just couldn't bring himself to truly believe she would cheat on him. The last thing he wanted to do was confront her about infidelity and hurt her with a false accusation. By the end of the day he was glad he listened to his heart and left the note in his desk rather than on her pillow as he'd planned.

First thing in the morning when Rebecca got up to get dressed; Norman pretended that he had to go in to his office on post for a few hours. When Rebecca left the house, however, he followed her instead of going to work.

She drove for more than an hour, and eventually turned down a private drive that led to a gated women's correctional facility. Norman followed at a discreet distance, and watched as the gate guard buzzed her into the facility. He waited on the side of the road for several minutes before driving up to the gate. The guard asked him for his identification, and then told him he wasn't allowed to go in because he wasn't on the visitation list.

"Can you at least tell me who my wife is visiting? She came through just before me," Norman said. When the guard looked skeptical, Norman pulled out a picture of the two of them together that he'd been keeping in his wallet since his last deployment. "If your wife was sneaking around visiting prisons behind your back, wouldn't you want to know what was going on?" Norman said as the old man looked at the picture.

"Well, the last names do match... and you have a picture," the guard sighed. "Rebecca has an employee badge. I'm not sure what her job is, but I do know that she also comes once a month to see that little girl who was in the news for killing her roommate up in Ashland City a couple of years ago."

"Shirelle?"

"Yep. That's the one. I'm sorry I can't let you in, but if you fill out this form to be added to the visitation list for Shirelle you might get in sometime in the next two months. All visitors have to be approved pending the inmate's behavior, and we only update the lists once a month. You have to have a valid driver's license or state i.d. to be approved. Paperwork tends to be a little slow around here."

"Thanks," Norman said as he accepted the papers and drove off. He didn't go far. He parked at a convenience store along the main road and watched for Rebecca's car to come back into view.

Her next stop was the Fort Campbell Credit Union. He didn't even know she had an account there. He watched from the nearly full parking lot as she went in and then came out a short time later with a smile on her face. She practically skipped back to her car. He didn't like all this sneaking around, but he stayed hidden so he could get to the bottom of whatever was going on with his wife. He was surprised she still hadn't noticed him following her around. After her trip to the bank, she stopped by a fast food restaurant and ate in her car alone. She then made a couple of phone calls before driving to the Austin Peay State University Campus.

Norman parked in one of the lots and quickly trailed behind her into one of the administrative buildings. He peeked around the corner she'd just rounded, and then stepped back when he saw her talking to several people. They were an older, distinguished, scholarly looking bunch. Shortly after Rebecca got there they all stepped inside a conference room and stayed in there for the next few hours.

After Rebecca zipped out of the conference room, Norman decided to stop following her. He wanted to know what the meeting had been about, so he entered the room and introduced himself to all the people still seated around the table.

"Can I help you?" an older woman with a head full of snow white hair said to him. She was seated at the head of the table and appeared to be in charge.

"Yes," Norman cleared his throat. "My name is Norman Gregory. I'm Rebecca's husband. I know she just left, but I came in because I'm trying to find out what she's been up to lately, and I get the feeling that you guys might be able to help." He realized he probably sounded foolish, but he didn't care what these people thought of him at the moment. He only cared about getting to the bottom of Rebecca's mysterious behavior.

"*You're* married to that precious little thing?" the woman smiled. "She's talks about you all the time, but somehow I thought you would be smaller. She's always going on about how sweet you are, but she never mentioned what a great big tall fellow you are. I'm Martha Flannigan, the head of the advisory committee that's been giving Rebecca guidance on a project she's been working on for more than a year now."

"Why don't you have a seat, and we'll see if we can answer your questions," a portly man in a suit said as he got up to close the door behind Norman.

Martha and the other members of the advisory committee spent a couple of hours telling Norman all about the Cece Graves Scholarship Fund for women. Before he left the conference room, he arranged a meeting with his investment manager and made a last minute contribution to the fund his wife had started. Rebecca had started it in her mother's honor because of the hardships she had faced trying to raise two kids and work without even a GED. The fund included provisions to pay for tutoring, child care, and even books for women who qualified, and unlike other scholarships, it was mostly based on need and the will to succeed rather than on an outstanding GPA. The committee had disagreed with Rebecca on that point, yet she had convinced them to accept her terms because the women who would need such a scholarship might have a lower GPA than traditional students who didn't come from such tragic circumstances. Information about the program was to be made available at local women's centers and pregnancy crisis centers to reach those who needed it most.

Norman marveled at Rebecca's gumption as he drove home that night. She had managed to take all the negative energy from her recent experiences and her troubled past and channel it into something positive, radiant, and giving. He couldn't believe he ever doubted her, and he vowed never to do so again... but he would have to have a serious talk with her about her need to do everything on her own. She could have saved them both a lot of heartache and lonely nights if she had just talked to him about her intentions in the first place.

Norman returned home to find Rebecca curled up in bed hugging his pillow with his note lying beside her. He cursed silently to himself because he knew she must think he'd left her. He removed his clothes and got into bed with her. He pulled her close to his chest and kissed her until she woke up.

"Norman?" she said uncertainly.

"You weren't supposed to see that note... I'm sorry Honey," he said gently.

"I've been working two jobs so that I could save up a lot of money for scholarships," she blurted out. "I haven't been doing anything bad... please believe me Norman. You can still trust me."

"I know," he responded as he kissed her forehead and held her close again. "Don't worry about it. Just get some sleep; I'm not going anywhere and neither are you. I love you."

The next morning Norman woke up feeling as if a great weight had been lifted from his chest. He watched Rebecca as she lie snoring softly beside him. She hadn't even bothered to remove her clothes from the night before, and in the early morning light her face looked as if it had aged years since they'd gotten married. The dark circles under her eyes and unhealthy looking frailness of her body were things that he hadn't really thought much about until that moment.

When she finally did wake up he had breakfast waiting for her on a tray beside the bed.

"Good morning," he greeted her cheerfully.

"I'm sorry I didn't tell you what I was doing," she began immediately.

"Don't even worry about it right now. Please just eat something. You look like a sad little skeleton," he told her sternly.

She raised her eyebrow at him, but she didn't argue with his assessment. She dug into her breakfast like she hadn't eaten in days.

"You know, I really wanted to tell you..." she said between bites of her strawberry topped waffles. "I just had this feeling that this was something I was supposed to do, but I didn't want to argue with you about money. I guess I kind of figured that if I was the one working for the extra money you wouldn't be able to tell me no."

Norman watched her eat for a few minutes before he responded carefully, "What made you think I wouldn't want you to start a scholarship fund? That's a good cause to spend money on," he said.

"You still don't know how much money I used to start it," she said hesitantly. She looked extremely uncomfortable as she continued,

"It's all money from my jobs and my savings from before I met you.... So please don't get mad and feel like I took money from you."

"We're married, so if you want to get technical about it what's mine is yours and vice versa," he said. He wasn't cutting her any slack with the look he gave her. "Just how much money are we talking here?"

She looked up at him momentarily and then took another huge bite of her breakfast. She ate in silence for another few minutes, all the while practically squirming from the look in his eyes.

"How much?" he prompted again when the tray was clear.

"One hundred and fifty thousand dollars...." She said in a barely audible whisper. Her heart was pounding in her chest, and she felt the room spin a little as he removed the tray from her hands and set it upon the table.

When he didn't say anything for a few minutes she cleared her throat and said, "All of it came from my savings, my therapist salary, and my extra job. I've been working on this for almost two years, and this is one of those things that you'll either never understand or you'll just accept how important it is to me. I know it's a lot of money, but we aren't poor..."

"Would you have eventually told me about this if I hadn't gotten suspicious?" he finally asked.

"I don't know," she answered honestly.

"And that right there is the root of this problem... Rebecca we are married!" he said fiercely. "This is exactly the type of thing you need to come to me and talk to me about. How do you expect me to have a good reaction when you hide something this big from me? And how do you expect me to feel when you never even gave me the opportunity to understand your reasons for doing this? You never even tried talking to me."

"I didn't want you to talk me out of it. This is the biggest thing I've ever done in my life. I don't think I could stand having you against me on this," Rebecca admitted.

"It's not that I'm okay with you keeping things from me, because I'm not," Norman said. "But I'm still too relieved that you're not cheating on me to think of much else."

"What do you mean?" she asked uneasily.

"I mean we should talk about this again after I've had a few days to think about it," he clarified.

Rebecca cringed and shrank back under the covers, hiding almost her entire face from him. "It's too late for that," she squeaked.

"I know you think the final decision is yours alone, but I still think we need to discuss the final amount before you go ahead with this idea," his voice reminded her of a drill sergeant ready to pounce on an unsuspecting private who'd made a grave mistake.

She gathered up the courage to be honest anyway. "I've already met with an advisory committee at the school and given them the money.... I can't take it back now."

"Call them right now, and tell them you want to schedule a meeting to make some last minute changes. I'm sure they'll work with you." His voice sounded unrelenting from her imaginary safe haven under the covers.

"Norman, I can't," Rebecca said with finality. When she finally did emerge from the covers she didn't see the thunderous expression that she'd expected. Instead, he merely looked exasperated with her. "I know it's a lot of money, but I'll make it up to you. If it means that much to you I'll make it up somehow.... Just don't ask me to go back on my word and take back something that means so much to me."

"Why does it mean so much to you? Can you at least explain that to me?"

Rebecca looked at her husband. He was sitting across from her looking as handsome as ever, and while the expression on his face was both stern and exasperated, the expression in his eyes was slightly vulnerable. If she hadn't seen that hint of uneasiness in his eyes she may never have found the nerve to open up to him. He was the most wonderful man she'd ever encountered, but she had to remember that he was just a man. And maybe, just maybe, her inability to share her deepest feelings had somehow hurt his.

For the first time since Norman's deployment she talked to him about the time she'd spent alone. She told him about growing up with a mother who valued independence above all else. She told him about her own personal struggle to make her imposing mother proud once she'd reached adulthood, and she opened up for the first time about Ronnie's death. Norman had no idea how deeply the girl's death had been affecting his wife until she'd finally explained about her unusual closeness to Shirelle. Apparently Shirelle had reminded Rebecca of her own mother.

When they finished talking Rebecca thought she still needed to convince him she was doing the right thing, but in truth Norman had made up his mind about the scholarship fund before he ever broached the subject to his wife. He'd only grilled her about it so that she would talk to him about what had been on her mind for the past year and a half.

Chapter 25

Somehow Norman and Shelly had managed to bully Rebecca into hosting a fundraiser for her new scholarship fund. The event was to happen less than a month after Norman and Rebecca's big talk, and much to Norman's chagrin he hadn't been able to convince her to discuss changing the amount of her own personal contribution. She adamantly refused to give any less than the hundred and fifty thousand she had worked so hard to accumulate. Some of Norman's brothers and even some of his extended family and associates were to attend the event, and due to the sheer number of relatives and friends her husband had Rebecca was more than a little nervous.

She'd rehearsed her speech a million times in her head and about ten times in the mirror and in front of Shelly, but the preparation did little to dispel the nervous energy that gripped her as she walked through the doors of the fancy banquet hall. Immediately, she regretted letting Shelly talk her into making this event a full blown charity ball.

There was a veritable sea of glittery ball gowns and suits mingling with each other and discussing the topic of the day. When a hush fell over the place at her entrance, Rebecca had no doubt that she was that topic.

Norman felt her steps grind to a halt as more and more people took note of their arrival, but he didn't want to drag her forward as if she were a naughty child. He stopped beside her and whispered in her ear, "You look lovely tonight."

He heard her take in a deep, steadying breath and saw her square her shoulders, and he knew she was ready to face the world with or without him at her side. But when she reached out for his hand anyway, he couldn't have been more touched.

After the initial mingling and introductions, Rebecca felt slightly less anxious. Most of the people at the ball were connected to Norman's family in some way, and the rest were directly related. It seemed that many of them had been curious about her since they'd heard about Norman's rushed second marriage. She couldn't have asked for a better setting to be introduced to the main body of his acquaintances. They all seemed to collectively embrace her philanthropic endeavor and her reserved and sweet nature made her an instant favorite among them.

For the most part Norman was content to step back and watch her shine. After all the hard work she'd put into this event he was glad to finally see her looking proud of herself. She was a far cry from the Rebecca who had finished her first marathon with tears in her eyes, and then refused to acknowledge her own hard work.

When it was time for Rebecca to make her big speech in front of everyone, Norman felt anxious for her. He knew her well enough to see she was terrified as she approached the podium. Public display wasn't something she would ever be comfortable with, and Norman crossed his fingers and hoped that she would get through it without mishap.

He smiled encouragingly at her as she situated herself at the microphone and began with a simple, "Good evening."

Rebecca swallowed as she looked out at the more than three hundred pairs of eyes watching her every move, and the rehearsed speech that she'd worked so hard on suddenly left her head. She looked down and realized she'd left her notes back at the table with Norman. She couldn't even remember the opening quote, and everyone was waiting in expectant silence for her to continue.

She opened her mouth to speak and said the first thing that came to her mind.

"I remember one of the first things my mother ever taught me... she taught me to rely on myself and no one else, because people were not to be trusted. For a long time I believed her; she had my best interest at heart, and she lived by her own advice. I never once saw my mother asking for a handout or acting like the world owed her something after harsh circumstances forced her into a life of desperation.

"And more recently, after working with young women who come from backgrounds similar to my mother's, I've learned that this misguided sense of independence is actually a symptom of the inability to trust. Emotionally, it is far easier for a woman who has been victimized to scrape out a meager existence on her own than it is to learn to trust again, and accept help, and lean on someone else. Many of the women I hope to reach out to through this fund are just like my own mother and the girls I've had the honor of working with in therapy. They are victims of rape. They are victims of domestic violence. And on some level they are even victims of their own inability to believe in a better life for themselves and their children.

"One of the first things I learned about the young girls who typically end up on the street is that they have come to believe in the prevailing ghetto mentality of the inner city streets and projects. I've heard it countless times during my years at the youth center... 'If you were born in the ghetto and raised in the ghetto you're going to die in the ghetto.' And anyone who dares to hope for a better life can easily be looked upon as foolish.

"So here I am before you making a foolhardy request for you to help better the lives of perfect strangers.... I'm the product of a mother who was raped at the age of 13 and kicked out on the street when it became obvious that she was pregnant from the event. I know from personal experience how important programs like this are to women like my mother. She is just one of a staggering number of women who didn't get the right type of help when she needed it most, and I am here asking for donations so that there are fewer women left to fend for themselves after being victimized. I'm here because I truly believe that this scholarship program will send a powerful message to those women who need it most. I recognize the amount of commitment it takes to get through college, and this is the type of program that will stay with them through the entire journey. I'm here because I want those young girls who are now in situations that seem hopeless to know that there is hope, and above all else I want them to know that not everyone who was born in the ghetto and raised in the ghetto has to die there as well."

As Rebecca finished her impromptu speech she met with a roomful of silence. For one agonizing minute she thought she'd gotten too personal, and that everyone was looking at her in disapproval. It was only after she blinked away her own tears that she noticed that others were taking a moment to dry theirs as well. As she left the podium to rejoin her husband the room filled with applause. But it wasn't the boisterous applause of an enthusiastic crowd... it was an applause that was rich in respect and deep understanding of the gravity of the situation. Several older ladies caught her eye and smiled reassuringly at her as she passed by, and a feeling of peace settled over her. All of her hard work had not been in vain; they understood.

Norman stood and embraced Rebecca when she got back to their table.

"That wasn't the speech you worked so hard on," he said as he held her for a moment.

"I was so nervous I forgot it... and that was what came out," she admitted ruefully.

"Speaking from the heart is better anyway," he assured her.

Immediately following Rebecca's speech, Shelly took the podium to deliver a computer presentation she and Rebecca had prepared together. It focused on some of the areas that Rebecca hoped to impact with her foundation. She informed every one of the dismal statistics regarding the reporting of rape and domestic violence, and then she described some of the ways that Rebecca hoped to help. Rebecca had done her graduate research on the effect that certified Sexual Assault Forensics Examiners had on the reporting of rapes. In her research she'd learned about the positive ramifications of having a certified SAFE center in more hospitals. SAFE centers were places where victims of domestic violence and sexual assault could go for treatment and evidence collection, but unlike a regular emergency room SAFE centers provided a more compassionate and private level of care. They were designed to decrease any additional emotional trauma to the victims. Rebecca hoped to raise awareness and encourage more emergency rooms to implement a SAFE program. The three main points of the presentation had been the need to increase awareness, the need to increase the reporting of such events, and the need to offer the victims long term help in dealing with the aftermath. Rebecca was adamant that with enough support her foundation could make improvements in all three of those areas.

After Shelly's presentation there was a moment of silence for victims worldwide, and guests were asked to consider how much of a donation they were willing to make. Rebecca knew that her own contribution would likely be the largest, but she was still hopeful about the amount of money that could be raised. She couldn't help thinking that if each person in the room could pledge just $600 for the year, it would more than double the impact of the foundation. She had to admonish herself not the get her hopes up too high... great things didn't happen overnight. She'd slaved away for many months just to save enough money to get it started, and it would take even more time for it to grow from there.

During Shelly's presentation Shane had sat at the table and observed Rebecca and Norman. The first time he'd seen them together at their wedding he hadn't really understood what Norman saw in her, but tonight he did.

"Rebecca, explain to me again how you came up with so much money all on your own," Shane said.

She looked at him from across the table and smiled. "It wasn't that hard."

Norman stared down at her with an incredulous look on his face. "I guess running marathons isn't that hard either," he said.

Rebecca glanced down at the table in obvious embarrassment. "It was nothing," she hedged. When she looked up again she saw Shelly approaching. She jumped up and said, "I'm going to go see what Shelly needs, she's waving at me."

Shane hadn't seen Shelly wave. Obviously Rebecca was uncomfortable and wanted to escape his scrutiny.

Norman wasn't so bashful though. As soon as his little wife was out of earshot he said, "I've never seen anyone work so much in my life Shane... at least not someone who didn't have to. She was working two jobs behind my back to save up all that money."

"Two jobs huh? And you didn't know?" Shane asked.

"Well, one of them was part-time. She usually left around four in the morning and got home past eight at night... I figured she was working extra hours because she didn't want to be around her mother. Cece isn't exactly an easy person to be around. Her and Becky barely talk. It's the strangest thing...it's obvious that they love each other, but there is just so much between them."

Shane nodded. He'd been just as moved by Rebecca's words about her mother as everyone else had; he'd just kept it hidden. He steered the subject away from Cecilia. "But I don't get it... Why would she work herself to death when she could have just used some of what Old Money Bags gave you?" he asked.

"She doesn't know about that," Norman answered after a long pause.

Shane had picked up his glass to take a sip of wine, but at his brother's admission it went down wrong and he sputtered for a few seconds before he managed to exclaim, "You never told her?!"

"That's right."

"You've been married almost two years now. Don't you think you should?"

"I know I should, but there just never seems to be a good time to bring it up."

"So to her all that money is a real sacrifice…"

"I hadn't thought of it that way."

"Well you should," Shane said as he looked across the room and caught sight of Shelly and Rebecca talking near the tables where donations were being tallied. It was easy to spot the two of them because Shelly's bright hair stood out anywhere. "It's like you married Mighty Mouse… she must really care about this."

"I think this is partly her way of showing she cares about her mother," Norman sighed as his gaze followed Shane's across the room. "It's like she's trying to make up for what her father did."

"When are you going to tell her? Or *are* you going to tell her?"

"I'm going to tell her tonight when we get home," Norman sighed.

Shane felt badly for his little brother. He looked stressed about what was to come. "For what it's worth, I don't think she'll react the same way Julie did. Julie has always been a selfish bitch."

"That's not what I'm worried about. Rebecca's mother raised her well; she's the least selfish person I know. She won't even buy herself new clothes without a good reason. I just hope her feelings aren't hurt that I've been keeping this from her for so long," Norman explained as he raked his fingers through his hair in aggravation.

Shane almost laughed at him, but he caught himself. Juliana had really done a number on his brother's confidence when it came to women, and Shane knew Norman wouldn't see the humor in his present situation. "You two are priceless." he said.

"Why?" Norman demanded.

"She hides her extra job and raises a small fortune for charity behind your back, and you can't find one opportunity in two years of marriage to come clean about who your grandparents are. I'd love to be a fly on the wall for that conversation."

"Enough about my life," Norman cut in. "How's the flower business been treating you lately, Hightower?" he snickered.

"Like I haven't heard that one before," Shane returned. His friends had been calling him that for years, ever since he gave up his career as a fire fighter and partnered up with a florist who retired and ultimately left the flower business to him. Shane had been seriously considering going back to the high demand life of a fire fighter, and his brother's good natured ribbing just tipped the scales. "Actually, I was just accepted for a position with the Nashville Fire Department. I start in a couple of weeks," he lied. He hadn't even applied yet, but he knew he'd be a shoo-in once he did. He had more than 15 years of experience with the New York City Fire Department.

"You know I was just kidding…" Norman said. Shane didn't miss the worried look that crossed his brother's face.

"I know you were, but I wasn't. It's the only thing I've ever really been passionate about, and I've been away from it for too long. It's time I put the past behind me and went back to it."

"You sure you want to go back?"

"It's not like I have to go back to New York. I'm staying in Nashville."

"Well good luck," Norman said. Shane couldn't miss the concern in his face. He looked like he wanted to say more, but before either of them could speak again Shelly and Rebecca returned to the table.

Shane turned to Rebecca and asked, "How's your mother's recovery going?"

"It's been about nine months since it happened, and she's already walking again." Rebecca smiled when she spoke, but there was a look of lingering sadness in her eyes.

"Why didn't she come tonight?" Shane asked.

Rebecca cleared her throat and glanced at Norman and Shelly. "She still needs some time…this would have been too public for her."

Shane wanted to know more about the woman who had inspired tonight's ball, but he could tell Rebecca was reluctant to say more. He smiled and took another sip of his wine. Shelly subconsciously fingered the small scar that started just below her hair line, and Rebecca stared down at the table with a pensive look on her face. Nine months hadn't been enough time for all of them to heal after their night with the maniac. He wondered what scars Cecilia struggled with tonight. Was she still hurting as Shelly and Rebecca appeared to be? Was she alone? His one glimpse of her all those months ago had stayed with him. When Norman put his arms around Rebecca's shoulders Shane looked away. He should stop asking questions about Rebecca's mother; her life was none of his business.

The night of the ball Cece confined herself to her room. Her boss Mrs. Lee had allowed her to take extended leave from work, assuring her that her job would be waiting for her when she was well enough to return.

It had been nine months now... nine months since her life had taken this crazy, unimaginable turn. Physical therapy was grueling, but it was the only part of her day she actually looked forward to. The physical therapist always pushed her to keep trying, especially when it seemed that her recovery had stalled and she couldn't possibly do more no matter how hard she tried. The hard work paid off, but it did so in agonizingly small installments. In six months she'd gone from not being able to move her legs at all to being able to walk with the assistance of a walker.

She hadn't told Rebecca that she'd been practicing walking unassisted in her room at night for the past few weeks. Cece knew her daughter would insist on helping, and she didn't want her overly sympathetic daughter to see how many times she fell. She had a multitude of bruises from her recent attempts to walk alone. She'd gotten to the point where she could make it around the full perimeter of the room if she used the wall for support. If she tried it with no support at all, she could only make it a portion of the way before the exhaustion became unbearable. Her physical therapist always told her that each step was a victory, but Cece felt that the real victory would come when she could go back to her life and stop depending on her daughter for every little thing.

The moonlight shone in through the open window, giving her just enough light to see her way around the room. The pale yellow paint on the walls looked too happy in the daylight, but at night it was subdued and not too annoying. Usually Cece hated the dark, but somehow the darkness seemed appropriate for her clandestine attempts to walk on her own.

She was sweating when she approached the open window on her second trip around the room, and she paused to enjoy the cool breeze that came through. She leaned out the window so the breeze could cool her overheated face and the sound of her daughter's soft laughter floated up towards her. She drew back into the shadows of the darkened room. She didn't want to be seen, but she didn't immediately leave the window.

She stood there and watched Rebecca and Norman. Rebecca was laughing because Norman had picked her up and was now spinning her around on the back lawn. They still wore their formal attire from tonight's ball. Cece had never seen the two of them so affectionate and unguarded before. When she was around, Norman tended to keep his hands to himself. What Cece thought she knew about their relationship was so at odds with the idyllic scene she was witnessing now.

Norman stopped spinning and sat Rebecca down on the ground, but he didn't let her go. His hands stayed around her waist and she draped her arms over his shoulders and clasped her hands behind his neck as she looked up at him. Cece heard their voices again, but she couldn't make out any of the words they said to each other. They seemed so relaxed tonight. When they started kissing Cece felt like she should look away, but she didn't. Even after her legs started to tremble and threatened to let her down, Cece remained by the window.

Norman spread a blanket across the grass, and the two of them lay down together. Every once in a while Norman would point up at the sky. They appeared to be discussing the stars. When Rebecca sat up and rubbed her arms Norman removed his tuxedo jacket and draped it around her shoulders. He then ran his fingers through her hair until it came loose and was falling all around them; Rebecca had always had way too much hair, but it was so gorgeous Cece had never been able to cut it short.

They lay back again wrapped in each other's arms and stayed silent for a long time. The entire time Cece watched, Norman kept his arms around Rebecca and her hands continuously flitted around, caressing his shoulders and chest. When their kissing and touching turned more intimate Cece took a step back, and immediately hit the floor. For a short time she'd forgotten about her physical limitations. She lay on the floor next to the window, too exhausted to even attempt to get up, and fell asleep.

The past month with Norman had been almost like the honeymoon they never had. When they weren't busy with work they spent all of their free time together. They were making big plans for the summer, because Dylan was supposed to stay with them through his entire summer break. The absence of the insane pressure of keeping things from her husband had done wonders for their relationship. They'd reconnected and grown closer while planning the charity ball and Rebecca still couldn't believe how well the evening had gone.

After all the donations and pledges had been tallied, Shelly interrupted the dancing to announce that they'd raised just over five million dollars in one night. Rebecca had been stunned, absolutely stunned. Even now as she and Norman enjoyed some quiet time in the back yard she was still stunned.

"What are you thinking right now?" his warm breath tickled her ear.

"You have to ask?" Rebecca panted, still out of breath from what they'd just done.

Norman smiled up at her, and there was a naughty twinkle in his eyes when he spoke again. "This is my new favorite place to make love, but only when you're on top," he grinned.

Rebecca giggled. "We should probably go back inside now." She was still straddling him, and she sat up to fix her dress. Norman had pulled it down to expose her chest in the heat of the moment; she hadn't protested of course.

"Wait," Norman whispered and grasped her hands. "Just let me look at you... I love the way you look tonight with all the stars shining behind you."

"This has been one of the best nights ever... nothing could top our wedding night, but this one was pretty awesome too," she smiled and leaned down to kiss him again. "I still can't believe we raised so much money in one night! I'm glad I listened to you and Shelly about having a ball."

"And I still can't believe how much work and research you've put into this. My brother Shane called you Mighty Mouse because you work so hard."

Rebecca wrinkled her nose. "I don't work any harder than you do...thank you so much, for everything."

"What did I do?" he chuckled.

"I saved up a lot of money, and I have a feeling that most husbands wouldn't want their wives to just give that kind of money away... so thank you for understanding how important this is to me and supporting this decision. We both have good careers, so between the two of us we can save up that amount of money again in a few years if we live frugally. Plus we're still young, so it's not like we're going to retire soon... Remember how I promised I'd make it up to you? Well,

I've already come up with a financial plan for the next five years, and I can--."

Suddenly Norman was kissing her again, cutting off her speech. He sat up and held her close to him, and she completely lost her train of thought. "What were we talking about?" she asked.

"How great you were at the ball tonight," he murmured against her neck.

"I still can't believe we raised over five million dollars in one night. I feel like we won the lottery," she sighed. "Do you have any idea how much we can do with that kind of money? How many women we can help reclaim their lives? And I have to find out who donated so much money. One of the members of the advisory committee told me that four million of tonight's total came from a single donor, but they wouldn't tell me who it was. I think Shelly might know though; she was acting kind of suspicious when I asked her if she knew anything. She's not a very good liar you know."

"I know," Norman chuckled. He pulled her close and hugged her again. Usually she was the quiet one, but tonight Rebecca was being a chatterbox.

"Is something wrong?" she finally thought to ask. Was he so unusually quiet because he felt emasculated by her success tonight?

"Not at all..."

"Sorry, I guess I'm just really excited about tonight. I hope you're okay with this... I mean just because I started the foundation doesn't mean we can't both be involved. I know it's a lot of money to see go to someone else, but it's for a good cause Norman."

"Rebecca, I'm not worried about the money," he insisted a bit gruffly.

"Then what is it?"

"There's something I need to tell you, and I don't want you to take it the wrong way."

"What is it?" she breathed. The conversation had just taken a serious turn, and her emotions were rapidly coming down from their previous high.

"I know who donated all that money," he said. If Rebecca didn't know him so well she might have thought that his worried tone was contrived just to pick on her, but Norman wasn't the type of man to play silly practical jokes.

"Who was it? Was it someone who wants the money back?"

"No... it was me."

"You?"

"Yes." Norman pulled away from her to look down at her face in the moonlight.

"How is that possible?" she asked.

"It's such a long story," Norman sighed. "Have you ever heard of Edgar Howard and Marlene Watson?"

"Of course I have. They've been the two richest people in the world for the past ten years now...everyone in the world knows who they are," she answered.

"Did you know they used to be married?" Norman asked.

"I had no idea... I guess that explains why they supposedly hate each other now."

"Hate doesn't even begin to describe how they feel about each other. They've been divorced for about fifty years now. It happened because their only daughter ran away with the young man in charge of the stables out at one of their estates. Edgar disowned her and completely cut her off, and Marlene never forgave him. Neither of them ever remarried or had any more kids...it really is a sad story."

"Where is their daughter now? She's going to be the wealthiest woman in the world soon... aren't they both in their late nineties?"

"Their daughter has been dead for more than thirty years now...she died when I was six."

"Your mother?" Rebecca whispered.

Norman nodded.

"So Marlene and Edgar are..."

"My grandparents."

Rebecca was silent for a long time as Norman's confession sank in. His secret was way bigger than hers had been, but oddly enough she wasn't angry with him. It did explain why he happened to know so many people with deep pockets who were willing to drop everything to attend a last minute charity ball. It also explained why he never seemed overly concerned about how much money she spent. Why hadn't Norman told her about this sooner? Did he not trust her?

"I think my grandmother always felt bad about what they'd done, and when my mother died she was distraught. I guess she always thought there would be time to make up with her later...but time ran out when she wasn't paying attention. She has no idea how to deal with her grief or how to go about having a real family relationship with us, so she's tried to reach out the only way she knows how. She set up a trust fund for each of us after she heard about our mother's death. All eight of us get a hundred million dollars each. Her only stipulation was that on our tenth wedding anniversary we'd only gain access to our trust fund if she approved of our spouse. Of course our father didn't tell us about any of this... We all grew up with no idea who our mother's parents were. All we knew was that they'd disowned her, and that she chose our father over her inheritance. We knew it was a lot of money, we just didn't know it was *that* much money. I got my first visit from her lawyers the day after I filed for divorce. Isn't that ironic? She approved of Julie just because her father was a rich banker, not because she's a good person. Julie never even finished college; she dropped out because it was too much of a bother for her."

"And you got to keep the money even though you were getting a divorce?" Rebecca asked. She hardly knew what she hoped his answer would be, but she scarcely breathed as she waited for him to continue.

"Yes. I was married ten years, and that was the stipulation. Even more ironic is the fact that Julie never saw a penny of all that money," Norman let out a humorless chuckle.

"Why didn't she?"

"Because when we married her parents insisted that I sign an iron-clad prenuptial agreement. They were rich and I was just a sergeant at the time; I signed it because I loved her. I would've signed anything just to get her to marry me... It stated that no matter how long we were married; if we ever split each of us would leave with whatever assets we entered the marriage with. It was designed to keep me from trying to take any of her money if we split up, not that I would have done such a thing. Since the trust fund had been set up in my name before I was even a teenager it counted as a premarital asset of mine, even though I didn't even know about it until the day after I filed for divorce. In the divorce she had no legal entitlement to that money because of the document that she and her parents had made me sign before we married. By then her father had gone bankrupt, so they really wanted it. They tried everything to get it. When they realized they didn't have a legal leg to stand on they tried to go the reconciliation route."

"Is that why she's been telling everyone that you guys are getting back together?"

"Yes, but I'm not some teenaged idiot with a crush on the popular cheerleader anymore. Even if I'd never met you I still wouldn't go back to her. No one in my family can stand her after the divorce. I avoid her as much as I can...I love Dylan so I treat her with respect for his sake."

"Has she ever tried to use Dylan to get money out of you? He's your son, so can't she sue you for an astronomical amount of child support?"

Rebecca tried to look into his eyes, but he looked away before he spoke again. "She doesn't have a legal leg to stand on there either... she tried that, and the court required me to get a paternity test. It turns out that I'm not Dylan's biological father either. With Abigail I *had* to step aside, because Julie is actually in a relationship with her father. But Dylan... he's been mine for so long, and Julie doesn't know who his father is. I'm the only father he has, so I agreed to pay child support for him in exchange for her letting me continue to be in his life. We never told him the truth. My family knows the truth, and they're on my side. You have no idea how much I wish he really were my son. I hate the fact that she can change her mind anytime and I can lose him."

"But he looks so much like you..."

"I know. That's the same thing I thought. Even Shelly thought there may have been a mistake. We ordered another test just to be sure, and the results were the same."

"Do you get along with your grandparents?"

"Our grandfather has never acknowledged our existence, and our grandmother attempts to control our lives with money...it's not exactly easy to get along with people like that."

Rebecca felt downright melancholy when she saw the expression on Norman's face. She pulled him into her embrace and held him for a long time without speaking.

"I'm sorry I didn't tell you about all this sooner," he said when he looked at her again. He had a single tear rolling down his cheek, and Rebecca wiped it away with her thumb.

"I imagine talking about it reminds you that you lost your mother at such an impressionable age. I can understand why you wouldn't want to bring all this up. It makes me sad just thinking about it, especially the way Julie treated you. All you are to her is an endless supply of money and material things. I can't imagine how that must have felt when you still had feelings for her."

"So you're not upset with me?" he asked.

"Do you remember that talk we had the day I found that scar on your chest? You told me that I should trust you to understand and talk to you about everything, and you said that we were both stronger after all our experiences apart and that we needed to grow stronger together…"

"You remember that?"

"Of course I do. Anyway, my point is that it took me a while to tell you a few things because I was afraid you wouldn't understand. I decided to start this foundation the day Ronnie died…I couldn't believe that you would be on my side, so I never talked to you about it. I'm not upset with you. I'm just glad that you finally gave me the opportunity to understand this part of you."

When she shivered in the cool air he stood up and then pulled her to her feet. He held her against his chest and said, "Let's get some sleep. We have a big day tomorrow. We have to meet with my investment managers and discuss this new foundation of yours."

"*Ours*," Rebecca corrected with a yawn. She bent down to pick up the blanket.

"You're tired Sweetie, let me get that."

"I got it." She smiled over her shoulder at him as she started walking back up the hill towards the back door.

Norman caught up to her and scooped her up. "You want to carry the blanket, fine. I'll just carry you."

The next morning Norman awoke to the sunlight streaming into the room and an empty spot beside him. He felt as if the weight of the world had been lifted off his shoulders last night after he'd told Rebecca about his grandparents. He'd gained access to the money on the worst day of his life, and it had been nothing but a burden and a concrete confirmation how little his ex-wife had actually cared for him as a person. In the years since the divorce debacle he'd seen it as an unwanted curse on his life, but all that had changed last night. It may have come into his life on a negative note, but he didn't have to let it remain that way. Obviously his mother-in-law had felt that way about Rebecca, or she wouldn't have invested the time and effort to raise her properly.

He checked the bedside clock; it was almost six o'clock. Usually at this early hour Rebecca could be found playing her piano on her days off. Norman got dressed and made his way downstairs so he could hear her play. He opened the doors to the music room and found her standing near the window deep in thought. Any number of things could be on her mind. It could be the meeting they'd scheduled to finalize all the details of her foundation, it could be her mother, or it could be the topic they'd discussed just last night. He had a feeling it was last night.

"You look thoughtful this morning," he remarked.

"I am. I've had a pretty busy morning so far," she said with a smile.

"Oh really? May I ask what you were busy doing so early in the morning? You obviously weren't cooking my breakfast..."

Rebecca laughed and gave him a playful punch. "I'll get right on it as soon as I help my mom out of bed."

"So what were you doing Becky?" he asked.

"I was going through the house thinking about all the beautiful gifts you've given me... Can you guess which one is my favorite?" She looked up at him with a smile lurking about her lips, ready to break out any second.

Norman thought about it for a moment. He had given her quite a few gifts in the two years they'd been together, but the piano was the one she used the most. He smiled with certainty and said, "The piano."

She looked over at the piano, and then she looked back at him. "You're *way* off," she grinned up at him. "The best gift you've ever given me is your love. As long as I have your love I'm set for life."

The Indigo Plume Publishing Co. proudly presents

THE PROSTITUTE'S DAUGHTER

ADRIENNE D'NELLE RUVALCABA

Coming soon in paperback

Keep reading for a preview of Adrienne D'nelle Ruvalcaba's next novel. The romance continues with the story of Cece Graves.

Prologue

The poetic justice of the situation was not lost on him as he stared at her beautiful, serene face. The day he truly knew what it meant to love both completely and unconditionally happened to coincide with the day he truly knew what it meant to lose everything.

A silent tear escaped his eye as he looked down at her face again. She appeared to be sleeping, and at peace, but he knew that her soul was anything but peaceful right now. Yes, today was the first time in his life that he'd ever truly felt the all consuming power of love, and of loss.

He reached out a trembling hand to touch her smooth cheek. Her eyes remained closed as he'd known they would, yet the absence of her warmth was still startling to his raw senses. The cold, waxy cheek, that just three days ago had been supple and warm, brought home the reality as almost nothing else could. Before he'd touched her he could have gone on telling himself that she was just sleeping. Today, he truly knew what it meant to love... and to lose.

He wasn't ready to let her go, and a sudden, overwhelming need to climb into the casket with her and sleep for eternity threatened to overtake him. His life was over anyway, so why not join her? He contemplated it for a crazed moment that stretched into near infinity, but then the gentle whisper of his love for her brought him back to the edge of his sanity. She would want him to make it right somehow, and he couldn't make it right if he was dead.

A fellow mourner squeezed his shoulder in a show of support, and his single tear gave way to a torrent. Grief came up to smite him with a forceful blow that left him weak, breathless, in pain, and unable to speak coherently or stand without support. Violent sobs came from the nothingness within him and brought him down to his knees. He felt the side of her cool silver casket against his forehead, and he heard his own strained voice, fraught with anguish, and somehow detached from his body and his control.

"They can't get away with what they did to you."

When he finally regained control of his voice his tears transformed yet again. The torrential sobs slowly became gentle keening sounds as he clung to the casket. Someone was telling him that it was okay to let go, but they didn't know that it wasn't okay, that it would never be okay. Eventually numerous people surrounded him with their useless platitudes and their ubiquitous, overly helpful hands.

Chapter 1

"It's kind of slow around here for a Friday night," Shane Gregory's long time friend Augustus said to him. The two were on duty at the fire station, and there hadn't been one call all evening. Not that Nashville Tennessee was a hotbed of fires and accidents, but usually they would have responded to at least one call by 8pm on a Friday night.

"Maybe people are finally taking all those public safety announcements seriously," quipped Shane around a mouthful of his Kung Pau chicken.

"Yeah, right," Gus said. "Rush hour wasn't so bad today, but just wait until all the drunks take the wheel later tonight."

Shane grunted in agreement as he continued shoveling food into his mouth. For the past five Friday's in a row his dinner had been interrupted by an emergency call, and he was determined to finish tonight.

Gus eyed him with amusement in his bright green gaze.

"And for Pete sake, close your damn mouth when you eat man! You need a woman to teach you some manners," Gus said as he watched Shane eat.

Gus was the only man Shane would take such admonishments from. The two had known each other since college, and Shane had been the best man at Gus's wedding ten years ago.

Shane swallowed and said, "Magda doesn't seem to mind the way I eat."

"That's because she's never seen you in your natural habitat," Gus laughed. Shane was a constant fixture at his dinner table, and he did have impeccable manners when it counted.

When there were no women around, however, Shane was very much a man's man.

Shane was too busy shoveling food to respond to that one. He really didn't want to have to leave his dinner again, so he continued eating at his insane pace.

"Animal," Gus muttered as he got up from the table.

Shane's spoon was laden with the last bite and poised halfway between his mouth and his plate when the alarm sounded.

Shane was suddenly all business as he and the other firefighters quickly donned their turnout gear and took their places on the screaming fire truck. There hadn't been an apartment fire in their area in some time, and the call that had just come in was for an address that Shane was already familiar with. It was an older, ten story building.

Gus and Shane were on the company's advanced search and rescue team. The two of them had been firefighters in New York City for a number of years before Gus decided to relocate to Nashville. Shane relocated years later because he was originally from Tennessee, and life in New York had quickly grown stale for him without his good friend. Now they were two of the best veteran fire fighters on the force. They were a perfect pair when it came to dragging people from burning buildings. Gus was big, burly, and built very much like an ox. He also had the tenacity to take on an enraged bull if the situation called for it. Shane was a slightly less bulky man, but at 6'6" he was just as solid and intimidating as his search and rescue partner. Other firefighters in the company often joked that the two of them could probably pack a herd of horses out of a burning barn if they had to.

"Looks like we got a doozie," Captain Shipman said as they arrived at the site and prepared to enter the building.

The first hose team was already hooking up and advancing the line directly to the fire floor as Shane and Gus donned their masks and did a quick radio check. Shane looked up at the building and a strong sense of dread hit him when he saw the burned out windows of the apartment on the fourth floor. He and Gus would take the fifth floor, the floor directly above the fire, the floor with the greatest risk of death or injury.

It was something that they'd done many times before, in both New York and Nashville. They were the best in their company. With over 30 years of combined experience and enough muscle to move mountains, they were expected to be the best and they loved living up to their reputation. This time, however, things were different. This was the first time Shane had ever run into a burning building where someone he knew was in the kill zone.

He charged up the stairs, taking them three at a time until he reached the fifth floor. The first search and rescue team stopped at the fourth floor to search the apartments for people needing assistance. The hose team suppressed the fire on the fourth floor as the rescue team began the meticulous search through all the apartments. They checked each apartment thoroughly, looking in cabinets and pantries, under beds, and in closets as they called out to people who might be trapped somewhere. Shane and Gus were the only two to advance into the uncertainty of the fifth floor.

Shane tried to tamp down his desperation to get to her. He had to do his job with a clear head. The smoke filled hallway was almost clear of people. Most had gotten out before the firefighters ever arrived, but they still had to quickly sweep the floor for trapped tenants. They carried out one elderly couple who were then whisked away to the hospital to be treated for serious smoke inhalation. The moments that it took to get back to the search were agonizing for Shane. His little brother would never forgive him if he let his wife's mother die in the fire. *Please just let her be alive*, Shane prayed as he approached her apartment.

She lived in the apartment at the end of the hall, the one farthest from the stairs. The apartment next to it had been completely blown out. Some sort of explosion had taken out the floor the ceiling and wall between the two apartments. There was one charred body in a twisted grotesque position halfway through the wall of the two apartments. Shane approached, but it was apparent that the person was beyond help. He couldn't tell if it was a man or a woman.

"Shane!" Captain Shipman called on the radio. "What is your location?"

"I'm on the alpha side of floor five," Shane answered.

"Good. Dispatch has a victim on the phone. A woman trapped in the bathroom of 525."

Intense relief washed over Shane. He turned away from the unfortunate person in the wall and quickly entered her apartment. With the wall blasted out, and everything inside either flaming or charred black it was hard to believe that she was in the bathroom on the phone. How could anyone be alive in here? The superheated air alone was enough to kill most people.

The evening of the fire had started out on a peaceful note. Cece had just wrapped up one of the most important cake orders she'd ever received. The mayor's daughter, a young lady named Lynette Reid, was getting married in the middle of the summer, and Cece Graves had been honored with the task of making her wedding cake. It would be her first society wedding, and was certain to be a boon to her small bakery.

She was soaking in her tub, head back, eyes closed, and lips curled up in a rare smile when she felt the explosion. First disbelief, then dread assailed her. She froze and listened in expectant horror. When the second set of explosions shook her apartment and confirmed her fears, she got out of the tub and reached for her bathrobe. She opened the bathroom door and looked down the hall to see the entire front half of her apartment on fire. Her living room wall was nearly completely blown out, and there appeared to be someone calling out for help.

She advanced toward the moans coming from the front room and saw her neighbor sprawled half in her apartment and half in his. His clothes flamed, and as she looked another explosion drove her back. She dashed back to her bathroom and grabbed her cell phone off the counter.

"911, what is your emergency?" a calm, female voice asked.

"There's an apartment fire, and some explosions coming from next door. I'm at 2700 West Forrest Avenue in apartment 525. Everything is on fire, and I can't get out. I'm in my bathroom," Cece panted in a rush of adrenaline.

"Ma'am, you need to find an exit. Is there a fire escape, or an alternate exit from your apartment?" the dispatcher asked.

"It's on fire!" Cece said in a shaking voice. "Something over there keeps exploding! What should I do?"

"The fire crew is on the way ma'am. Are you still in the bathroom?"

"Yes!"

"Good. Can you open the window?"

"Oh God.... Oh God, oh God, oh God."

"Ma'am, I'm going to need you to stay with me."

"There's no window," Cece choked out in a coarse, horrified whisper. "I'm going to die in here."

"Listen carefully ma'am. Firefighters are on the way. You need to do exactly as I say until they get there."

"Okay," Cece said. She had to fight the panic as smoke started seeping over the top of her door. Her power went out, and she could only see a limited area with the eerie blue glow from her cell phone display.

"Turn on the water, and wet a towel. Do you have a towel?"

"Yes. I have a closet full of them."

"Good. Put one wet towel under the door and another one over the top. You want to keep as much smoke out as you can until they get to you. Use another wet towel to wrap around your face. Only breathe the air through the towel, and stay as low as you can. Do *not* breathe in the smoky air."

"Okay, I can do that," Cece panted. Terror had dried her throat and sapped her of her strength, but she still did as the dispatcher instructed.

"Good," the woman said in a falsely soothing voice. "Now leave the water running and put as much water as you can on the walls around you, the door, and the floor. Use it to keep the fire out of the bathroom and stay low."

The woman continued to talk to Cece and tell her that help was on the way, but Cece's hope of rescue deteriorated as the fire closed in on her tiny bathroom. Eventually the water started making a hissing sound when it hit the hot walls and door. Smoke and flames licked at the top of the door and the ceiling, and the temperature in the bathroom steadily rose. Breathing through the wet towel was harder than it had first seemed, and Cece almost panicked several times while talking to the dispatcher. The tub was full to overflowing, and the water was still running onto the floor.

"I can't! I can't! Oh God help me!" Cece said as she looked up and saw the ceiling catching fire. The fire must be above her, and at any moment it would come crashing down to kill her. Smoke was filling the room, and the temperature still kept rising. In desperation she flung water up at the ceiling, but all it did was hiss and pop and quickly become steam.

"I'm going to die," she whispered into the phone with finality just before she plunged herself into the tub. The water coming from the tap was still cool enough to keep her from overheating. Every few seconds she raised her head out of the water and took a breath through the soaked towel as the water continued to run. She wasn't sure why she wished to cling to life when it seemed that a ghastly death was certain. Perhaps it would be better if she just breathed in the water and let herself drown. Drowning had to be less painful than burning to death.

Just as she was about to take in a painful lungful of water she felt a pair of rough, gloved hands yank her from her imaginary safe haven. Her eyes flew open and the nightmarish sight before her caused the panic she'd fought so hard against to take over for a split second. She saw a huge, imposing masked shadow over the backdrop of a ceiling that was alive with undulating flames. It looked so much like what she'd imagined hell itself must be like. She was yanked into a world of intense heat, crackling wood and shattering glass, and slung roughly over the shoulder of the demon that seemed determined to carry her to the underworld.

"Don't breathe! And wrap that towel around your head!" the demon shouted above the roar of the fire and the rescue sirens. It had a deep, gravelly voice and a strong grip around her legs.

She quickly complied, and moments later it seemed like she was flying past all the smoke and flames and into a cooler environment. She couldn't see anything, because her face was shrouded in her wet towel, but she did realize that the demon was actually a fireman. She clung to him for her life.

"Shane, what's your status?" a voice on the radio asked.

The fireman answered, "525 is alive and on the way out."

"Listen, we got ladders to evac the seventh floor, and there are some rescue teams from another company helping out up there. Clear the fifth floor and you and Gus get out of there," the captain commanded.

"It's clear. We did it before the call about 525," Gus answered because Shane was busy trying to get to the stairwell with Cece.

The hose team fought the flames near the front of the hall as Gus and Shane approached the stairwell. It seemed as if the monster was to be contained soon... on this floor anyway.

Shane carried the soaking wet Cece down to the third floor before it finally occurred to him that she could probably walk on her own. He stopped in the middle of the stairwell and gently set her down.

"You're lucky you didn't cook yourself in that tub of water back there," he chastised her immediately. He'd seen more than a few people who'd tried the same thing end up dead before the search and rescue team could reach them.

Cece didn't respond. She just pulled her sodden bathrobe tighter around her body.

When she finally did look up at him with red, tear filled eyes she still didn't say anything; she frowned, turned away, and walked the rest of the way down the stairs to the paramedics.

Shane watched her for a moment and tried to dispel the uncomfortable memory of their first meeting a few years ago. She didn't remember that meeting, because she'd been busy trying to drag herself across the hospital floor to get away from some imaginary phantom from her past. Over the past few years, he hadn't been able to get that moment out of his mind. When she looked at him tonight, making eye contact through his mask, he'd been struck hard by the same sense of mystery that had gripped him during his visit to her hospital room. It was obvious that she didn't recognize him, but then again he hadn't expected her to. After all, they'd never actually been introduced. She probably didn't know he existed.

Gus caught up to him on the stairs while he was still standing there contemplating whether or not he should follow her and introduce himself properly. He had almost done so a number of times over the past three years, but in the end the memory of his first sight of her lying broken and paralyzed in the hospital always stopped him. What excuse could he have for wanting to meet her? According to her daughter she had an intense need to be left alone by everyone, especially men. He could respect that need.

"What the hell was that all about?" Gus demanded.

They walked down the stairs past the hose team, and Shane remained silent.

"Well?" Gus persisted.

"What?" Shane finally said.

"I've never seen you move like that. You could have been killed going in there to get her, and you didn't even slow down. You saw it was sagging and structurally unsound. Why did you go in there anyway? You're lucky it went down after you grabbed her instead of while you were grabbing her."

Shane looked at his good friend and said simply, "I know her. She's family." Gus was right; it had been a close call. A split second after he'd seen her in the tub, half of the ceiling had collapsed in front of the door and it took part of the floor with it on the way down. The weight of the tub full of water, Cece, and himself had all combined to cause the remainder of the floor to sag towards the gaping hole. It felt like his only option at the time had been to grab her and jump across the hole before the rest of the floor went down. If Gus hadn't been right there to give him a hand when he stumbled upon landing he might very well be dead right now.

"We've got a major collapse on the alpha side of four, five and six. If you're still in that area get outta there!" Captain Shipman was saying over the radio. "I repeat, major collapse on the alpha side of four, five and six!"

The primary search and rescue on all the floors was now complete, and every rescue team, with the exception of Shane and Gus, had retreated from the burning building.

"We're heading out the front door of the building right now, captain," Gus said into his radio.

Less than a minute later they were standing near the commander watching as multiple hose teams suppressed the raging fire.

"Helluva job guys," he said to all the search and rescue teams. Shane and Gus had found a total of ten people on the fifth floor in need of rescue. Of those ten, only Cece had been in the kill zone. The other tenants on the opposite side of the floor had been far enough away from the fire to not have to worry about the flames, but there would be heavy smoke damage to their units.

"Take a rest. Can't have my best guys overheating," Captain Shipman said to them.

"Take your mask off man, you're scaring people," Gus said to Shane.

Shane had been so lost in thought he hadn't removed his mask. Maybe that's why Cece hadn't recognized him. He removed it, conscious of the fact that his face was probably dripping with sweat and beet red from the heat and exertion of running through a burning building. The night air on his face felt good, and he closed his eyes for a moment and wiped some of the sweat off with the back of his forearm.

"So, how do you know 525? She doesn't exactly look like she could be related to you," Gus asked.

"You remember my little brother Norman? He's the one who got remarried about four years ago... 525 is his wife's mother," Shane answered.

"Are you kidding me?" Gus said in disbelief as he stared at someone off in the distance.

Shane followed his gaze and caught sight of Cece standing near the paramedics watching the fire. She was still clutching her bathrobe and looking very much like a little deer in the headlights.

"No kidding," Shane said. They both stared at her as she stared at the fire.

"I got a mother-in-law, but she doesn't look anything like that," Gus said with a touch of awe in his voice.

"Hey man, don't ogle her like that," Shane said.

"Why not? Everyone else is..."

Shane looked around, and saw that Gus was right. Other guys from the primary search and rescue teams were getting an eyeful as well. Even some of the male fire victims were staring at her rather than at the destruction of their own property.

"She doesn't like to be stared at," Shane gritted out. He grabbed a grey blanket from one of the paramedics and approached Cece with it.

"Cecilia, you look like you could use this," Shane said as he walked up to her and draped the blanket around her shoulders. Her hair was still damp, and her bathrobe clung to her in a very revealing way.

"How do you know my name?" she asked as she looked up at him.

Her brown eyes bored into his midnight blue ones, and he felt it again. Why did this woman have the power to tie his tongue in knots?

"My brother," Shane stammered out as she continued to stare up at him. She dropped her gaze, and suddenly he could think again. "I'm Norman's brother," he finally said.

"Oh. So, you're related to that Neanderthal my daughter married."

"Yeah," Shane said.

"That explains why I feel like I've seen you before."

"Yeah," Shane said again.

"Is everyone in your family so tall?"

"Yeah." Why couldn't he think of another word? "Have you been evaluated by the medics? Smoke inhalation is deadly if not treated."

"I have," she answered. "It's a good thing I had that wet towel, they said that everything looked good after they checked my nose and throat."

"Good. You sound fine, and you aren't coughing. Those are both very good signs," Shane said. She hadn't looked up at him again, but he could see her shoulders slump slightly when she looked back at the burning building.

"Do you have somewhere to go?" he asked gently.

She straightened her posture and looked up at him again. "I can stay with my daughter for the night," she said quietly, dismissively.

"Just let me know if you need anything." He was about to turn and walk back towards Gus when her hand on his arm stopped him.

"Do you know which fireman is the one who got me out? I'd like to thank him properly. I was too rattled earlier to do so," she said with quiet vulnerability in her voice.

Shane felt a furious blush creeping up his neck as he said, "It was me."

She looked up at him again with tears in her eyes. They were the most subtle, unshed tears he'd ever seen, and she blinked them away so quickly he questioned whether they'd been there in the first place. "I thought I was going to die in there. Thank you so much," she said at last.

14005750R00146

Made in the USA
Charleston, SC
14 August 2012